A Woman Scorned

MARCIA CLAYTON

ISBN-13:978-1-0687456-0-7

Published by Sunhillow Publishing

For my sister, Gilly, my biggest fan and supporter
and, of course, in memory of my lovely son, Paul, who was
taken from us far too soon.

Also by Marcia Clayton

The Hartford Manor Series

Betsey: The Prequel

The Mazzard Tree

The Angel Maker

The Rabbit's Foot

Millie's Escape

A Woman Scorned

Annie's Secret

Acknowledgement

Thank you to my husband, Bryan, for his patience and encouragement and, as usual, for being the first person to read this book to spot any serious plot holes!

To my sister, Gilly, niece, Sharon, and friend, Sylvia, for proofreading my book and offering unwavering support.

To my talented daughter-in-law, Laura Clayton of LC DESIGNS, for producing yet another beautiful book cover.

I want to express my heartfelt thanks to author Celia Martin for editing my book and providing me with many valuable suggestions and excellent constructive criticism.

I must also thank the many other authors and readers who have befriended me on social media and provided help, advice, and much-needed moral support. I appreciate it.

Last, but not least, the biggest thank you goes to you, my readers. I have received some wonderful feedback from readers, who have told me how much they have enjoyed my books. Their reviews and messages encourage me to continue writing. A simple message, particularly from a stranger, saying they loved my story, means so much to me.

MARCIA CLAYTON

The Main Characters of Hartford

The Carter Family

EDWARD CARTER (b1812)
Married **BETSEY LOVERING** (b1814)

Their children:

1. **EVELINE CARTER** (b1837)
    Married **Charlie Chugg** (b1835)

    Their adopted children are:
    - Twins Joseph and Matthew (b1875) children of Eveline's late brother, William.
    - Amelia (b1876) daughter of Eveline's late brother, William.
    - Martha, (b1884) orphan, parents unknown.

2. **GEORGE CARTER** (b1840)
    Married (1) Alice Brown (1840 – 1880)

    Their children:
    - Harriet (b1860)
    - Francis (b1862)
    - Alfred (1865 – 1869)
    - Theresa (b1868)

    Married (2) **MARY ANN BROWN** (b1848)
    - Nellie (b1883)
    - Sophie (b1884)

3. **FREDERICK CARTER** (b1841)
    Married (1) Lucy Fuller (1843 –1881)

    Their children:
- Llewellyn (b1872)
- Rosella (b1876)
- Alfie (1877 – 1877)
- Grace (1879 – 1879)
- Eddie (b1880)

    Married (2) **CHARLOTTE MACKIE** (b1860)
- Illegitimate daughter Doris (b1884)
- Nicholas (b1885)

4. **TOM CARTER** (1841 – 1880)
    Married **SABINA BAILEY** (b1846)

    Their children:
- **ANNIE** (b1864) married (1) Harry Rudd (1851 – 1881)
  Their daughter: Selina (b1881)
  Married (2) **ROBERT FELLWOOD** (b1863)
- Mabel (1866 – 1866)
- Willie (b1869)
- Mary (b1871)
- John (1872 - 1880)
- Emma (1874 - 1880)
- Edward (b1876)
- Stephen (b1878)
- Helen (b1880)
- Danny (b1880)   Foundling (Son of Charles and Eleanor Fellwood)

5. **WILLIAM CARTER** (1845 – 1881)
    Married (1) Lottie Chang (1850 – 1880)

    Their children:
*   Identical twins Joseph (b1875) and Matthew (b1875)
    (now adopted by Charlie and Eveline Chugg)
*   Amelia (b1876)   (now adopted by Charlie and
    Eveline Chugg)

    Married (2) **SARAH MARTIN** (b1845)
    Their son:
*   Bentley (b1882)

The Lovering Family

Adam Lovering (1780 - 1824)
Married (1) Ellen Richardson (1784 -1821)
Their children:

*   Barney (b1810) married Bronwen Evans
*   **BETSEY** (b1814) married **NED CARTER** (b1812)
*   Norman (1817 – 1821)

Married (2) Greta Thompson (1784 – 1825)
Their daughter:

*   **EMILY LOVERING** (b 1823)
    Married Lenny Gibbs (1815 – 1872)
    Their daughter:
*   **Rosemary Gibbs (1843 – 1885)**
    Her children:
*   **MILLICENT** (b1870)
*   **JONATHAN** (b1880)

The Fellwood Family of Hartford Manor

Ephraim Fellwood (1770 – 1840)
Married Helena Thompson (1775 – 1820)
    Their children:

a) **Joshua Fellwood** (1803 – 1868)
    Married Marianne Simpson (1805 – 1825)
    Their son;

- **CHARLES FELLWOOD** (b1825)
  Married: **Eleanor Chichester** (b1838)
  Their children:

1. David Fellwood (1861 – 1881)
2. Lily Fellwood (1862 – 1864)

3. **ROBERT FELLWOOD** (b1863)
    Married **ANNIE RUDD** (b1864) nee Carter
    Their children:

- Selina (b1881) (Annie's daughter)
- David and Thomas (twins b1885)

4. **VICTORIA FELLWOOD** (b1863)
    Married Frank Eastleigh (1863 - 1885)
    Their children:
  - Caroline   (b1882)
  - Joshua (b1884)
  - Francis (b1885)

5. **Sarah Fellwood** (b1870)
6. **DANNY** (b1880) (Adopted by Sabina Webber)

b) **Thomas Fellwood** (1805 – 1823)
    Married Gypsy Jane (b1805 – 1841)
    Their son:

- **SAM FELLWOOD** (b1821) married Gypsy Jenny (b1824)

Their son
- **MARROK FELLWOOD** (b1840)
- married Laura Smith (1842 – 1885)

Their children:
- Jinnie and Elizabeth (twins) (b1876)
- Martin (b1880)
- Paul (b1882)

c)   **George Fellwood** (1807 – 1833)
d)   **MARGERY FELLWOOD** (b1814)
Married Clarence Montgomery (1810 – 1870)

The Hammett Family
Isaac Hammett (1806 – 1880)
Married: **Liza Jones** (b1810)

The Chugg Family
Alfred Chugg (b1815)
Married Jane Watts (1820 – 1884)

12 children - one son still living at home:
Jimmy Chugg (b1855)

CHARLIE CHUGG (b 1835) (Alfred's brother)
Married: **EVELINE CARTER** (b1837)

Their adopted children:
- Identical twins Joseph and Matthew (b1875)
- Amelia (b1876)
- Martha (b1884)

The Webber Family

PETER WEBBER (b1815)
Married Mary Jane Watson (1818 – 1866)

Their son:
ARTHUR WEBBER (b1836)
Married (1) Drucie Reynolds (1840 – 1866)

Their children:
- Christopher Webber (b1856) married Clarice Gubb
- Dudley Webber (b1858)
- Elsie Webber (b1863)
- Maria Webber (b1866)

Married (2) **SABINA CARTER** nee Bailey (b1846)

Their child:
- **KATEL WEBBER** (b 1885)

A WOMAN SCORNED

CHAPTER 1

GRANTLEY MANOR,
BRAMPFORD SPEKE

The bedridden woman hurled the sparkling crystal glass with surprising strength. Narrowly missing the terrified maid, it smashed against the far wall, and the contents left a sticky plum-coloured stain trickling slowly down the expensive flock wallpaper.

"I told you to bring me a drink, you imbecile, not that watered-down rubbish! If you value your job, do as you're told."

"Yes, ma'am, but the doctor instructed that you were only to have fruit juice, you see."

"Simpkins, remind me, does the doctor pay your wages, or do I?"

"Well, you, of course, ma'am."

"Then, for goodness' sake, do as you're told. You're lucky I'm so weak, or I'd give you the hiding you deserve."

As the maid hurriedly left the room, Lady Lilliana Grantley sank back against her pillows, coughing violently. A fit and healthy woman all her life, she had little sympathy for anyone afflicted with disability or illness. Having recovered from the typhoid that had claimed her husband's life shortly before Christmas, she had then contracted influenza, which quickly developed into pneumonia and left her fighting for her life. Even now, in the middle of February, she could scarcely believe how little strength she had or how depressed she felt.

She did not miss her husband, for they had never been close, though this was not of her choosing. Both were from wealthy families, and their marriage was arranged years before the ceremony took place. She had been content with her parents' choice of husband, for Sir Edgar was a handsome and intelligent man, albeit a few years older than her, and perhaps naively, she had thought he returned her love. However, he had made love to her only once during their entire sixteen years together, and that, she eventually realised, was only to consummate the marriage on their wedding night.

As the weeks and months passed by and her spouse steadfastly ignored her, she wondered what she had done wrong. He treated her kindly, provided her with everything she wanted, and was gracious and caring when they appeared in public. However, in private, he treated her almost as a stranger, avoided her if possible, and refused to discuss the matter.

After her first suicide attempt, he reluctantly explained the situation to her. He was in love with someone else and always had been. Someone he was not permitted to marry, but someone he would never abandon. He was deeply sorry for the position their forced marriage had put them in, but suggested that perhaps they could live together amicably enough and that she should take a lover if she so wished. Bitter at his callous words and manner, she took him at his word and, over the years, had taken many lovers, each time hoping to become pregnant with the child she longed for, but it had never happened. Realising that so many men could not all be at fault, the unhappy woman was forced to accept that the problem must lie with her and that she would likely remain forever childless.

For the first few months, Lady Lilliana did not know who her husband's mistress could be. He was discreet, and the servants, who had known him from birth, were loyal to their master and kept his secret. However, when Lenny Gibbs, a long-serving agricultural labourer, was killed in a farming accident, folk were curious when his widow, Emily, and her daughter, Rosemary, were not evicted from their tied cottage but allowed to continue living there. Naturally, the gossip eventually reached Lilliana's ears, and she tackled her husband about the matter. He confessed that his mistress was Rosemary Gibbs, a girl he had known since childhood, and furthermore, she was carrying his illegitimate child. This news, of course, enraged his barren wife even more.

From that time onwards, Emily, Rosemary, and her children lived in their tied cottage rent-free and were supported by generous handouts from the wealthy landowner, though Rosemary worked as a cleaner to give the appearance of supporting them all. By this time, the neighbours were aware of the affair, but as Sir Edgar was popular and his wife disliked, folk turned a blind eye. Rosemary and Sir Edgar were discreet, and though the gentleman made sure that his daughter, Millicent, and then, a few years later, his son, Jonathan, wanted for nothing, he never acknowledged them as his children, and they were unaware he was their father.

The maid returned with a glass of claret for her mistress and, bobbing a curtsey, enquired if madam required anything else.

"Yes, although the doctor says I must remain in bed, he has agreed that I might open my post, so please bring it to me."

In due course, the maid returned with a dozen or so envelopes on a silver platter and set it down at the side of the bed, within easy reach of her ladyship. Dismissing her nervous employee, Lady Lilliana quickly rifled through the letters. Mostly, they were from kindly friends and relatives, either expressing their condolences on the loss of her husband, wishing her a speedy recovery, or both. She skimmed through the letters, tossing them aside until she found the ones she had most looked forward to receiving.

She recognised the elaborate handwriting on the expensive linen paper of two envelopes and tore them open eagerly. As expected, they were from Sir Clive Robinson, a wealthy shipping magnate whose fleet of ships transported raw materials, manufactured goods, and agricultural products worldwide. Being a married man with four children, Sir Clive had, of necessity, always been discreet about their relationship, particularly as much of his wealth had come to him via his wife, and his father-in-law still held many of the purse strings. After a string of lovers over the years, Lilliana truly fell in love with Sir Clive and was faithful to him. However, she had not seen her lover since before Christmas, for during the festive period, his presence was naturally expected in his family home in London. Over the years, it had always been easier for the pair to meet when Lilliana resided in the Grantley townhouse in the capital.

In his first letter, dated late January, Sir Clive expressed concern for her well-being. He had heard of her illness from typhoid and begged her to contact him as soon as possible. Having received no response and by this time having heard of Sir Edgar's death, the second letter, dated the tenth of February, was phrased even more urgently. Fearing for her life, he begged her to contact him at the first opportunity. Sighing deeply and resolving to write back as soon as possible, Lady Lilliana turned her attention to the remaining two letters lying on the tray. They were also postmarked in London and written a month or so apart, but she did not recognise the handwriting.

Tearing open the first letter, dated mid-January, she saw it was from her husband's solicitors, Parkham, Glover, and Brown. They had been notified of Sir Edgar's death and offered their sincere condolences. The second letter, from the same solicitors, though written by a different hand, requested her attendance at their offices at the earliest opportunity to attend the reading of the will, which was, of course, to be expected. However, it was the final paragraph that enraged the weakened woman.

The letter asked if she knew of the whereabouts of Emily and Rosemary Gibbs, as Sir Edgar had left strict instructions that they, too, must be present at the reading of the will. Furious that her husband should heap this final embarrassment upon her and assuming he had left the Gibbs family an inheritance, Lady Lilliana rang the bell impatiently, and her maid came running.

"Yes, ma'am; can I fetch something for you?"

"Yes, Simpkins, get me another large glass of wine and keep your disapproving frown to yourself. Then fetch my writing set; I have an urgent letter to write, which must be posted today."

Lady Lilliana, however, did not even finish her first letter before her maid returned to tell her she had a visitor.

"So, who is it? Spit it out, girl, or do you expect me to guess?"

"It's Sir Clive Robinson, ma'am, but I wasn't sure if you would receive him in your bed-chamber, though he is insistent upon seeing you."

Lilliana quickly considered the options. It was hardly seemly for the gentleman to see her in bed, though, of course, he had done so on numerous occasions, but she knew she was not strong enough to dress and go downstairs.

"Oh, how kind of him to visit. I've just opened a letter from him, sending his condolences on the loss of Sir Edgar, and it would be pleasant to chat with him for a while. Simpkins, help me into my thicker bedjacket; it will be a little more respectable, and I'll receive him here as I'm not well enough to leave my bed."

"Of course, ma'am."

"Thank you. Now, you may sit outside the door to act as a chaperone, and I'll call you if I need you; otherwise, do not disturb us. Please show Sir Clive in."

The two lovers greeted each other formally for the sake of the maid, but as soon as they were alone, Sir Clive gathered the frail woman into his arms and showered her face with kisses.

"Oh, my dear, I've been so worried, and I couldn't leave London without causing suspicion until now. As it is, I think my inquisitive father-in-law suspects I have a mistress, though my wife seems blissfully unaware. How are you?"

"I think I'm on the mend at last, thank goodness, but I've been horribly ill, and I've missed you so much, my darling. I'm so weak that the doctor will not yet let me out of bed and insists on bleeding me regularly, though I'm not convinced it does any good. Still, no matter, you're here now, and I feel so much better for seeing your handsome face and hearing your voice. I have only just opened your letters, for the doctor would not let me deal with my correspondence until today. At least your visit has saved me from replying when everything is still such an effort."

Lady Lilliana went on to tell him of the two letters she had also received from her husband's solicitors in London and of her anger that the presence of Emily and Rosemary Gibbs was required at the reading of the will.

"But, why would Edgar insist they attend? I don't understand?"

"As you know, Rosemary had long been his mistress. They were childhood friends, and, if possible, he would have married her, but he knew if he did so, he would be disinherited of the Grantley estate and title. Looking back, I think he did his best to discourage me from marrying him, but he was a handsome young man and considered quite a catch, and I had always been brought up knowing I would one day marry him. I loved him and thought he returned my love, but after our marriage, it soon became clear that was not the case."

"Even so, why would he want the Gibbs women at the reading of the will?"

"Presumably, he's left them an inheritance, maybe even the tied cottage they've enjoyed living in rent-free since Lenny Gibbs died. I don't know why they must be at the reading, but hopefully, that will never be possible."

"Why is that? How can you prevent it? The solicitors will find out where they live from Edgar's estate manager and contact them there if they haven't already."

"Ah, but they're no longer living in the cottage. Thankfully, I turned Emily, the older woman, out before I was taken ill with this beastly influenza, and her daughter, Rosemary, had just died of typhoid; I saw her body myself."

"Oh, my goodness; where did the old woman and her grandchildren go?"

"I believe the vicar was going to take Emily to the Exeter workhouse, but I doubt she made it. She was terribly sick on the day I saw her, and she certainly didn't look as if she was long for this world. It was a bitterly cold day when I evicted her, and by the time she reached Exeter, I reckon hypothermia would have finished the job."

"That's a little callous, my dear, I must say."

Lady Lilliana glanced at him sharply. "Maybe, but that family had been a thorn in my side for more years than I care to remember, and but for them, I might have had a happy marriage, if not a family. As it is, I've had to suffer the humiliation of not only his affair being common knowledge on the estate and in the village but the presence of his two bastards living within a stone's throw of my home."

"Oh, dear, I can see you're understandably bitter about the situation; it has put you in a terrible position for years. Edgar's parents should never have insisted on the marriage in the first place. However, what of the two children; how old are they, and where are they?"

A deep frown creased the haughty lady's face. "The girl, Millicent, is fifteen, and the boy, Jonathan, is around five, I believe. My husband even had the audacity to name him after his father. Can you believe it? As to where they are, that I would dearly like to know. When I entered the cottage where the old woman was lying ill, they were not to be found. I had the entire village searched and had men scouring the countryside, but to no avail. The girl is in possession of a valuable brooch, which she stole from this house, so when she's apprehended, she'll be sent to jail or, better yet, hanged."

"How did she come by the brooch?"

"I believe that after my husband's death, she entered this house and stole it. Knowing their benefactor had died and that in all likelihood I would evict them from their cottage, no doubt she was searching for something to sell to support her family for a few months."

"Do you have any proof of this?"

"Yes, Anna, my faithful companion, saw the girl sneaking around the house and then spotted her leaving the grounds. It was later that day that I noticed the brooch was missing. The police interviewed Anna, and she gave them a statement and is willing to swear to it in court if necessary. My father-in-law, of course, died several years ago, and my mother-in-law just last year. As my husband was an only child, all her jewellery came to me, and this brooch was her favourite piece. It has a large sapphire in the centre, surrounded by tiny diamonds. I treasured it and want it back, but more importantly, the thieves must be punished."

"My goodness, how terrible. In that case, let's hope she and her brother are apprehended soon. Would you like me to find out how the search is going?"

"That would be marvellous if you could. I had two of my farm labourers searching for them, but since being so ill, I've been unable to find out if they have made any progress. Perhaps you could interview them while you're here and advertise in the newspapers again. I did so once and offered a reward, but no one came forward. Someone must be sheltering the pair of them, so no doubt, if the reward is large enough, someone will betray them sooner or later."

"What will happen to the estate now that Edgar has passed away?"

"I investigated that a long time ago, and as he had no legitimate heir or any close relatives, everything will come to me. Once all that is settled, I intend to make a will in favour of my nephew, Oswald. He's a worthy young man, and I've always been close to him. He's the son of my second brother, so he's not in line to inherit a fortune from anyone else. So far, he has no inkling of my intentions, and I look forward to telling him as soon as the formality of reading the will is taken care of. However, it must wait until I'm stronger, though I will write to the solicitors to advise them of this as soon as possible. Anyway, my darling, how long will you be in Devon?"

"I plan to stay a couple of months or so, and hopefully, we can resolve these matters. Perhaps you could travel to London with me when I return. It would be appropriate for me to accompany you as a family friend."

"I'd like that very much."

CHAPTER 2

BRAMPFORD SPEKE

Brampford Speke, a peaceful little village situated only a few miles from the bustling city of Exeter, would probably not have existed at all but for the position of Grantley Manor. Farm labourers and workmen were always in demand on this large and prosperous estate. The village was surrounded by green rolling hills and picturesque scenery, and despite the bitter temperature that morning, the vicar was content with his lot.

Gregory Swann was an elderly man, born in the village some seventy years earlier and raised to follow in his father's footsteps as a man of the cloth. Indeed, he still lived in the same house where he was born and knew that the only way he would ever want to leave would be carried out feet first. Kissing Edith, his wife of more than fifty years, goodbye, he let himself out of the back door and crossed the icy yard to the stable, where he saddled his pony and set off to visit his parishioners.

Despite his warm hat, scarf, and gloves, the portly man shivered violently in the sub-zero temperatures, and his breath hung in the air. The grass and hedgerows glistened with a hard frost, and ice covered the village pond where a couple of ducks skidded on the surface, futilely seeking a morsel to eat.

He planned to visit several needy folk that day, some physically unwell, others depressed with their daily struggle for survival, and a few simply lonely and who would benefit from seeing a friendly face. He decided his first port of call would be Ollie and Agnes Darch, who lived in the row of tied cottages that housed the labourers working on the estate. Shortly before Christmas, the Darches had both suffered from typhoid, a disease which had carried many to their graves, causing him and the local undertaker far more work than usual over the festive period. Thankfully, the couple had recovered, and the epidemic appeared to be over, but he had heard that Ollie was now suffering from lumbago.

Having visited the couple many times before, Gregory drove the pony and trap to the rear of the cottage and loosely tethered the pony under a lean-to, where the animal would have some shelter from the biting wind. He knocked on the back door and was welcomed by a friendly smile from Agnes, a woman in her late fifties.

"Good morning, Vicar. I wondered if you would call; I guess you've heard Ollie's poorly?"

"Good morning, Agnes, yes; how is the patient?"

"I'm afraid the patient is most impatient and wants to return to work, but as he can barely stand, I think that will have to wait a day or two. Anyway, come in and get warm, and I'll pull the kettle forward on the stove and make us a cup of tea; it'll help to keep out the cold. You go on up to the bedroom and sit with Ollie; you know the way, and he'll be glad to see you for a chat. I found some comfrey on my walk along the riverbank yesterday, so I've mixed it with some willow bark, and I gave him a dose of that a while ago. Hopefully, it might ease the pain."

"Yes, it should do; my mother always swore by that old cure when she had aches and pains. My father used to get lumbago, too, from time to time, and she often applied a mustard poultice; have you tried that?"

"It's funny you should say that because that was my next job. I've ground the mustard seeds to make the poultice, but that can wait until after your visit. A chat with you will probably do him just as much good. I'll bring the tea up as soon as it's brewed, and you can sample one of the biscuits I made yesterday."

As Gregory climbed the steep, narrow stairs, he gripped the wooden bannister to help himself up but was still a little out of breath when he reached the top. He was pleased to hear there may be some biscuits coming his way, for Edith was making him cut down on his food to help him lose a few pounds. The vicar was not keen on the idea, though he knew his wife did it for his own good. Being a man who cared deeply for his flock, he visited anyone in need and who was willing to receive him. He was usually offered some refreshment despite many living on the breadline, and unfortunately, he knew that Edith's efforts were unlikely to bear fruit unless he, too, tried a little harder.

Ollie was lying flat on his back in the bed and winced as he lifted his head to see who was visiting.

"Oh, hello, Mr Swann, I thought you might call when you heard I was laid up. Thanks for coming."

"Of course, Ollie; how are you?"

"Not good, as you can see. I can't believe I've put my back out again, and this time, all I did was sneeze. It's so frustrating and so painful; I must get back to work tomorrow, for as you know, no work means no pay, and though we have a little put by, it will soon go if I'm not earning. I'm saving all I can for when the day comes that I can't work at all. Goodness knows how we'll manage then."

"Yes, I know it's difficult for a manual worker like you, Ollie. I'm lucky because though I get a bad back from time to time, I can still do most of my work, though folk have to come to me. Still, Agnes was telling me she's dosed you with her herbal remedy, so I hope that helps. She's preparing a mustard poultice, too, and I swear by that, myself. If you return to work tomorrow, do try to be careful, won't you; perhaps they could find you a few lighter duties for a day or two."

"I don't think there's much hope of that, but I can ask."

The vicar sat on an upright chair at the side of the bed, leaving the comfy armchair on the other side for Agnes. Hearing her slow footsteps on the stairs, he pushed open the door and took the heavy tray from her. He set it on the marble washstand and nudged the empty bowl and pitcher along to make room.

"I would have carried that up for you, Agnes, if you had called me."

"Oh, thank you, but not to worry, Vicar, I suspect you would have struggled just as much as me, and I'm used to it, though I won't be sorry when Ollie's better, for these stairs wear me out. Now, have a couple of biscuits because I know you like them, and I'll pour the tea. I'll help Ollie to sit up a bit, and then I want you to tell me what happened to Emily Gibbs after she left here."

With much huffing and puffing and groans from her husband, Agnes helped Ollie to sit up and propped some pillows behind him before passing him some biscuits and a cup of tea. She then settled in the armchair and looked expectantly at their visitor.

"There's not a great deal I can tell you. After that callous woman, Lady Grantley, evicted Emily without so much as a moment's notice and left her sitting in the snow, I put her on my cart, made her as comfortable as I could, and took her to the workhouse in Exeter. It's a few miles, as you know, and the journey took longer than usual, for the roads were in a terrible state. It was such a bitterly cold day that by the time we got there, I was frozen to the marrow, and she was barely conscious. I was so annoyed that such a kind old lady was thrown out in such a cruel manner, and then for Lady Lilliana to forbid me to offer Emily shelter in the vicarage was unbelievable, but unfortunately, she held the upper hand, and she knew it."

"Yes, exactly. We would have taken Emily in and let her stay here, but living in Brampford Speke, we're all beholden to the Grantley family, as they own everything and do as they like. This would never have happened when Sir Edgar was alive, but you could see she meant what she said when she told us that if we sheltered Emily, she would evict us, too. So, did the workhouse take Emily in all right?"

"Oh, yes; I knew they would. I mean, she was homeless, elderly, and seriously ill, so there could be no one more needy than she was. They were not best pleased to hear she was suffering from typhoid, as that kind of thing is so infectious, but at least they didn't turn her away. As she was barely conscious and couldn't stand, let alone walk, she was taken to the infirmary, and I saw her tucked up into bed and had a word with the doctor. He examined her and told me he'd be surprised if she survived the night."

"Oh dear, poor Emily, have you heard any more since then?"

"No, sadly not, though, now you've reminded me, I may visit the workhouse the next time I'm in Exeter and enquire how she is. I'm curious, though. Who hid Millie and Jonathan from Lady Lilliana and her men that day, and where are they now?"

Ollie and Agnes looked at the vicar in surprise.

"We all assumed you'd given them refuge in the vicarage despite Lady Grantley's threats. We were going to ask you where they are."

"Oh, I see. No, I haven't seen the children since their mother, Rosemary, died. I visited the house a couple of days before she passed away and prayed with them for her and Emily to recover, but I've not seen them since. When we reached Exeter, I tried to ask Emily where they were, but like I said, she was not strong enough to talk. Oh dear, I hope they're all right. Did they have any other relatives that you know of?"

"No, I don't think so. Emily was orphaned as a young child and brought up in the workhouse, and she and Lenny Gibbs only had Rosemary, as far as I know. Of course, we're all aware of who their father was, but sadly, he can't help them now. Lady Grantley's actions are understandable to some extent, for she's been in an impossible position for years. However, none of it was the fault of Emily or her grandchildren."

"No, quite so. Not to worry, as I go on my rounds today, I'll make a few discreet enquiries to find out if anyone knows where the children are, and if I discover anything, I'll come back and tell you; I know you were fond of them."

"Oh, yes, please do. For all these weeks, we thought you must have found someone to take them in. Not knowing where they are is worrying, especially in the depths of winter. I hope someone has offered them a home."

A little later, having happily devoured several more of Agnes's delicious biscuits, the vicar left the kindly couple and went thoughtfully on his way.

CHAPTER 3

HARTFORD

Betsey Carter was sitting in a chair next to the bed where her husband, Ned, lay resting. Ned was in his mid-seventies and had been instructed by the doctor to take life slowly to ease the strain on his weakened heart. His wife was ensuring he did just that, and consequently, he was seldom allowed out of bed much before mid-morning. They were enjoying a quiet cup of tea together when screams from the kitchen below reached their ears.

"Oh dear, those boys are fighting again. Honestly, they just don't get on, and I think it's mostly Bentley's fault."

Betsey hurriedly put her cup and saucer onto the washstand.

"I'll sort them out, Ned, and be right back."

However, by the time she reached the two red-faced boys, they were being hauled apart and scolded, Bentley by his mother, Sarah, and Jonathan by his elder sister, Millie. Sarah shook her son angrily.

"There, now you've disturbed your granny and made her come all the way downstairs. What do you have to say for yourself?"

Bentley thought the world of his granny and couldn't bear to think she might be angry with him, so he hung his head and muttered an apology. Millie was mortified that her little brother should cause trouble when this kind family had recently offered them a much-needed roof over their heads and was also cross.

"And you, Jonathan, how could you be so naughty when everyone here has been so kind to us? You should be ashamed. Why were you fighting?"

Jonathan, who was considerably smaller than his opponent despite being a year older, was also shamefaced.

"I'm sorry, Millie, but it doesn't matter which toy I pick up; Bentley says I'm not allowed to touch it because it's his, but Aunty Betsey said I could play with whatever I liked. Bentley pushed me over and snatched the spinning top from me, so I thumped him."

Bentley was four years old, an intelligent child, and the youngest son of Betsey and Ned's late son, William. Sarah, William's second wife, had not always got on with her in-laws. However, she had now lived with them at The Red Lion Inn for several months, which had proved beneficial to all concerned. Bentley, the spitting image of his late father, was something of a favourite with his granny and could usually twist her around his little finger. However, Betsey would not tolerate bad behaviour and looked sternly at her grandson.

"Is this true, Bentley? Tell me the truth now, or you'll be in even more trouble."

"Yes, Granny, I did take the top because it's mine. Why can't Jonathan play with his own toys?"

"We've talked about this, Bentley, and you know Jonnie has no toys. How would you like it if you didn't have any toys? I'm disappointed in you, but I'll leave your mother to decide what to do with you now."

Betsey turned on her heel and remounted the stairs, knowing she should leave Sarah and Millie to deal with the situation. She entered the bedroom and retrieved her cup of tea as Ned raised his eyebrows questioningly.

"Oh, it was as I thought: Jonathan and Bentley fighting again. Bentley refuses to share his toys with Jonathan, regardless of how often Sarah and I tell him he must. He's behaving so badly."

"It is understandable, though. He's been the only child living here until now and had everything his own way. I don't think it's all about the toys either; you've always spoilt him, and now he doesn't like sharing your affections. You've spent a lot of time with Millie and Jonathan since they turned up here out of the blue, and Bentley's nose has been put out of joint."

"Yes, that's true, I suppose, but I've felt so sorry for the pair of them. It must have been so difficult for them to leave their home in Brampford Speke and walk the fifty miles here in the middle of winter. They've had no time to grieve for their mother, and we still don't know what's become of their granny, Emily. I was hoping she'd have turned up here by now, but of course, we don't even know if she's still alive. The workhouse isn't the best place to recover from typhoid. We must search for her soon, Ned; she's my half-sister, after all, although I never knew she existed until a few weeks ago."

"Yes, we must do that, for I know you won't rest until you know what's happened to her. I'm afraid it will have to wait a while, though, for we can't go roaming the countryside searching for her at our age, and the rest of the family has enough on their plates. George still doesn't seem himself, does he? I don't think he's ever been right since that rat bit him last year, and his arm still keeps festering. Fred's up to his eyes getting organised to move here, as well as renovate Robert Fellwood's canal boats. We can't put any more on either of them right now."

"No, you're right, as usual, my love. I think maybe it's time we swapped places with Fred and Charlotte, though, and let them take over here. Fred's finished repairing the barn out the back now and has been gradually transferring all his carpentry stuff there, so I think he's ready for the move."

"How about his cottage; is that ready for us to move into?"

Betsey looked a little shamefaced and grinned. "Yes, he's reinstalled the cupboards that he moved to Bluebell Cottage when we intended to live there, and they're back in his kitchen again. Now that Millie and Jonathan have turned up unexpectedly and will live with us, I think it's better we move to Fred's cottage because it has more space. We'll need to find new tenants for Bluebell Cottage, though, and the rent will come in handy when we no longer earn a living here."

"At least if we move to Fred's cottage with Millie and Jonathan, it will put a bit of distance between Bentley and Jonathan, which won't be a bad thing. Perhaps we should think of a name for the cottage when we move there; we can't keep calling it Fred's cottage. Any ideas?"

"Yes, I'd like that; no, nothing springs to mind, but I'll give it some thought. I think I'll invite Charlotte and Fred here for their tea tomorrow, and then we can talk about the move. It will be nice to see them, and all the children, too, of course. I hope Llewellyn will come, though he always seems so busy these days since he's started learning the carpentry trade from Fred, but he has to eat."

The following day, Betsey busied herself making a large pot of beef stew with plenty of dumplings, for she knew it was Fred's favourite, and she never missed an opportunity to spoil one of her children if she got the chance. Having lost two of her sons, she knew how important it was to take nothing for granted and to spend as much time with her family as possible. Pneumonia had claimed Bentley's father, William, and her other son, Tom, had succumbed to consumption, though he had fought the illness for several years. His wife, Sabina, still lived in the village and was remarried to a man called Arthur Webber. They had recently celebrated the birth of a little girl called Katel, Sabina's tenth child.

With Sarah, Bentley, Millie and Jonathan, and Fred and Charlotte and their five children, there would be thirteen of them present for tea, so Betsey decided to include Louis Blaquiere, a man who had worked for them for a few months, to even up the numbers. She hoped the group would fit around the large kitchen table, and, after all, several of them were children, and two were only babies. By six o'clock, everyone was squeezed around the table as Betsey ladled generous helpings of her tender stew onto their plates.

"Oh, good, beef stew and dumplings, and it smells delicious; you know it's my favourite, Mum. I was hoping you'd make this for tea."

Betsey surveyed her son fondly. "Aye, I thought you'd be pleased, Fred. Enjoy it then, everyone, and there's plenty more if anyone has room, though I've made an apple crumble for pudding, so I shall expect you all to sample that with a dollop of my fresh clotted cream later."

They all tucked in happily and caught up with each other's news. Betsey had carefully seated Jonathan and Bentley at opposite ends of the table to ensure they were as far apart as possible. Ned sat back and stretched contentedly as he laid down his spoon.

"That was very tasty, my dear, as always. Now, while we have a breather before our pudding, I want to talk to you all about our move. Now that I'm a bit better, Betsey and I think we should move as soon as possible. So, Fred and Charlotte, what do you think? Are you ready to move to the inn and take up the reins here?"

Charlotte beamed at her father-in-law. "We were hoping you'd say that, Ned. Yes, we're ready and can't wait to move here, but we didn't want to rush you and Betsey until you felt up to it. Do you have a moving day in mind?"

"Betsey and I talked about it earlier, and we think the sooner, the better, so how about this Saturday? You're leaving most of your furniture in the cottage for us, and we're not taking much from here, so it's not like there's a lot to move. Do you think we can do it all in one day, or do you want to move here on Saturday, and we'll move to your cottage on Sunday or Monday?"

"I think we can do it all in one day, Dad, but we want to get one thing straight: you and Mum will be doing nothing on moving day. Eveline and I have already discussed the matter, and we think you should stay with her and Charlie for a few days at Hollyford Farm while we sort everything out. I don't want any arguments now."

Eveline was Betsey and Ned's only daughter, and having married farmer Charlie Chugg late in life, they had no children of their own. However, following William's death, they adopted Amelia, Joseph, and Matthew, his three children from his first marriage, and also another little orphan girl called Martha.

"Oh, Fred, what a marvellous idea. I would dearly like to help, but I don't want your dad getting overtired with it all. What about Millie and Jonathan, though?"

"We thought it might be best if Jonathan goes with you, Mum, and Millie too if she wants to, though she could be a big help here. It will be a pleasant change for you to spend some time with Eveline and the children and for Jonathan to get to know them all. We're a big family, and it's not easy to understand where everyone fits in." He smiled at Millie. "What do you say, Millie? Do you want to go to the farm with Jonathan, or will you stay here and give us a hand? We thought you could get our cottage ready for Betsey and Ned and you and Jonathan."

"Oh yes, I'd love to help. You've all been so kind to us, taking us off the streets and giving us a home; I'm willing to do anything you want me to. Jonnie, will you be all right without me?"

Her little brother nodded. "Yes, if Aunty Betsey and Uncle Ned are going, I'll be all right, and I'd like to see all the farm animals."

"Good, now that's all sorted out, I'll dish up the pudding. Ned, you were going to mention that old trunk to Fred before we forget about it."

"Oh yes, I was; thank you for reminding me, my dear. Fred, you don't have to worry about this until you've sorted yourself out, but there's an old trunk up in the attic that's been there for a very long time. My dad discovered it back in the 1830s when the inn last had a new roof, and we reckoned it had already been there for over a hundred years then. Those two cream jugs on the mantelpiece were found in it, and your mother took a fancy to them, but there were a few other things in the trunk that we didn't quite know what to do with at the time, so we put them back again. We think the trunk was put there by Jago Carter, my great-great-great-grandfather. Silas and I were so excited when Dad opened it; we hoped it would be full of treasure. I remember there was a green leather bible with a name on it, which I've forgotten, and a lot of Spanish pieces of eight. We were afraid to sell them in case we were accused of stealing the money, but I think after all these years, it would be safe to do so. The coins might be worthless, but I wanted you to know about the trunk before I meet my Maker. You never know; if they're worth anything, the money might help towards the cost of a new roof when you need one, and that won't be too many years away."

"That sounds intriguing, Dad, and I'll investigate once we've settled in, but if the contents are worth anything, then it will belong to you and Uncle Silas. We'll have less talk of you meeting your Maker, too; I want you and Mum to enjoy a long and happy retirement. You've certainly earned it."

Not long after their visitors had departed, Betsey and Ned went to bed. Ned needed a lot of rest these days, and Betsey was content to retire early with him and lie reading her book if she was not ready to sleep. However, they had much to discuss that night, and her book lay unopened on the dressing table.

"It will be the end of an era when we move to Fred's cottage; I've never lived anywhere else, and you've been here since you were six years old."

"That's true, Ned, but it's the right thing to do; you're not regretting our decision, are you?"

"No, not at all. You've been spoiling me for the last few months, not letting me lift a finger, but you're no spring chicken yourself, and you need to take it easy, too. That will never happen while we're living here. I'm looking forward to our retirement. With nothing else to do, I might be able to manage a short walk around the village or go across the road to George's shop and pester him for a while, and we can probably call on Sabina and Eveline and spend more time with our grandchildren; there are enough of them."

"Yes, I'm looking forward to it, too. I know you had reservations about us taking in Millie and Jonathan, but I've already grown fond of them, and I think Millie will be a big help around the house. She'll care for her little brother, so I think it will work out all right."

Betsey twisted the pretty gimmel ring Ned had given her for an engagement present around on her finger. Although her hands were swollen with arthritis and she had gained a little weight over the years, the ring still fitted, and she treasured it.

"Do you remember when you gave me this ring, Ned? It was Christmas time, and we had the house to ourselves for once. We sat in front of the fire and roasted some chestnuts, and then you dropped down onto one knee and proposed to me. I was so surprised, especially when you broke the ring in half, and we wore half each until we were wed."

"I know you were, but I'd wanted to ask you to marry me for a long time. I hated it when you were courting that horrible Daniel Abernethy; doctor or not, he was a scoundrel, and even if I couldn't have you, I didn't want to see you marry him."

"No, I know, but I was dazzled by his handsome face, and I thought he loved me; thank goodness I came to my senses in time. I wonder where he is now?"

"Far, far away, I hope."

CHAPTER 4

HARTFORD

The following day, Betsey and Ned were delighted to receive an unexpected visit from their eldest granddaughter, Annie. She was accompanied by her three children, Selina, who was five, and nine-month-old twins, David and Thomas. Annie was the eldest daughter of Tom Carter, who had died of consumption over six years earlier, and she still missed her father. Annie was now the wife of Robert Fellwood, the heir to Hartford Manor, and her life bore no resemblance to her early years when the Carter family had struggled to survive.

Although only twenty-three, Robert was already in charge of the Hartford Estate, for although his father was still alive, he had suffered a severe stroke a few years earlier and was seriously handicapped. Following his marriage to Annie, Robert refurbished the derelict west wing of Hartford Manor, and he and Annie now lived there with their family. Robert's parents, Eleanor and Charles, disapproved of his marriage to Annie, for she was a former servant and, they felt, an unsuitable match for their son. They lived in the central part of the Manor House and, sadly, had little to do with their son and his family.

Annie tapped lightly on the back door of The Red Lion Inn and peered into the kitchen, where she spotted her granny, Betsey, kneading some pastry.

"Hello, Gran. I see you're busy, as usual. I thought you and Grandad were going to retire?"

"Hello, Annie, what a nice surprise. Hello, Selina, my lovely. My goodness, how these two bonny boys are growing. That's it; bring the pram into the warm, and I'll get us all a cup of tea. Yes, we will retire soon, but what brings you here today?"

Annie removed the children's coats and then her own. She pushed the pram into the corner of the room and lifted the two babies out, sitting them on the rag mat and putting a few toys in front of them. Selina sidled up to her granny.

"Could we have some of your biscuits, please, Granny Betsey?" She smiled up at the older woman with wide blue eyes.

"I expect I can find one or two, seeing as you've asked so nicely. I'll let this pastry rest and see to it later; I'm ready for a sit-down, anyway."

"I'm here because I've heard that you're moving to Uncle Fred's cottage in a few days, and Charlotte tells me that you and Grandad are going to stay at Hollyford Farm with Aunty Eveline and Uncle Charlie while they move everything. I think that's wise, Gran, because you'd only wear yourself out doing everything if you were here. I've come to offer to take you and Grandad to the farm in the carriage. I know Grandad's not too well, and it would be a lot warmer than on the pony and trap, and we certainly don't want the pair of you getting wet through if it rains. Would you like that?"

"Oh, that is kind of you, my dear; thank you, and yes, I would appreciate that. I've been worried about Ned getting cold and wet on the journey."

"Good, we'll collect you early on Saturday morning, then. I'll bring the children, and we'll spend the day with you at the farm and then fetch you again when the cottage is ready. I believe Jonathan's going with you, too, isn't he?"

"Yes, that's right. Millie will stay here and help get our cottage sorted out, but we'll take Jonnie with us to get him out of the way. He and Bentley have not taken to each other, to say the least, and the last thing everyone will need on the moving day is for those two boys to be squabbling all day long."

"Mum's offered to look after Rosella, Eddie, Doris and Nicholas at the Lodge House to leave Charlotte and Fred free to deal with the move, so I expect Bentley could go there too if it would help."

"Goodness, we have such a lot of children in this family. Someone asked me the other day how many grandchildren I have, and I honestly didn't know. I'll have to count them sometime when I have nothing better to do. It's kind of Sabina to say she'll have the children, though, and I'm sure it will be a big help. Sarah, Louis and the other servants will deal with the stagecoaches that call at the inn throughout the day, and Llewellyn will see to any work at the carpentry yard, leaving Charlotte and Fred free to get on with the move. Hopefully, it should all go like clockwork. I'm looking forward to my little holiday at Hollyford Farm; I don't see so much of our Eveline since she got married, and Ned will enjoy a natter with Alfred Chugg and a little wander around the farmyard."

As promised, early on Saturday morning, Annie arrived in the Fellwood carriage, which Dodger Watkins drove. It was a bit of a squeeze with Betsey, Ned, Annie and the four children, but Annie and Betsey held the babies on their laps, and they all were comfortable enough. It took just over half an hour to reach Hollyford Farm, and Ned, in particular, thoroughly enjoyed the journey, as he had been unwell for several months and had barely stepped outside the inn.

It was a dry and sunny day, although there was quite a nip in the air, and Annie tucked warm blankets around her grandparents' legs. As the carriage pulled into the farmyard, Eveline saw them arrive and went outside to meet them. She led the way into the warm kitchen, where Amelia, Joe, and Matthew eagerly awaited their cousins' arrival. Amelia was delighted to have another little girl's company, and she and Selina soon disappeared to her bedroom to play. Joe and Matthew had only met Jonathan once, but they made him welcome, and the three boys went outside to introduce Jonathan to the farm animals. With the children out of the way, Annie, Betsey, and Eveline sat around the kitchen table and chatted while Martha played on the floor with the twins. The little girl was now a sturdy two-year-old and fully recovered from her difficult start in life. Eveline explained that Charlie and his Uncle Jimmy were working in the fields but would be in at lunchtime. Normally, Charlie's elder brother, Alfred, would have been with them, but he was a bit under the weather and taking a day off. He and Ned took themselves off to the study, where, having been friends all their lives, they enjoyed smoking their pipes and putting the world to rights.

Many of the Carter family were busy in Hartford that day. Since Annie's marriage to Robert Fellwood, her mother, Sabina, and her siblings had lived in the Lodge House, a substantial building at the entrance to the driveway of the manor. Once used as a gatehouse, a gatekeeper had vetted visitors to the manor in the past, but that custom had long since died out, and until it was refurbished for Sabina, the house had stood empty for more than twenty years. Now tastefully decorated and furnished, it was Sabina's pride and joy, and she often found it hard to believe she was lucky enough to live there.

Sabina and her late husband, Tom Carter, had raised nine children together, but only two, Stephen and Helen, now lived at home. Annie, of course, was married to Robert Fellwood, and Willie and Edward worked at nearby Sugworthy Farm. Mary cared for an old gentleman at the far end of the village and lived in. Sadly, one child, Mabel, had lived for only a day, and poor Johnny and Emma had passed away from diphtheria. In addition to Stephen, Helen, and Katel, the new baby from her second marriage to Arthur Webber, Sabina cared for Danny, a foundling she had adopted.

Charlotte had gratefully delivered her children to Sabina bright and early that morning, and Stephen, Helen and Danny were looking forward to the company of their cousins. Bentley had been given the choice of staying at the inn with his mother, Sarah or playing with his cousins, and he had decided to spend the day with his Aunt Sabina. Sarah hoped and prayed he would behave himself, but she knew Sabina would stand no nonsense.

Sabina was pleased that the day was dry and sunny, for the Lodge House had a large garden, and, thanks to her son-in-law, Robert, it had a swing, see-saw, and slide. Having cooked a large breakfast, which all the children had enjoyed, she ushered them outside to play. She had not always had the luxury of feeding her family well, but she knew children with full bellies were always less trouble than hungry ones. She settled the babies, Nicholas and Katel, into their cots for a mid-morning nap and, having found a selection of toys to keep two-year-old Doris amused, sat down for a quiet cup of tea with Liza Hammett.

Liza was a former neighbour and was now in her seventies. She had lived with the Carter family since the untimely death of her husband, Isaac, who was killed when a tree fell onto their cottage in a storm. She had been of enormous help to Sabina after the death of her husband, Tom, which occurred around the same time, and the two were now close. They had not been sitting there long when, after a brief knock on the back door, Sabina's eldest son, Willie, poked his head into the kitchen.

"Hello, Willie. I wasn't expecting to see you today. What brings you here? Is Edward all right?"

"Hello, Mum, hello, Liza. Yes, Edward's fine, and he loves working at Sugworthy Farm. I heard that Fred and Charlotte are moving to the inn today and Granny and Grandad to their cottage, so I came to see if I could help. Since Robert sent a couple of extra workmen to the farm, and with Edward there as well, I can take the odd day off now and then. Marrok Fellwood will be moving in there soon with his family; I think his broken leg is mended now. Where could I be of most use, do you think?"

"We're fine here, and so far, all the children are playing nicely. Annie's taken Betsey and Ned to Hollyford Farm for a few days to get them out of the way until everything's sorted out, and I think Fred and Charlotte have plenty of help from Sarah and Louis at the inn. I think it might be best if you give Millie a hand. Fred and Charlotte are moving Betsey and Ned's belongings to the cottage and leaving Millie to get everything shipshape. You met Millie at Christmas, didn't you?"

"Yes, that's right, I met her and Jonathan, and I felt so sorry for them. Is there any sign of their granny yet?"

"No, not yet, and once this move is over, someone must organise a search for her. The children need to know what's happened to her before they can get on with their lives, and, of course, she's Betsey's half-sister, so now she needs to find her, too."

Sabina did not miss the smile on her son's face when she suggested how he might spend his day, and she tried to hide her amusement at his next question.

"Yes, of course. Does that mean Millie and I are related then?"

"Oh, my goodness, now you've asked me. Let me see. Your granny, Betsey, and Millie's granny, Emily, are half-sisters, so no, not closely related. Why do you ask?"

"Oh, I just wondered, that's all."

"If you're asking because you rather like Millie, and I did notice how you couldn't take your eyes off her at Christmas, then I can tell you that there would be no reason for you not to marry her one day, should you want to. Does that answer your question?"

To Liza's and his mother's amusement, Willie's face was scarlet. "You're getting ahead of yourself, there, Mum, but yes, I did like her."

"No need to be embarrassed, Willie. She's an attractive girl. Would you like something to eat before you go?"

"No, thanks. Florrie cooked me a huge breakfast at the farm, so I'll get on; I'm sure there will be plenty to do."

"Very well, and bring Millie here for dinner later if you want; I've done loads of baking to feed everyone today, so two more will make no difference."

Willie strolled the short distance to his Uncle Fred's cottage, where Louis and Fred had finished unloading the first cartload of Betsey and Ned's belongings. They were surprised but pleased to see Willie, especially when he offered his help for the day. Fred had also noticed Willie's interest in Millie at Christmas and suspected this was the real reason for his visit that day.

"That's kind of you, Willie, but I think Louis and I have things under control at the inn. It might be best if you stayed here and helped Millie; there's quite a lot to sort out."

Willie entered the cottage happily, finding Millie struggling to lift a heavy box.

"Millie, let me carry that; it's far too heavy for you."

Millie's face reddened as she saw the young man. "Oh, hello, Willie, it's all right; I can manage, but what are you doing here?"

"I came to offer my help for the day, and Mum and Uncle Fred said I should give you a hand. Let me take that box, and I'll carry it upstairs. Perhaps you can sort out where everything will go if I bring the stuff up?"

"That will be a big help, thanks, Willie."

The girl smiled at him happily and decided the day had suddenly got a whole lot better.

CHAPTER 5

HARTFORD

The Carter family worked hard that day, and Millie and Willie enjoyed one of the best days of their lives and giggled as they realised their names rhymed. At one o'clock, after a couple of hours of hard work lugging the boxes up the narrow stairs of the cottage, Willie was ravenous, and he invited Millie to the Lodge House for some dinner.

"Are you sure your mum won't mind me coming?"

"No, she suggested it, and anyway, she's minding all Uncle Fred's children today, and there are so many people there that she'll barely notice two more."

As they left the cottage, Willie tentatively reached for Millie's hand and, delighted that she seemed happy about it, held it all the way to the Lodge House. Across the road, his cousin, Theresa, was cleaning the inside of her father George's shop window, and she smiled when she saw them holding hands. She knocked on the window and waved, and with a wide grin, Willie waved back. At the Lodge House, they were ushered into seats around the kitchen table and were soon tucking into Sabina's legendary bacon and egg pie and Liza's delicious bread and butter pudding. Millie tried hard to remember the names of the many children present, and they enjoyed making her guess.

Bentley was on his best behaviour and got along with Stephen, Danny, and Eddie, who, being older, stood no nonsense from him anyway. Watching them playing together, Sabina, who knew Bentley was quite a handful, thought he would benefit from attending school and mixing with the other children. Being an only child, he had ruled the roost for far too long and needed the corners knocked off him as she thought of it. She resolved to suggest this to Sarah and find out if the schoolteacher would allow him to start school after Easter, although he was only four. She knew the teacher might refuse, for children usually had to be five years old to start school, but Bentley looked older. He was a stocky child, tall for his age, and undoubtedly clever enough. Failing that, once Rosella and Eddie were living at the inn, they would, no doubt, take him down a peg or two.

The folk at The Red Lion Inn had also been frantically busy. The inn employed several workers these days, for as well as serving refreshments and offering a bed for the night to stagecoach travellers en route to Exeter and London, Betsey's Kitchen, the other food outlet housed in the old shippen, offered cheap and wholesome food to be taken away to eat, or consumed at the rough wooden tables. Betsey had started the venture in the thirties when the inn struggled to stay afloat. Back then, there were many labourers employed locally to build Lord Hartford's canal, and they had been delighted to buy a pasty or a bowl of stew to keep them going. The local folk soon joined the queue for food as they found the helpings generous and good value for money. Although the canal workers had long since finished their task and left the area, plenty of farm labourers, limekiln workers, and, more recently, holidaymakers enjoyed a daily visit to Betsey's Kitchen.

On moving day, Sarah oversaw the inn's meals and kept an eye on Betsey's Kitchen, but the staff were well-trained, and everything ran like clockwork. Louis Blaquiere also helped in the bar but mainly supervised the outside staff who looked after the stagecoach horses. Often, the horses only required rest, food and water, but for longer journeys, the horses were exchanged for fresh ones. Fred's wife, Charlotte, had found Louis unconscious on Hartford Beach and saved his life before he drowned in the rising tide. When he awoke, badly injured from a beating, he found he had lost his memory, and not knowing where to go or what to do, Betsey and Ned had offered him a temporary job at the inn and somewhere to lay his head. A few months later, his memory had returned, and now they wondered how they had ever managed without him. Louis had decided to stay, for he was courting Betsey and Ned's granddaughter, Theresa.

Betsey and Ned thoroughly enjoyed themselves at Hollyford Farm and could not remember when they had last had a day away from the inn. Annie, Selina, and the twins left the farm after lunch so that the carriage could travel back in daylight to Hartford Manor, and they promised to return on Tuesday. Betsey was delighted to see Ned enjoying a stroll around the farmyard with Alfred. The pair had been friends since their school days, and Betsey hoped they could meet more often now that they had left the inn. Over the next few days, she was even more convinced they had done the right thing in handing the inn over to Fred. It would be an excellent opportunity for him and Charlotte, and they deserved it, for they were a hardworking couple. Hopefully, it would give Ned a new lease of life after a difficult winter blighted by illness.

Eveline enjoyed spoiling her parents and would not let either of them lift a finger to do anything. She was delighted they could spend some quality time with Joseph, Matthew, and Amelia and get to know Martha better. With the farm a few miles from the village, the children saw less of their grandparents than their cousins. Jonathan was having a great time playing with Joseph and Matthew, and the three boys spent much of their time exploring the farm while Amelia enjoyed making rag dolls with Eveline and Betsey. This was a venture Eveline had embarked on whilst working at her brother George's shop. A visitor from London noticed the dolls for sale one day and asked if she would supply his toy shop in London. Nowadays, she struggled to keep up with the demand and was glad of Amelia's help, for the little girl was a quick learner and skilful with her needle. Eveline was delighted that with her mother's help and that of Amelia, they produced enough dolls to fill the next order in record time.

Before Willie left the cottage that day, he plucked up the courage to ask Millie if he could see her again. Her wide smile gave him his answer, and thus encouraged, he gently kissed first her hand and then her lips. The young man agreed to return to the cottage the following Sunday to accompany her to church for the morning service and then stay for lunch. Knowing his granny would have no objection to this, he mounted his horse and enjoyed the gallop back to Sugworthy Farm.

After Willie left, Millie strolled around the cottage, checking that everything was to her liking. The dwelling had four bedrooms and was newly decorated, with much of the furniture made by Fred. The largest bedroom at the front of the cottage was for Betsey and Ned. She had made the bed and placed a bunch of snowdrops in tight buds on the windowsill, thinking they would be in full bloom by the time the couple returned on Tuesday. Charlotte had offered for Millie to stay at the inn for a few nights rather than be alone in the cottage, but the girl declined the offer. She would enjoy being there on her own for a few days and wanted to cook a tasty meal for Betsey and Ned when they returned. Although not an experienced cook, her granny, Emily, had taught her how to make a rabbit stew, and Millie planned to do just that and include some light, fluffy dumplings. Betsey had left her some money to stock the larder, and she decided to visit the butchers and George Carter's shop in the morning. She wasn't quite sure yet what to make of Uncle George; he had not seemed as welcoming as the rest of the family, but then she had heard he wasn't in the best of health. She hoped one of his daughters, Harriet or Theresa, would serve her when she called.

On Tuesday morning, Millie felt nervous when the Fellwood carriage drew up outside, and Dodger Watkins helped Betsey and Ned down the steps. Jonathan, Annie, and Selina were with them, though Annie had left the twins at Hartford Manor. Millie opened the door with a broad smile and nervously watched them wander around the cottage as she hugged her little brother.

"Oh, Millie, it's so cosy, and what's that delicious smell?"

"I bought some food, like you said, Aunty Betsey, and I've made a pan of rabbit stew and dumplings for our dinner. I thought you might be hungry when you arrived, and it's one of Jonnie's favourite meals. When I went to the shop, Theresa told me that today is Pancake Day, so I've also made some batter. If you and Selina want to stay, there's plenty of stew, Annie?"

"Yes, thank you, I'd like that, and I'm sure Selina and Jonathan would love to try tossing a pancake later."

They enjoyed the rabbit stew, and Millie made the pancakes and let the two children toss them. Fortunately, only one ended up on the floor. Having eaten two pancakes, dusted with sugar and doused in lemon juice, Ned pushed his plate back contentedly.

"Well, you certainly can cook, my dear. That was a tasty meal, and what I liked most about it was that Betsey didn't have to lift a finger. Yes, I think you'll fit in here very well."

"Thank you, Uncle Ned; I intend to care for you and Aunty Betsey as best I can. I'm so grateful you took us in when we had nowhere to go."

Seeing a sad frown cross the girl's face, Betsey patted her hand.

"Don't worry, Millie; we haven't forgotten about your granny, and I'll get someone to search for her as soon as possible. We've had such a lot on since Christmas, and we were hoping Emily would have made her own way here by now, but as she hasn't, we'll have to do something about it. We need to know where she is."

"There is something I must tell you, Aunty Betsey. I didn't do all the work in the cottage myself; Willie came and offered to help. His mum and Charlotte said he didn't need to help them, so they sent him here for the day."

Betsey grinned. "Did they now, and how did you feel about that, my dear?"

Millie's red face belied her feelings, and the others laughed.

"I enjoyed his company, and I hope this is all right, but he's invited himself here for the day next Sunday. He said he'd accompany me to church and then stay for dinner. He said you wouldn't mind."

"Cheeky boy; he knows his old granny too well. No, of course, I don't mind. We'll be delighted to see him, and I could see he was quite smitten with you at Christmas. Who am I to stand in the way of true love?"

CHAPTER 6

BRAMPFORD SPEKE/EXETER

It was a bright sunny day when the doctor finally permitted Lady Lilliana to take a stroll around the magnificent landscaped grounds of Grantley Manor. The winter had, without a doubt, been the longest and most tedious she had ever known. Weakened by typhoid before Christmas, she had then fallen ill with influenza, followed by a bout of pneumonia, and, unbeknownst to her, the doctor had feared for her life. However, with her appetite improving, she gained strength with every day that passed, but was glad to rest on a comfortable seat near the lake. It was a spot sheltered from the chilly wind, and she raised her face gratefully to the warm spring sunshine.

"Oh, Clive, you have no idea how grateful I am to feel the sun upon my face; there were many days in the last couple of months when I thought I might never enjoy this simple pleasure again. I'm so pleased to be sitting here, especially with you, my darling."

"I'm delighted you've recovered your health, my dear, and now you have the whole summer to look forward to. Do you think you'll soon be well enough to travel to London? I must return in the next few weeks, for my father-in-law is already suspicious of the amount of time I spend in Devon, and unfortunately, I can't risk upsetting him if I'm to continue living as I do."

"Yes, I think so. I'm feeling so much better, and I must attend the solicitor's office in London for the reading of Edgar's will. It's only a formality, of course, but until it's done, I can't tell my nephew, Oswald, that I intend him to inherit the house and estate from me eventually. I cannot wait to see his face when I tell him the good news; he'll be so surprised and pleased. I wonder if he might decide to come and live here; I'd like that, for I enjoy his company."

"Has there been any further news on the mother of Edgar's mistress and her two bastard children? A few weeks ago, I spoke to the two men you sent looking for them before Christmas, but they had no progress to report."

"No, sadly not, and that reminds me, I must speak to them myself. I've been so ill that I've not checked on their progress, but surely they must have located the children by now; I mean, how far can two penniless waifs get on foot and in winter? I must do that when we return to the house."

Some thirty minutes later, Bill and Larry, the two workmen, had been summoned to the drawing room and were distinctly uncomfortable as they stood before her ladyship. Their employer wasted no time on pleasantries, asking straightaway if they had found Mrs Gibbs and her two grandchildren.

"We understand the vicar took the old lady to the workhouse, ma'am, but we haven't visited to find out if she's still there. We were told she was unlikely to live."

"And what of the two children?"

"We traced them as far as Crediton, where folk recognised them from our description, ma'am, but then the trail went cold. We continued searching for them right up until Christmas, but no one we spoke to had seen hide nor hair of them. The weather was atrocious, with heavy snow and ice, and it was difficult to believe they could have survived out in the open in such temperatures. We came to the conclusion that they had probably perished. Either that or someone had taken them in, meaning it would be impossible for us to find them until the weather improved."

"So, have you continued your search now that the weather is better?"

"No, ma'am, we were needed here on the estate as there was so much work to do, and we thought it was better to do that until we could speak to you again to find out your wishes."

Lady Lilliana looked at them haughtily, her displeasure plain for all to see. The two labourers kept their eyes on the carpet and shuffled uncomfortably as they wondered if they would keep their jobs. Their mistress was never lenient with any member of staff who displeased her.

"I thought my instructions were clear. I told you to search until you found the pair of runaways, or I told you to stop. Which part of that instruction did you not understand? Go, get out of my sight while I decide whether or not to sack you, for you certainly deserve to be dismissed for not obeying my instructions to the letter."

The two men backed away, muttering to each other. They had worried about this outcome for weeks, but in truth, did not know where else to look for the two runaways. They firmly believed they must have perished and were probably lying dead in a ditch somewhere, or someone had taken them in, and they were keeping out of sight. Neither man blamed them; they would have done the same in their shoes.

Sensing his lover's anger, Sir Clive reached for her hand.

"Don't upset yourself, my dear; we will find them, and to be fair, it sounds as if the men didn't know where else to look, so it might be a little harsh to dismiss them, though naturally, that must be your decision. However, only last week, I placed more advertisements in all the local papers offering a substantial reward, so no doubt, sooner or later, someone will come forward with information. I've always found that money will usually loosen tongues."

Calming down a little, Lilliana forced a smile back onto her face. "Thank you, Clive, that is kind of you; I do hope so."

"In the meantime, if you think you're fit enough to travel, why don't we visit the Exeter workhouse and find out what has happened to Mrs Gibbs? You never know; the two children might be there too and right under our noses all the time. In fact, the more I think about it, the more likely I think that will be the case. They had little money and were travelling in the middle of winter in bitter temperatures. Without a doubt, someone would have taken them to the workhouse to be with their grandmother."

"Oh, yes, that might be it; you are clever, my darling; yes, let's do that. I'm determined to find them, for the girl must be punished for stealing my brooch. I'll see her in jail or hanged if it's the last thing I do."

A few days later, and fortunately, with her doctor's blessing, Lady Lilliana, accompanied by Sir Clive, travelled to Exeter, where they decided to spend the night and visit the workhouse the next day.

"I've booked us into the Royal Clarence Hotel in Exeter, my dear. Have you ever stayed there?"

"Oh, yes, I have, though a while ago now; how wonderful, Clive. I believe it is quite the most comfortable hotel I've ever stayed in, and the apartments are so elegant."

"Indeed, and although situated in such a pleasant spot overlooking the Cathedral Green, it's only a stone's throw from the Exeter Union Workhouse in Bartholomew Street; we can probably walk there in the morning if the weather is favourable. I hope I have not been presumptuous, my dear, but I have arranged for us to have adjacent rooms with an adjoining door. It's so long since we've been able to spend any quality time together."

"Perfect. You think of everything, Clive. It's a pity you're still married, for now, my beastly husband is no more; we could finally have been together."

"Although that would be marvellous, I'm afraid it is out of the question, as you know."

"Yes, yes, I know, but one day, maybe."

The next morning, after a delicious breakfast, Lady Lilliana and Sir Clive decided to walk the short distance to the workhouse. It was a large and imposing building, and several inmates worked in the gardens as they approached.

"My goodness, what a huge building; how many people do they have here?"

"I've heard it can accommodate up to five hundred people, though I don't think it's full yet. I'm told the infirmary alone has beds for over a hundred poor souls."

They entered the building and approached an elderly woman sitting at a desk. It was obvious that this couple was not seeking admission, and the woman smiled up at them pleasantly.

"Good morning; how may I help you?"

"Good morning, ma'am. We want to enquire about an inmate, please, and, if possible, have a word with her."

"Of course; what is the inmate's name?"

"It's an old lady called Emily Gibbs, and her two grandchildren may be with her. They're called Millicent and Jonathan Gibbs."

"I see. Do you happen to know when they were admitted?"

"Yes, Emily Gibbs would have been admitted a week or two before Christmas."

"Please take a seat whilst I check our records. I'll try not to keep you too long."

Some fifteen minutes later, the woman approached Lady Lilliana and Sir Clive, shaking her head.

"I'm afraid none of the people you seek are in the workhouse. Emily Gibbs was admitted on the twenty-first day of December and spent three weeks in the infirmary. However, somewhat unusually, she discharged herself and has not been readmitted. It's unusual for inmates to discharge themselves from the infirmary, for if they are there, they are unwell and would return to the workhouse's normal accommodation before leaving to face the outside world. As for Millicent and Jonathan Gibbs, there is no record of them ever having been admitted here."

"Are you sure?"

"Oh, yes, ma'am; I keep the register myself and have done so for many years. I pride myself on my bookkeeping. You can rest assured that what I have told you is correct."

"Are you sure the old woman didn't die?"

"Perfectly sure, ma'am. If that had happened, then that is what I would have recorded."

"I see; did the old woman leave a forwarding address, or is there any record of anyone collecting her?"

"No, I'm afraid we don't keep that information, ma'am. People come to the workhouse voluntarily and can leave whenever they wish; it's none of our business where they go."

CHAPTER 7

HARTFORD

Willie and Edward Carter entered the spacious kitchen of Sugworthy farmhouse and were greeted by a tantalising aroma which awakened their taste buds and made their mouths water. They were ravenous, for they had been up since half past five and, having milked twenty cows and cleaned out the shippens, they were more than ready for a hearty breakfast. Willie had worked at the farm for several years, having started as a young boy. He was soon to be promoted to the position of farm manager, for although young, he had kept the place going for the last couple of years when the previous tenant, Tommy Houle, became too ill and infirm to keep on top of things. Willie's hard work was now to be rewarded by Robert Fellwood, the owner of the farm, which formed part of the Hartford estate. Annie Fellwood, Willie's sister and Robert's wife, would have dearly liked Willie to be the next tenant. However, Robert felt he was a little young for that position and, in any case, wanted his newly found second cousin, Marrok Fellwood, to take over.

Marrok was the son of Sam Fellwood, an old man who had lived most of his life as a gypsy and a tramp. Sam had always known he was a Fellwood, but he had no way of proving it until one day, fate took a hand, and his parentage was recognised. To his amazement, Sam discovered he was the heir to a considerable fortune left to him by his late father, Thomas, and since then, his life had changed beyond all recognition. However, although able to enjoy all the comforts of life, Sam only wanted to find his son, Marrok, whom he had reluctantly abandoned as a child over forty years earlier. Fortunately, the pair had recently been reunited when Sam discovered Marrok and his four children living in the Barnstaple workhouse. Marrok had now recovered from a broken leg, and he and his family would soon be moving to Sugworthy Farm.

Edward Carter was Willie's younger brother and had moved to the farm a few months earlier. Edward was only ten and had been deaf since birth. He was also mute but had a magical way with animals and had been a godsend to Willie while the farm was so short-staffed. The two brothers, accompanied by another couple of farmhands, scrubbed their hands at the sink and then eagerly sat around the table.

"My goodness, Florrie, my nose tells me something smells even more delicious than usual; what is it?"

The housekeeper smiled at Willie, for whom she had a soft spot. "Yes, you're right, lad. I've cooked some hogs' pudding to go with your bacon and eggs this morning, so that and a slice or two of crisp fried bread should fill your belly."

Edward grinned happily, and the labourers and Florrie all tucked into their delicious breakfast together. Willie was in an exceptionally good mood, for he had the rest of the day off and was planning to take Edward with him to Hartford. Edward, of course, knew nothing of this, but Willie knew he would be delighted to see his mother, Sabina, and his siblings. Willie had other plans, as he had arranged to escort Millie, her brother, Jonathan, and his grandparents to church and then join them all for tea. He couldn't wait to see Millie again and wondered if she felt the same.

The young lady in Willie's thoughts was upstairs making the beds when she heard the sound of a horse's hooves in the yard. Millie glanced out of the window, and her face lit up when she saw it was Willie, for she had been worried he might not come. Hastily tucking the last sheets and blankets into place, she hurried down the stairs to the parlour and found Betsey welcoming her grandson inside.

"Hello, Willie. How lovely to see you. I thought you might have Edward with you."

"Hello, Gran; yes, he did come with me, but I've left him at the Lodge House with Mum. Have you settled into your new home?"

"Yes, thanks to you and Millie, we're all shipshape and enjoying living here. It's such a treat not to have to do so much cooking and cleaning and tend to all the travellers at the inn; I don't know myself. Millie barely lets me lift a finger, and I'm being spoilt."

"You deserve it, Gran." Willie was greeted by his grandfather, Ned, smoking a pipe in his favourite chair by the stove, and Jonathan, whittling a piece of wood with his pocket knife. Finally, he turned his attention to Millie. "Hello, Millie, how are you?"

"Oh, I'm fine, thanks, Willie; how about you?"

Having dispensed with the pleasantries, Ned advised Willie that he would miss the church service that morning.

"It's bitterly cold out, and I'd rather stay here in the warm; if I have to have a weak heart, I intend to make the most of it." Ned grinned boyishly.

"I don't blame you, Grandad; I'd do the same in your shoes. How about the rest of you? Are you all coming to church?"

"Yes, we are, but after church, Jonathan and I will call on your Uncle George; I'm afraid he's still not well. Now, we've all had a cooked breakfast and won't want much until teatime, but how about you, lad? Are you hungry? I can find you a pasty to tide you over until then if you like?"

"No, it's all right, Gran; Florrie cooked us all an enormous breakfast, so I won't be hungry until teatime."

"All right, and perhaps after church, if you and Millie would like a little time to yourselves, I thought you might take her for a walk around the village. Although it's cold out, I think the sun will shine, and plenty of spring flowers are in bloom. What do you think, Millie?"

"Oh, yes, I'd love that; I've explored a little but not gone far. I must be back in time to cook the tea, though, Willie. I'm roasting a shoulder of lamb; will you be able to stay?"

"I'd love to, thanks; is there any mint sauce?"

"Yes, I found some in a sheltered corner of the garden earlier."

Leaving Ned to enjoy a little time to himself, the others walked the short distance to the church, where several other members of the Carter and Fellwood families joined them.

When the service had ended, Betsey, accompanied by Jonathan, first checked that Ned was all right and then walked to her son George's cottage. George was a devout Christian, and his mother knew he must be feeling poorly to miss his regular weekly visit to the church. George owned the village shop, a successful and lucrative business which sold many items, including clothes, shoes, and groceries. Having lost his first wife, Alice, to diphtheria some six years earlier, George was now married to her sister, Mary Ann, who had recently given birth to a daughter, their third child in as many years. In truth, George would have preferred not to have started a second family at his age, for he already had three grown-up children, Francis, Theresa, and Harriet, from his first marriage. However, nature had taken its course, much to the amusement of some of his family. On the other hand, Mary Ann was delighted to become a mother, having long given up the hope of marrying and resigned to life as an old maid.

After knocking briefly, Betsey and Jonathan entered the cottage by the back door and stepped into a cosy room where Cissie, the housekeeper, was busily peeling potatoes at the sink. Beside her, her son, Mickey, was scrubbing carrots.

"Hello, Cissie; how are you?"

The middle-aged woman looked far older than her forty-five years; her thin face was wrinkled and marred by a long and ugly scar down one side. It seemed life had not been kind to her, and, in truth, that was the case. Cissie and her son, Mickey, had been rescued a few months earlier from a miserable existence in one of the most notorious brothels in the nearby town of Barnstaple. As a reward for their help in rescuing George's eldest daughter, Theresa, who had been abducted, she and Mickey now lived with the family in Hartford and were never happier. Cissie smiled widely at the older woman.

"Oh, I'm grand, thank you, Betsey, and still thanking my lucky stars for the day your menfolk rescued Mickey and me from that terrible man, Noah Berryman, at The Tucker's Arms. We're leading such a different life now, I can tell you."

"I'm pleased to hear it, Cissie. Where is everyone?"

"Miss Teresa has gone for a walk with her young man, Louis Blaquiere, and they will be here a little later for their dinner. I believe her sister, Miss Harriet, is in her room reading, and Master Francis has stayed at the shop in Barnstaple today, though he often does come here for Sunday lunch."

"What about George and Mary Ann and the little ones?"

"Mr George has stayed in bed today, for he's feverish again and not feeling well. The mistress is in the sitting room with Nellie and Sophie, who are playing with their toys, and I believe she's feeding the little one. The doctor has only allowed her out of bed in the last day or two, for 'tis barely a fortnight since Etheline was born. Would you and

Jonathan like to stay for dinner? It's roast chicken, and there's plenty of it."

"No, thank you, Cissie. Millie's cooking a joint of lamb for our tea, and we had a fried breakfast, so we won't starve. We'll leave you to it and go and see George and Mary Ann."

"Very well, but I'll bring you a pot of tea and some scones; I'm sure this young man will find room for one or two."

Betsey led Jonathan to the sitting room, where Mary Ann had fed the new baby and was patting her back to bring up her wind. She smiled at the sight of her mother-in-law, and the two toddlers made a beeline for their granny. Nellie quickly ran into Betsey's arms, and Sophie crawled as fast as she could. Betsey hugged them both, then set them back on the floor to play with Jonathan.

"How are you, Mary Ann? How's the baby doing?"

"I'm fine, thanks, Betsey, and yes, Etheline is thriving, and she slept for six hours last night, which I was thankful for. How about you? Have you settled into Fred's cottage?"

"Yes, we have, and I think we'll be happy there, thank you. Jonathan's sister, Millie, is doing most of the work around the house, and Ned looks more rested. As for me, I've never had so much free time, and I honestly don't know myself. We just need to find my half-sister, Emily, now, and then we can live the rest of our lives peacefully, I hope. But, more importantly, how is George? Is he pleased to be a father again?"

"I think if he's honest, he wouldn't have had more children from choice, but now they're here, he's fond of them. I wish this one could have been a boy, for he only has one son. Still, at least she's whole, and that's all any of us can ask. As for George, no, he's a bit under the weather. He seems to improve, and we think he's on the mend, and then he relapses. This has happened several times, and the doctor thinks he has rat-bite fever. Apparently, it can come and go like this for some time, and there's no cure."

A little later, Betsey mounted the stairs to visit her eldest son. He was fast asleep when she entered the room, and she sat on a chair beside him and observed him with worried eyes. She could see that George was feverish, and yet he shivered from time to time. After ten minutes or so, he opened his eyes and smiled at her.

"Hello, Mum; you should have woken me. How long have you been sitting there?"

"Not long, and I'd rather you rested. How are you feeling?"

"Not great, but I'm all right. I keep getting bouts like this, then I feel a bit better for a few days, but then the fever returns. It's a real nuisance, but the doctor says this is how rat-bite fever can affect people. I can't believe I was so stupid as to get bitten."

"It wasn't your fault; it was just one of those things. The glands in your neck seem swollen; is your throat sore?"

"Yes, and I have a throbbing headache that won't go away. But how are you and Dad? Have you settled into Fred's cottage? I'm sorry I couldn't help."

"Yes, we've settled in and are pleased with the move, but now I want to organise a search for my half-sister, Emily."

George grinned. "Yes, I thought you'd want to do that; I hope you find her."

He rubbed his eyes tiredly, and leaning over him, Betsey kissed his forehead and told him to get some more rest.

"I'll come and see you again tomorrow, George; it's easy now that I'm a lady of leisure and only live across the road. I'm going home now to mix up some medicine to help with that headache, and I'll give the potion to Mary Ann later. Doctors know a thing or two, but not much will beat one of Gypsy Freda's old remedies."

CHAPTER 8

Willie clutched Millie's hand and hurried her away from the churchyard, where folk were catching up with each other's news. It was a pleasant morning, and now that the earlier frost had cleared, it was quite warm as the sun shone from a dazzling blue sky.

"Where would you like to go for a walk, Millie?"

"I've only explored the village so far, as I didn't want to get lost. Take me on your favourite walk."

"Very well; in that case, we'll take the footpath which runs inland to the edge of the moors. It then turns towards the coast, and we can walk back beside the sea. It's quite a long walk, is that all right?"

"Yes, that sounds perfect; a walk that has everything."

Willie led the girl across a couple of fields which had recently been ploughed and were ready for planting, and the ground was rough and muddy underfoot. Assuring her the track would become easier, they crossed a stile and found themselves in a large orchard.

"These are huge trees, Willie. What are they? Apple trees?"

"No, these are mazzard trees, and this village is famous for them. It's a sort of cherry, and many farmers have mazzard greens, as they're called. It's become a profitable crop since the railway arrived in Hartford because the fruit can be sent further afield. I've heard a lot of it, even goes to London."

"How do people pick them? The trees are so high."

"Yes, mazzard trees always grow tall, and most farmers make their own ladders because you can't buy one long enough to reach the top. The pickers hang their baskets onto the branches, leaving both hands free for picking. The trees will blossom in a month or two, and then we'll come again because it's a beautiful sight. My sister, Annie, used to come here when she was courting Robert Fellwood, and I saw them kissing several times. I'd love to have jumped out and scared them, but with Robert being a gentleman, I didn't want to upset him. Landowners have a lot of power, and some would have turned us out of our cottage for less. Mind you, now I know him better; I know he's a kind man who can take a joke."

After crossing three orchards, the ground began to rise steeply, and both walkers grew red in the face. They became breathless, and their legs began to ache. Willie glanced at the girl.

"Are you all right, Millie? When we reach the top, there's an old tree trunk we can sit on to rest and an awesome view out over the bay."

"Phew, yes, keep going; is it much further?"

"No, not too far."

Ten minutes later, they staggered up the final few feet of the cliff, and Millie exclaimed in wonder at the incredible vista before her. The cliffs were covered in bright yellow gorse, which stood out vibrantly against the cloudless blue sky. Tiny clumps of pink flowers were dotted here and there amid many primroses.

"Oh, Willie, what an amazing view."

"Yes, I think this is my favourite spot. Whenever I come here, I always think I should have brought a picnic; then I remember that enormous hill and know I wouldn't have wanted to carry it. Shall we sit on this tree trunk and get our breath back for a few minutes?"

They sat side by side and enjoyed watching the gulls wheeling and circling over the cliffs; the only sound was the birds' screaming calls to each other. Far out at sea were a couple of small fishing boats, and below them on the rocks, some seals were basking in the sun.

"Thank you for bringing me here, Willie. The countryside around Brampford Speke, where I lived, is stunning, but we don't have any coastline."

"Do you miss living there?"

"I miss my mum and granny, but of course, they wouldn't be there even if I went back, and I've nowhere to go back to now. I would have liked to go to my mum's funeral, but Gran insisted we leave as soon as possible; she even made us leave at night so no one would see us."

"Why, what was the rush?"

"Well, I didn't know it until after Mum had died and Gran told me, but Sir Edgar Grantley of Grantley Manor was my father. Sir Edgar always called on us regularly, but I never knew Jonnie and I were his illegitimate children. It seems he'd had a relationship with my mother, Rosemary, for years, even before he married Lady Lilliana, and he refused to end it when he was forced to marry the woman his family had chosen for him. He and Mum continued to see each other secretly, even after his wife found out. As you can imagine, Lady Lilliana hates my family and me. Gran said she would, no doubt, evict us from our cottage and make trouble for us. It seems that's true, for she has the police searching for me to arrest me for stealing a precious brooch."

"Oh no, where is the brooch?"

"I did have it, but I didn't steal it. Sir Edgar gave it to my mother when his own mother died, and Gran pinned it on my bodice before I left home. When I found out the police were looking for me and the brooch, I left it with a kindly old lady who gave us a bed for the night when we were making our way here. Aunty Betsey says that now Uncle Fred has moved to The Red Lion and us to his cottage, she'll get someone to search for my gran as soon as possible. I think she'll be in the Exeter workhouse, but she may have passed away, for she was seriously ill when I left her. I'd love to visit my mum's grave and pay my respects, but I daren't show my face in Brampford Speke ever again, not with a price on my head. I don't want to hang! I'm terrified Lady Lilliana will find us as it is."

Willie was horrified to see tears running down Millie's face, so he put his arm around her and hugged her.

"Aw, don't cry, Millie; I'm sure it will all work out, and we'll find your gran. I know you wouldn't have stolen the brooch. I wonder if Robert could help. He knows a lot of rich folk; he may even know Lady Lilliana. Perhaps he could convince her you didn't steal the brooch and help to find your gran."

"Lady Lilliana knows I didn't steal the brooch; that's a story she's made up to make trouble for me. From what I've heard, she's paid a servant at Grantley Manor to swear she saw me creeping out of the house on the day the brooch went missing. She wants me sent to jail or hanged; she's that bitter. I know now that Gran was right to send us away when she did. She probably saved my life. Well, so far, anyway."

"When we get back, I'll ask Gran if she'll have a word with Annie and Robert. I don't see them often, but Gran does, and I'm sure they'll help you."

Willie still had his arm around Millie, and he used his free hand to brush the tears from her cheeks before kissing her gently on the lips. When she responded, he kissed her more passionately, then pulled away and grinned broadly.

"I like you, Millie. Can I see you again?"

"I'd love that, Willie; I like you, too."

They rose happily from their seat and walked hand in hand back to the village along the cliff path, enjoying more views of stunning scenery.

Robert and Annie visited Fred and Charlotte at The Red Lion that afternoon. It was the only day of the week when no stagecoaches called at the inn, so it was quieter than usual. With the lunchtime rush over, Charlotte and Sarah were enjoying a quiet cup of tea in the sitting room with all the children.

Selina peered around the door and beamed when she saw Bentley. Frequently partners in crime, they were always egging each other on and often up to no good.

"Selina, hold the door open for me, too, then."

Selina pushed the door wide open to allow Annie to enter, pushing the twins, David and Thomas, in their pram.

"Hello, Sarah, hello Charlotte; Fred said I'd find you in here. Is it all right if we join you for a while? Robert wants to have a chat with Fred about the canal boats."

"Yes, of course; come in and have a cup of tea. Do you want to put the twins on the floor to play with Doris?"

Annie placed David and Thomas on the floor where Doris was already playing with a selection of toys. Charlotte was breastfeeding Nicholas.

"My goodness, he's growing, Charlotte; how old is he now?"

"Nearly four months, and yes, he likes his food."

"Where are the other children?"

"They're all outside; it's such a lovely day. Rosella and Eddie are playing with some of their school friends, and Llewellyn is with Fred; he's becoming quite skilled at carpentry and is such a help to his father. I expect he wants to hear what Robert says about the boats. He's been working on them with Fred."

Robert sauntered down the grassy path behind the old coaching inn. He went past the stables and Betsey's Kitchen, through the kitchen garden and an orchard, before spotting Fred and Llewellyn at the end of the large meadow, which sloped gently down to the canal. They saw him approaching and waved, and he waved back.

"Hello, Fred, hello, Llewie; I came to see how you're getting on with renovating the barges into pleasure boats since I closed the canal."

"Hello, Robert; yes, good, we've nearly finished two of them. Come and have a look."

Leaving the third boat they were working on, the men walked a short distance along the canal to where the other two barges were resting on wooden cradles, allowing access to their undersides. It was easy to see where new wood had been inserted to replace that rotted, and the boats looked watertight. They sported flat wooden roofs, wide side windows, and a stunning figurehead; on the first, a carved woman, and on the second, a sailor.

"Oh, Fred, I love the figureheads; did you carve them?"

"Aye, we shouldn't have wasted time doing them when there's so much else to do, but I thought they'd make the boats more attractive to visitors. I carved the woman, and Llewie did the sailor; I think he's done a grand job."

"You've both done an amazing job, and the visitors will love them, especially when they've been painted."

"Yes, that's the next job with these two, and I'd like them to have a few more coats of paint while we have them out of the water because that won't happen often. The trouble is it all takes time, and that's something I don't have much of, especially now we're running the inn. Charlotte, Louis, and Sarah bear the brunt of things, but I like to help as much as possible."

"That's why I've come to talk to you, Fred; you can't do everything. I want to get this project up and running in time for Easter, and that's only a month or so away. Annie tells me Easter Sunday is on the twenty-fifth of April, so fortunately, it's quite late this year."

"Yes, but Robert, it's not only the boats that we need to finish; we need to build a jetty here, too, if we want the visitors to come to the inn."

"I know, Fred, and that's why I think we should form a partnership. You can supply the know-how and expertise and oversee the project, and I'll provide the finance for the materials and employ extra staff. What do you think?"

Fred passed a hand over his eyes and squinted at his brother-in-law in the bright sunshine.

"I think that sounds like a great idea; thank you. Several folk are unemployed in the village since you closed the canal, and whilst they understand why you had to close it, they still need to eat and would be glad of the work. I've been neglecting my carpentry business for the last week or two, but with help, we can get it all back on track again. What would we have to do?"

"I know we're related by marriage, and we're friends, but I think we should visit a solicitor and get a formal agreement drawn up; it's never wise to mix business with pleasure. I'll open a joint bank account in our names and put some money in it, which you can access to pay for the materials and wages. Could we get it up and running by Easter if we employ more men?"

"I should think so, and we can but try. I'll do my damnedest, Llewie, too, I'm sure. He spends all his spare time working here as it is."

"So, what's left to do to these two boats?"

"They both need painting inside and out, and I need to fit the seats and build a few shelves at the rear. We could carry a few refreshments for folk to buy then. I've been thinking about the paintwork too. Maybe we could ask Peter Webber to do some artwork. You know, he's that chap with no hands who does the most amazing paintings. It's beyond me how he does it, but he uses a brush in his mouth or one strapped to his arm. I've seen some of his work at the Manor House, and he's so talented. I thought maybe he could paint a picture inside each of the boats."

Robert grinned. "Yes, I know Peter. He lives at Enderby with my Uncle Sam. That's a great idea, Fred; I'll ask him. We'll need to think of some names for these barges, too."

"Llewie came up with a couple of suggestions; tell him, Llewie."

Llewie looked embarrassed. "I thought the boat with the figurehead of the lady could be *The Hartford Lady* and the one with the sailor could be *The Jolly Sailor.*"

"I love it; they're great names, Llewie. What about the third one?"

"It depends on what we carve for the figurehead, but I thought maybe *The Red Lion?*"

"If you think you can carve a lion, that's a very appropriate name."

"I guess we'll also need three animals to pull the barges along the towpath. We could carry on using the mules, but they aren't very elegant; what do you think, Fred? Could donkeys pull them, or would they be too heavy for them?"

"I think donkeys could manage it because an animal can move forty times as much weight in a barge as in a cart; that's why the canals were so popular. There's barely any friction on water, you see."

"Hmm, I don't know. Donkeys aren't very glamorous, are they? I was wondering about shire horses; would they be suitable?"

"Yes, they'd do the job perfectly, but three shire horses would set you back a pretty penny. Mind you, I'm not sure we'd need three. Perhaps we could manage with two. I doubt we'd have enough visitors to fill all three barges at the same time, at least not to start with."

"All right, I'll give it some thought and ask Jack Bater how much two or three shire horses would cost me. Now, about going to Barnstaple, could we go tomorrow?"

"Aye, the sooner I get some help, the better."

CHAPTER 9

Sam Fellwood sighed contentedly as he swirled a generous brandy around the glass he held in his lap. Seated in a comfortable armchair with his feet resting on a padded footstool before a roaring log fire, he could not have been happier. It was a far cry from how he had lived most of his life as a gypsy and a tramp. He still found it hard to believe how much his life had changed since the day he had inherited a fortune. However, in Sam's opinion, the best thing to have happened by far was that he had been reunited with his son, Marrok, who was now sitting in the opposite armchair, equally content and also savouring the excellent brandy.

The third man in the room was Peter Webber, a close friend of Sam's, and the pair lived together in a cottage owned by Sam's Aunty Margery on the Enderby estate. The men were cared for by Peter's grandson, Christopher, and his wife, Clarice, who was expecting their first baby in June. Unfortunately, Peter was unable to hold a glass like the other two men, for sadly, he had lost both his hands in a terrible mining explosion some years before. However, despite his life-changing injuries, he had discovered a surprising talent for painting pictures. After much practice at holding a paintbrush in his teeth or strapped to a harness on his forearm, he made far more money selling his artwork than he ever had down a mineshaft. It was Peter that Fred Carter intended to ask to paint murals inside the canal boats. Fortunately, Sabina Carter had thought of a clever way for Peter to drink unaided, and he leaned over a small table to his side to sip a little brandy using the ryegrass straw inserted into his glass.

Like his father, Marrok rested his bare feet on a footstool, and he wiggled his toes and circled his ankles in the air.

"I'm so pleased to have that plaster off my leg and be able to do this. Not long ago, I thought I'd never walk or work again. Those doctors did an amazing job. I have much to be thankful for."

"We all do, lad, but how is your leg now? Is it still painful?"

"No, not too bad, Dad." The young man smiled as he uttered the word, barely believing he was sitting opposite his father after so many years apart. "It aches a lot, and the doctor said it would, but it's getting stronger every day. I want to visit Sugworthy Farm tomorrow. Would you both like to go with me?"

Releasing the straw from his mouth, Peter replied. "Thanks, Marrok, but I'll say no this time because I've promised to spend the morning painting with Margery. I'd like to come sometime, though, perhaps when you're settled in. Anyway, you should have some time alone with your dad. Are you taking the children with you?"

"Yes, they want to come; we're all impatient to see our new home and strong enough now, having recovered from our stay in the workhouse. I'm so grateful to Robert for offering me the tenancy. I never expected to have my own farm; it's a dream come true, and I can't wait to start. How about you, Dad?"

"Yes, I'd love to come and see the place, please. How are we going to travel there, though?"

"Aunty Margery offered me the use of her carriage for the day, so I thought we'd visit the farm and then go to

Hartford Manor and see Annie and Robert. As it's a Saturday, the children will be home from school, so they can play with Selina."

Early the following day, after a delicious fried breakfast, Marrok walked the short distance to Enderby House to collect the carriage. It was ready and waiting for him, and he assured the farm manager that he was more than capable of managing the horses himself and would not require a driver. He carefully drove the carriage to Primrose Cottage, where Sam and the four children were waiting.

The meagre diet inside the workhouse had caused Marrok and the children to lose a lot of weight, and sadly, their mother, Laura, had perished from cholera whilst they were living there. However, Clarice's cooking using wholesome food swiftly put that to rights, and the family was now fit, healthy, and eager to see their new home.

Sam boarded the carriage first, followed by nine-year-old twins Jinnie and Eliza, then six-year-old Martin and three-year-old Paul. Marrok took his time, and as the journey took them nearly an hour, Sam kept his grandchildren entertained by telling them tales of when he was a boy and living a rough life as a gypsy.

The carriage stopped in the farmyard, and Willie appeared from the barn to welcome the visitors. He had not known they were coming and had only met Marrok a couple of times. The two men shook hands, and Willie introduced his younger brother, Edward, and a couple of other farmhands. Assuring his new boss that the horses would be cared for, Willie led the way into the old farmhouse.

Florrie, an old lady who had been the housekeeper there for many years, was wiping her hands on a towel and eyed the visitors warily.

"Marrok, this is Florrie; she's lived here all her life, for her mother was the housekeeper before her. If you want to know anything about Sugworthy Farm or the folk that have lived here, then there's not much that Florrie can't tell you. She also cooks the most delicious meals."

"Hello, Florrie; how are you?"

"I'm well, sir; thank you for asking, and I'm pleased to see your leg has healed."

"Yes, it has, thank you. Now, Florrie, a little bird told me that you're concerned about keeping your job here. Is that right?"

"Yes, sir. I must confess I've had more than a few sleepless nights since Mr Houle died. I've only ever lived here, you see, and I'm not sure where I'll go if I'm no longer needed, though, of course, that's not your worry, and you must do as you see fit. If you can give me a little notice, I'd appreciate it, though."

"There's no need to worry, Florrie; I'm told you're an excellent worker and have this place running like clockwork. Your job is safe for as long as you want it. The thing is, can you cope with four noisy, and sometimes naughty, children in the house? It's me who should be worried you'll want to leave."

The change in the woman's face was heartwarming as she smiled broadly and took Marrok's hand.

"Oh, sir, you don't know what that means to me; you really don't. I've lived here since I was born, and my mother and grandmother before me. I've never married, for I never found a man I wanted to spend the rest of my life with, and so I've never had a family, more's the pity. I love children, though, and there's nothing I'd like better than to care for yours. It'll be a pleasure to cook for some youngsters. It would have broken my heart to leave Sugworthy Farm."

"Excellent; I'm glad that's settled. Now, could you show us around the farmhouse?"

"Aye, that I can. Now, although most of it's tidy, I'm afraid I don't clean all the rooms every week as there are eight bedrooms, and only two have been used in recent years: one for Tommy Houle and his late wife and one for me. If I'd known you were coming, I'd have scrubbed everything."

"Then I'm glad you didn't know, Florrie; I wouldn't have wanted to cause you too much work. To begin with, we won't need to use all the bedrooms, and the rest can wait for the time being. I'll need a room, one for the girls and one for the boys; I think they'd prefer to share for the time being. I bet it's quiet and dark here at night."

"It certainly is, sir, apart from the old barn owl who screeches most nights and wakes me up."

Marrok glanced at his father. "Dad, I've been meaning to ask whether you'd like to come here to live with us. If so, we'll need another bedroom for you. I didn't want to ask you in front of Peter, as I didn't know where it would leave him, Christopher, and Clarice if you moved here. I wouldn't want to see them lose their home."

"Ah, son, I was wondering if you would ask me that question, and yes, without a doubt, I'd love to live here with all of you. We've spent so many years apart, I'd love it, though, like you, I wouldn't want the Webbers to have to move. Let me think about it. Now I have so much money I could pay to rent Primrose Cottage for them or possibly even buy it if Margery would sell it to me."

"That's great, Dad; I hoped you'd come here to live. It would be good for the children to have their grandfather around."

"To be honest, it will suit me far better to live here than at Enderby, though I'll miss Peter, for I enjoy his company. Primrose Cottage is so lavishly decorated and furnished with the most expensive furniture that I'm always worried I'll damage something, although Margery always tells me not to worry about it. Here, in the farmhouse, it's much more homely, and I can potter about the farm and do a few jobs. I worked for Charlie Chugg at Hollyford Farm for a few months, when he let me live above the stables, and I enjoyed helping out on the farm. These past few months have been interesting living the life of a gentleman, but I need something to do."

"Good, that's settled then. Right then, Florrie, would you lead the way, please?"

Sam, Marrok, and the children followed the housekeeper up a steep staircase that led onto a spacious landing. Sunlight streamed through a window, and Marrok and Sam were thrilled with the view of the rolling hills on the edge of Exmoor.

"Now, this was Mr Houle's bedroom. I've stripped the bed, washed the sheets, and cleaned it from top to bottom, so perhaps you'd like this bedroom, sir?" Florrie looked questioningly at Marrok. "It's the largest room and the most comfortably furnished. It has quite a view, too."

Marrok crossed the room and peered out of one of the two large windows. "Oh, yes, this will suit me down to the ground, Florrie, but we must get one thing straight: you can't keep calling me sir. My name is Marrok, and that's what I'd like you to call me. I'm sure Dad will say the same."

"Yes, of course, Florrie, call me Sam; although we're both lucky to have been recognised as belonging to the Fellwood family, it's not long since I lived in a rickety old hut, and Marrok and the children were in the workhouse. You'll get no airs and graces from us, and I want us all to be friends."

"Very well, sir, sorry, Sam." Florrie smiled at the old man. "This next room is mine at the moment, but I don't mind moving to any of them as long as I can stay here. I had this room because it was easier to nurse Mrs Houle and then Tommy when they became ill. It's a pleasant room, as you can see, but there are plenty of other rooms I can move to, and it might be sensible for the children to use this room next to their father."

"Yes, that might be best if you're sure you don't mind, Florrie."

"No, of course not. Now, I'm afraid that this is where things start to go downhill. You see, no money has been spent on this farmhouse for quite some time. Tommy barely made a living for the last few years and wasn't one to spend money even before that, so barely any maintenance work has been done. You'll see what I mean as we go around."

The following two bedrooms were in reasonable condition, though they would benefit from a thorough spring clean. The furniture was covered in dust sheets, and the windows were grimy, though neither man thought less of Florrie for that. It was a large house for one woman to manage and nurse the owners. Both rooms were of a decent size, with a double bed in each, a large oak wardrobe, and a marble-topped washstand.

Moving on along the landing, Florrie warned them to watch where they were walking, as here and there were buckets collecting rainwater, for the roof leaked.

"I'm afraid this end of the house has barely been used in years, and I think the roof needs replacing. I mentioned it to Mr Houle many a time, but my words fell on deaf ears. These last four bedrooms are in a poor state."

Florrie pushed open a door with some difficulty, for it was swollen with dampness. As they entered another spacious room, they saw three buckets strategically placed to catch rainwater.

"My goodness, Florrie, it must take you all your time to keep these buckets emptied when we have a downpour."

"Yes, it does, and the other three rooms are the same. I usually open a window and pour the water outside, but even that's becoming difficult as the windows are so hard to open. I'm afraid these rooms will need some work before they can be occupied. However, the next one's not too bad, so I'll move into that one; then, you can have the four best rooms."

They surveyed the other bedrooms, which were all damp and mouldy, and the men could see why Florrie had given up trying to keep them clean.

"Right, I think we've seen enough, Florrie, to know the place needs a new roof or at least a lot of repairs. That first bedroom you showed us is enormous, so we'll move another bed in there, and Dad and I will share that room. The two boys can move into your room as they still tend to wake during the night, and it's better if they're close to me; then the girls can have one of the other two decent rooms and you the other."

"Oh no, sir, oh, sorry, Marrok, I don't want to put you out. I'll be all right in the fifth bedroom. There's room for my bed to be away from where the roof leaks."

"No, it's too damp and will make you ill, Florrie. No arguments now; my mind's made up. Now, shall we explore downstairs?"

Florrie led the way, and they surveyed the spacious ground floor. There was a large kitchen, which was cosy and warm, with a Bodley stove, a dining room, a parlour, a sitting room, a study, and a dairy. Outside, a lean-to housed a copper for washing and an old mangle.

Although the downstairs was also neglected and needed refurbishment, it was in better condition than the bedrooms because no rainwater was leaking into the rooms. The Fellwood family was overjoyed to think they would soon be living in this wonderful old house.

CHAPTER 10

Leaving the children in Florrie's capable hands, Marrok and Sam went to find Willie, as they wanted to explore the outbuildings and land. Unused to entertaining children and knowing there were no toys in the house, Florrie was momentarily unsure how to deal with her unexpected guests. She thought back to her childhood, when there were barely any toys, and tried to remember what she had done with her time. Suddenly, she beamed at the children.

"I know what we could do. Would you like to do some baking? We could make some cakes and jam tarts for your dad and grandad to eat later."

"Oh, yes, please; we used to do baking with Mum, but we haven't done any since we had to go into the workhouse and she died."

"Let's do that, then. Now, remind me, my dear, what's your name?"

"I'm Jinnie, and that's Eliza, and we're twins. The boys are Martin and Paul."

"That's it; I'll try to remember. Right, I think I'll put you two girls making the pastry, and the boys can help me to make some cakes. I'll put another log or two on the fire to get the stove hot, and then we can start."

Marrok and Sam found Willie in the barn, where he was harnessing two sturdy carthorses. Two friendly black-and-white collies greeted them.

"Hello, Willie; what are these two called?"

"Oh, that's Rex and Rover, and they're a great help herding the sheep and cows."

The two men patted the dogs and watched Willie deftly fasten buckles and straps.

"What are you doing this morning?"

"I'm getting Bert and Sadie ready to work in the fields. We've ploughed the land we want to till this spring, but the ground needs to be broken down before we can sow any crops, and it's nice and dry today. Of course, you might want to change what we'd planned to grow now that you're taking over."

Willie explained to Marrok and Sam what he had intended to plant that year, and they agreed.

"That sounds all right to me, Willie; we'll stick with that for this year, especially as you already have the seed. I'd probably have chosen the same crops as you, anyway. Would you mind showing us around the farm buildings before you start? If you can spare the time, I'd like to ride around the farm and see the lie of the land, too."

"Yes, that's no problem. I'll ask one of the other farmhands to make a start in the fields, and I'll join him when we've finished."

Willie led them into a huge barn, which still housed a generous amount of last year's hay, a mound of mangolds, and, in another corner, a pile of potatoes. Marrok could see daylight shining through the roof at the far end, and the floor beneath was damp.

"I see repairs are needed here, too. We looked around the house earlier, and it needs a lot of work."

"Yes, I'm afraid it will be the same story wherever you look. Mr Houle hadn't spent anything on maintenance for years, and the fences and gates are in a sorry state, as are the shippens and stables."

"I can help with the cost of the repairs, Marrok; we can do a bit at a time and get it put to rights."

"Thanks, Dad; that's kind of you; that will be a big help because, as you know, I have no money of my own."

There were three large shippens where the cows were milked twice daily and sheltered through the winter. The two stables could accommodate eight horses, though the farm only had two carthorses and a stallion, previously ridden by Tommy Houle. At the bottom of the farmyard were two pigsties housing four pigs, a large henhouse surrounded by numerous chickens, and a flock of geese that ran hissing and squawking at the visitors.

"The geese are better than any guard dog, especially now when they're nesting; they can give you a nasty nip if you get too close."

When they had finished touring the outbuildings, Willie offered to take Marrok and Sam around the land on horseback.

"If I ride Tommy's horse, you two could ride the carriage horses; would that be all right?"

"Yes, that's fine. What about you, Dad? Do you want to come or stay with Florrie and the children?"

"I haven't ridden much for some time, so I expect I'll feel about ninety tomorrow, but I'd like to see the farm and get back to riding, so I think I'll come with you."

The three men set off to explore the two hundred acres of land, and Sam and Marrok were delighted with what they saw. Despite seeing work to do wherever they looked, the land was mainly flat and fertile. A small brook meandered through several fields, providing an excellent water source, and the views in every direction were stunning.

"You've done a great job of keeping it going with so little help, Willie. I think we'll make a sound partnership, you and me, and I can't wait to get to work."

"When are you planning on moving here?"

"Next week, I think. Fortunately, there are enough usable bedrooms, and the rest can be renovated once we live here. I'm going to visit Robert at Hartford now, and as long as he approves, then I'd like us to move in next week."

The three men returned to the farmhouse, where they found the children playing with a litter of kittens. Florrie had prepared a tureen of leek and potato soup, and they enjoyed a bowlful with some crusty bread before sampling the children's efforts at rock buns and jam tarts.

Leaving Sugworthy Farm, Marrok carefully drove the carriage to Hartford Manor, where Dodger met him and promised to take care of the horses. The visitors knocked on the door of the west wing and were admitted by Ethan Bater, the farm manager's son. Sam and Marrok were delighted when Ethan told them that Robert and Annie were at home and ushered them into the sitting room.

"Hello, Marrok, Sam, and everyone; we weren't expecting to see you today."

"No, I'm sorry to arrive unannounced, Robert; I hope it's convenient?"

"Yes, of course; how are you all?"

"We're all fine, thank you, and I'm so pleased to have the plaster off my leg. We've been to view Sugworthy Farm, and what a wonderful farm it is. I can't thank you enough for letting me be the tenant."

Annie grinned at the four children. "Selina's in the nursery; would you like to go and play with her? She'll be so pleased to see you."

The children nodded, and Annie rang the bell for a maid to escort them to the nursery. When the children had left, Marrok and Sam continued to tell Robert and Annie about their visit to the farm.

"I'd like to move in next week if that's all right with you, Robert?"

"Yes, of course, the sooner the better; is the farmhouse habitable?"

The two men grimaced, and Marrok explained. "I'm afraid everything's in a bit of a state, though Willie's done well to keep the place going. The animals are healthy and well-fed, and he's ploughed the fields ready to plant spring crops, but the house, outbuildings, and all the gates and fences need repair. Fortunately, four of the eight bedrooms are all right, but the other four are damp and mouldy because there's so much rain coming through the roof, which I think will need replacing. The downstairs is a little better, but the whole place needs a lot of attention."

"I'm not surprised. I should have asked Tommy to leave years ago, but his family had lived there for so many generations that I couldn't bring myself to do it. I don't mind helping with the cost if you can oversee the work. It should be in good repair before you take over the tenancy, so I have some responsibility as the owner."

"I've already told Marrok that I'll help with the cost of the repairs, Robert, and I'm delighted to be in a position to do so. I have to sort out a few matters with your Aunty Margery about the Webbers continuing to live in Primrose Cottage, but Marrok has invited me to live at the farm with him, and I can't wait."

"Oh, that's good, Sam; we wondered if you'd move there. After so many years apart, that will be so nice for both of you. Thanks for your offer to pay for the repairs; perhaps we can deal with it together. What about Florrie, Marrok? Are you going to keep her on?"

"Yes, I've put her mind at ease about that. The children took to her this morning, and if the soup she gave us for lunch was anything to go by, then she's an excellent cook. There is one other thing I wanted to ask you about. The children have been attending Enderby School, but when we move to Hartford, they'll need to go to the local school, though it will be a bit of a walk for them. I wondered if you could direct me to the headmaster's house if he lives in Hartford. I thought I'd call on him this afternoon and suggest the children start after Easter. I'd like them to have a week or two at the farm to settle in before they start school."

Annie and Robert exchanged glances, which Sam and Marrok noticed.

"What? Is the school full or not good?"

"No, it's not that, Marrok, but Annie and I have been discussing Selina's education and trying to decide whether to send her to school or employ a governess. Annie and all her siblings attended Hartford School, but I had a governess until I was nine and was then sent to a boarding school." Robert took Annie's hand. "Annie, you know my preference, but I'll leave this decision to you, though I will want David and Thomas to attend a boarding school when they're older."

Annie looked slightly concerned at this news but decided that was a conversation for another day. "Thank you, Robert. I know Selina will be much happier attending the school with all my younger siblings, so that's my choice. Marrok, if you like, I could accompany you to the village a little later, and we can speak to the headteacher, Mr Atkins, together. He's a great teacher, and he's been at the school for years; he even taught me. Now, speaking of Easter, Robert and I plan to invite all the family here on Easter Sunday, which falls on the twenty-fifth of April this year. We'll have a garden party and an easter egg hunt if the weather is kind to us, or if not, it will have to be indoors; do say you'll come. You too, Sam."

"Yes, that sounds wonderful; thank you. We wouldn't miss it for the world."

CHAPTER 11

CREDITON

Rosa Baker's hip was hurting, and she decided it was time to visit the bakery in Crediton and enjoy a cake and a cup of tea before catching the train back to Eggesford. She usually enjoyed her weekly shopping trip, but it was getting ever harder, and she wondered how much longer she would be able to manage it. She entered the busy tearoom and was pleased to see that her favourite table by the window was unoccupied. The lady behind the counter noticed the weary expression on Rosa's face and, smiling brightly, told Rosa to sit down and that she would bring the refreshments to her.

"There we are, my dear; I guessed you'd want your usual. I hope I was right. You seem a little tired this morning. Is everything all right?"

"Oh, thanks, Mary; bless you. Yes, but my hip is particularly painful, and I didn't get a wink of sleep last night. I haven't finished my shopping, but I had to rest. I'll sit here now and have a look at the newspaper until it's time for my train if that's all right with you."

"Yes, of course. You're one of our regulars; you sit there as long as you like."

Rosa, thankfully, took a sip of her strong, sweet tea and bit into the piece of fruit cake she treated herself to every Friday. Reaching into her shopping bag, she retrieved her newspaper and spread it on the table before her. She read a few articles with interest, but as she turned the page, she was horrified to see another advertisement offering a reward for information leading to the apprehension of Millicent and Jonathan Gibbs. Fortunately, there were no photographs, but the detailed description would make them easily identifiable by anyone who saw them. The reward had been doubled to twenty guineas, a small fortune, and the old woman knew many would be tempted. She feared for the youngsters and hoped they had reached their destination in Hartford safely and had been taken in by their relatives.

Leaving the bakery in plenty of time to stroll to the railway station, she boarded the train and was relieved to find an empty seat. Although only four stops to Eggesford, she knew she would struggle to stand all the way. She left the train and glanced worriedly at the steep hill to her cottage, wondering how she would carry her heavy shopping all the way home. Her thoughts went back to the day she had met Millie and Jonathan on the train and had offered them a bed for the night in return for some cleaning. They helped her carry her shopping and then cleaned her home from top to bottom in return for their tea and somewhere to lay their heads for the night.

Half an hour or so later, and with enormous relief, she entered her cottage and dumped her shopping inside the door, deciding to rest before putting it away. As she sank into her favourite armchair, she glanced around the room, which had not been cleaned since the two youngsters had worked so hard in the new year. She had been so grateful to see her home respectable again, but now it needed cleaning once more, and she was not fit enough to deal with it.

Having allowed herself to recover for a few minutes, she struggled to her feet and reached under the wooden mantlepiece, where she dislodged a loose stone. Reaching into the cavity beyond, she retrieved a small leather pouch which held her life savings and a brooch she had promised to keep safe for Millie. She settled back in her armchair and, as she had done many times since the children left, turned the brooch over and over in her gnarled old hand. It was so pretty, especially with the sunlight playing on it through the grimy window. A large sapphire surrounded by diamonds and with a gold clasp, it was such a dazzling piece of jewellery. However, she knew it had brought nothing but trouble to the young girl who had worn it on her bodice, for she had been wrongly accused of stealing it. Rosa had no doubt the girl was innocent and wondered if she would ever see Millie again.

Unfortunately, Rosa Baker wasn't the only one who had seen the advertisement in the newspaper. Simon Higgins, the landlord of The Farmer's Arms at Kings Nympton, was also reading it at that very moment. He could hardly believe his eyes, for without a doubt, it concerned the same youngsters who had stayed at his inn earlier in the year. But for a terrible blizzard which had made travel impossible, Simon would have handed them over to the police himself and claimed the reward without a second thought. However, with his plans foiled by the inclement weather, he had imprisoned them in a bedroom for a day or two, waiting for the road to Crediton to clear.

His intentions towards Millie had been far from honourable during their stay. In desperation, she had cried out from the bedroom window, trying to attract the attention of a family who had also sheltered at the inn and, with the roads now clear, were about to leave. Luckily, the gentleman and his wife heard her plea for help and agreed to take the two runaways to the police station and claim the reward. The landlord had protested mightily at this, saying he had found the pair and the reward should be his. Sir Roger Everson agreed, paid him the ten guineas, and set off to Crediton to get his money back.

That was the last Simon had seen of the two children or the Everson family. Thankfully, the reward money had helped him through a sticky patch, so he had given the matter no more thought. However, he was puzzled about why the children were still on the run.

Luckily for Millie and Jonathan, Sir Roger and his wife, Lady Jasmine, had encouraged the young girl to tell her story and, when she had finished, believed every word she said. Sir Edgar Grantley had been a close friend of theirs, and they were shocked to hear he had passed away. Furthermore, they knew of his miserable marriage and that he had, for many years, kept a mistress. Knowing his embittered wife, Lilliana, they could readily believe Millie's story that the lady was trying to make trouble for her and her brother.

Simon couldn't for the life of him understand what had happened. It didn't matter from his point of view, for he had received the reward money, though he would have liked to spend a night or two entertaining himself with the young girl, but why would the gentleman have paid him the ten guineas and not claimed it back? He called out to Dora, the old woman who worked for him.

"Dora, come here a minute."

The servant hurried to find out what her master wanted.

"Yes, what is it, Mr Higgins?"

"Do you remember that pair of runaways that stayed here when we had all that snow?"

"Aye, sir; of course, I do. That gentleman and his wife took them away in his carriage."

"That's right. So why do you think another reward is being offered? Here, look; see this."

Dora stared at the newspaper but could not read the words, which meant nothing to her.

"Why, what does it say?"

"Oh, I forgot how ignorant you are. It says there's a reward of twenty guineas for information leading to their arrest. It doesn't make sense. That man paid me the ten guineas and was going to claim it back from the police station in Crediton. Do you know what their plans were?"

Millie had confided in Dora that they were making their way to Hartford in the hope of finding some distant relatives, but she had no intention of telling her employer that. Simon was an unkind man who couldn't keep his hands to himself where women were concerned. Consequently, all the maids had left the inn, leaving only Dora, who was too old to interest the lecherous landlord, to do all the work.

"No, sir; she didn't tell me anything, and like you say, it doesn't make sense."

Dora resumed her work with a tiny smile playing around her mouth. She didn't know what had happened but assumed it could only be good for Millie and Jonathan, and she fervently hoped they had reached safety.

Having returned to the sitting room, Simon continued to study the advertisement. After a few moments, he reached for a pen and paper and, in his scrawly handwriting, began to compose a letter to Sir Clive Robinson. Although the innkeeper had no idea where the youngsters were now, he thought that for the price of a stamp, it might be worth sending the letter. He hoped the gentleman might be willing to part with a small reward in return for what little he knew.

CHAPTER 12

HARTFORD

It had long been the ambition of Robert Fellwood to offer shooting and fishing breaks at Hartford Manor, and encouraged by how well his plans for developing the canal were coming along, he felt it was time to investigate the matter further. He had already discussed his ideas with his great aunt Margery, who had been offering similar holidays at her mansion at Enderby for some time. The Hartford Manor estate was blessed with much fertile and productive land, and the farming business was prospering. However, hundreds of acres were spread across Exmoor, where crops would not flourish, but the landscape was ideal for fishing and shooting.

The main stumbling block to Robert's plan was providing accommodation for the visitors. Enderby House was huge, and sensibly, after the death of her husband, Clarence, Lady Margery had selected a few of the best rooms for herself, and the rest was devoted to providing luxurious rooms and suites for the guests. It was a lucrative business, and the house and landscaped gardens were well maintained with the profits. It was mainly men who participated in the expeditions, but they were often accompanied by their wives, who enjoyed each other's company and the sumptuous food on offer.

The difficulty at Hartford Manor was that since Robert had taken over the management of the estate following his father's stroke, he, Annie, and their family had lived in a small part of the west wing, leaving his parents to reside in the main house. Charles and Eleanor had never approved of their son's marriage to Annie, a former servant at the manor, and the two families saw little of each other. Although Robert visited his parents occasionally, they had never met their grandchildren and refused to be in the same room as Annie.

Robert had pondered this problem for some time and decided to pay his Aunty Margery another visit. She was the wisest person he knew and with whom he was very close. At their previous meeting, she suggested he speak to her estate manager for in-depth advice about how to proceed. Having made his decision, Robert went in search of Annie to find out if she would like to accompany him. He found her sitting on the nursery floor, playing with David and Thomas, and Selina was drawing a picture.

"Ah, there you are. That's a wonderful picture, Selina; I love the trees. Is it our garden?"

"Yes, and in a minute, I'm going to draw you and Mummy, and David and Thomas and me."

Robert sat on the floor beside his wife and the two boys, who were beginning to shuffle around and try to crawl.

"I'm going to visit Aunty Margery this afternoon to ask her advice about the fishing and shooting parties I've been talking about, and I wondered if you'd like to come and bring the children."

"Oh, yes, Mummy, can we see Aunty Margery? I like going to see her."

"That would be nice, but we've already promised to see Granny Betsey and Grandad Ned after lunch, and they'll be disappointed if we don't go. I think you were hoping to play with Jonathan, weren't you?"

"Oh, yes; I forgot."

"We'll come next time, Robert, but thanks for asking. I want to find out how Millie and Willie are getting on; it's the latest romance in the family, and Gran says they're quite besotted with each other. Anyway, if we don't come, I expect you'll ride Prince, won't you? You're always saying you don't ride as much as you'd like to these days."

"Yes, I will; I just thought I'd ask."

Within the hour, Robert was galloping across the rugged moorland where he hoped to offer the shooting expeditions. His journey also took him past Shebworthy Pond, where he knew many local folk already fished for a free meal. His first date with Annie had been in this very spot when she offered to take him fishing, and he remembered it fondly, thinking he had fallen in love with her on that day. Knowing how hard it was for some folk to feed their large families, he would be reluctant to tighten up on the poaching and would need to give the matter some thought.

When he arrived at Enderby House, he was shown into the sitting room, where he found Marrok and Sam, who had also just arrived. After the pleasantries were over, Sam explained the reason for their visit.

"Marrok has kindly invited me to move to Sugworthy Farm with him and the children, and I must admit, I'm thrilled because there's nothing I'd like better, but I'm concerned about what will happen to the Webbers." He glanced at Lady Margery. "I've enjoyed living in Primrose Cottage with Peter for the last few months, and I wouldn't want him to have to leave his home. I thought about offering to take him, Clarice, and Christopher with us to Sugworthy, but we already have Florrie as the housekeeper, and you know what they say about two women in a kitchen. Not only that, but there aren't enough usable bedrooms. Perhaps I could purchase the cottage from you, Margery, or, failing that, pay their rent."

"I'm so pleased for you, Sam, and yes, of course, you must live with your son. I must confess, I rather saw this coming, so I've already given the matter some thought. Peter and I have become close friends, and I wouldn't want him to move away. We love our time sketching and painting together, and we've had some enjoyable days out in the carriage. I want the Webbers to continue living at Primrose Cottage, though they may be reluctant to do so, as they may see it as charity once you leave. I'm going to suggest that Christopher works part-time on the estate, and then it could become a tied cottage. I know he has to attend to all of Peter's personal needs, but that doesn't take all day, and he doesn't have enough to do. He told me so himself a while back."

"Oh, that's such a relief. I'm so pleased; can I tell them when we get back? I know it's been playing on their minds too, and with Clarice expecting her baby in a couple of months, I didn't want them to worry."

"Yes, do that; I was going to tell them myself when I next saw them. When are you moving to the farm?"

"This weekend. Fred recommended a builder to me, and he'll call next week to discuss the work that needs to be done. I was hoping Fred would do some of it himself, but he's got too much on, what with the canal project and taking over The Red Lion. Anyway, we'll tell the Webbers the good news and leave you two some time together."

After Sam and Marrok had left, Robert explained the reason for his visit to his aunt, and as usual, she grasped the nettle firmly by the hand.

"Surely, the solution's obvious. You and Annie need to swap places with your parents. They must move into the west wing and let you and Annie live in the main house. You need to do as I've done; select the rooms you need and develop the rest into accommodation for your visitors."

"You make it sound so easy, but you know how set in their ways they are. I can't see them agreeing to it, and there's also Victoria to consider. She's been living with them since Frank was murdered last year."

"I don't think Victoria will stand in your way, and actually, she asked me a while back to keep an eye out for a suitable property for her to purchase. She doesn't want to continue living with her parents forever, and I've found a splendid house for her in Lynton; I think it will be perfect. It's got fantastic views and impressively landscaped gardens. There's even a cottage on the grounds, which may be suitable for Frank's mother. Victoria feels sorry for Catherine, losing her son and husband in such a short time, and she's going to suggest she moves to Devon so she can see more of her grandchildren."

"You're right, of course, but I'm reluctant to upset Mama and Papa."

"Would you like me to visit, and perhaps if I put in my pennyworth, it might help things along?"

"I believe you can read my mind, Aunty Margery, and yes, that would be marvellous, thank you. I was hoping you'd say that."

"It wasn't that difficult to guess your thoughts, my boy. Now, do you want to find my estate manager and pick his brains about the practicalities of your business venture? You might as well while you're here." Robert nodded.

"Go on, then; I'm sure he'll be a big help to you, and when you've finished, come back here, and we'll have some tea together."

CHAPTER 13

Later that evening, with the children settled in bed, Annie and Robert sat together in the study, enjoying a glass of Madeira wine. There had been a cold snap for several days, and they were sitting before a roaring fire, enjoying its warmth. Robert put his arm around his wife's shoulders and drew her close as he sipped his wine. Annie relaxed against him and enjoyed watching the flames flickering in the fireplace.

"How did you get on at Enderby today? I've not had a chance to ask you until now."

"Very well. Aunty Margery immediately came up with a way of accommodating the visitors we hope to attract. To be honest, I'd already thought the same thing, but I knew it would upset my parents."

"I presume the solution is for us to swap places with them?"

"Yes, it's the obvious answer. Would you mind?"

"No, not at all. I'm happy to be living in Hartford Manor and be able to feed my children. You only have to remember my past to know it takes little to make me content. Most days, I can't believe how lucky I am. What about Victoria, though? Hartford Manor is her home, too, and I wouldn't want to upset her."

Robert put down his wine and kissed his wife warmly. "I thought you'd say that, thank you. I went to see Victoria earlier on, and we discussed the matter. She's been looking for a suitable house in the area for her and the children to move to, as she doesn't want to continue living with Mama and Papa. Aunty Margery has been helping her and thinks she's found the perfect house in Lynton. They plan to view it in a couple of days, and I thought we might go with them. Would you like that? Victoria wants you to come."

"Oh, yes, I'd love to. I've never been to Lynton, but I've heard the views are amazing."

"Yes, it's a picturesque spot. Victoria hopes Catherine, Frank's mother, might move to Devon to be nearer her grandchildren. Frank was her only child, and now he and her husband, Monty, have passed away; there isn't anything to keep her in London. She's a pleasant lady, and I hope she does move here; she's had a rough time lately."

"Would she live with Victoria?"

"No, there's a cottage on the grounds of the house Victoria is viewing that might suit Catherine. Victoria wants her to live close by, but not in the same house. We thought we would see if this house is suitable for Victoria first, and if it is, tell Mama and Papa all our plans at the same time. Aunty Margery has offered to help convince them."

"Obviously, I won't come; that would upset them even more."

"Yes, I know, and it's so stupid; I hope they'll come to accept you one day. It's them that's missing out, not us."

Two days later, Robert and Annie joined Victoria in the courtyard and boarded the Fellwood carriage, which Dodger Watkins drove. They were joined by Victoria's younger sister, Sarah, now a young lady of sixteen. They were to collect Aunty Margery from Enderby House and waited in the carriage for the elderly lady to arrive. She didn't keep them waiting long, and they were soon on their way.

Dodger drove the carriage carefully along the narrow, twisting lanes until they arrived at Wrinkleberry House, where they spotted the land agent waiting for them on the steps. It was a grand house, some two hundred years old, and needing modernisation. With fifteen bedrooms, it would be big enough for Victoria and her household staff and still leave adequate accommodation for visiting guests. As the Fellwoods left the carriage, they exclaimed in delight at the far-reaching views. The house was perched on the edge of the clifftop with a commanding view of the Bristol Channel, and the extensive and well-manicured lawns were surrounded by flower beds, now full of daffodils, tulips and wallflowers, all magnificent in the warm spring sunshine.

Victoria gasped in delight. "Oh, Aunty Margery, what a view."

Robert shook the agent's hand and introduced his family. "Thank you for meeting us here, Mr Dunn; I hope we haven't kept you waiting too long?"

"No, I've only been here a few minutes. May I suggest I show you around and then leave you to wander about on your own and get a feel for the place? No one has lived here for over a year since the last owner died, and the family have only recently decided to put the property on the market. I'm afraid you'll have to use your imagination as to how comfortable the house could look, as much of the furniture is covered in dust sheets. However, I can assure you it is a most desirable property and bound to generate much interest once it goes on the market."

"Oh, is it not yet for sale?"

"Yes, it is, but only in the last few days, and as I've been keeping an eye out for a suitable property for Lady Margery, I thought I would offer you first refusal."

"That's kind of you, Mr Dunn, thank you. I can quite see that with these stunning views, the property will not be on the market long. Shall we proceed?"

An hour or so later, the agent left the family and went to sit in the sunshine on the steps. From the exclamations of delight as he conducted the tour, he rather suspected he had found a buyer, and it was worth waiting to find out.

Annie, Victoria, and Sarah immediately fell in love with the property, which, although dusty and neglected, had stunning views from every room, high corniced ceilings, ornate fireplaces, and excellent proportions. Having thoroughly explored the interior, they ventured outside to inspect the stables and outbuildings before strolling through the extensive grounds.

"Oh, look, Victoria, the stables are in good repair and can easily accommodate a dozen horses or more."

"Trust you to take more interest in the stables than in the house, Sarah, but yes, you're right, and I love everything I've seen so far." Sarah and Victoria were keen horsewomen. "Robert, can we walk around the gardens now, please?"

Her brother nodded, and taking Lady Margery's arm and his wife's hand, they walked down a pathway through the dappled shade under the trees and out to a viewing platform where they rested on two benches and admired the view.

"I love the place already. It's perfect, and I can't wait to move here. We must view the cottage to see if it's suitable for Catherine, but to be honest, if it isn't, then I'll get one built. I must have this house."

Lady Margery glanced at her niece. "I thought you'd love it here. I came here once as a girl and remembered it was impressive. However, may I suggest you keep your enthusiasm to yourself when we rejoin the agent? I'm sure we could put in a lower offer."

"Would you like me to negotiate for you, Victoria?"

"Yes, please, Robert; I'd be grateful, thank you."

An hour later, after the cottage was explored and approved, Robert discussed the price of the house with the agent and made an offer, which Mr Dunn thought would more than likely be accepted for a quick sale. Delighted with their morning's work, the party proceeded to an inn in

Lynmouth for some lunch before travelling back to Hartford Manor, where they planned to call on Charles and Eleanor Fellwood and make them aware of their plans.

Charles and Eleanor were enjoying the spring sunshine on the south terrace of Hartford Manor when the footman came to advise that they had visitors. Charles was in his wheelchair, where he had spent most of his time since his stroke a few years earlier, and his wife was relaxing in a garden chair. Eleanor instructed the footman to show the visitors to the terrace and organise refreshments. Annie, of course, had returned to the west wing, knowing her presence would not be welcomed. Eleanor was delighted at the sight of her three children, and Charles smiled his familiar lop-sided smile as they welcomed their visitors and urged them to make themselves comfortable.

"This is a surprise; how nice to see you all. I can't remember the last time we were all together."

"No, it's been a while. How are you, Charles, and you, Eleanor?"

"Oh, not too bad, thank you, and better for this warm sunshine, but what brings you here, Aunty Margery?"

Victoria took up the conversation. "I asked Aunty Margery a while ago to let me know if she heard of any properties on the market that might suit me and the children. I'm grateful to you for letting us all stay here since Frank died and for your support, but I think the time has come for me to purchase my own house."

"There's no need for you to move out, Victoria; this will always be your home. Why haven't you mentioned this before?"

"I know, Papa, and that you and Mama would prefer me to stay, but although I want to live nearby, I need my own house. I didn't want to worry you both until I found something suitable, and now I think I have."

"Oh, so you're not returning to London, then?"

"No, Mama, I've always preferred living in Devon and will do so now that I can do as I please. We viewed a house in Lynton this morning, and it's perfect. Robert has made an offer for me, and if it is accepted, I'll be moving as soon as the house is ready. Actually, I've fallen in love with the place so much that if I had to pay the full price, then I would."

"I'm pleased to hear you'll stay in Devon, for I've loved having you and the children here. We've enjoyed watching our grandchildren growing up, and we'll miss them."

Robert resisted the urge to mention that his parents had three more grandchildren living next door and instead said brightly.

"Lynton isn't far away, and maybe you'll be able to stay occasionally."

"There's a cottage on the grounds that would be perfect for Frank's mother. I'm going to write to her later to suggest she move to Devon; I think she'd benefit from being near her grandchildren, too."

"That's a wonderful idea; she was heartbroken at losing her son and husband within a few weeks of each other, and we enjoy her company too. We'll be rattling around in this huge house on our own, though; I wish you'd reconsider and stay, Victoria."

Robert seized the opportunity to introduce his plans and smiled at his parents.

"I have some news too, Mama, and I may have a solution. The Hartford farms are profitable, but the maintenance and running costs of the Manor House increase by the year, and I've been considering ways to make the estate more sustainable. I've discussed this with Aunty Margery because, as you know, she's an astute businesswoman, and having taken her advice, I intend to offer fishing and shooting weekends and holidays here at Hartford Manor as she does at Enderby House."

"That sounds like a sensible idea, Robert. The countryside of Exmoor is perfect for shooting and hunting, and Shebworthy Pond is teeming with fish, though you'd have to employ more gamekeepers to keep the poachers at bay. The locals seem to think they can help themselves to the fish there whenever they like."

Robert was delighted to hear his father approve of his plan and, thus encouraged, continued.

"I'm glad you agree, Papa. However, there is one hurdle we need to overcome. You see, the guests would need somewhere to stay, and the obvious place is Hartford Manor, but we don't have enough room in the west wing. I want Annie and me to swap places with you and Mama. The two of you do not need a house this size, especially as you rarely entertain anymore."

Eleanor was white-faced and thin-lipped but said nothing for a few moments. Eventually, the deafening silence was broken by Lady Margery, who gently took her niece's hand.

"Eleanor, I can see you're horrified at this suggestion. I'm sure the more so because you disapprove of Annie. However, surely you can see it's the most sensible way forward. Robert is already running the estate and one day will inherit the Fellwood title from Charles. It's fitting that he and his family live in the main part of the Manor; they will one day, anyway; this is simply bringing that date forward a little."

Eleanor, her eyes downcast, refused to answer, and Robert took her other hand.

"Mama, I respect your feelings about Annie, though I wish you would reconsider the matter, for you have three grandchildren living next door, whom you could also enjoy. However, that's up to you. Day to day, life would go on as it is now. You and Papa can keep to yourselves, as we will, and as far as the west wing is concerned, I think you'll be pleasantly surprised. I had it refurbished when Annie and I got married, and it is quite luxurious. There's even a bathroom with hot running water in the bath and a flush toilet. Neither facilities exist in your accommodation. Perhaps you would like to come and look around?"

"You're quiet, Charles. What do you think?"

"I think it makes sense, my dear, but I don't want you to be unhappy. Why don't you do as Robert suggests? Have a wander around the west wing and see if you think we could be comfortable there."

To Robert's amazement and delight, Lady Fellwood reluctantly agreed.

CHAPTER 14

KINGS NYMPTON

Sir Clive Robinson had extended his stay in Devon by several weeks by advising his wife in London that he was ill with influenza and unable to travel. This was untrue, but he knew it was unlikely she would check up on his story, and even if she did, it would not be easy to prove. He suspected his wife knew of his infidelity and was not overly concerned about it. He wondered if she, too, had taken a lover, although they still enjoyed sharing the marriage bed whenever he was at home and had four children to prove it. It was an amicable arrangement which suited everyone. Everyone, that was, but his father-in-law, a strict and religious man who would never condone such a lifestyle. Sir Clive knew he must maintain a respectable persona or his lavish lifestyle could be seriously curtailed.

Lady Lilliana continued to recover from the pneumonia which had threatened to take her life, and she hoped to accompany Sir Clive to London after Easter. She eagerly anticipated the trip, for she liked London and wanted to attend the reading of Sir Edgar's will and lay that matter to rest.

The couple were enjoying lunch together on the terrace of Grantley House when the butler arrived carrying their mail on a silver tray. There were a couple of routine letters from friends of Lady Lilliana, enquiring about her health and inviting her to various social gatherings, and intriguingly, there was one letter for Sir Clive. They knew immediately that this must be connected to their search for the two Gibbs children, for Sir Clive's mail was normally delivered to his own address. Eagerly, he tore open the letter and perused the scrawly handwriting.

"What does it say?" Lady Lilliana was impatient for news.

"It's from the landlord of an inn called The Farmer's Arms at King's Nympton; do you know it?"

"No, I've never been there, but I think it's near Umberleigh; what does he want?"

"He's seen our advertisement in the newspaper and says he has news of Millicent and Jonathan. Naturally, he wants to claim the reward money. How far is it to Kings Nympton?"

"I'm not sure; probably thirty miles or more; why, do you think it's worth going?"

"Yes, I think so. We have no other leads, and we need to find the pair of them before the London solicitors do. It would take all day in the carriage, though we could probably stay at the inn overnight, or perhaps we could go by train. Which would you prefer?"

"I enjoy travelling by train, but there's no privacy, and besides, it would give us the perfect opportunity to spend the night together."

Sir Clive grinned. "I like your thinking; let's do that then. Shall we go tomorrow? If there's no room at the inn, I'm sure we can find another not too far away."

The following morning, bright and early, Sir Clive's carriage called at Grantley House and collected Lady Lilliana. According to the carriage driver, Lady Lilliana had been right in her calculations, and the journey was expected to take five or six hours, depending on the state of the roads.

They found the roads to be in terrible condition, and after a rough journey of over six hours, being constantly jolted about, the pair were ravenously hungry and exhausted. With immense relief, they saw the sign for The Farmer's Arms swaying in the strong breeze.

Leaving their driver to arrange stabling for the horses, they entered the establishment, and Lilliana looked around in dismay at their shabby surroundings. However, they were warmly welcomed by the landlord, and Sir Clive arranged for them and their driver to stay overnight. He demanded the best room on offer for him and his wife and asked for a meal to be brought to them. It wasn't until they had eaten that Sir Clive advised the landlord of the purpose of their visit and asked him to join them for a drink and tell them what he knew of the two runaways.

Simon was delighted and advised that he had news that might lead to the youngsters' immediate apprehension. He asked for the reward to be paid before he imparted the information. However, Sir Clive was an astute gentleman, and he assured Simon that he would be paid if, and only if, he felt the news was valuable. Having no choice but to agree, Simon told his tale.

"The pair you're searching for arrived here in the middle of a blizzard in early January. They had no money and sought shelter from the storm. With the weather like it was, I couldn't turn them away and agreed that if they would do a few jobs, they could earn their keep for a day or two."

"Were they alone?"

"Aye, just the pair of them. The girl had long red hair and was about fifteen or sixteen, and the boy was much younger, probably five or six."

"How do you know they are the youngsters we're seeking?"

"I didn't until another carriage arrived, and the passengers also asked for shelter for the night. They were well-to-do folk on their way to Barnstaple and had hoped to get there that day, but it was impossible with the weather like it was. It was a gentleman with his wife and two young children. Anyway, leaving them to eat their meal, I got chatting with their driver, and he was saying how, in Crediton, he'd heard of a reward being offered for two runaways from Brampford Speke. He described them, and I realised it was the pair working in my kitchen."

"So, why didn't you take them to Crediton and claim the reward?"

"I intended to do that as soon as the snow cleared, and in the meantime, I locked them in a bedroom as I didn't want the gentleman or his driver to see them and put two and two together. Times are hard, and I needed that reward money to help me through the winter. Unfortunately, on the day the family was about to leave in their carriage, the girl shouted out of the bedroom window, attracting their attention, and accused me of imprisoning her and threatening to force myself on her. All lies, of course, but the lady in the carriage insisted on hearing their story."

Scrutinising the man before them, Sir Clive and Lady Lilliana could easily believe that Millicent had probably been telling the truth, and she shuddered slightly.

"I explained that they were thieves and would take them to Crediton that day to claim the reward. The gentleman said that it wasn't far out of their way, so they could take them instead. He paid me the ten guineas reward money and said he would claim it back at the police station, and that's the last I saw of them."

"I see. So, you've already been paid the reward money?"

"Yes, but I've given you useful information now, surely."

"What I don't understand is why the reward money was never claimed from the police and why the pair was never handed in. Why do you think that was?"

"I've no idea."

"Do you remember the gentleman's name?"

"Yes, it was Sir Roger Everson; I have a good memory for names, and it's not often we have a sir staying here. I don't think I ever heard his wife's name."

Lady Lilliana and Sir Clive each took a sharp breath, for the gentleman was known to them.

"Are you sure?"

"Aye, does that information help you at all?"

"Yes, I think it does. All right, I'll pay you five guineas and not a penny more."

The landlord, pleased, for he had expected to get nothing, smiled happily and thanked his customers kindly.

Amazed at the landlord's tale, the lovers considered their next move. They decided that, as Roger Everson usually resided in London, interviewing him would have to wait until their visit there after Easter. However, in the meantime, they decided to spend the night at the inn as planned and then travel to the police station in Crediton, which would be on their way to Brampford Speke.

"I can't believe Roger would aid and abet two runaways, although his wife, Jasmine, is soft-hearted. Especially as he knew it was me who wanted to apprehend them. He's been a friend of mine and Edgar's for years. Why would he let them go? It doesn't make sense."

"I don't know, my dear, but at least it gives us another lead. He obviously didn't hand them in, though goodness knows why, but at least he can tell us where he took them. Maybe he took them back to London with him for some reason, and that's why we can't find them in Devon.

The following day, after a surprisingly comfortable night, Sir Clive and Lady Lilliana left the inn and travelled to Crediton, a sizeable town around fourteen miles from Brampford Speke. They left early with the intention of returning to Grantley House within the day. At the police station in Crediton, they were delighted when the policeman on duty was aware of the two youngsters in question.

"Yes, I've seen the advertisements concerning these two, and I thought I'd found them earlier in the year. Two youngsters who matched their description were walking along the High Street. They had blankets wrapped around them against the bitter cold, and I even challenged them, but a man came out of one of the shops and claimed they were his children. I was suspicious, but I could hardly argue with him, for why would he claim they were his children if they weren't?"

"When was this?"

"Oh, a couple of days after Christmas, 'twas bitter weather."

"Where did they go?"

The man told them off for leaving the cart, and after he had finished his shopping, they left with him. I hung around until they drove off, but there was nothing more I could do."

"Which way were they headed?"

"Back towards Newton St Cyres."

"Did he tell you their names?"

"He did, but I can't remember what he said. It wasn't Millicent and Jonathan, though."

"So, you didn't get a visit from a gentleman called Sir Roger Everson a few days after that, wanting to hand them in and claim the reward?"

"No, the reward has never been claimed as far as I know, and now it's been doubled; I wish I could claim it myself. Police wages aren't that great."

Thanking him for his help, Sir Clive pressed a few shillings into his hand, and he and Lady Lilliana continued their journey to Grantley House. They were disappointed not to have traced the children and vowed to seek answers from Sir Roger Everson as soon as possible.

CHAPTER 15

HARTFORD/BARNSTAPLE

Charlotte and Fred had been living at The Red Lion Inn for a few weeks and had settled in well. They were fortunate that the staff were well-trained and needed little supervision, and as Betsey and Ned lived just down the road, they were always on hand to answer any questions that arose. Sarah and Louis had been a godsend to the new landlords, and thankfully, Bentley was getting on all right with Fred's children. Being older than their cousin, Rosella and Eddie were adept at keeping the precocious little boy firmly in his place.

Sarah had spoken to Mr Atkins, the headmaster, and asked if Bentley could start school early. She explained he was a bit of a handful and needed something to occupy his mind, as he was usually naughty when bored. The headmaster looked the little boy in the eye and sternly asked if he would like to come to school and if he did, if he would behave himself. Bentley, grinning cheekily, answered in the affirmative, so it was agreed he could attend on a two-week trial after the Easter holidays.

Early one Friday morning in mid-April, Sarah and Charlotte were busily loading the cart with produce ready for Louis to take to the Barnstaple Pannier Market to sell. This was a regular practice, for it was a large weekly market attracting farmers from far and wide and the best place to sell surplus goods. The inn kept two cows, and the milk was used to make butter, cheese, and clotted cream. Much of it was used in the meals for the stagecoach travellers who visited the inn daily, but there was always plenty left over. With the days getting longer, the fifty or so hens that wandered around the land at the rear of the inn were laying more eggs, and Charlotte carefully loaded a box containing several dozen into the centre of the cart, where she thought they would be the safest. Having added jars of homemade jam and chutney, potatoes, onions, and swede to the load, Louis was finally ready to leave. He waved goodbye to the two women and looked forward to his day out.

He stopped in the village to collect Betsey, Millie, and Jonathan, who had asked if they might accompany him to the local town, for the youngsters badly needed some new clothes. Millie was concerned that someone in Barnstaple might recognise her, for she knew an advertisement had been placed in the newspapers asking for information about her. To be on the safe side, she had coloured her abundant red hair with a brown dye made from crushed walnut shells. She tied it into a tight bun and wore one of Betsey's bonnets. Ned lent Jonathan one of his caps, and Betsey tried to reassure the girl.

"I'm sure it will be all right, Millie. If anyone asks about you, I'll say you're my niece, Anna Smith, and nephew, Leonard, from Cornwall. It will be nice to have a day out together. I want to show you George's other shop, and you can meet his son, Francis, who runs it. I'm hoping we might see Eveline in the market, and we can chat with her, too."

Robert Fellwood was also planning a visit to Barnstaple that morning, though he was more interested in the cattle market than the Pannier Market. Following his discussion with Fred about the canal boats, he wanted to purchase two shire horses to tow them. He had discussed the matter with Jack Bater, his estate manager, and, unsurprisingly, Jack had pointed out that donkeys would be far cheaper and equally efficient. However, Robert felt the shire horses would be more attractive to visitors and worth the extra money. The two men decided to travel on horseback, knowing they could each lead a shire horse back to Hartford if they purchased suitable beasts.

They arrived in the town in plenty of time for the auction, which started at ten o'clock. After leaving their horses at a stable yard, they joined the many other farmers hoping to sell or purchase livestock. The market sold every kind of animal, including poultry, pigs, and sheep, which could be viewed in the many pens. They spotted Marrok and Willie eyeing up some piglets.

"Hello, Marrok, hello, Willie; I think you both know Jack?" The two men nodded. "Have you settled into Sugworthy Farm all right, Marrok?"

"Yes, fine, thanks, Robert; the builder came yesterday and gave us an estimate for the work needed to repair the farmhouse, and he's going to make a start next week. The outbuildings and barns need attention, too, but I can handle that myself. I need to get the house weatherproof as soon as possible, though; it's so damp and cold."

"Don't go falling off any more roofs, Marrok; that leg of yours needs time to strengthen."

"You don't have to worry, Robert; I'll be careful. I don't want to go through that again. Are you here to buy some animals?"

"Yes, I'm going to bid on a shire horse a bit later; how about you?"

"Willie and I are here to buy some provisions, but I like the look of these piglets. There are only four pigs at the farm and plenty of room for more, so I might buy a dozen piglets to rear for pork. We've brought the horse and cart so we can easily transport them home."

"And how are you, Willie? Are you pleased with your new position as farm manager?"

"Aye, very pleased, Robert; I'm grateful to you and Marrok for promoting me. I thought the other workers might resent it, with you being my brother-in-law, but it's been all right so far."

"Good. Now, we must leave you, as the auction will be starting soon, but we'll go to The Golden Fleece for some lunch around noon; would you like to join us?"

"Yes, I'd like that. See you later, then."

Robert and Jack eased through the crowd, leaning on the barrier and watching the auction. Each beast was ushered into the ring, and the farmers gathered around to make their bids. The auctioneer sang out the prices, speaking at an unbelievable speed. Robert loved attending the auction, even if he was not buying or selling, and would have been content to stay there all day soaking up the atmosphere and enjoying the fascinating scene.

There was only one shire horse on sale that day, and Jack had already run his expert hands and eye over him before the auction started and assured Robert he was in excellent condition. Jack advised what he thought would be the top price Robert should pay, and armed with this knowledge, Robert made his bids. Unfortunately, another buyer was also keen on the animal and countered each of Robert's bids with a higher one. However, Robert was determined to own the animal, and his persistence eventually paid off, though he paid far more than he intended. He looked at Jack ruefully afterwards.

"I expect you'll tell me I paid far too much?"

"It was a bit on the steep side, but I think he'll be worth it; he's a grand beast. No, I would have done the same. There's the owner, look; let's ask him a bit more about the horse."

Robert introduced himself and Jack to the farmer and discovered his name was Jim. He congratulated him on rearing a fine animal.

"I only wish there had been another shire horse here today, as I need two to pull some canal boats."

The farmer looked at Robert with more interest. "I think I can help you there, sir, because, as it happens, I have another shire horse that I want to sell. I've been breeding them for years, but I've sold my farm as I'm retiring soon, and my daughter isn't interested in taking it on. I could only bring one horse with me today, but if you have a mind to come to the farm, you can inspect the other horse and see if he would suit you. I don't think you'll be disappointed, for he's a sturdy beast."

"Yes, I'd like to do that. When would be convenient?"

"The sooner, the better; tomorrow, if you like."

"Yes, that would be all right, though it would have to be late afternoon as I have other commitments during the day."

The farmer could tell Robert was a gentleman and was impressed that he was buying his animals himself. He looked at him thoughtfully. "Have you ever fished for elvers?"

"No, why?"

"Well, they're plentiful at this time of year, and we caught tons of them last night. We'll catch more for the next few nights, and it's quite a sight. I wondered if you'd like to join us. You can stay the night in the farmhouse; it will be too dark to ride back to Hartford afterwards."

Robert's curiosity was piqued, and he could not refuse the offer.

"I'd like that; thank you. What time shall I come?"

"Well, come in daylight, for you don't want to ride in the dark. You can have something to eat with us, and we'll venture out with the nets around midnight because that's when high tide will be."

Robert thanked Jim and promised to see him the following evening, and he and Jack walked towards The Golden Fleece for lunch.

As they strolled along, Robert suddenly had a thought.

"Jack, do you trust me to pass judgment on the second horse? Be honest. Do you think I should let you go to the farm? I won't be offended. It's more important that we buy a sound animal."

"No, I think I've taught you everything I know, Robert, and I'm sure you'll make the right decision. Besides, that farmer has an excellent reputation and wouldn't sell you a poor beast. I've been elver fishing before, too, and it's quite something to see; no, you go, you'll enjoy it."

Millie and Jonathan had spent a few weeks in Barnstaple before Christmas, when they were trying to get to Hartford. Needing to earn some money to buy food, Millie had been befriended by a young prostitute who took her back to the house she shared with several others. At the time, Millie was worried she was being duped into a life of prostitution, but Jess had been true to her word and had only expected Millie to clean the house and mind the many children of the prostitutes so they could go out to work.

Unfortunately, one of the prostitutes, called Liz, had brought a policeman back to the house one day, and he had recognised Millie from the notices circulated to all police stations. However, Millie was one step ahead of Liz, and she and Jonathan hastily fled under the cover of darkness, sheltering with a kindly neighbour until they could arrange a ride on a cart to Hartford. The farmer who had come to their rescue was none other than Charlie Chugg, Eveline's husband from Hollyford Farm.

Betsey and the two youngsters had a great time browsing the shops in Barnstaple. They visited George Carter's shop near the Albert Clock and met Betsey's grandson, Francis, where Betsey treated herself to a new pair of boots, Ned to some tobacco, and the two youngsters to some much-needed new clothes. Betsey drove a hard bargain.

"Now, Francis, I want you to charge me your best prices, and then remember I'm your granny and knock off a bit more."

"Gran, that's taking advantage."

"Yes, that's right, lad, I am, but your father can afford it, and he wouldn't have a shop if it weren't for me and his dad. He wouldn't begrudge me, and you know it."

"Aye, that's true, Gran; how does ten shillings sound?"

"Perfect; thank you. Now, please don't leave it too long before you come to Hartford and visit us in our new home. Your grandad hasn't seen you for a long time, and it would cheer him up to hear how you're getting on. Bring your young lady to tea if you like."

With Francis promising to visit soon, they made their way to the Pannier Market, which was crowded with people seeking a bargain. They found Eveline sitting at her stall in the middle of the market, looking slightly flustered as she served her many customers. She spotted her mother, and a wide grin spread across her face.

"Hello, Mum, hello, Millie and Jonathan; how are you all?" Sorry, excuse me while I serve this lady. Mum, sit down and rest your legs for a minute."

Between serving customers, Eveline managed to chat briefly with her mother and was pleased to hear that she and Ned had settled into their new home. Seeing how busy it was, Betsey kissed her daughter on the cheek and said she would catch up with her at the Manor House on Easter Sunday when Annie had invited them all for the day. Moving on, they walked through the market and, a little further on, had a brief chat with Louis. Betsey handed him a hot pasty she had bought for his lunch.

"We'll see you later, Louis; we're going to The Golden Fleece for some lunch now, but we'll come back here at half past three to ride home with you."

"Aye, all right, Betsey; thanks for the pasty. I'll see you later."

The Golden Fleece Inn was situated across the road from the cattle market on an ancient thoroughfare called Tuly Street. The tavern had been there for centuries and was favoured by farmers when they had completed their business in the market. Betsey and Ned had often called there for a tankard of ale on their rare visits to the town together, and Betsey decided she would like to take Millie and Jonathan there for some lunch.

They entered the crowded hostelry, and Betsey looked around, hoping to find a vacant table. However, she could see no free seats, but then spotted Marrok and Willie sitting with Robert and Jack.

"Oh, look, that's lucky; we can join them; come on."

Willie smiled with delight as he saw his grandma, accompanied by Millie and Jonathan.

"Hello, gentlemen; would you mind if we joined you? There are no other free tables, and I could do with resting my legs."

"No, of course not, Betsey; we can easily squeeze up and make room."

Seeing the delight on Willie's face, Robert rose and asked Millie to take his seat.

"Millie, why don't you and Jonnie sit on the bench beside Willie? I can perch on this stool."

The other folk seated at the table hid their amusement, for they could see that the two teenagers couldn't take their eyes off one another. Robert ordered them all a bowl of lamb stew and a thick shive of bread and refused payment.

"No, that's all right; it's my treat today."

"Were you successful in bidding for the shire horse, Robert?"

"Yes, and luckily, the farmer has another back at his farm that I'm going to look at tomorrow; how about you, Marrok? Did you purchase your piglets?"

"Aye, though I think their squealing may drive us mad on the way home."

The group was not of people who would normally meet for lunch, and they all enjoyed catching up with each other's news. When they had finished eating, Betsey, who was convinced Willie was holding Millie's hand beneath the table, suggested they might like to go for a walk before meeting Louis.

"Oh, yes, I could show you around the town, Millie: would you like that? Marrok, are you in any hurry to leave for an hour?"

"No, that's all right, lad; I'm happy to sit here for a while chatting. My leg still aches, and it will benefit from a rest. You take your time and come back here when you're ready."

"Millie, can I come?"

Betsey quickly intervened. "Jonnie, you might want to stay here with me because I've noticed there's apple pie and custard, and I don't know about you, but I could certainly eat a bowlful. What do you think? Shall we have some?"

Betsey knew Jonnie's favourite pudding was apple pie and custard, and she was confident he would be unable to resist.

"Oh, yes, please, Aunty Betsey; do you want to stay and have some, Millie?"

"No, I'm full, thanks, Jonnie, but you enjoy your pudding, and I'll see you later."

Once outside the inn, Willie took Millie's hand.

"That was kind of Gran, wasn't it? She knows I have feelings for you, Millie."

"Do you now? Have feelings for me, I mean."

"I think you know I do. Shall we walk along the river towards Rock Park? It's pleasant along there."

"Yes, I'd like that, but I hope I don't see anyone who remembers me from when I lived here for a couple of weeks. I escaped from the police in the nick of time, and there's still a big reward on my head."

"I don't think you need to worry; you look so different with your hair dyed brown and Gran's bonnet on. Come on, I'll look after you."

They strolled down to the River Taw and across the entrance to the Long Bridge, which had been there since medieval times. As they walked along Taw Vale, Millie suddenly exclaimed in horror for coming towards her with her latest punter was none other than Liz, the prostitute who had reported her whereabouts to the police.

"Oh no, I don't believe it. Willie, I can't let that woman see my face. Kiss me!"

Millie suddenly pulled Willie under a large oak tree, threw her arms around his neck and kissed him passionately. Willie naturally responded and was delighted to remain in the embrace for several minutes. Millie nestled her face in his neck and whispered.

"Have they gone?"

"I'm sorely tempted to say no so we can stay like this, but yes, they've walked on. Why, who was it?"

"It was one of the prostitutes I lived with when I stayed here, and she never did like me. Do you think she noticed me?"

"She did glance back at you, but then walked on, so no, I don't think so. You're not wearing the same clothes you wore then, are you?"

"No, this is an old dress of Theresa's. When I arrived in Hartford, I only had what I stood up in, so people have been giving me and Jonnie a few things to wear."

"I'm sure she didn't realise it was you. I think she might have thought she had competition the way you were kissing me." Willie grinned. "Not that I'm complaining, mind."

Millie slapped his arm. "Behave yourself, Willie Carter. Needs must, as they say."

"Fair enough, but I think you might have feelings for me, too, after that kiss?"

"I might have."

CHAPTER 16

BARNSTAPLE

It was late afternoon when Robert arrived at Lower Beara Farm on the outskirts of Barnstaple. The directions given to him by Jim the day before were easy to follow, and he found the farm with no problem. He cantered into the yard and spotted Jim grooming the shire horse.

"Hello, Lord Fellwood; did you find us all right?"

"Yes, thanks; is this the horse that's for sale?"

"Yes, he's the only one I have left now. I shall be sorry to leave the farm, for I've lived here all my life, but I think it's the right thing to do. Unfortunately, we never had any sons, just one daughter, and she's happily married to a solicitor and living in the town, so they don't want to take it over. My wife, Mary, and I have bought a little cottage in Newport. It's about a mile out of Barnstaple, so within walking distance, and it has a good-sized garden out the back that will be enough for me now that I'm older. Anyway, take a look at the horse, by all means, but I don't think you'll be disappointed. We call this one Toby, and t'other one was Larry, though, of course, you can call them what you like."

Robert thoroughly examined the horse and thought, if anything, he was even stronger than the one he had purchased the day before.

"It's a fine horse, Jim, and yes, I'd love to buy him. Is he the same price as the other one?"

"He is to you, sir. I was going to ask a little more for this one, as he's a bit sturdier than Larry, but as you've purchased the two, that's saved me extra work, and I'm grateful. Now, come inside and meet Mary. She's roasted a chicken, and you'll love her parsley stuffing; I do, anyway."

After a delicious meal, Robert and Jim enjoyed a couple of whiskies and chatted in front of a roaring fire. Mary sat with them for a couple of hours, sipping at a glass of homemade wine and knitting some baby clothes for a much longed-for grandchild due any day. At eleven o'clock, yawning widely, she bid the men goodnight and said she hoped they caught a lot of elvers.

"Are elvers only around at this time of year, then, Jim?"

"Aye, 'tis only a short season of a few weeks during the spring. The young eels or elvers migrate from the oceans into the freshwater rivers and swim upstream to find a suitable place to grow to full size."

"When do they return to the oceans again?"

"When they're fully grown, they're called silver eels, and they travel back to the ocean in the autumn. I'm told they travel all the way to the Sargasso Sea in the North Atlantic to spawn. It's amazing; Mother Nature is so clever."

"How do we catch them?"

"When the tide turns, the elvers are swept into the rivers, and so we peg nets across the estuary, and the eels swim into them and are caught. The nets are called fyke nets, and they're funnel-shaped and get narrower and narrower, making it difficult for the fish to swim back out again." Jim threw back the last of his whisky. "Come on, then, we'd better get out there. You'll soon see what I mean."

It was a starry, moonlit night, and Robert was astounded by the number of people waiting around the estuary of the River Taw. Despite the late hour, men, women and children carried buckets, nets, and sieves, indeed anything to catch the slippery little eels and get a few free meals. Jim led Robert to where his men stood in the water, ready to pull the fyke nets out when full.

When the tide turned, Robert could not believe his eyes, for suddenly, the river and the ground around his feet seemed to be alive with millions of tiny, translucent eels about three to four inches long. As well as swimming upstream, they slithered over the long, wet grass, and the children squealed in delight as they captured them by the bucketful.

There seemed to be a never-ending flow of elvers, and Jim told Robert that most folk would be there all night, or at least until the tide turned or the supply of elvers reduced.

"Goodness, they'll be so tired; don't they have to work tomorrow?"

"Aye, of course; some might be lucky enough to grab an hour or two of sleep before they turn in for work in the morning, but I expect most had a nap after supper and will go straight to work at dawn. I doubt many children will be at school for the next week or two, but it's more important to gather free food when it's available. Families will eat the elvers fresh for the next couple of weeks, but they'll also be dried, pickled in vinegar, or some folk like to salt them; they'll keep for some time then, though the taste is altered. Folk aren't fussy when there's nothing else. Anyway, have you seen enough? Shall we leave them to it and have one more nightcap before we turn in?"

Robert was feeling the cold and could only imagine how the men, women and children, many of them barefoot, could withstand the icy water around their feet and legs. He nodded gratefully.

"Yes, I like the sound of that; thank you, Jim. I've enjoyed watching this so much, and I take my hat off to these folk. How hard they're working."

Jim smiled to himself, thinking it never did any harm for the gentry to see how the other half lived.

Robert spent a comfortable night in a cosy bed and, in the morning, was awakened by a maid, who knocked on his door and brought him a cup of tea.

"Good morning, sir. The missus says if you'd like to join her and the master for breakfast, she's cooking some elvers, and she thought you might like to sample them."

"Thank you; I'll be down in a few minutes."

Robert swiftly dressed and wandered downstairs to the kitchen, where Mary was sprinkling some elvers with salt and stirring them around in a colander. He watched with interest.

"Why are you doing that, Mary?"

"'Tis the best way of cleaning them, sir. Elvers are a bit slimy, and if you wash them in salt and then dry them, it gets rid of it. Next, I'll roll them in flour, fry them in a bit of lard, and, when they're cooked, add a few beaten eggs. Have you never eaten them before?"

"No, but it sounds interesting; I can't wait to taste them."

While Mary was cooking the eggs and elvers, the young girl cut thick shives of bread and toasted them before the roaring fire. She then put a couple of slices on each plate and spread them with fresh farm butter, ready for Mary to put the omelettes on top. Robert cautiously took his first mouthful and grinned.

"Oh my, they're delicious. I wasn't sure if I'd like them, but they're so tasty."

"Aye, I didn't think you'd be disappointed. Would you like to take some home for your family? We have plenty."

"Yes, please. My wife was a servant before she married me, and her family has lived in the village for years, so I expect she's eaten them in the past. I'm sure she'll enjoy them, anyway. Are there any other ways of cooking them?"

"Yes, you can do what you like with them. Some folk like to cook them, then mince them up and mix them with parsley and mashed potatoes like a kind of fish cake. That's tasty; I do that sometimes, or you can eat them fried without the eggs, but this is our favourite. I'm glad you enjoyed them."

After breakfast, Robert thanked Jim and Mary for their hospitality and wished them well for their retirement. Leading the new shire horse behind him and with a pannier full of elvers strapped to each side, he bade them farewell and rode slowly back to Hartford.

Leaving the shire horse in Dodger's capable hands, he asked the stable boy to send the two panniers to the kitchen for Maisie and Mrs Potts. He went in search of Annie and told her of his night fishing for elvers.

"Oh, lovely, I enjoy a feed of elvers. I expect some of our villagers might have been at the estuary last night. Folk will travel a few miles to get a catch, as they can be saved for the winter when there isn't much else to eat. Did you bring enough back for me to let Mum have a few? She and Liza love them."

"Yes, there are loads in the two panniers I've sent to the kitchens; I'll leave it to you to share them. I want to hear what Jack has to say about the second shire horse I bought; I don't think he'll be disappointed."

Annie had already planned to visit the kitchens and enjoy a cup of tea with her old friends, Maisie and Mrs Potts. Although she was now the lady of the house, she had never forgotten how kind they had been to her when she was a servant at the Manor. The cook and the housekeeper smiled as she entered the warm kitchen.

"Hello, ma'am, how nice to see you." As there were other servants present, Mrs Potts greeted her mistress formally.

"Hello, Mrs Potts, hello, Maisie, how are you both? I've come to see the elvers that Robert caught last night."

The three women admired the many tiny fish in the panniers and agreed there was plenty to let Sabina have some. Annie spoke to Ethan Bater, one of the footmen.

"Hello, Ethan, can you deliver one of the panniers to my mother at the Lodge House, please? Tell her it's from me, and she can do with them as she pleases." As the young man hurried off, she turned back to Maisie. "I want to talk to you about the food for Easter Sunday, Maisie. I've invited an awful lot of people, so I hope you can cope?"

"Aye, ma'am; what would you like me to prepare?"

"I'm hoping the weather will be sunny as I'm going to organise an easter egg hunt for the children, and I thought we could sit outside and enjoy a picnic. There's no need to cook a proper meal; can you make things like sausage rolls, quiche, cold ham, salmon and that sort of thing? We'll also need a few puddings, hot cross buns, and perhaps three simnel cakes. Now, more importantly, I want to hear all your news. I've heard gossip that you are to marry Martin; is that right?"

"Yes, that's right, Annie; sorry, ma'am. We're getting married in June. As Martin also works on the estate, Mr Fellwood has agreed we can have the cottage that was lived in by old Billy, the gardener. Sadly, he died a month or so ago, though he was in his eighties."

"Yes, I was sorry to hear about Billy passing away, and Robert was quite upset as he'd been a gardener here since Robert was a child. Still, I'm delighted for you, Maisie; if you come to my room later, we could see if one of my dresses would fit you for your wedding day if you like."

"Oh, yes, thank you; that would be grand; do you remember how we once tried on some old dresses of Miss Victoria's and wore them to the staff Christmas party?"

"I do, indeed, and Miss Wetherby tried to send us to bed early because she said we were dressed inappropriately. It was only thanks to Mrs Potts that we were allowed to stay until the end. You were always kind to me, Mrs Potts."

Annie dispensed with protocol and hugged the old lady.

CHAPTER 17

HARTFORD

Having formalised his new business partnership with Fred Carter, Robert lost no time in employing workers to build a jetty in the meadow behind The Red Lion, leaving Fred time to settle into his new role as landlord of the inn and finish refurbishing the three canal boats. The work hadn't stopped there; wooden picnic tables, children's swings, a see-saw, and swing boats had also been installed. Fred hadn't been sure about the swing boats, for they were quite expensive, but Robert assured him they would soon see a return on their investment.

Fred had completed the work on the three barges, which were smartly painted in dark green and had large side windows, which would afford the passengers an excellent view of the lush countryside and wildlife along the canal. At the front and back of the boats were black panels decorated with paintings of roses and forget-me-nots and edged in bright red. The last finishing touch around the front of the boats was a colourful border with a diamond-shaped pattern of yellow, blue, red and white. Each barge bore one of the names suggested by Llewie: *The Jolly Sailor, The Hartford Lady,* and *The Red Lion.* The names had been painted onto panels by Peter Webber on his easel and then fitted onto the barges. Each panel bore a picture relevant to its name.

Robert and Fred were delighted when everything was finally in place and decided to have a trial run. Each boat could carry twenty-five passengers, including the driver, so they invited all the family to take a trip on the Sunday before Easter. The two shire horses had already practised pulling the canal boats a time or two, and a donkey was used for the third until they could judge whether the project warranted the purchase of a third horse. Visitors would board the barges at The Red Lion Inn and pay for a single fare to the next village, where the canal ended or a return trip. The barges would carry snacks and drinks, which could be purchased from the driver.

The weather dawned bright and clear on the eighteenth of April, and when Betsey and Ned arrived, they found it hard to believe the work that had been carried out in their meadow.

"Oh, my goodness, there are so many people, Ned. I can't believe we have such a large family, and seeing them all together is lovely. Let's look at the new jetty."

The elderly couple meandered their way to the water's edge and onto the new wooden jetty. It was sturdily built, and from there, they could admire the three barges. They were impressed.

"Robert and Fred, what a wonderful job you've done. The barges are amazing, and I can barely recognise the old meadow; we never made full use of it."

"I'm glad you like it, Dad. We're still letting the chickens run around, though we may have to make an enclosure for them if we get a lot of visitors; the crowds might put them off laying."

"You'll need more servants at the inn if these boats ever arrive full of passengers. How many folk do they hold?"

"Each one can carry twenty-four passengers seated, plus the driver, Mum, and the trip will take three hours there and back. To begin with, we'll run one trip a day, but if we get busy, we could do one in the morning and one in the afternoon. No doubt it will only be from Easter to the autumn, but we're hoping to make enough money during that time to recoup the expenditure. Only time will tell, as they say. Now, I'll ask the family to board so we can get going."

Ned and Betsey boarded the first barge, *The Hartford Lady*, to be driven by their grandson, Llewie. They were followed by Eveline and Charlie and their children, twins Joseph and Matthew, Amelia and Martha. Sabina, Arthur and Liza climbed on next with Mary, Stephen, Helen and Danny, and Fred carefully handed baby Katel to Sabina once she was seated. Millie and Jonathan, who had accompanied Betsey and Ned, also stepped cautiously into the barge, and Sarah and Bentley sat behind them. Millie was disappointed that Willie could not join them, but unfortunately, he had to work that day.

The next barge was *The Jolly Sailor*, and this one carried the Fellwoods: Robert and Annie, Selina, Thomas and David, and Victoria with her three children, Caroline, Joshua, and Francis. Unfortunately, Robert's younger sister, Sarah, was unwell that day and could not join them.

The final barge was *The Red Lion*, and the passengers were Fred and Charlotte and their children, Rosella, Eddie, Doris, and Nicholas. To Betsey's delight, she noticed her eldest son, George, arrive at the last moment with his wife Mary Ann, daughters Harriet and Theresa, and toddlers Nellie and Sophie. Mary Ann held six-week-old Etheline, the latest addition to the Carter family, in her arms. Theresa was delighted when, at the last minute, her young man, Louis Blaquiere, jumped aboard.

"Goodness, Ned, I can't remember the last time all the family was together; probably a wedding or a funeral, I expect. I hope the inn has enough food for everyone when we get back, and I'm surprised Fred, Charlotte, Sarah, and Louis are all here; I would have thought at least one of them should have stayed at the inn to make sure everything runs smoothly."

Ned took his wife's hand. "It's not your worry any longer, my dear, and after all, everyone knows this is a trial run, so we'll manage whatever happens. Now, relax and enjoy the day and let the younger ones do the worrying."

One by one, the barges left the jetty, the first two being towed by Larry and Toby, the shire horses, and the last by Dobbin, the donkey. The third boat lagged behind a little, but Robert and Fred were interested in seeing that Jack Bater was right and that a donkey could pull a barge satisfactorily. Nevertheless, the shire horses certainly looked the part; their leather harnesses and trappings were highly polished, the decorative horse brasses gleaming brightly in the warm April sunshine. Their dark brown coats were well-groomed, and the long white hair which encircled their hooves was thoroughly brushed. The only thing that Robert thought was missing was some bright red ribbon to decorate their manes, and he made a mental note to purchase some in time for the Easter weekend.

The barges meandered slowly along the canal, and the passengers enjoyed the scenery, for the trees were clothed in vibrant green, and kingcups grew in profusion along the banks. The hedgerows, too, were full of wildflowers, and Betsey was delighted to see so many of her favourites: primroses, bluebells, cockrobins, and buttercups. When they reached the third bridge to cross the canal, as previously arranged, the driver of each boat asked the passengers to be silent and enjoy the tranquillity of the waterway.

The only sound was the quiet swishing of the water lapping against the barge, the steady clop of the horses' hooves and much birdsong. Silently, the drivers pointed out a stork sitting quietly on the bank and, a little further on, a swan nest with young cygnets. The folk fortunate to be sitting beside the windows could gaze into the clear depths of the canal and spot trout swimming around and occasionally leaping into the air for flies, and a few passengers were delighted to see two baby otter cubs frolicking on the far bank. After a few minutes, the drivers invited the passengers to continue talking and advised them they had drinks available if anyone wanted one.

"Oh look, there's a kingfisher, Ned," Betsey exclaimed in delight as the vividly coloured blue and orange bird darted through the air. "It's years since I've seen one of those, and listen; I think I can hear a cuckoo."

When the barges reached the next village of Rockingham, the drivers skilfully drew alongside the jetty and announced that the passengers could disembark to stretch their legs and that the return journey would commence in half an hour. The short break gave folk a chance to relieve themselves if they needed to, buy a drink or a snack from the small shop, or chat with each other.

In the queue of people waiting to leave the barge, it was unfortunate that Jonnie and Bentley ended up next to each other. Jonnie, the eldest, edged slightly in front of Bentley, much to the other boy's annoyance. A scuffle ensued as they pushed and shoved each other, and within minutes, both boys had fallen overboard!

"Oh, my God! They've fallen in! Quick, grab them, someone. Is the water deep?"

The water was, in fact, only about four feet deep, but nevertheless above the heads of the two boys. Fred, who was the nearest, jumped in and grabbed Bentley first and then Jonathan and pulled them out. He deposited them on dry land and scolded them before leaving them to be dealt with by an angry Sarah and Millie.

"We've learnt one thing, Robert. We must put some railings where folk disembark and maybe take their arm to help them off the boats. The drivers could do that. We don't want any of our passengers falling in. These two shouldn't have been squabbling, but boys will be boys, so it could happen again."

Millie and Sarah took the two boys to the village shop, where an elderly woman provided towels to dry them off. They were both chilled, for although it was a sunny day, there was still a nip in the air, and the water had been freezing. However, they received little sympathy and, to their dismay, were both soundly scolded by Betsey.

The family milled around, catching up with each other's news, and Betsey and Ned sat with George and Mary Ann.

"I'm so pleased to see you all here today; are you feeling better, George?"

"Yes, thanks, Mum; it's strange how this fever keeps coming and going. I was feeling ill all last week, and I still don't feel great, but hopefully, I'm on the mend. I haven't felt right since that rat bit me last year, and the doctor is convinced I have some sort of recurring infection."

Betsey turned her attention to the newest arrival in the Carter family. "And how is baby Etheline doing? That's such a pretty name."

"She's doing well, thank you, Betsey. I must confess I was hoping to give George a son this time, seeing as he only has one, and now, five daughters, but the main thing is she's thriving. Would you like a cuddle?"

"Oh, yes, I'd like that, Mary Ann. I love babies, though they all bring their worries, and it doesn't change, no matter how old they get." Betsey glanced anxiously at her eldest son as she spoke.

The return journey was uneventful, and the barges arrived safely at The Red Lion. This was when the staff at the inn would be tested, but Betsey and Ned were impressed that everything ran smoothly. Sarah, Louis, and Charlotte quickly disappeared into the inn to supervise while Fred went to seek out some dry clothes.

Most children made a beeline for the new swingboats, painted bright yellow, red, and green. Llewie took charge and made them form a queue. Four boats hung from a sturdy wooden framework, and each one held two passengers and was accessed by wooden steps. Llewie helped the children in, handed each of them a rope, and told them to pull hard. He gave each swingboat a hard push to start them off, and then it was up to the passengers to keep them going. Within minutes, Joseph and Matthew, Danny and Stephen, Rosella and Amelia, and Helen and Selina were squealing in delight. Llewie allowed them each a few minutes, then skilfully lifted a wooden beam from under each boat and brought them juddering to a halt. The children dismounted and were quickly replaced by the next lot of passengers. Robert and Fred watched thoughtfully.

"I think we could charge the tourists for using the boats, Fred; what do you think?"

"Yes, I was thinking the same, Robert. It need only be a ha'penny each or even a farthing, but it would soon mount up. We'll see how it goes next weekend at Easter."

CHAPTER 18

It was a warm spring day, and with the twins Thomas and David sitting in their pram and Selina running on ahead, Annie walked down the long driveway from the Manor House. The crocuses and daffodils had mostly finished blooming, but the woodlands to either side were carpeted with bluebells and white wood anemones. It didn't take long to reach the Lodge House, where her mother, Sabina, lived with her family.

As Annie opened the garden gate, she was greeted by Helen, Stephen, and Danny, eagerly awaiting her arrival. It was Easter Saturday, and Annie had asked that all the children attending her get-together at the Manor House the next day bring a painted hard-boiled egg.

"Hello, Annie. Have you brought the eggs?"

"Hello, you lot; yes, Maisie has boiled two each for you to decorate, then you can pick the best one and eat the other. I have them here in my bag."

Helen opened the back door and shouted. "Mum, Liza, our Annie's here."

Liza smiled at Annie as she dried her hands. "Hello, Annie, love, how are you?"

"I'm fine, thanks, Liza; how about you?"

"Yes, all good, thank you. Your mum's putting Katel in her cot for a nap, but she'll be down in a minute. I'll get the kettle on, and you can tell us your news."

"Thanks, Liza."

Annie took the twins out of the pram and sat them on the floor. They were crawling everywhere now, and she hastily shut the door to stop them from escaping into the hallway. She went to a cupboard and pulled out a box of toys to keep them amused, then surveyed the expectant faces of her daughter and siblings.

"Now, give me a minute, and I'll find the eggs and the paints, and then you can decorate them. I've brought a few eggcups in case Mum didn't have enough. Ah, here we are; put the eggs in the egg cups and then it will be easy to paint them. I've brought some glue, raffia, ribbons and wool, and I thought you might stick some of that on the eggs; it could be hair or a beard if you're making a face. I'll leave it up to you, but the eggs will be judged tomorrow, and there will be an extra-large easter egg for the winner, so do your best."

By the time Sabina entered the kitchen, the four children were engrossed in their task, and she embraced her eldest daughter.

"How are you, love?"

"I'm all right, thanks, Mum; are you looking forward to tomorrow?"

"Yes, it was grand to have the family together last week when we went on the barges, and now here we are doing it again. It was such a good idea of yours to have Katel christened tomorrow. Is everyone coming?"

"Most people are, yes. Charlotte and Sarah can't because they're so busy at the inn, and neither are Fred or Llewie as they're driving the barges, but I think everyone else will be there. Louis wasn't sure if he could make it, but Theresa persuaded him, and Fred agreed he was due a day off. I can see wedding bells there before too long, though I don't know how Uncle George will take it."

"I think he seems all right with it, although Louis is quite a bit older than Theresa. George has mellowed in recent years, and he's not in the best of health by all accounts. What's the plan for tomorrow?"

"I've suggested that we all go to the church for the christening, and then everyone will come to the Manor House. Robert will collect the decorated eggs from everyone later today and take them to Grandad to judge them. Jack Bater will hide them around the garden in the morning while we're all in church. You know, Robert, any excuse for a gallop on Prince, so he was happy to ride to Hollyford and Sugworthy to collect the eggs from there."

"The children are so excited about this; we've never had an easter egg hunt before."

"No, I know. Maisie's preparing lots of food for lunch, which will be spread out in the dining room for folk to help themselves. There are so many people coming, we thought it would be easier than a sit-down meal, and everyone can chat with each other. I didn't want anything formal, just a get-together for us all to enjoy ourselves. After lunch, weather permitting, we'll sit in the garden and watch the children find the painted eggs. I've ordered enough easter eggs for them all to have one, but whoever finds the most eggs, and whoever wins the competition for the best-painted egg, will get a bigger one."

"That sounds marvellous; we're so lucky these days."

Fortunately, Easter Sunday dawned bright and sunny, and Annie, Robert, Victoria and Sarah decided to walk the short distance to the church with their children. They were greeted at the door by the Reverend Rees, and they strolled down the aisle to their customary front seats, greeting family and friends as they went. Sabina and Arthur sat in the front pew on the other side of the church, with Sabina nursing baby Katel, ready for her big moment. Willie, Mary, Helen, Stephen and Danny sat alongside their mother. In the pew behind them were Katel's godparents, Arthur's brother,

Dudley Webber, Amelia, daughter of the late William Carter, and, somewhat surprisingly, Millie Gibbs, a newcomer to the family.

Arthur had left the choice of Katel's godparents to his wife, and Sabina, having given the matter much thought, decided to include her stepson, Dudley, who now worked with his father in the market garden. Now in his thirties, Dudley had not yet found a young lady to settle down with, and Sabina thought it would be beneficial to draw him into the family a little more. The young man doted on all her children and was often to be found cuddling Katel. Similarly, with the godmothers, she had chosen Amelia, who, despite being only ten years old, loved babies. Furthermore, Sabina had been fond of her father, William, and knew he would be delighted with her choice. With such a big family, there were so many eligible godparents for the child, but Sabina thought it would be a kind gesture to show Millie that she was truly accepted into the Carter family. Katel, dressed in a lacy white christening gown, behaved impeccably, barely whimpering when the vicar dipped his hand into the font and drew a cross on her forehead with the water.

When the service was over, the children were keen to leave the church, and most folk walked the short distance to the Manor House. Betsey and Ned, however, travelled in their pony and trap, conserving their energy for the day ahead. A sumptuous feast awaited them, for Maisie had been preparing food for days. Annie surveyed the loaded table and was delighted that her family could enjoy such a delicious spread.

When the meal was over, Robert invited everyone outside, where the adults sat on comfortable seats beneath parasols and the children on blankets on the lawns. He declared the easter egg hunt open, and the youngsters ran off, each carrying a small basket to search for the painted eggs. Jack Bater had done an excellent job of hiding them, and it took the children some time before all the eggs were found. When the eggs were counted, it was found that Bentley had found the most, and to his delight, he received a large chocolate easter egg.

Next came the results of the competition for the best-decorated egg. The winner had been chosen by Ned, who had no idea who had painted which egg. He had found it a difficult decision to make, but one egg in particular caught his eye, and it belonged to Marrok's daughter, Jinnie. The little girl was delighted and promised to share her egg with her siblings. However, there was no need to worry as Annie had bought enough smaller eggs for all of them.

Whilst they were all relaxing in the sunny garden, Betsey asked Annie if she thought Robert might listen to Millie's story and see if he could help to get her name cleared.

"Yes, of course, he will, Gran; I'll fetch him."

Millie was sitting next to Willie on a blanket, and when Robert arrived, he sat next to her and asked her to tell him everything. He had heard the bare bones of her story but wanted to hear it from her first-hand. She sighed and explained their desperate flight after their mother's death.

Betsey and Ned listened to Millie's tale in silence, but when she had finished, Ned spoke up.

"We wondered, Robert, being as you're a gentleman, whether you could visit Lady Lilliana and tell her that Millie is innocent."

"Yes, I could do that, Ned, and would gladly, but I doubt it would do any good. For her, this isn't about the brooch; it's about making trouble for her husband's illegitimate children. It might be best to visit this old lady in Eggesford and get the brooch back. Then, if we take it to Sir Edgar's solicitors and explain the story, Millie will be in the clear. I think I have Roger's address somewhere; I know he lives in London. I'll write to him tomorrow and ask if he knows which solicitors Edgar Grantley used. In the meantime, Millie, we need to get the brooch back and find out what's happened to your granny. Where do you think she is?"

"She promised to follow us here as soon as she was feeling better, but as she hasn't arrived, I'm worried she might have died, or she could be in the Exeter workhouse." Millie's eyes filled with tears, and Willie quickly put his arm around her.

"Aw, don't cry, Millie, she might be all right. We simply have to find her."

"Willie's right, Millie. Annie and I are going to Cullompton in a couple of weeks to visit our friends Geoffrey and Clara Turner. Geoffrey's a doctor who works in London, and he's going to operate on Danny's other leg soon. They've invited us to stay with them for a few days to discuss the arrangements for going to London. I suggest you come with us because Cullompton isn't far from Eggesford or Exeter. We can call on Rosa Baker on the way to collect the brooch and then on to the workhouse in Exeter to see if your granny is there. Would you like to do that?"

"Oh, yes, please. What about you, Jonnie? Will you be all right with Aunty Betsey and Uncle Ned if I go?"
Jonnie was sitting nearby and listening to all that was going on.

"Yes, I'll be all right, Millie. I'm starting school next week, and I don't want to miss the first day."

"Good, that's settled then. I'll let you know which day we're going, Millie."

"Thank you so much, sir. I do so want to find my granny."

"You're welcome, and please, call me Robert."
Robert sauntered off to chat with a few other people, and Willie whispered in Millie's ear.

"Would you like to walk down to the river, Millie, so we can be alone for a while?"

Millie nodded happily, and the young couple wandered off hand in hand.

CHAPTER 19

Mr Atkins welcomed the children back to school on the Tuesday following Easter Monday. Often, the holiday went on a little longer after the religious festival, but Easter was late that year, and the headmaster wanted the pupils to practice their maypole dancing ready for the customary celebrations on the village green on May Day.

Several new pupils were starting school that term; among them, Jonathan Gibbs, Bentley Carter, and Selina Fellwood, as well as Marrok Fellwood's three children, Jinnie, Eliza, and Martin. Sarah walked with Bentley from The Red Lion Inn to the school that first morning, and they met Millie along the road, escorting Jonathan. The two women took the boys into the classroom and instructed them to be on their best behaviour. As they left, they had a word with Annie, who was with her daughter, Selina, followed closely by Marrok, who had brought his three children on his horse and cart for their first day, though warning them that most days they would have to walk. With some anxiety, the adults left the children and hoped all would be well.

Jonathan, Bentley, Selina, and Martin were all with Mr Atkins, but being a little older, the twins, Jinnie and Eliza, were in another class. Not knowing of the rivalry between Bentley and Jonathan, Mr Atkins sat them next to each other and, with Selina and Martin sitting at the desk behind them, proceeded to teach the class their alphabet. Bentley and Selina were already able to read and write, and Bentley was scornful of Jonathan's untidy attempt to write his letters.

"I thought you'd already been to school?"

"Yes, but only for a couple of weeks; then the school closed because so many people had typhoid. Can you write your letters?"

"Aye, my Gran taught me; writing's easy. I can read, too. You must be stupid."

"No, I'm not."

"Oi, you two, no talking; get on with your writing. I don't have talking in my classroom." Mr Atkins frowned at the two boys.

However, after lunch, it was a different tale when the children assembled in the playground to learn how to dance around the maypole. Jonathan was a natural dancer and quickly grasped the steps and how to weave in and out of his classmates, whilst Bentley appeared to have two left feet and no sense of rhythm whatsoever.

"No, no, Bentley; you're going the wrong way again. Look, watch Jonathan; he's doing it correctly."

It did not please Bentley to hear his rival praised, and with a deep frown, he longed for the dance lesson to be over.

When the children came out of school that day, Selina wore a broad smile, and a torrent of words came tumbling out of her mouth as she eagerly told Annie all that had happened at school.

"Did you have a nice time?"

"Oh, yes, I loved it! There were so many children to play with, and I sat beside Martin. Helen, Stephen, and Danny are all in my class, too."

Since moving to the Manor House with Annie and Robert after their marriage and leaving the Lodge House,

Selina had missed the company of Annie's siblings and was delighted she would now see them every day.

Sarah, Millie, and Marrok were also waiting at the school gates for their children. Jinnie and Eliza also wore happy smiles, but Bentley and Jonathan looked less than content.

"How did you get on today, Bentley?"

"All right, I suppose."

"You don't look very happy; was the teacher pleased you could already read and write?"

"Yeah, that was all right, but we had to dance around a silly maypole, and I kept getting it wrong."

"Oh, you'll soon get the hang of it; there are a few days until May Day. How about you, Jonathan? How did you get on with the dancing?"

"I loved the dancing, but Bentley says I'm stupid because I can't read and write."

"Of course, you're not stupid; you've only been to school for one day. Bentley's lucky because his granny taught him to read and write. You'll soon pick it up."

Mr Atkins soon realised it had not been wise to sit Bentley and Jonathan together, for they clearly disliked each other intensely. However, he decided they would have to get used to it or be punished if their bad behaviour continued. He made a few allowances, it being their first week at school, but pupils sat where he put them, and that was that.

A couple of days later, at break time, some bigger boys were teasing Bentley about his terrible dancing. The more anxious the little boy became, the more he muddled the steps, and that morning, he had got the whole class in a right tangle with the streamers hanging from the maypole. For once, Jonathan felt sorry for his enemy as the boys shoved him and told him that, thanks to him, they had all danced far longer than usual. Jonathan ran off to fetch Eveline's two boys, Matthew and Joseph, knowing that at eleven, they could help. Sure enough, the twins came to their cousin's rescue and drove the bullies away. Bentley was surprised that Jonathan had helped him, and that afternoon, when Mr Atkins told them to chalk a line of the letter H on their slates, he let Jonathan see what he was doing rather than putting his arm around his work to hide it as he usually did.

Jonathan whispered. "Thanks, Bentley; I couldn't remember how to draw the letter H."

"Copy me from now on, Jonnie. I think the letter H looks like one step on a ladder; that's how I remember it."

"Oh, that's clever, thanks. When we dance around the maypole tomorrow, why don't you get in behind me and follow me? That might help."

And so, to everyone's relief, the two boys buried the hatchet and, within the week, were the best of friends.

May Day fell on a Saturday, and the celebration took place on the village green as usual. The maypole had been freshly painted white, and with streamers of red, white and blue, it looked magnificent. Many of the cottages had been decorated with flowers and branches in the hope that the woodland spirits would bring good fortune to their inhabitants. At school, the children had made hoops out of thin, pliable branches and decorated them with crepe paper and flowers, ready to be judged by the vicar later in the day.

The Red Lion Inn faced the village green and, for centuries, had provided refreshments for the May Day revellers. Fred and Louis brought the old trestle tables out from the cellar and assembled them on the grass. In the kitchens, Sarah, Charlotte, and several maids baked an enormous amount of food: rabbit stew, crusty bread, pasties, sausage rolls, cakes and jam tarts. Fred fervently hoped that business would be brisk.

The Easter weekend had been a roaring success, with many visitors travelling on the barges, and the inn had made an excellent profit. Fred was mightily relieved, for he had taken out a considerable loan to provide his part of the capital needed to build the jetty. He and Llewie would be driving the barges again that day, but he resolved to employ more staff as soon as possible, for he was finding it difficult to cope with everything, and his carpentry business was sadly neglected.

Fortunately, it was sunny, and by midday, the village green was teeming with people. All the Carter family were present, and Sabina, Annie, Eveline, and Betsey sat with Tilly Rudd and Robert's Aunty Margery and enjoyed the opportunity to chat while the children played. Sarah and Charlotte were too busy working in the inn to join them, but popped out occasionally with food or drinks and stopped to have a word.

The celebrations commenced at two o'clock, with the May Queen cutting a ribbon and welcoming everyone. The villagers, having heard Millie's sad tale of being destitute and homeless, had, with a little prompting from Betsey, chosen her as the May Queen, and the girl was overwhelmed by their kindness. Willie Carter had begged Marrok for the day off, and knowing romance was in the air, Marrok was willing to oblige.

Annie had provided one of her dresses for Millie to wear, and she looked beautiful. Like Annie, she had vibrant red hair, and the pale green dress suited her perfectly. She cut the red ribbon, declared the celebrations open, and was carried shoulder-high around the green by Willie and a few others. This was the signal for the Morris Men to commence dancing, and many side stalls offered their wares or a chance to win a prize.

Francis Rudd, the village blacksmith, was, as usual, offering to arm wrestle anyone for a penny. A hugely strong man, he had, over the years, developed a reputation of being unbeatable, usually winning easily. Millie walked around the green, arm in arm with Willie, and they watched as Dudley Webber tried his luck against Francis. The crowd laughed loudly when Francis, with a wide grin, forced Dudley's arm to the table for the second time and pocketed the penny, one of many that day.

"Willie, why don't you have a go?"

"Nah, I'd stand no chance, Millie."

"Go on, I'll treat you. One of the customers gave me a penny earlier; perhaps it will bring you luck."

"Oh, all right, then."

Willie reluctantly sat opposite Francis and put his penny on the table. The crowd suddenly took more interest, for Willie had worked at Sugworthy Farm for several years, and hard work and nourishing food had built up his strength. He was broad-shouldered, stood over six feet tall, and his muscles bulged through his shirt. He was, undoubtedly, a strong young man. A whisper ran through the crowd, wondering if this could be the time when Francis was finally defeated.

The two men put their elbows on the table and gripped each other's hands. Refusing to look into his opponent's eyes, Willie pushed with all his might, and for several seconds, the two were locked in a fierce battle. The watchers were intrigued as sweat appeared on the brows of both men, and at first, it seemed that Willie might win, but then Francis rallied more strength and, slowly but surely, pushed Willie's arm flat to the table. The two men flexed their arms momentarily and then prepared for the second round. Again, it was a hard-fought contest, and their arms inched fore and back as the tussle continued, but to the crowd's delight, this time it was Willie who was triumphant. Millie was overjoyed, threw her arms around his neck, and kissed him soundly on the lips. The crowd cheered, Willie grinned in delight, and Francis looked bemused, for he couldn't remember when he had last had to go three rounds with anyone. There was a delay for a few minutes as the crowd began to bet each other on who would win this intriguing contest.

"Come on, Willie; you can do it." Millie squeezed his arm and urged him on.

The two men retook their positions, and Willie, determined now to win for Millie, pushed with every ounce of strength he could muster and made it look surprisingly easy as he quickly forced his opponent's arm to the table. Francis immediately rose to his feet, shook Willie's hand, and handed over the money.

"Well done, Willie; I honestly can't remember the last time someone beat me, but you did it fair and square. I intend to get my revenge next year, though, so mind out."

The men surrounding the wrestlers clapped Willie on the back and congratulated him; several threw their pennies onto the table and said he had earned them for providing such an entertaining contest. Pocketing the large copper coins, Willie took Millie's hand and led her away.

"That was amazing, Willie; well done."

"I can't believe I beat him; it's well-known Francis always makes a packet on May Day. Let's get something to eat and a drink; there's room on that bench beside my mum, look. You sit down, and I'll fetch us something."

When Willie returned carrying a tankard of ale and a pastie each for him and Millie, there was a loud cheer, for Millie had been singing his praises.

"Are you going to the barn dance tonight, Millie?"

"Yes, I'm looking forward to it. How about you; can you go, or do you have to get back to the farm?"

Yes, I'm going and staying at the Lodge House with my mum tonight, though I need to ride back early in the morning. I shall play my fiddle; Dad taught me when I was a nipper, and I play every year. I'm glad you're coming, Millie; I'm hoping you might let me have a dance."

"I'd love that, Willie. I was hoping you'd ask me. If I know any of the tunes you play, maybe I could sing a couple of songs; I'm told I have a tuneful voice and often sang in school concerts."

"Oh yes, that would be grand. When we've eaten this, let's go into the barn and have a practice."

CHAPTER 20

EGGESFORD

A couple of weeks after the May Day celebrations, Annie and Robert left Hartford Manor in their carriage, driven by Dodger Watkins. They called on Betsey and Ned to collect Millie, who would accompany them to Cullompton. Millie was keen to go, for she was desperately worried about her granny and anxious to rescue her from the workhouse where she suspected she must be. Jonathan had settled in at school and was the best of friends with Bentley. The two little boys now played together all the time, so he was content to stay with Betsey and Ned whilst his sister went travelling. Annie, however, was uneasy about leaving the twins for the first time, though she knew her nursemaid, Naomi, would take excellent care of them. To put her mind at rest, Sabina assured her she would visit the boys and Selina daily to ensure they were content.

The main reason for Annie and Robert's visit to their friends, Geoffrey and Clara Turner, was to discuss the best time to take Danny to London for the operation on his second foot. Sabina was torn between accompanying her adopted son or staying with her baby daughter, Katel, whom she was still breastfeeding. Annie had it in mind to offer to go to London with Danny, but first, she wanted to see how the twins fared without her for the weekend, for she knew the trip to London would be for at least a month.

Having decided to combine their social weekend with the opportunity to clear Millie's name and find her granny, Robert felt it was best to visit Eggesford first, to see Rosa Baker about the brooch, then on to the Exeter workhouse, hopefully, to collect Emily, and finally spend a day or two with their friends in Cullompton.

They left Hartford early in the morning, the carriage stopping at The Portsmouth Arms, an ancient coaching inn near the village of Umberleigh, for a late lunch. The inn, believed to date from the fifteenth century, also operated as a tollhouse, collecting the fees for the Turnpike Trust. As the travellers alighted from their carriage, a train thundered past in close proximity to the hostelry.

"Goodness, the railway is right beside the inn; that's handy."

"Yes, I considered travelling by train because it's much quicker than by road, and the line runs through Umberleigh and Eggesford on the way to Exeter and then on to Cullompton, but with all our luggage, I decided it would be easier to use the carriage. I heard the inn's named after the Earl of Portsmouth, as he was involved in the construction of the railway. Anyway, let's get inside; I'm starving. Dodger, would you like to join us?"

"No, sir, thank you, but I'll see to the horses and then have a bite to eat with a friend of mine who works here."

Robert led the way into a low-ceilinged room with dark wooden beams and a huge fireplace where a fire was burning brightly. With the thick cob walls and small windows, the room was dimly lit, but as their eyes adjusted to the gloom, they could see it was clean and well-maintained. Seated at a table by the window, Robert ordered them a tankard of ale each and a bowl of beef stew and dumplings, which the landlord assured them was freshly made.

"Mm, this is delicious, and I'm certainly ready for it."

"Yes, me too; how far is it to Eggesford from here?"

"Not far now; about another four or five miles, I think. We'll visit the old lady and get your brooch back, Millie, and then stay overnight at The Fox and Hounds Inn. It's in Eggesford, so it's quite convenient. I've never stayed there, but a friend recommended it."

A couple of hours later, they arrived at Rosa's cottage, and Millie knocked on the door. Eventually, they could hear the heavy bolts being drawn back, and the door opened slowly. An old lady peered out timidly, but when she saw Millie, a broad smile appeared on her face.

"Aw, hello, Millie; I'm so pleased to see you, my dear. Please come in."

Leaving Dodger with the carriage and horses, Millie, followed by Annie and Robert, entered the tiny parlour, where Rosa invited them to be seated.

"How are you, Rosa?"

"Oh, I mustn't grumble, but never mind me, did you find your relatives all right? I'm guessing you did."

"Yes, Jonnie and I had quite a few adventures after we left you, but eventually, we got to Hartford and found our Aunty Betsey and Uncle Ned, and they've given us a home. This is Annie and her husband, Robert. Annie is the granddaughter of Aunty Betsey, so my cousin, I think."

"I'm so pleased to hear that, Millie. Those horrible men didn't catch up with you, then?"

"No, but we had a few narrow escapes."

"I'm afraid they're still searching for you, my dear. I went to Crediton shopping only a week ago and bought a newspaper like I always do, and there was another advertisement asking for information about you. The reward money had doubled to twenty guineas, so Lady Lilliana is still determined to find you."

Millie was shocked. "Oh dear, she's so bitter, I don't think she'll ever give up. What was it Gran used to call her? Oh, yes, I know, a woman scorned; yes, that's how she used to describe her, a woman scorned, though I don't know why she said that."

"That's quite a famous saying, Millie, though I think the actual words were slightly different. It was a quote in a play called *The Mourning Bride,* written by a well-known playwright called William Congreve."

"Goodness, sir, how do you know that?"

"Oh, I went to a public school, Rosa, and that was one of the plays we studied. I suppose Sir Edgar did treat Lady Lilliana disgracefully."

"Yes, of course, he did, but it's not Millie's fault. Now, have you come to collect the brooch?"

"Yes, please, and thank you so much for keeping it safe for me. Robert is the heir to Hartford Manor and is highly respected, and he thinks that if we give the brooch to Sir Edgar's solicitors, it will clear my name."

"Now, that is sensible, and I've kept it safe for you. Can you fetch it to save me from getting up?"

Millie reached under the mantlepiece and, removing the loose stone, retrieved a small leather bag, which she handed to the old lady. Rosa reached inside and slowly withdrew the sparkling brooch with her swollen fingers. She gazed at it for a few seconds.

"My, it is beautiful; I must admit I've enjoyed looking after it for you. I've often taken it out and admired it in the sunlight from the window or the candlelight of an evening. Mind you, I'm relieved to give it back to you; I've worried about it getting stolen or me dying before you returned."

"Oh, Rosa, don't say that." Millie handed the brooch to Robert, and Annie peered at it.

"Oh, it's so pretty; see how it sparkles. I can see why Lady Lilliana wants it back. What's the big stone?"

"It's a sapphire surrounded by diamonds, and I'd say the clasp is solid gold; it must be worth a small fortune."

"I'm glad you have it back now, but I'm forgetting my manners, for I haven't even offered you a cup of tea. I'll pull the kettle forward to boil and make you one now."

"It's all right, Rosa, I'll do it; I know where everything is."

"Bless you, maid, thank you, though I don't want you looking around too much; you left this place spick and span, and I'm afraid not much cleaning's been done since. I'm so crippled up with arthritis that I can barely move, and life becomes ever harder. I must get someone to bring my bed downstairs, for I struggle to climb the stairs these days."

When she returned with the tea, Millie nervously cleared her throat. "Robert, I need to ask you something, please. Rosa was so kind to Jonnie and me that I'd like to help her again. I wonder if I could stay here tonight and clean through again, and you could collect me in the morning?"

"I'd like to help you, Millie. Robert, how can we arrange this?" Annie looked at her husband questioningly.

"We all seem to be thinking along the same lines, so here's what I suggest. Rosa, Millie mentioned you'd like to sell the two fields behind your cottage. Is that right? Or have you already sold them?"

"Yes, I want to sell them, but I haven't done so yet. The farmer I thought would buy them has fallen on hard times and doesn't have the cash, so I wasn't sure how to go about it. I must sell them, though, because that money would make my final years far more comfortable, and I've no family to leave it to."

"Right, that settles it, then. I suggest I take Rosa with me in the carriage to The Fox and Hounds Inn, where she can have a hot meal, and we can have a chat about selling her property. While we're gone, you two can clean Rosa's house if that's what you want to do, or if not, you can come with us, and we'll employ someone to do it."

"That's a great idea, Robert. I'm happy to roll up my sleeves and clean the house, and I know Millie is, too. Is that all right with you, Rosa? You must say if you don't want us to."

"Oh no, I'd love you to, and I'd appreciate your advice, young man; I don't want to get ripped off."

"That's settled then, but first, let's shift your bed downstairs; I'll just call Dodger, our carriage driver, and he can help. Where do you want it to go?"

"Oh, my, if you're sure, that would be wonderful. Thank you. I have three rooms downstairs: this one, where I spend most of my time, the kitchen, and a small room through that door, where I would like my bed if you can manage it."

Fortunately, there was little furniture in the future bedroom, and Annie and Millie swiftly swept and washed the floor while Robert and Dodger dismantled the double bed, brought it downstairs, and reassembled it. Millie searched the airing cupboard for clean bedding, and in no time, the bed was fully made.

"Oh, thank you so much; it will be such a relief not to climb those stairs every night. I've been terrified of falling and lying there all night."

"What about your clothes, Rosa? Shall we bring down your chest of drawers and the wardrobe? I think there's room."

"Yes, if you can manage it, but I don't want you hurting yourselves."

Within the hour, the bedroom furniture and all of Rosa's clothes had been moved downstairs. Leaving the two women to clean through the house, Robert helped Rosa into the carriage, and Dodger drove them to The Fox and Hounds Inn, where they were expected.

Annie and Millie were no strangers to hard work, and they swept, scrubbed, and dusted until the little cottage was as clean as a new pin. It was a blustery, sunny day, so they also washed all the bedding and a pile of dirty clothes they found in one corner and put them on the line to dry. Satisfied with their efforts, they sat down to enjoy a cup of tea whilst they waited for Robert and Rosa to return.

Rosa was having the time of her life. She had lived in the tiny hamlet of Eggesford since her marriage some sixty years earlier and had walked past the grand Fox and Hounds Inn many times, never expecting to set foot inside. The owner welcomed Robert, and the pair were ushered onto a sheltered terrace overlooking the rolling hills. Having ordered a substantial meal for Rosa, Robert enjoyed an ale while chatting in the warm sunshine.

"Rosa, thank you so much for your kindness to Millie and Jonathan; they could have perished in the freezing temperatures last winter, but for your generosity in letting them stay."

"Oh, 'twas nothing, sir; I enjoyed their company and was so pleased they cleaned my house for me. They gave me more than I gave them."

"Were you never tempted to contact the police, give them information, and claim the reward? Or even sell the brooch? Many would have done so in your shoes."

Rosa was shocked. "No, of course not; it never entered my head."

"No, I'm sure it didn't, Rosa, for you're a kind and trustworthy woman, and I'm going to pay you the reward for not claiming it."

Robert reached into his pocket, retrieved a handsome leather wallet and removed four crisp white five-pound notes.

"Here we are, Rosa. When you go into Crediton to do your shopping, I suggest you exchange one of the five-pound notes for coins at the National Provincial Bank to spend as you need to and keep the rest for a rainy day. That's a branch of my bank, and you can be sure then that you won't be cheated."

Rosa looked at Robert with tears in her eyes. "Oh, sir, there's no need to do that; I was delighted to help them."

"I know, but I insist; now, with that money, will you be able to employ someone to help you around the house?"

"Yes, and it will be a huge help; thank you so much. It will tide me over until I can sell the fields."

"Good, now, about the fields. I'll ask my farm manager, Jack Bater, to inspect them, and then he can advertise them locally and see if we can get a buyer. Is that all right with you?"

"Yes, please; I don't know how to thank you."

CHAPTER 21

Having spent a restful night and eaten a delicious breakfast at The Fox and Hounds Inn, Robert, Annie, and Millie were ready to travel to Exeter early the next morning. Dodger Watkins had stayed in the servant's quarters of the inn and also enjoyed a hearty breakfast. As instructed, he was ready and waiting with the carriage at half past eight. Robert and Dodger had known each other since childhood and got on well together.

"Good morning, Dodger. Did you have a comfortable night?"

"Yes, thank you, sir, and a tasty breakfast."

"Excellent, let's get on our way to Exeter, then. You need to stay on this road, and I think it's about twenty-five miles. Hopefully, we might get there by lunchtime."

"Aye, sir, I'll do my best. You might need to tell me where to go once we reach the city, if you wouldn't mind. I haven't been there before."

"Yes, that's fine; I know the way to the Royal Clarence Hotel because I've stayed there before. When we get closer, I'll ride beside you and give you directions."

Ironically, Robert had chosen to stay at the same hotel as Sir Clive Robinson and Lady Lilliana, though thankfully not at the same time. It was conveniently situated in the city centre and within easy walking distance of the Union Workhouse.

The roads on the outskirts of the city were in far better condition than those in North Devon, and they arrived at the hotel at midday and had a light lunch before walking to the workhouse on Bartholomew Street. Like Lady Lilliana and Sir Clive, a few weeks earlier, they approached the elderly lady sitting at a desk in the hallway. She asked how she might help them, and Annie and Robert nodded to Millie to ask her questions.

"I'm looking for my granny, Emily Gibbs, please. I think she might have been admitted not long before Christmas. We want to take her home with us if she's here."

"That's strange; she must be a popular lady, for you're the second lot of visitors to ask about her in the last week or two."

"Really? Who else was asking for her?"

"Another lady and gentleman; I don't remember their names, but I can only tell you what I told them. Emily Gibbs was admitted here just before Christmas and spent a few weeks in the infirmary before discharging herself."

"Are you sure? Perhaps you could double-check?"

"No, I don't need to because I checked when the other couple was here, and I keep the records myself, so I know what I'm telling you is accurate. I'm sorry I can't be of more help, and I do hope you find your granny."

Bemused, they left the building and walked back to the hotel, where Robert ordered them all a hot drink while they discussed the information they had received.

"I don't understand it; why would Gran discharge herself from the infirmary when presumably she was still unwell, and where is she now? If she set off from Exeter to get to Hartford, she should be there by now; it's been five months since we left home."

"Oh, Millie, I don't know; would she have returned to Brampford Speke?"

"I wouldn't have thought so because if she was in the workhouse, Lady Lilliana must have evicted her from our cottage, and she wouldn't have anywhere else to go."

"What about the neighbours; would they have taken her in?"

"I suppose Ollie and Agnes next door might have done, or possibly the vicar."

"Look, try not to worry; we'll stay the night here in Exeter and then visit our friends in Cullompton, but on the way home, we'll visit Brampford Speke and talk to the neighbours and the vicar and see if they can shed any light on her whereabouts."

"Thank you, but what if Lady Lilliana sees me? I might get arrested."

"No, don't worry about that; it's unlikely she'll see you, and anyway, you're with us, and we have the brooch, so she can't accuse you of stealing it. I was thinking of taking it back to her, but I think it's best we take it to Sir Edgar's solicitors so there's a record of its return. Otherwise, she might deny she has it and still accuse you of taking it. Now, we have the rest of the day to ourselves, so I suggest we make the most of it and see a little of the city."

They stepped outside their hotel, which was beside the 12th-century cathedral, and decided to pay it a visit. Robert escorted them inside and pointed out the ancient Gothic architecture and intricate carvings, but Annie and Millie were more in awe of the beautiful stained-glass windows illuminated by the bright spring sunshine. Duly impressed, they continued to explore the city, strolling along the historic quayside, a bustling hub of activity where shops, businesses, and warehouses lined the waterfront.

"Shall we walk to the Northernhay Gardens? It's too nice to go indoors, and it's a pleasant spot."

Both women nodded, and Robert escorted them to the landscaped parklands, which contained impressive flower beds and statues. It was peaceful after the bustle of the city, and they rested a while on a bench, enjoying the birdsong and the antics of two squirrels, before strolling back to their hotel.

The following day, as before, Dodger was ready and waiting with the carriage to take them to their friends in Cullompton, a journey of a dozen miles or so. The weather was again in their favour, and in little more than an hour, they turned into the driveway of a large house. Annie had not been there before and was impressed.

"Oh, Robert, it's such a lovely house."

"Yes, it's easy to see why Clara likes living here so much and why Geoffrey wants to retire."

Before they reached the front door, a butler opened it, welcomed them inside, and ushered them into the drawing room, where the Turners were enjoying their elevenses. Geoffrey rose to his feet, a broad smile on his face.

"Robert, my boy, and Annie, how delightful to see you both, and who is this charming young lady?"

"Hello, Geoffrey, hello, Clara." Robert bent to kiss his hostess's hand. "This is Annie's cousin, Millie Gibbs. I hope you don't mind us bringing her with us; it was a last-minute decision with no time to tell you."

"No, of course, we don't mind; we have plenty of bedrooms. I'm pleased to meet you, my dear, and Annie; you're looking well."

After the pleasantries were over, Robert explained why they were accompanied by Millie and about their visits to Eggesford and Exeter.

"How strange. You must be so worried about your granny, my dear. I do hope you find her soon. Geoffrey and I are acquainted with Lady Lilliana, and we also knew Sir Edgar before his untimely death; it was so sad. We knew all was not well between them, but still, she should not take her spite out on you. Is there anything we can do to help?"

"I don't think so, thank you, ma'am. Robert has kindly offered to take me to Brampford Speke on the way home to see if my gran has returned there, and if not, we don't know where else to look. I'm worried she might have tried to make her way to Hartford and perished somewhere along the way."

"Oh, dear, I do hope not. We must all hope for the best."

The visitors spent the next few days being spoilt by the Larkbeare House staff. They strolled around the house's extensive grounds, enjoying the carpets of bluebells in the woods and the many shrubs covered in vibrant green shoots and blossoms in the landscaped garden. Clara Turner took a keen interest in her garden and revelled in the opportunity to show it off. They explored the small town of Cullompton, with its narrow streets, small shops, and weekly market, and in the evenings, after their meal, the men retired to enjoy a port together and a game of cards whilst the ladies chatted and put the world to rights. Millie enjoyed it all but was anxious to continue her search for Emily.

Sir Geoffrey advised that he would be returning to London by the end of the month and that he could arrange for the operation on Danny's foot to be carried out in June.

"As you know, my colleague, Doctor Brown, will do the operation, for he's an orthopaedic surgeon, and it's not my speciality. I'm glad Danny's willing to have this final operation, for I think it will make all the difference to him and get rid of his limp once and for all. He's had a difficult time, poor lad, but he's borne it all with such fortitude. Will Sabina be coming to London with him? I know she has a young baby, for I delivered the child. Katel was her name, if I remember correctly."

"Yes, that's right, and as she's still breastfeeding, she's torn about the best thing to do. She wants to be with Danny, but it's a long journey for such a small child, and she doesn't want to wean her yet."

"Would Danny be willing to go without his mother?"

"Yes, I think so, especially if Annie accompanies us. We've not quite decided yet."

Annie took up the conversation. "This is the first time I've left the twins, though they're nearly a year old, and I want to see how they've been in my absence. I've weaned them, so that's not a problem, and I have every confidence in our nursemaid. I'll decide when we return, but we'll sort something out."

Having thanked the doctor and his wife for their hospitality, Robert, Annie, and Millie left, and the carriage headed for Brampford Speke.

"Is there an inn at Brampford Speke, Millie?"

"Yes, it's called The Agricultural Inn."

"I think we'll see if we can stay there for the night because by the time we get there and see the vicar and your granny's neighbours, it will be a bit late to head home. We'll visit the vicarage first; the vicar should know what happened to Emily."

They arrived at The Agricultural Inn in time for lunch, and the landlord agreed to provide them with accommodation for the night. Robert asked him if he knew Emily Gibbs' whereabouts, but the man could not help. Leaving their luggage at the inn, they walked the short distance to the vicarage, and Robert knocked on the large front door. A maid answered and showed them into the sitting room whilst she fetched her master.

"Millie, how lovely to see you. How are you, my dear? We all wondered what happened to you and Jonathan." Gregory Swann beamed widely at the young girl.

"Thank you, Vicar; yes, I'm well, and so is Jonnie. When Gran heard Sir Edgar had died, she insisted we flee the village that same night, for she was afraid Lady Lilliana might make trouble for us. Gran thought some relatives of her father might still live in Hartford and offer us somewhere safe to stay. It took us weeks to get there, but thankfully, we found our family, who kindly took us in. This is my cousin, Annie, and her husband, Robert, the heir to Hartford Manor."

The vicar was impressed. "That's wonderful, Millie; I'm so pleased for you, and what about Emily? Have you been able to collect her from the workhouse, too?"

"No, the lady there said Gran discharged herself after a few weeks, and we don't know where she is. We were hoping you might know. What happened after we left?"

Gregory pursed his lips. "What happened was disgraceful, and it still makes my blood boil; your granny was wise to send you and Jonathan on your way. The day after you left, Lady Lilliana arrived at the cottage, stormed in, and demanded to know where you and your brother were. She said you had stolen a valuable brooch and were wanted by the police, though we all knew that was rubbish. Emily told her you had gone to relatives in Somerset, but the lady didn't believe her and had the whole village searched. When she couldn't find you, she evicted poor Emily, who was so sick she could barely stand."

"Oh no! I thought Ollie and Agnes would have taken her in; how did she get to the workhouse?"

"Ah, yes, they would have done, and so would I, but no, Lady Lilliana would have none of it. She got her man to deposit Emily in the snow outside, dressed in only her nightdress, and said if any of us offered her shelter, we would be evicted too, for as you know, she owns the entire village. Luckily, I came along as all this was happening, and I wrapped Emily up in blankets and took her to the Exeter workhouse on my horse and cart. I must be honest, my dear; I thought she might perish before we even got there, for she was so weak and ill. I find it hard to believe she discharged herself from the infirmary, I mean, where would she go? I'm sorry to say it, but are you sure she didn't pass away?"

"No, the lady at the workhouse was sure she discharged herself, so she must have recovered from the typhoid. I wondered if she had come here to you or Ollie and Agnes?"

"No, she hasn't returned to the village, and she wouldn't because she knew if anyone offered her a home, they would be evicted. Perhaps she intended to travel to Hartford to find you and Jonathan."

"Yes, and that's the only explanation I can think of, but it's nearly five months, and she should have arrived by now. I'm worried she's perished along the way. Jonnie and I found it hard to travel so far, but it would have been nearly impossible for Gran. We don't know where to look for her."

Millie was distraught when they left the vicarage with no answers, and Robert and Annie took her to visit Emily's neighbours in case they had any further information, though they were not hopeful. Agnes was delighted to see Millie but could tell her no more, and disheartened, they returned to the inn to spend the night before journeying home the next day.

CHAPTER 22

HARTFORD

Peter Webber and Lady Margery had not seen Sam since he and his family moved to Sugworthy Farm nearly a month earlier, and they missed him. It turned out the arrangement with Peter's grandson, Christopher, had suited everyone, and now, after attending to Peter's needs each morning, he worked on the Enderby Estate for the rest of the day, once more attending to his grandfather at lunchtime when he went home for his dinner. As Peter had become better acquainted with Clarice, Christopher's wife, he now allowed her to care for him, too, and she took it all in her stride. However, Clarice had been taking it easy for the last few days as she had given birth prematurely to a baby boy, and although mother and baby were doing well, the doctor had insisted that she rest for at least two weeks.

Christopher was over the moon at becoming a father and worked even longer hours to make up for the time Lady Margery insisted he had off to care for his grandfather and bedridden wife; she also sent one of her maids to live there for a couple of weeks to help out. The Webbers were overwhelmed by her generosity.

"I wish you'd let me pay the maid's wages, Margery; 'tis only right, and I have some money put by now from selling my paintings."

"Nonsense, Peter; you're a dear friend, and it's not like I can't afford it. Maybe I should be paying you for all your advice on my painting."

"Oh, you more than repay me by taking me out in your carriage; I would never have visited half the places we've been to if it wasn't for you."

"Now, it's funny you should mention that because I think it's time we had another little jaunt; how do you feel about travelling to Sugworthy Farm tomorrow to see how Sam and Marrok are getting on? I know you miss Sam, as do I, and it would be nice to see them."

"Oh, yes, I'd love that; do you think they'll mind if we just turn up?"

"I think they'll be delighted to see you, and me too, I hope. That's settled then."

They set off in Lady Margery's carriage the next morning and were at Sugworthy Farm within the hour. It was a hive of activity for two workmen were thatching the farmhouse roof, and another was installing a new window. Sam was repairing a gate, and Marrok was helping Edward and Willie to clean out the shippens. As it was a Saturday, the children, too, were running around playing, and Eliza and Jinnie were collecting eggs from the hen houses. When he heard the carriage, Sam glanced up from his task and smiled when he recognised his visitors.

"Margery, Peter, I'm so pleased to see you. I was only thinking yesterday that I must ride over to Primrose Cottage to see how you all are. Are Clarice and Christopher all right?"

"Hello, Sam; yes, they're both fine, thank you, especially now they have a little boy, and I have a new great-grandson."

"Oh, splendid, but he wasn't due yet, was he?"

"No, there was a month to go, but he got impatient. Still, he weighs nearly five pounds, so not a bad size, and he's thriving; Clarice, too. They're going to call him Peter, after me."

Sam clapped his friend on the back. "Congratulations, Peter, please give them my best wishes. Come inside and have some tea, though I expect Florrie will be all of a tizzy at a lady calling."

"Oh, she mustn't worry on my account, Sam; you know that. Hello, Marrok. Have you settled in all right?"

"Yes, thank you, ma'am, sorry, Aunty Margery. We love it here, though there's an awful lot of work to do. Come in and see for yourself."

Sam was right, and Florrie was anxious about having a lady in her kitchen, but Margery put the old woman at ease as only she could, and they were soon chattering away as if they had known each other all their lives. A little later, Marrok and Sam showed their visitors around the house.

"We haven't done much downstairs yet apart from helping Florrie to give everything a thorough clean. I need to employ another couple of maids to help her, for it's far too big a house for one woman to manage, but I haven't got around to that yet. We've been busy upstairs, though; four of the bedrooms were in a terrible state because of the roof leaking, and now that the new timbers have been fitted and the thatch is nearly finished, I've employed a couple of builders to take the ceilings down and redecorate. Come and see." Marrok opened each door, showing the rooms at different stages of completion. "The work's coming along nicely, thanks to Dad's generosity in paying for everything, though Robert offered to contribute too. We still have a long way to go, for most of the windows need to be replaced and a few doors, but we're getting there slowly."

"I think you've worked wonders in such a short time, Marrok; how about the land? Is that well-managed? I know the area; many years ago, I worked here as a farm labourer."

"Oh, did you, Peter? That's interesting. Was that in Tommy Houle's day?"

"Aye, and his father before him. I knew his grandfather, too, before he passed away. Good farmers were the Houles; 'tis a pity Tommy never had a family, but there 'tis, and if they had, you wouldn't be here now, so every cloud has a silver lining, as they say."

After a couple of hours, Lady Margery and Peter left Sugworthy Farm, promising to return soon and urging Sam to visit them as soon as possible. Marrok had invited them to stay for dinner, but they declined his invitation as they wanted to see more relatives before heading home. The carriage quickly covered the few miles between the farm and the village of Hartford and dropped Peter off at the Lodge House to visit his son, Arthur.

"We'll collect you again later, Peter. Would five o'clock be all right with you?"

"Yes, of course, Margery; whatever you say. I'll have me dinner with Arthur and Sabina and catch up on their news, and then be ready and waiting for you."

"Good, thank you. If we leave then, we'll still be home before dark now that the nights are drawing out. See you later."

Knowing Robert and Annie were visiting the Turners in Cullompton, Lady Margery went straight to the front door of Hartford Manor and was quickly ushered inside by the butler.

"How are you, Hobbs?"

"Very well, m'lady; thank you. If you would like to follow me, the family are in the sitting room."

Lady Margery was pleased to find her niece Victoria and three children, Caroline, Joshua, and Francis, with Charles and Eleanor.

"Hello, Margery, how nice to see you."

"Thank you, Eleanor, you too. Are you all well? My goodness, how these children are growing."

Eleanor nodded and glanced proudly at her three grandchildren. "Yes, they are, and they're such a delight; it's been marvellous having Victoria living here with her family, though sadly, not for much longer."

"Have you been successful in purchasing the house in Lynton, then, Victoria?"

"Yes, Aunt, I have, and I'm so excited. The sale is nearly complete, and I'll have the keys in a few days. I can't wait to move in; it's such a wonderful house with amazing views. Mama and Papa, you'll love it."

"Hm, maybe, though I'd rather you stayed here."

"We've been through this, Mama, and Lynton isn't that far away."

"It's nearer than London, I'll grant you that."

"What about Frank's mother? Does she want to live in the cottage on the grounds of your new house?"

"Catherine's not seen it yet, but I've offered it to her, and she's going to come and stay for a month once we've moved in and then decide. It's up to her, but I think she was pleased to be asked."

"Excellent; I'm delighted your plans are coming together. Times have been difficult for you recently, and you deserve a little happiness. And how about you two? Have you decided to move into the west wing and let Robert take over the main house so that he can develop his business?"

"We haven't decided yet. We need to survey the west wing and see what we think of it."

"So what's stopping you? Oh, you won't go there in case you meet Annie. Well, Robert and Annie are away at the moment, visiting Geoffrey and Clara Turner in Cullompton. They're arranging for Danny to have one more operation to straighten his feet." Lady Margery said this hesitantly, realising that she had nearly given the game away by referring to the child as Charles and Eleanor's son. Knowing, to her disgust, they had rejected the boy at birth because of his extensive disabilities, she could never resist an opportunity to remind them of it. However, knowing Victoria was unaware that Danny was, in fact, her brother, she felt it wasn't her place to enlighten her. "I could take you there now if you like. I'm sure they wouldn't mind, for Robert is keen to get on with his plans to offer fishing and shooting parties and to do that, he needs the space to accommodate the visitors."

Charles studied Eleanor. "That seems like an excellent suggestion, my dear; why don't you do that? Victoria, perhaps you could accompany your mother? I'll be content with whatever you decide; as long as I spend the rest of my days in Hartford Manor, I don't care which part of the house it is."

Eleanor considered the matter for a moment or two. "All right, if you're sure they won't mind. It seems rather rude to visit when they're away."

"Well, considering you won't visit if Annie is at home, it seems to be a way forward. Shall we go now?"

Victoria rang the bell for the nanny to take the children back to the nursery, and the three women walked the short distance to the front door of the west wing, where Ethan Bater admitted them after advising that the master and mistress were not at home. The butler knew Lady Margery and Lady Victoria, for they visited regularly. He also knew that Lady Fellwood disapproved of his mistress, and he looked a little unsure.

"It's all right, Bater; I'll take full responsibility for this visit, and I assure you it's something Master Robert would approve of."

"Yes, ma'am, of course; where would you like to go?"

"We want a look around the building; nothing for you to worry about, and as I say, I will take full responsibility and speak to my nephew upon his return. Do you know when he expects to be back from Cullompton?"

"Not exactly, ma'am, but probably in the next day or two, I believe."

With the butler uneasy, Lady Margery led the way around the west wing, and Lady Eleanor was impressed, though she played down her feelings.

"I must admit, they've made it comfortable, and there is plenty of space for us. Some of the downstairs rooms would be suitable as a bedroom for Charles with access for his wheelchair. Have we seen it all?"

"Yes, apart from the servants' quarters and the kitchens, and I don't think you need to see them."

"No, of course not."

Lady Margery and Victoria had, in fact, also avoided the nursery and rooms used by Annie and Robert's children, Selina, Thomas, and David. It was apparent that Lady Eleanor was unaware that her grandchildren were in the house. They descended the stairs and were horrified when Ethan opened the door to admit Robert and Annie back from their travels.

Of the group, it was difficult to say who looked the most shocked. Annie and Robert could scarcely believe their eyes. Ethan lowered his eyes and hoped he would not be dismissed. Lady Margery, Victoria, and especially Eleanor looked embarrassed and wished the ground would open up and swallow them. It was Lady Margery, of course, who recovered first and put a broad smile on her face.

"Robert, Annie, welcome home. I hope you had an enjoyable trip. You must tell me all about it soon. Now, you must be wondering what we're all doing, trespassing in your home. Well, as you might expect, I'm afraid it's all my fault, and you certainly mustn't blame Bater for letting us in. I called on Charles and Eleanor unexpectedly and asked if they had decided to move from the main house to the west wing. When it was apparent they hadn't even looked around, I thought now would be a good time."

The old lady stared at Robert, willing him to understand that she had been trying to help, and eventually, he found his voice.

"Yes, of course, Aunty Margery; you know you're welcome here any time. We were a little surprised to find you all here."

Before more could be said, there was the sound of running footsteps on the stairs, and a little girl suddenly appeared, a nursemaid on her heels.

"Mummy! Papa! You're home. I saw your carriage from my window."

Naomi, the nursemaid, curtseyed. "I'm so sorry, ma'am. Miss Selina ran down the stairs before I had time to stop her."

Selina sensed something was wrong and wondered why her parents' faces were so serious. She glared at Lady Eleanor.

"You don't like me, do you? And you don't like my mummy. Well, I don't like you, either. So go away!"

Annie reached for her daughter and shook her arm. "Selina, don't be so rude. Apologise immediately."

The little girl wore a sulky expression. "You always say I must tell the truth, Mummy."

"Selina!"

"I'm sorry."

Everyone in the room knew the child was lying, and white-faced, Eleanor hurried through the front door.

CHAPTER 23

Victoria rushed after her mother, leaving Aunty Margery to apologise to Robert and Annie for invading their house in their absence. Ignoring the old lady for the moment, Robert reassured the nursemaid that she was not to blame for Selina's sudden appearance, and Annie hugged her daughter.

"Hello, Selina. Did you miss us?"

"Yes, lots, Mummy; I wanted to see you and Papa."

"Yes, I know; that's all right, Selina, but you were quite rude to the lady, and that was naughty. You mustn't speak to her like that again."

Selina's lip trembled slightly, but she wore a defiant expression. "Well, she doesn't like me, Mummy. Even when I smile at her, she always frowns. Who is she anyway?"

This was a difficult question, but Annie never lied to her children.

"That is Lady Eleanor, and she's Papa's mama. She lives next door with Papa's father, Charles, Aunty Victoria and Aunty Sarah."

Selina was astonished. "So, if she's my granny, why doesn't she like me? Granny Betsey and Granny Sabina like me?"

Robert took over the difficult conversation, but decided the fact that he was not the child's father could wait until she was old enough to understand.

"I'm afraid my mama is rather silly, Selina. You see, she has always been a rich lady with lots of servants, and she would have liked me to marry a lady too, but I fell in love with your mother. Now, I wouldn't change your mother for the world, but she used to be a servant, and that's why your grandmother doesn't like her."

"But Aunty Margery is a lady, and she likes us."

"Yes, I do, Selina, very much; I'm afraid Lady Eleanor is being silly as Papa says, and we all hope she'll realise it one day. Anyway, there is nothing for you to worry about, for you have lots of people who love you."

"Selina, go to the nursery with Naomi, and in a few minutes, I'll come to see you, Thomas and David."

The nursemaid led the child away, and Lady Margery attempted to put matters right.

"I must apologise, my dears, for what must you think, returning home to find Victoria and me here in your house with your mother? However, I assure you I had your best interests at heart. Peter and I visited Marrok and Sam at Sugworthy Farm this morning and then decided to come to Hartford. I dropped Peter off at the Lodge House to chat with Arthur and Sabina, and then called on Charles and Eleanor, and naturally, I enquired whether they had decided to move to the west wing. Eleanor was obviously curious to see the west wing, but would never come here whilst you were present, Annie. Knowing you were away, I thought it would be a convenient time to show her around, but I'm sorry if this has upset you."

"No, that's all right, Aunty Margery; it doesn't matter. It was a shock, that's all. I don't know who was the most horrified, us or my mother. Out of interest, what did she think of our home? Did she like it?"

"Do you know, I think she was impressed, and with careful handling, I believe she will agree to the move. I'll leave you now and try to pour oil on troubled waters next door, and I know Annie is desperate to spend some time with her children. But did you find Millie's grandmother?"

"No, sadly not, but we'll tell you all about that another time. Good luck with my mother."

As soon as Lady Margery left them, Annie tore up the stairs to the nursery and hugged her babies and then Selina, for she had missed them so much. Naomi assured her that all had been well and that Betsey, Sabina, Victoria, and Sarah visited the children every day. Having given all three a small gift, she settled down to play with them for the rest of the afternoon.

Downstairs, Robert heaved a sigh of relief as he sank into his favourite chair and rang the bell. When Mollie appeared, he asked her to fetch him a cup of tea and a slice of Maisie's best cake and turned his attention to the stack of letters waiting on his desk. Most were correspondence concerning the estate, and they could wait a while, but one was from Sir Roger Everson, and Robert read it eagerly. He was pleased to learn that the gentleman was staying in Devon for a couple of weeks and invited Robert to lunch at the Royal and Fortescue Inn in Barnstaple that Friday. Robert quickly penned a reply and rang for a footman to ensure his acceptance was delivered promptly.

The following day, feeling he had put the matter off for long enough, Robert visited his parents. His mother was furious about Selina's comments and ranted and raved about the child's disgraceful manners and how humiliated she had felt.

"It was unfortunate, Mama, but Selina cannot comprehend why you appear to dislike her. I explained to her that you would have liked me to marry a rich lady and were disappointed that I married her mother, a former servant. She still doesn't fully understand but accepts the explanation. Annie reprimanded her for speaking as she did, and she has been told to treat you with respect in future. Now, I'm glad you have explored the west wing, although the situation was a little confrontational; what was your conclusion? Would you be prepared to move there?"

"I must confess, I was impressed with your refurbishments, and it is a pleasant home. I've discussed the matter with Charles, and we think it would suit us. Therefore, we will move there, though I think we'll stay with Margery for a week or two whilst the change takes place. She offered for us to do so yesterday before she left."

"Oh, that's excellent news; thank you, Mama, and I think you'll be more comfortable there, Papa. We had all the plumbing replaced and a new bathroom installed before we moved in, and I'm sure you'll enjoy using the new facilities."

Robert and his father had not been on good terms for some time, and Charles was pleased with the opportunity to discuss something positive with his son.

"I think the shooting and fishing weekends are an excellent idea, Robert, and I know Aunty Margery has found them lucrative at Enderby. These large houses become ever more costly to run, so you're wise to expand your business. You already manage the estate efficiently, according to Jack Bater, and when I pass away, you'll inherit the title and become Lord Fellwood. Now is an appropriate time to take your rightful place in the main house. With Victoria moving out shortly and you with a growing family, you need the space far more than we do."

"I'm so pleased; thank you again, Papa. If possible, I'd like us to move in before our trip to London next month. We visited Geoffrey and Clara Turner in Cullompton last weekend to arrange a date for Danny to have the third, and hopefully final, operation on his foot, and we've agreed on mid-June. We have other business in the capital, and the sooner we can go, the better. Could you move in the next week or two?"

"Yes, there's no point putting it off. I'll send a message to Aunty Margery to tell her when to expect us."

Robert was feeling pleased with himself and hastened to the west wing to tell Annie the news.

"I'm surprised they agreed. I never thought they'd move out of the main house."

"No, neither did I, but I think Mama was rather taken with our living accommodation, and it will suit them far better than the main house. Victoria's moving to her new house next week, and Mama and Papa will stay with Aunty Margery whilst we transfer to the main house. It won't be as comfortable as the West Wing, for we'll need to carry out a lot of renovations, but I think we should move in and then take our time deciding what changes to make. If we offer accommodation to visitors, I want them to be separate from us; it's essential that we keep our privacy. I'll call in an architect to discuss the plans."

"Can we afford to do this? It sounds expensive."

"Yes, it will be costly, but I've discussed my plans with Mr Billery, who approves. It should bring a handsome profit once it is all up and running. Anyway, how did you get on at the Lodge House? Is Sabina going to come to London with Danny or not?"

"No, she isn't. She doesn't want to leave Katel, and Danny is happy to go without her. He loves spending time with you and Percy, but I've decided to go with you. I'd love to see London again."

"Excellent. I was hoping you'd come, and I'm sure the children will be content with Naomi, though, of course, they'll miss you. I'm glad I can meet Roger in Barnstaple on Friday to find out about Edgar's solicitors; it will be interesting to hear what he says about the family, and it's easier to talk face-to-face than by letter. I want the brooch returned and Millie's name cleared before we leave for London."

On the following Friday, Robert rode to Barnstaple and left his horse in the stable yard at the rear of The Royal and Fortescue Hotel. He was a little early for his luncheon appointment with Sir Roger Everson and entered the bar, thinking he would enjoy a tankard of ale while waiting.

However, he had no sooner sat down on a comfortable sofa than he espied Sir Roger in the doorway and called out to him.

"Roger, hello Roger, over here." He waved his arm and then shook the gentleman's hand warmly. "How nice to see you again. I trust you and the family are in good health?"

"Hello, Robert. Yes, thank you. Yours too, I hope. How old are your children now?"

"Yes, thank you. Annie and I have a five-year-old daughter called Selina and twin boys, David and Thomas, who will be one next month."

"How splendid. We have Jessica, who's nearly five, Ernest, aged two, and Jasmine is expecting our third child in a few weeks."

"Oh, congratulations. I hope all goes well."

"Thank you. Shall we continue our conversation in the dining room, where there is more privacy?"

When comfortably seated, they ordered poached salmon with dill sauce, new potatoes, and asparagus and waited for the waiter to leave before continuing their conversation.

"I'm much obliged to you for meeting with me, Roger. I know you're aware that my marriage is a little unconventional, and not everyone approves."

"No, I know. I heard that you'd married someone below your station, Robert, but I'm no snob, and if you love the girl, then I don't blame you, though I know many will not approve. I'm fortunate, for my marriage to Jasmine was arranged from birth, and we played together as children, but we genuinely love each other and are content. However, I'm not sure I would have been prepared to marry her if we didn't. Anyway, how can I help?"

"It's a strange tale. My wife's grandmother, Betsey, was neglected as a child, particularly after her mother died when she was six. Her father, Adam Lovering, was an alcoholic, and he couldn't cope with Betsey and her brother on his own. One day, he abandoned them and was never seen again. Sadly, the little boy, Norman, died, but Betsey was taken in by the family next door and raised as their daughter. She married, had a family, and still lives in Hartford with her husband, Ned Carter.

"Not long after Christmas, two children, Millie and Jonathan Gibbs, arrived in the village searching for Adam's relatives. They found the grave of his wife, Ellen, and son, Norman, made enquiries and were put in touch with Betsey. They were amazed that she looked so much like their granny, Emily. It turned out that after Adam left Hartford, he married again and had another daughter. Emily Gibbs and Betsey Carter are half-sisters, sharing Adam Lovering as their father, but with different mothers."

"Goodness, this is quite a story, and I think I can see where it's leading. I met Emily Gibbs and her daughter, Rosemary, many years ago when I stayed at Grantley House in Brampford Speke. Edgar Grantley was my close friend, and I spent a lot of time with him when we were young. We played all over the estate, and children from the village often joined us in our games, though our parents would probably not have approved. I remember Rosemary Gibbs because, as a teenager, she was beautiful, and Edgar was quite besotted.

"However, he was forced to marry Lady Lilliana because the union had been arranged since they were children. He begged to be released from the betrothal, but to no avail, and the marriage took place. I was one of his few friends who knew Rosemary Gibbs continued to be his mistress until the day he died. Of course, eventually, Lady Lilliana found out about his infidelity and was bitterly unhappy, which was understandable. I believe she had always wanted a family, but despite many relationships, which were the talk of London town, she never had a child."

"Yes, I see. That's what I've heard from Millie and Jonathan, whom I believe you've met?"

"Yes, that's right, though quite by chance. Jasmine and I were travelling to Barnstaple in our carriage and hoping to get there before nightfall when we were forced to seek shelter from a blizzard at The Farmers Arms in Kings Nympton. It was not the most desirable of establishments, and the landlord was quite an unsavoury character, but any port in a storm, as they say. Anyway, we were there for a couple of nights waiting for the roads to clear, and then, as we were about to depart, I heard a girl crying for help from a bedroom window. It was Millie, and she was begging us to take her and her brother, Jonathan, with us, for she feared the landlord, Simon Higgins, would force himself upon her. To be honest, the man gave my wife the creeps, even though she had me to protect her, so I think Millie's fears were probably well-founded.

"Simon Higgins was furious and said he had imprisoned them until he could take them to Crediton to claim the reward money offered by Lady Lilliana of Grantley Manor for their capture. My wife insisted we take them with us, and I agreed with her, so I paid the reward money to Mr Higgins, and we took the children with us."

"But you didn't hand them in and claim the reward?"

"No, when Millie told her story about Lady Lilliana accusing her of stealing a brooch, I believed her, and I was sad to hear Edgar had died. I didn't know he had fathered two children by Rosemary, but I'm not surprised, for their relationship lasted many years, although they were discreet. The children also look like their father. We took them all the way to Barnstaple and paid for them to stay here at The Royal and Fortescue Inn for the night, as we arrived late, and it was bitterly cold. When we went down for breakfast in the morning, they had vanished, and we continued our journey to Cornwall. I'm so glad they made it safely to Hartford and found relatives prepared to take them in."

"Thank you for telling me all that; it corroborates their story, though I believed it anyway."

"How can I help you?"

"Millie does have the brooch in question, but she didn't steal it. It used to belong to Edgar's mother, and he gave it to Rosemary Gibbs, though Lilliana had all the other jewellery. Lilliana is making up the charges against Millie because she wants to get her jailed or hanged in revenge for her husband's unfaithfulness. She's already evicted poor Emily Gibbs from her cottage in Brampford Speke. She was taken to the Exeter Workhouse but is no longer there, and we don't know where she is. I think the best thing is to take the brooch to Edgar's solicitors and clear Millie's name. I'm hoping you might know who his solicitors are?"

"Fortunately, I do. It's a firm called Parkham, Glover, and Brown, and they have an office on Oxford Street in London. I know because I once went there with Edgar to witness some documents."

"Oh, I didn't realise his solicitors were in London; I expected it to be a firm in Exeter."

"No, I think the family has used the same firm for many years, and as I spend most of my time in the capital, it was easy for me to call in and sign the documents as a witness. Obviously, I have no idea what the documents were; none of my business. I simply witnessed Edgar's signature."

"I'm so glad we've found this out now, for Annie and I are travelling to London next month, and possibly we could take Millie and Jonathan with us to get this matter sorted out."

"That's good. There is something I must tell you, though, Robert. I've also received a letter from Lady Lilliana asking me to call on her before I leave Devon. I've arranged to visit her in Brampford Speke on my way back to London next week. I'm puzzled as to why she wants to see me, for we were never close; it was Edgar with whom I was friendly, but I can only assume it must have something to do with Millie and Jonathan. Somehow, she must have heard of my involvement with them and is making quite an effort to locate them."

"I see; that is interesting, and thank you for telling me. This is asking a lot, but could you avoid mentioning that you transported the children to Barnstaple? Until we get this brooch to the solicitors, I'd like to keep Millie and Jonathan's whereabouts quiet."

"Of course. They're Edgar's children, and my allegiance was with him, and now his children; I never took to Lilliana anyway. Rest assured, I'll be discreet."

CHAPTER 24

Later that evening, Robert and Annie curled up together in their favourite spot on a comfortable sofa in the study. Although the west wing contained many grand rooms, they preferred this cosy room, where they often caught up with each other's news at the end of the day whilst enjoying a glass of wine. Robert told Annie all about his conversation with Sir Roger.

"Oh, my goodness; I'm so glad you discovered Sir Edgar's solicitors are in London before we left home. It would have been so annoying to learn that when we returned. What shall we do? Take Millie and Jonathan to London with us? He'd be company for Danny."

"Yes, that's what I thought. We could deliver the brooch ourselves, but I think it would be better if Millie did it in person. If she's with us, it will carry more weight that we've accepted her and Jonnie into our family."

"In that case, do you mind if I take them to Barnstaple next week and buy them some new clothes? When they arrived, they only had what they were wearing, and though Gran's bought them a few things, they still don't have much. It's Millie's birthday in a few days, too, so I'd like to buy her something."

"Yes, of course. You need to be careful, though. Don't forget there's a high price on her head."

"No, I know, but the last time they went, they were going to use the names of Anna and Leonard Smith from St Ives in Cornwall if they were introduced to anyone. I don't think they were, and people wouldn't expect them to be with a group of other people. I'll invite Gran and Charlotte, too; they say there's safety in numbers. I would ask Mum, but she doesn't like leaving Katel for long yet."

A few days later, with Dodger driving the carriage, Annie collected Betsey and Millie from their cottage and Charlotte from The Red Lion Inn. It was Millie's sixteenth birthday that day, and they planned to do some shopping and then enjoy a birthday lunch together. Once again, Millie had dyed her hair dark brown and wore Betsey's bonnet in case anyone recognised her.

Annie instructed Dodger to drop them at Francis Carter's shop near the Albert Clock and leave the carriage at the rear of The Royal and Fortescue Inn, where they were to have lunch. Robert was so impressed with the food when he ate there with Sir Roger that he suggested the ladies might enjoy it. Francis was pleased to see his granny and cousins and welcomed them into the shop.

Betsey hugged him. "Hello, Francis; how are you, lad? You get bigger every time I see you, but not too big for a cuddle from your granny, I hope?"

"No, Gran, I'll never be too big for that. Is this a social call, or can I help you with anything?"

Annie joined the conversation. "Yes, please, Francis. Robert and I are taking Millie and Jonathan to London next week to return the brooch, and they need some new clothes. You've heard Millie's tale and know about the brooch, don't you?"

"Yes, I do, and I hope you get it all sorted out. What about you, Gran, and Aunty Charlotte? Is there anything you need?"

"We'll browse, lad; you see to Millie, and we'll tell you if anything takes our fancy."

An hour or so later, Millie was beaming from ear to ear as she happily clutched her shopping. Annie had purchased two new dresses, a shawl, a pair of boots, and some new underwear for her, and for Jonnie, a new jerkin, a couple of shirts, and some new trousers. He also needed new shoes, but they decided to get them from Mr Martin, the cordwainer in Hartford, for they needed to be sure they would fit. Not to be outdone, Betsey bought Ned some new socks and herself a skirt, and Charlotte purchased quite a few new clothes for each of the children: Llewie, Rosella, Eddie, Doris and Nicholas.

"What about you, Charlotte? Is there anything you or Fred need?"

"No, thank you; I've spent enough for one day."

"Annie, why don't you leave the shopping here and collect it on your way home? There's no need to carry it around the town with you."

"Thanks, Francis; we'll do that and see you later."

Leaving the shop, the women walked past the Albert Clock and wandered over to the river, where some large ships were unloading their cargo, and a steam train whistled as it sped by on the railway bridge. Suddenly, Millie caught sight of Jess, the prostitute who had befriended her when she was in Barnstaple. The girl quickly lowered her eyes and turned away, but her disguise did not fool the sharp-eyed woman.

"Hello, Millie. I hope you weren't goin' to ignore me?"

"Oh, sorry, Jess; I admit I was hoping you wouldn't recognise me, but not because I don't want to speak to you. It's just that there's a reward on my head, and I don't want to attract attention."

"'Tis nice to see thee, Millie, but yer right about the reward, and thee 'ad a narrow escape the day ye left. Did thee realise Liz's punter, the policeman, 'ad recognised ye?"

"Yes, I thought he had, and that's why we ran away."

"It was quite funny; Liz was furious cos 'er was 'oping to share the reward, and 'er certainly got it in the neck from 'er mother, Fanny, fer betraying ye. Fanny was angry after all the help thee'd given us. Where did ye go?"

"We lay low for a few days and then got a ride on a cart to Hartford, where I eventually found our relatives. This is my Aunty Betsey and cousins Annie and Charlotte. How's Alice, next door to you? Is she all right?"

Alice had helped Millie and Jonathan in their bid for freedom, but Annie had no intention of divulging this information, although she trusted Jess.

"Oh, that's good; I'm glad ye found yer folk. Aye, Alice is fine. The police searched 'er 'ouse that night cos Liz knew ye was friendly wi' her, but they didn't find anything. Don't worry; I won't ask who hid ye and Jonnie, though I could 'azard a guess. I'm glad ye escaped anyway. Did ye knaw the reward 'as bin doubled now for information leading to yer arrest? That lady must be proper angry with ye, and Liz is desperate to find ye and claim it. Did ye come to town a few weeks ago? Liz thought 'er saw ye but wasn't sure."

"I do know about the reward, and, yes, I saw Liz when I was in Barnstaple last. I dyed my hair and wore a bonnet, hoping no one would notice me, but I thought she'd recognised me. Luckily, she was with a punter and couldn't do much about it. Anyway, Jess, we'd better go."

"What about yer granny? Did ye find 'er?"

"No, not yet, but we're still trying. Bye, Jess."

Leaving the young prostitute to continue her search for her next customer, the women walked to the Royal and Fortescue Inn, where they enjoyed a delicious lunch of roast beef and all the trimmings, followed by treacle pudding and custard, all paid for by Annie.

"Oh, my goodness, I'm so full. Thank you, Annie; are you sure you won't let us share the cost, my dear?"

"No, it's all right, Gran; my pleasure. I'm glad you enjoyed it."

"Annie, what are we going to do about Millie's granny? We must find out what's happened to Emily."

"Yes, I know, Gran, and we'll keep searching, but it's difficult to know where to look. We checked at the Exeter workhouse and were told she'd left, and then with the vicar in Brampford Speke, but he didn't know where she could be. It's a mystery. Robert and I have talked about it a lot, and we think maybe she's doing like Millie and Jonathan did and making her way here slowly, getting jobs along the way so that she can eat. It would take her a while, as she's old and was seriously ill. It's important we take Millie to London to clear her name over the theft of the brooch and get Danny's foot operation over and done with, but if Emily hasn't been found by the time we return, we'll increase our efforts to find her."

"Yes, I suppose that could be it. She must have felt better to discharge herself from the workhouse, so that's one good thing."

"Anyway, ladies, if you've had enough to eat, I suggest we explore a few of the shops in the High Street before we head home."

Having enjoyed their shopping trip, Annie asked Dodger to take Betsey and Millie home first, knowing her granny was tired. Millie hugged Annie warmly and thanked her for all her birthday gifts, saying it had been one of the nicest birthdays she had ever known. However, as she spoke the words, tears glistened in her eyes as she wished her mother and granny could have been there to share it with her. At The Red Lion, Charlotte also thanked Annie for an enjoyable day.

Charlotte checked with Sarah that her little daughter, Doris, and baby, Nicholas, were all right and thanked her sister-in-law for babysitting. Rosella, Eddie and Bentley came bounding into the room.

"Did you buy us anything, Mum?" To her delight, Fred's children by his first wife, Lucy, had recently taken to calling her 'Mum'.

"I might have done; have you behaved yourselves for Aunty Sarah?"

"Yes, they've been no trouble at all, Charlotte."

Happily, Charlotte showed them the new clothes she had bought for them and then produced a sticky bun each, and their eyes lit up.

"Ooh, thanks. Can we eat them now?"

"Yes, tea won't be for a while. There's a bun here for you, too, Bentley, and take this one out to Llewie, please. Is he still working outside?"

"Yes, he's making some nails, and we've been watching him."

"Where are Fred and Louis, and what's that noise?"

A loud thump from above made them all jump.

"Oh, George and Louis are helping Fred to bring down an old trunk from the attic. Do you remember Ned telling them about it? Well, they took it into their heads to investigate this afternoon, but I think it's proving quite a challenge to get it through the attic trapdoor and down the ladder. I think that crash must mean they've managed it, though."

Charlotte went to investigate, leaving the children to eat their buns. She found her husband mopping his brow and George leaning against a door frame, looking pale and shaky.

"Are you all right, George? You look a little wan."

"Hello, Charlotte, no, I'm not too good; I've got this blasted fever back again, and I feel as weak as a kitten. I'll be all right in a minute; I just need to rest. That trunk was heavy."

Louis fetched a chair for George to sit on, and Charlotte gave him a glass of water.

"Right, let's open this chest and see what's inside. Oh, yes, look. It says Jago Carter and 1640 on the inside of the lid; I remember Dad telling us that. I think he'd figured out that Jago was his great-great-great-grandfather because his name appears in our family bible."

Fred removed a faded red cloak and discovered a bundle of documents tied up with a piece of string. He untied the string and peered at the ancient papers.

"I don't know what these papers say as they're written in Latin. Do we know anyone who could read them?"

"The vicar, maybe? Or perhaps Robert; he went to a private school, so he might be able to read Latin."

Putting the papers to one side, Fred removed a pair of pistols, a dagger, and a large leather-bound, green bible. Two wooden boxes had the words *Merchant Royal* painted on their lids, and when he opened them, he discovered they were full of foreign coins.

"These must be the Spanish pieces of eight that Grandad was talking about; do you know, George?"

"No, I've never seen coins like that before, but again, perhaps Robert would know if they're valuable. I think you should show all this to him, Fred. He's taking Danny to London soon, isn't he? Perhaps he could take all these things with him and find someone who knows about this sort of thing. Anyway, I'll leave you to it. I must get home; I think I need my bed."

"That's a good idea, George; thanks for your help, and I hope you feel better soon."

CHAPTER 25

BRAMPFORD SPEKE

Sir Roger Everson was soon to return to London and, as promised, called to see Lady Lilliana at Brampford Speke en route. He was welcomed into the drawing room, where the lady greeted him with a warm smile.

"Sir Roger, thank you so much for coming."

The gentleman bowed over Lilliana's hand and kissed it. "My pleasure, Lady Grantley; are you fully recovered? I understand you've been quite poorly."

"Yes, I have, indeed; first, with typhoid, and then influenza and pneumonia. I confess I have never felt so ill or so weak, and I wondered if I would ever recover."

"Well, I'm glad to see you looking as radiant as ever, my dear, but my condolences; I was so sorry to hear of Edgar's death. It was quite a shock."

"Yes, it was for all of us, poor dear; I miss him dreadfully."

"I'm sure you must. Now, you intimated in your letter that there was something I might help you with?"

"Yes, indeed; it's a trivial matter, but one I want to resolve. You may remember that not long before my husband's death, his mother, Lady Grantley, passed away."

"Yes, the last time I saw Edgar was at her funeral. I wanted to pay my respects, for I spent a lot of time here as a boy, and she was always kind to me."

"Quite; well, following her death, she left all her jewellery to me, and I was particularly fond of one brooch, a sapphire surrounded by tiny diamonds. I'm sad to say that not long after my husband died, the brooch was stolen."

"How terrible. How did that come about?"

"My maid saw a young girl from the village leaving my room, clutching something in her hand, and it was right after that we noticed the brooch was missing."

"How strange she should take only one item."

"No doubt she would have taken more but was disturbed."

"Did the maid know the girl?"

"Yes, she's called Millicent Gibbs, and she lived with her mother, grandmother, and brother in a tied cottage on the estate. My husband had known the family for years, ever since childhood, and having such a soft heart had let them stay in their cottage even after Lennie Gibbs, an estate worker, had died. As you know, with a tied cottage, it is customary for the family to vacate the premises if the worker dies or leaves the job. It had long been a bone of contention between Edgar and me, for I felt he should give them notice to vacate the cottage and leave it free for a new worker. Anyway, I assume that on hearing of Edgar's death, the Gibbs family knew they would be evicted, and the girl chose to steal the brooch to provide them with some money."

"Ah, I think I understand now why you wanted to see me. Years ago, I knew Rosemary Gibbs. When Edgar and I were young, she and many of the village children used to stray into the grounds of Grantley Manor, and we would all play together. I remember her mother, Emily, and father, Lennie, who were a kindly couple. I can see why Edgar would have been reluctant to evict the family."

"Quite so, but with Edgar's death, I felt the time had come for change. Anyway, I've been trying to locate Millicent Gibbs as I want my brooch back. I placed advertisements in the newspapers and was contacted by Mr Higgins, the landlord of The Farmer's Arms, an inn in Kings Nympton, to say he had information. When I visited, he told me he had recognised Millicent and her younger brother, Jonathan, from the description in the advertisement. He met them when they sought shelter from a blizzard at his inn, and, realising who they were, imprisoned them in a bedroom and planned to hand them into the police station in Crediton and claim the reward. However, the snowy weather prevented him from doing that for a few days."

"That's right, and that's how I became involved. Jasmine and I were travelling to Cornwall and stopped at the inn for shelter as the weather was atrocious. We were stuck there for two nights, waiting for the roads to clear. When we were finally able to leave, my attention was drawn to a bedroom window where a young girl was crying out for help as she feared the landlord was going to force himself on her. My wife insisted I investigate, for Mr Higgins was an unsavoury character, and Jasmine, too, had felt uncomfortable in his presence. He admitted he had imprisoned the two children whilst he waited for the weather to clear and would then take them to Crediton to claim the reward. Under the circumstances, we offered to pay Mr Higgins the reward, take them to Crediton ourselves, and get the money back. He accepted this solution as it saved him a journey, and at least we knew the young girl wouldn't be molested."

"Yes, I can understand that, but why didn't you hand them in and claim the reward?"

"Oh, you know, Jasmine. She's so soft-hearted. She asked the girl if she had stolen the brooch, and Millicent insisted she was innocent and that it was a case of mistaken identity. She was convincing, and we were unaware that the brooch belonged to you, for the landlord hadn't mentioned the owner's name. If we'd known that, we would have acted differently, of course."

"It's a pity you didn't. So where did you take the pair of them?"

"We dropped them off in Umberleigh, where they said they were visiting relatives and didn't think any more about it."

"Did they mention where their granny was?"

"No, we didn't know anything about their granny."

"You see, that's different to what their granny told me; she never mentioned Umberleigh. Emily Gibbs said her grandchildren were travelling to relatives in Somerset."

"When did you see Emily? Is she all right?"

"No, she was seriously ill with typhoid and not expected to live, but I'm afraid I had to evict her as I needed the cottage for another worker. She was taken to the Exeter Workhouse."

"I'm sorry you felt the need to evict the old lady. She was such a kind soul, and her husband, too. I must say, Edgar would not have approved."

"No, maybe not, but he's not here anymore, and I have to do as I see fit."

"Perhaps Emily might know where the children are? Have you asked her? Mind you, I don't suppose she would tell you, even if she survived typhoid and the workhouse, that is."

"I know she recovered from her illness and discharged herself from the workhouse, but I don't know where she went after that, possibly to Umberleigh to join her grandchildren, from what you've said. I must resume the search there, but it will have to wait, as now I'm better, I must visit Edgar's solicitors in London for the reading of his will. I'm going next week. That's another tiresome matter, for I've received a letter from the solicitors asking if I know of Rosemary and Emily Gibbs' whereabouts. For some reason, their presence is needed at the reading of the will, and the solicitors have been trying to find them."

"How strange; do you know why Edgar wanted them to attend?"

"No, though I wonder if he left them the cottage they were living in. It's just the sort of thing he'd do to annoy me further. Anyway, Rosemary's dead, and the old lady's missing, so it probably won't matter. The whole thing is only a formality, of course, for everything will be left to me. Sadly, Edgar and I were never blessed with children, so unfortunately, I suspect his title will be returned to the crown, though I would love it to pass to my nephew."

"I don't think that will be possible, my dear, but I hope you get everything sorted out to your satisfaction, and I'm sorry we didn't hand the pair of thieves in when we had the chance. I wish you every success in apprehending them. However, I must be on my way, for I'm travelling to Exeter this afternoon."

Sir Roger left, curious as to why his friend wanted his former lover and her mother at the reading of his will. He decided it was probably as Lady Lilliana surmised, and Edgar had left the Gibbs family their cottage. He decided he must write to Robert Fellwood to tell him about the latest developments in the story. However, knowing the Fellwoods were about to leave for London, he sent a telegram instead. He consoled himself that if they didn't receive it before their departure, they would soon find out what was happening when they visited the solicitors with Millie to deposit the brooch.

CHAPTER 26

HARTFORD/LONDON

Although they had known each other for only a few short months, Millie and Willie had become inseparable, and since Marrok had moved to Sugworthy Farm and taken on new farmhands, it was easier for Willie to take the one day off he was entitled to each week. Every Sunday, he arrived at his grandparents' cottage in time to escort Millie and Betsey to church. Then, after a roast dinner with Betsey and Ned or at the Lodge House with Sabina and Arthur, the young couple would go for a walk to enjoy a little time alone, whatever the weather.

They had explored much of the countryside around the village, and Millie enjoyed picking primroses and bluebells or searching for birds' nests. Willie was an expert at locating birds' nests, and he loved spotting one and challenging Millie to find it. He was frequently highly amused when she could not see it, even when it was right in front of her nose.

"It's so obvious when you point the nest out, but birds are so clever at disguising them, aren't they? I love seeing them, though, especially when there are eggs or babies inside. Did you use to take the eggs when you were younger, Willie?"

"I admit I used to steal a few because, like all my friends, I had a birds' egg collection, but we only used to take one from each nest, so the birds still had some to hatch. That was until Edward started to come out with me, and then he'd get so angry if we took any."

"Oh, did he?"

"Yes; he loves any living creature and gets furious if they're harmed. He may be deaf and dumb, but he knows how to make his feelings known."

Millie grinned. "Why, what did he do?"

"Oh, well, if frowning and shaking his head didn't work, he'd start thumping the thief. I've got into more fights defending Edward than for anything else. He never cared if the boys were bigger than him; he'd always wade in with his fists flying."

"Good for him. Oh, no, it's starting to rain; Gran said she thought it might."

"Come on, let's run for it to the old linhay; we can shelter there until it eases up."

The courting couple had taken to frequenting an old cowshed in the corner of one of the village's mazzard greens. The shed needed repair, but one end of the building was sound and a good place to shelter in inclement weather. As it began to pour with rain, they ran the last few hundred yards and grinned at each other as they got their breath back.

There was a pile of dry hay in one corner, and they sat there, kissing and cuddling and enjoying each other's company. The boy was respectful and did not take liberties, but wanted their relationship to go further. Pulling away, he held Millie's face in his hands and gently tucked a stray curl behind her ear.

"I don't want to rush things, Millie, but I can't wait to see you each Sunday; I love you."

She smiled at him happily. "I love you, too, Willie Carter."

They kissed again, and when they drew apart, Willie focused on her beautiful brown eyes again.

"Will you marry me, Millie? I know you're only sixteen, but I'm certain you're the one for me."

"Oh, Willie, yes, I'd love to marry you; am I old enough?"

"I think so. My mum married at sixteen, but I don't mind waiting if you're not ready. I know you need to find your granny and get this business of the brooch sorted out."

Yes, I'm off to London in a few days with Annie and Robert and will be away for a month; I'll miss you so much, Willie. I hope you don't find someone else while I'm gone."

"Never! That will never happen, and by the time you get back, I'll have a ring for you, and we'll tell everyone."

"I don't need a ring; you can't afford it, but I agree we should wait until I get back from London before we tell anyone. You never know; I might end up in jail or hanged if we don't sort out the matter of the brooch."

He took her in his arms again and kissed the top of her head. "No, that won't happen; Robert will look after you. It's lucky our Annie's married to him because he's a rich gentleman, and he'll make sure the charges against you are dropped." He glanced out of the door. "I think the rain's stopped; we'd better get back."

Leaving the cowshed, they walked with their arms around each other, stopping momentarily to admire the pretty pink and white frothy blossom on the mazzard trees. Just before they reached the village, Willie drew the girl into a glade and, once more, kissed her passionately.

"Bye, Millie; I hope all goes well in London, and I'll be counting the days until you're back."

A few days later, Dodger took Robert, Annie, Danny, Millie, and Jonathan to Eggleston Station to catch the train to Exeter and then on to London. Sabina was tearful as she hugged her son, but she knew Annie would take care of him, and, reassured by his beaming smile, she waved goodbye to the carriage.

Robert had decided to travel to London by train this time as it was much quicker than by carriage. As usual, when they visited the capital, they were to stay with his cousin,

Percy, in Grosvenor Square, a wealthy district in the Mayfair area of London. This would be Danny's third and, hopefully, final operation to correct the deformities he had been born with. The first operation, to repair his cleft palate, had been hugely successful and had changed the child's life, making it possible for him to speak clearly and eat all foods. With two club feet, the boy had always limped and walked with a strange gait. Bullied and teased at school, he couldn't wait to get his second foot straightened. Danny was eager to see Percy, for the two got on well. A sworn bachelor, Percy preferred the company of young men, something he had to be highly discreet about. However, his considerable wealth made this matter much easier than it would otherwise have been.

Though they did not know it, the travellers had barely arrived at Eggleston Station before Sir Roger's telegram was delivered to Hartford Manor. Ethan Bater, the butler in the west wing, put the telegram to one side, knowing it would have to wait until his master's return.

Millie, Jonathan, and Danny thoroughly enjoyed the long train journey to Paddington Station, where Robert hailed a carriage and gave Percy's address. The carriage quickly covered the short distance, and they were soon welcomed into the impressive townhouse. Percy kissed the hands of Annie and Millie, then shook Robert's hand and that of the two boys.

"So, here you are again, Danny; I love you coming to see me. It gives me the perfect excuse to dig out all my model soldiers and toys and play at being a small boy again. I see you've brought a friend with you this time, so we'll have even more fun."

The following day, leaving Danny and Jonathan to recover from their long and arduous journey and explore the attics to dig out all of Percy's battalions of toy soldiers, Robert and Annie escorted Millie to Sir Edgar's solicitors. Their carriage took them to the offices of Parkham, Glover and

Brown, situated in Oxford Street. It was an imposing building, and Millie was overcome with nerves, wondering if her story would be believed or if she would be leaving, escorted by a policeman.

Having advised the receptionist that he was the son of Lord Fellwood of Hartford Manor in Devon and would appreciate a meeting with one of the solicitors, Robert and his party were asked to take a seat in the waiting room. After a short delay, they were ushered into a comfortable office to meet with two of the partners, Mr Glover and Mr Brown. The two distinguished gentlemen invited their visitors to be seated and rang a bell for some refreshments. After a tray of tea had been delivered, Mr Brown invited Robert to explain how they could help.

"Thank you for seeing us at such short notice, sir; I appreciate it. Sir Roger Everson, a friend of mine, gave us your details. He advised me that you act for the late Sir Edward Grantley of Grantley Manor in Brampford Speke in Devon."

"That is correct, sir; how can we be of service?"

"I'd like to introduce you to Millicent Gibbs, Sir Edgar's illegitimate daughter. She has a younger brother called Jonathan, who is also the child of Sir Edgar, but I'll let Millicent tell you her own story from here."

Mr Brown, the elder of the two solicitors, smiled at the young girl. "Don't be nervous, my dear. We won't eat you. Please tell us how we might help."

Millie began her story nervously and, once again, told of her and Jonnie's hazardous and frightful journey to Hartford to seek relatives.

"This is all fascinating, my dear, but how can we help?"

"Before he died, Sir Edgar gave my mother a precious brooch which once belonged to his mother. His wife, Lilliana, had all the other jewellery, but this brooch was the old lady's favourite, and Sir Edgar wanted my mother to have it and eventually pass it on to me. When Jonnie and I left home, Gran pinned the brooch onto my bodice out of sight and told me if I were ever desperate to sell it for food. Lady Lilliana knew her husband had given the brooch to his mistress, but she spread the tale that I stole it and reported the theft to the police. There is a reward on my head, and she wants me jailed or hanged."

"My goodness, that's quite a tale. So, again, how can we help?"

Millie reached into her bag. "I have the brooch here, sir; it's useless to me, and Robert thought that if we returned it to you, then it would prove I'd not stolen it, and my name would be cleared."

The solicitor took the brooch. "Ah, now I understand, and yes, we can help you with that. We'll issue you a receipt before you leave the office today, proving your innocence and clearing you of any wrongdoing. Now, please accept my sincere condolences on the death of your mother, but tell me, where is your granny, Emily Gibbs?"

A brief frown crossed the young girl's face, and she sighed. "I wish I knew. Gran insisted Jonnie and I leave home straight away to escape from Lady Lilliana, but she was too weak to travel. She stayed at the cottage, hoping Lady Lilliana would allow her to recover before throwing her out. She planned to follow us to Hartford when she was strong enough, but she's never arrived, and it's been six months now. We've looked for her and know she spent a few weeks in the Exeter Workhouse, but then discharged herself. We've checked with her neighbours in Brampford Speke, but they don't know where she is either. I'm so worried about her, but we don't know where else to look."

Robert intervened at this stage, a puzzled expression on his face. "I hope you don't mind me asking, sir, but why are you interested in Emily Gibbs' whereabouts?"

"That's a good question, sir. The fact is, we have a letter from Sir Edgar which was to be opened in the event of his death. Naturally, we have done that, and the letter states that both Rosemary and Emily Gibbs must be present at the reading of his will."

"Why? Does the letter say why?"

"No, and so the will has not yet been read. That's because we've been searching for the two women for months, and Lady Lilliana has been seriously ill and unable to travel to London. If it were only that the lady could not travel, we would have visited her and read the will in Devon, but we have been trying to establish the whereabouts of the Gibbs' ladies. However, Lady Lilliana is expected to visit this office at any time, and now that we know Rosemary Gibbs has passed away, and, I'm sorry, my dear, but in all likelihood, so has her mother, Emily, then I think we will proceed with the reading of the will. Are you residing in London or returning to Devon?"

"We're staying in London for a few weeks whilst my little brother, Danny, has an operation. Why do you ask?"

"I'd appreciate it if you would kindly leave your address with my secretary. I can't imagine why Sir Edgar wanted Rosemary and Emily Gibbs present at the reading of his will, but presumably, he must have left them an inheritance. If that is the case, then whatever it is will pass to you and your brother, Millicent. When I have some news, I'll be in touch."

CHAPTER 27

LONDON

Having received a formal receipt for the sapphire brooch, Robert, Annie, and Millie left the solicitors, with Millie feeling happier now that her name had been cleared. They stood at the side of the road for a few minutes whilst Robert hailed a carriage to take them back to Percy's house. Unbeknownst to them, they were observed by Lady Lilliana and Sir Clive Robinson from their own carriage, which drew to a halt outside the solicitors' office. Lady Lilliana suddenly clutched her lover's arm.

"Clive, look, don't get out; I'm sure that's Millicent Gibbs, Edgar's bastard."

"Surely not; what would she be doing in London?"

"Yes, I'm sure it is, and I feel I know the gentleman she's with, too, but I can't quite place him. Do you know him?"

"Hmm, you're right; his face is familiar. Oh yes, I do know him. It's Robert Fellwood, I do believe. He inherited the Hartford Estate in North Devon when his father took ill. There was a scandal surrounding him a few years ago because he married a kitchen maid; mind you, if that's her, I can see why he was tempted. She's quite a beauty; completely mad to wed her, though, of course."

"What on earth are they doing with the girl? It doesn't make sense. Clive, I'll go into the solicitors, and you follow their carriage to find out where they're staying. The girl might lead us to her granny, and then we can get the will read and hopefully get her arrested for stealing the brooch."

"As you wish, my dear; I hope you get on all right with the solicitors. Shall I come back to fetch you?"

"No, because we don't know how far you'll have to follow them, and I don't want to be waiting around. No, you go home afterwards, and I'll do the same. The solicitor can get a carriage for me; no doubt Edgar was paying them enough. I'll see you later."

Lady Lilliana left the carriage, and Sir Clive told the driver to follow the vehicle in front at a discreet distance. The lady entered the solicitor's office, gave her name to the receptionist, and asked if it would be convenient to see Mr Glover.

"Do you have an appointment, ma'am?"

Lilliana looked down her nose haughtily. "No, I don't, but I suspect Mr Glover will find time to see me; I'm sure my husband was one of his wealthiest clients, and I've travelled all the way from Devon."

"Of course, ma'am, please take a seat whilst I tell him you're here."

The two solicitors looked at each other in disbelief that Lady Lilliana should call on them so soon after Millie Gibbs and the Fellwoods had left. They wondered if their visitors had spoken to each other. Both men rose as the lady entered and kissed her hand before begging her to be seated.

"Lady Lilliana, please accept our heartfelt condolences on the death of Sir Edgar. We were so sorry to hear the sad news. We trust you are now in good health?"

"Thank you, and yes, I am fully recovered, but have you located Emily Gibbs yet?"

"No, ma'am, though we have learnt that her daughter, Rosemary, sadly perished from typhoid in the same epidemic as your poor husband. We've searched high and low for the old lady, but to no avail. However, we do have some news for you. I'm not sure if you saw our previous clients leave, but their business had a bearing on your husband's will."

"Really? Who were they?"

"A young girl called Millicent Gibbs was accompanied by Lord and Lady Fellwood of Hartford Manor in North Devon. Millicent is the granddaughter of Emily Gibbs that we have been searching for and is also distantly related by marriage to the Fellwoods."

"I find that hard to believe."

"Nevertheless, ma'am, they are satisfied with the family connection, and the Fellwoods brought Millicent here as she wanted to hand in a precious brooch. Apparently, Sir Edgar gave this brooch to her mother, Rosemary Gibbs, before his death, but Millicent is aware that you have offered a reward for information leading to her arrest for stealing it. She wanted to clear her name and return the brooch to you. It has been put into our safe, but we'll let you have it before you leave today. What made you think the girl had stolen the item?"

"My maid saw the girl leaving my bedroom, and soon after that, I noticed the brooch was missing. No matter; at least it's been returned, even if her story is untrue. I mean, ask yourself, why would my husband have given a valuable piece of jewellery to a peasant? No, I'm sure she took it because she knew her family would soon have to leave the tied cottage they should have vacated years ago. My husband was too soft-hearted to evict them, but I am not so sentimental. No matter, but what is going to happen about the will? I can't wait forever for it to be read."

"No, quite so, ma'am. Millicent Gibbs doesn't know where her grandmother is, and in all likelihood, I suspect the poor soul has passed away. We have discussed the matter and feel able to proceed with the reading of the will. In fact, we can do that now if you so wish?"

"Yes, of course; that's what I'm here for. It will only be a formality for my husband was an only child with no other relatives, so naturally, the estate will pass to me. I presume you have not read the will yet?"

No, ma'am. It's sealed with wax, and we'll open it in your presence. The will was only drafted a few months ago by our partner, Mr Parkham, who has since sadly passed away. The document is sealed, and naturally, we have not opened it, but I have it here and will do so now."

Mr Glover took an ornate paper-knife from his drawer and prised away the red sealing wax from the envelope. He opened the will, and three additional pieces of paper fell out. He spread the documents on the desk and pored over them, taking time to read every word before facing his client with a shocked expression.

"My dear, Lady Lilliana, I'm afraid you must brace yourself for a terrible shock."

The lady in question paled. "What do you mean?"

"In the will, Sir Edgar admits he was a bigamist, ma'am! Sadly, he was married before he pledged his vows to you. I am so sorry, but he was never your legal husband and may have gone to jail if this had been known when he was alive."

"Don't be ridiculous. Of course, he was my husband. We were married for years; we lived in the same house."

"Nevertheless, ma'am, your marriage was illegal as Sir Edgar was already married to Rosemary Gibbs. This document is their marriage certificate. They were married by special licence in Exeter in 1868."

"What? No, that can't be right, and even if it were, as you said, she's dead."

"Yes, ma'am, that we do know, but Sir Edgar has left Grantley House and the entire estate to his son, Jonathan Grantley. There is also a generous provision for his wife, Rosemary, daughter, Millicent, and their grandmother, Emily Gibbs."

"But his children are illegitimate; they can't inherit."

"No, ma'am, his children are legitimate. These other two documents are their birth certificates, and the marriage certificate is dated two years before his daughter, Millicent, was born. She told me herself, not an hour ago, that she's sixteen, and her brother, Jonathan, is five. I am so sorry, ma'am, for this must be a tremendous shock. However, Sir Edgar has been generous to you, too. He has left you a considerable sum of money, his London townhouse, a carriage and six horses, and a letter, which I'll let you read for yourself. He begs your forgiveness for his actions, but does say he did his best to dissuade you from ever marrying him."

"Let me see for myself." Lady Lilliana hissed the words at the embarrassed man and snatched the documents. She was silent as she read her late husband's letter. "Are you sure this is legal? I shall challenge the will."

"I assure you, ma'am, the documents are correctly drawn up, witnessed, and legal in every way; there are no grounds to challenge Sir Edgar's will, and he was undoubtedly of sound mind. No doubt, you will also have noticed that he mentions the sapphire brooch, which we discussed earlier, and states that he gave it to his wife, Rosemary. Therefore, it must be returned to her daughter, Millicent. He does state that all the other jewellery belongs to you."

Lady Lilliana put her head in her hands. "I can't believe he would do this to me!"

"I'm so sorry, ma'am, and for what it's worth, it sounds as if Sir Edgar felt guilty for the way he treated you. Unfortunately, it sounds as if his parents forced him into marrying you, but he clearly refused to accept the situation. It's terribly sad. May I get you some water, ma'am? You are so pale."

The lady silently accepted the glass of water and sat for a few moments, seemingly bemused.

"Let me see that will again. Look, it's witnessed by Sir Roger Everson. What a snake in the grass he is. I saw him not a week ago, and he pretended to be my friend. To think he knew about this all along."

"No, ma'am, that's probably not the case. Normally, a witness to a legal document, such as a will, does not see the contents. They are simply witnessing the signature. I suspect Sir Roger would have had no knowledge of the details."

"So, what will happen now?"

"I'll contact Mr Fellwood and ask him to bring Millicent and Jonathan Gibbs here so that I can inform them of the contents of the will and their inheritance. There are also letters for them from their father and one for his wife, Rosemary, though sadly, she will never receive it now. This will be quite a shock for them, too, and this is clearly why Sir Edgar insisted Rosemary and Emily Gibbs should be present at the reading of the document. To inherit the Grantley Estate, Jonathan Grantley must reside at Grantley House, and so, ma'am, I'm afraid you must vacate the property as soon as possible. Is there anything else I can do for you today?"

"No, summon a carriage for me, if you will. I must go away and think about all this; I will seek a second opinion. There must be something I can do to prevent this."

"As you wish, ma'am, though unfortunately, I do not think there is."

CHAPTER 28

Sir Clive was amazed when the carriage carrying Robert, Annie, and Millie headed for the West End of London and stopped outside a grand townhouse in Grosvenor Square. One of the most prestigious squares in Mayfair, the area was known for its elegant Georgian architecture dating from the early eighteenth century. Whilst he knew Robert Fellwood was from a wealthy Devon family, this connection put him in a completely different league, and he was intrigued to know how the young girl could be connected to such nobility. Telling his driver to stop a few hundred yards away, he watched as the butler admitted Robert, Annie, and Millie through the front door.

"Well, I never. If I hadn't seen this with my own eyes, I would never have believed it. I wonder who lives there?"

Sir Clive spoke more to himself than anyone else, but his driver offered information.

"If it helps, sir, I can tell you that's the residence of the Chichester family, and they've lived there for many years. Algernon Chichester died some years ago, and his wife, too, I believe, but their son, Percival, still lives there."

"Thank you, George; that is, indeed, most interesting."

The carriage took Sir Clive back to Lady Lilliana's house, where he impatiently awaited her return, keen to divulge this latest information. However, when the lady breezed into the drawing room, his news had to wait, as she had a face like thunder and quite a tale to tell.

"You're not going to believe this, Clive; that monster I called husband for so many years was a bigamist! He married me illegally, and I've been living in sin with him all this time."

"What? No, surely not! I attended your wedding."

"I know, but it makes no difference; he was already married to Rosemary Gibbs when we took our vows! How could he?"

"But, my dear, there must be some mistake; why would he do that?"

"So he wasn't disinherited, of course. His father would never have allowed him to marry a commoner, and if he'd known, he would have left his estate to someone else. My marriage to Edgar was arranged almost from the day I was born, and we were always told we would marry each other. We were given no choice in the matter. My family is considerably wealthier than the Grantleys, but theirs is an old family that can trace its lineage back to the Domesday Book, so it was a favourable match for both sides. As far as I knew, Edgar was content with the arrangement, as was I, though admittedly, he seemed less keen as the wedding day approached. Everyone thought it was just wedding nerves, as did I."

"I've never liked to ask, my dear, but was he a husband to you in every sense?"

Lady Lilliana scowled at the man before her. "No, Clive, he was not, and I never understood why. He made love to me on our wedding night and then never shared my bed again in all those years of marriage. I had no idea what I had done wrong and was desperately unhappy. Eventually, I learned of his affair and realised he had made love to me to consummate the marriage and make sure it could not be annulled. Presumably, the other reason was he did not want to give me a child, though, as it turns out, that would probably never have happened anyway."

"That is terrible, my dear. I'm so sorry, but did the solicitor read the will?"

"Oh, yes, he read the will, all right, because Rosemary Gibbs is dead, and her mother, Emily, presumed so, and this is the best bit. My darling Edgar has left Grantley House and the entire estate to his son, Jonathan Grantley. Tucked inside the will were his marriage certificate and the birth certificates of the two children. He certainly tied everything up neatly."

"But what about you?"

"Oh, there was a lengthy letter of apology for betraying me, and he's left me this townhouse and a considerable amount of money. Rich, isn't it? Seeing as much of his wealth originated from my dowry. I doubt he's given back what it cost my father in the first place."

"Perhaps you can contest the will? Yes, that's what you must do: contest the will. What's more, when the girl is arrested for stealing the brooch, she'll go to jail, which must have a bearing on the case."

"Oh, no! Thanks to Robert Fellwood and his kitchen maid slut of a wife, that's why the girl was at the solicitors. She was returning the brooch to clear her name, even though she claims Edgar gave it to her mother. As it turns out, that's exactly what he did, for that, too, is mentioned in his will."

"So, what happens now?"

"The solicitors say there's nothing I can do. Edgar was of sound mind, and the will was correctly drawn up and witnessed. If he were here, he'd be guilty of bigamy, but as he's not, nothing will come of that. Oh, I'm so angry! I'm glad that bitch of a wife of his died, and they can't be together, but nevertheless, everything will be inherited by those two despicable children!"

"Maybe not."

"What do you mean?"

"It's true you're up against some formidable opposition, for I, too, have some startling news. I followed the Fellwoods' carriage and could hardly believe my eyes when it drew up outside one of the grandest houses in Grosvenor Square."

"What! How on earth can they be connected to a house like that?"

"I don't know, but they were admitted through the front door, and my driver told me that Percival Chichester lives there. I think I may have met him somewhere in the past, but I can't quite recollect. Anyway, now that we know where the children live, maybe we can ensure they will never inherit. If they were out of the picture, would Sir Edgar's inheritance revert to you?"

"I don't know; probably, but there's still the granny, Emily Gibbs, though no one knows where she is. The solicitor thinks she may be dead. Lying in a ditch somewhere with any luck! What did you mean about the children?"

"As you know, I own a fleet of ships that sail to the Americas and Australia regularly; what say we abduct this troublesome pair and send them to a new life thousands of miles away? No one would ever connect them to me, and who knows, there are often accidents on such long voyages; they may not even survive the journey."

"Oh, Clive, what a wonderful idea, for I hate them with every fibre of my being."

"If we send them to Australia, that should be far enough away to prevent them from causing any further trouble. It's around ten or twelve thousand miles, so the journey would take several months, and they would never have the means to return. If Emily Gibbs ever turns up, and I think it's unlikely, I doubt she'd have a claim; I'm sure the inheritance would come to you. Any court would see it as a way to right the unforgivable wrong Edgar did to you."

The lady suddenly beamed at her lover. "In that case, yes, that sounds like an excellent plan, but how are you going to get your hands on the children?"

CHAPTER 29

Mrs Miggs had been the cook in the Chichester household for many years, and there was not much she didn't know about the family, past and present. Having started as a tweeny at the tender age of twelve, she had progressed steadily to her now prestigious and well-paid position and counted herself fortunate. She adored young Master Percy, as she still thought of him, although he was now a handsome young man of five and thirty years. He was known for his frequent house parties and large gatherings, and if she sometimes wondered why there tended to be rather more young men present than women, she felt it was none of her business.

Over the last few years, she had enjoyed the visits of the Fellwood family, for Lady Fellwood always had time for a kind word and sometimes even joined her for a chat and a cup of tea in the kitchen. There were certainly no airs and graces to that young woman. Lord Fellwood, too, was kind and considerate, but most of all, she looked forward to seeing the sadly deformed child, Danny. He had such big brown eyes, and even when his cleft palate marred his countenance, he had such a winning smile. She had quite lost her heart to him.

On the morning of Danny's final operation on his foot, Mrs Miggs insisted on serving breakfast to the family. With the help of a couple of kitchen maids, she served up a delicious cooked breakfast with sausages, bacon and eggs, accompanied by thick slices of hot toast, made with bread baked only that morning and smothered in the best farm butter.

"Oh, Mrs Miggs, what a delightful spread you've laid on for us this morning. Your meals rival those of our own Maisie and Mrs Potts at Hartford Manor, and their one ambition in life seems to be to spoil us with their wonderful food."

"Well, sir, I know the young gentleman has a difficult day ahead of him, and I wanted to make sure he had a decent breakfast. If you'll beg my pardon for being forward, sir, I wanted to wish Master Danny well, and I hope everything goes all right at the hospital. He's such a brave young man."

"Yes, he is, Mrs Miggs, and thank you; that's not forward of you at all. Danny, what do you say?"

"Thank you, Mrs Miggs; I love your breakfasts, especially the sausages. I think they're my favourites."

"You're welcome, sir, and I look forward to seeing you back here again soon."

When the cook and the maids had left, the family talked about the day ahead.

"Millie, as you know, we have to take Danny to the hospital today, and I believe Percy has a business meeting, so Robert and I wondered if you and Jonathan would like to come with us or if you'd prefer a quiet day here at the house. We might be at the hospital for some time, waiting to see the doctor and settling Danny in, and you might be bored, though you're welcome to come."

"I think we'll stay here; thank you, Annie. We'll be all right with Mrs Miggs, and I'd rather leave you to concentrate on Danny today. We can explore the grounds and maybe even take a short walk around the area."

"That's fine, then, if you're sure. We thought we'd take you sightseeing tomorrow because we won't be able to see Danny for a few days, and it would be nice for you to explore a bit of London whilst you're here. If you go for a walk, you must take a maid with you and not go too far."

Shortly after breakfast, Annie, Robert, and Danny travelled the short distance to the hospital. They were shown to a waiting room, and it wasn't too long before Geoffrey Turner arrived to greet them.

"Hello, my dears; I'm pleased to see you all again. How are you, Danny?"

"I'm fine, sir, thank you, but I want to get this operation over with."

"Yes, of course, you do; well, hopefully, this will be the last one, and I'm confident it will be as successful as the other two. We'll have you running around in no time."

"Oh, I do hope so."

"Doctor Brown tells me this operation is less complicated than the one on your other leg, so it should mend more quickly. He would have been here to meet you himself, but he's operating on another little boy. Anyway, if you're ready, I'll take you to the ward where you can play with the other children for the day, and he'll operate on you first thing in the morning. Annie and Robert, do you want to come with us?"

"Yes, if that's all right, Geoffrey, we'd like to see him settled in."

Half an hour later, Robert and Annie left Danny playing with two other boys, one recovering from an operation and another, like Danny, waiting to have surgery the next day. Annie hugged her little brother as she left, but he smiled at her bravely and told her he would be all right. Robert took her arm firmly and led her away before the tears he could see shining in her eyes started to fall.

"Come on; he'll be all right. This is his third operation, and he knows what to expect, and it was his choice to have it done. This is the hardest part, leaving him on his own; Sabina was always far more upset than Danny when she came with him. What shall we do today? It's still only lunchtime, and Millie and Jonnie are happy to spend the day with Mrs Miggs so we can do something together."

"Perhaps we could visit Highgate Cemetery before we eat? I want to tend my Uncle William's grave, but it's not somewhere I'd want to take Jonnie and Millie. Would you mind?"

"No, of course not; we don't come to London often, so it's an opportunity to pay our respects. I quite like the cemetery, though that sounds a bit weird. It's beautiful in a way, with the old tombstones and the sculptured angels with ivy growing all over them. I find it peaceful after the hustle and bustle of the city. What would you like to do after lunch?"

Annie's eyes gleamed. "How about a little shopping?"

Robert groaned. "Yes, all right, but I think I'll buy a newspaper and sit in a tea room while you browse; would you mind?"

"No, that's fine, but don't wander off. I'd be in a real panic to find myself alone in London; there are far too many people, and I'd never find the way back to Percy's house."

"Don't worry, I won't lose you, and you can take as long as you like."

Back at Percy's house, Millie and Jonathan had spent the morning exploring the extensive grounds. The gardens were cleverly landscaped and, being mid-June, full of flowers. Gorgeous roses of every hue scented the air with their fragrance, and the bees were busy collecting pollen. Other flower beds contained vibrant peonies, delphiniums, lupins and foxgloves, all bordered by small bushes of lavender. It was so quiet and peaceful that it was hard to believe that only a short distance away, crowds of people were going about their daily business, with carriages, horse-drawn trams, and trains adding to the chaos in the streets.

"Oh, Jonnie, I've never seen such amazing flowers; they smell so wonderful. Look, I think I can see some water down there; shall we explore a bit further?"

Jonnie was not quite so taken with the flowers as Millie, but when he espied the lake, he was more interested. "Yes, I'd like that; there might be frogs and tadpoles."

Like many small boys, Jonnie was fascinated by frogs, toads, and newts and usually collected some frog spawn in the spring to watch it hatch into tadpoles. The lake was much bigger than they had first thought, and they decided to walk around it.

"Oh, yes, look; there are loads of tadpoles, and they're beginning to get their back legs. I wonder if mine at home have changed into little frogs yet; I hope Aunty Betsey's taking care of them."

"Yes, of course, she will; in any case, they look after themselves as long as their water doesn't dry up. They may have all jumped away by the time we get back home. Let's sit here for a few minutes."

It was a warm sunny day, and they sat on the grass beside the lake and idly watched the wildlife. Many blue damselflies and vivid green and red dragonflies darted above the water's surface, and several of the mallards and moorhens had a string of young chicks paddling behind them. They could see a swan with cygnets at the edge of the lake, and they knew to keep their distance, for swans could be fierce, particularly if they had young to protect.

Eventually, Millie stretched her arms lazily. "Shall we go back to the house now, Jonnie? We could have something to eat and then explore the streets this afternoon; it's far too nice to sit indoors."

Like all small boys, Jonnie brightened at the mention of food and happily agreed with his sister's plans. Mrs Miggs was in her element, spoiling the pair of them. Having eaten a delicious ham sandwich made with more of the fresh, crusty bread they'd enjoyed earlier, they found room for a piece of carrot cake and washed it all down with a glass of cool lemonade.

"Thank you so much, Mrs Miggs, that was delicious."

"You're welcome, my dear; what will you do with yourselves this afternoon?"

"We're going to take a walk around Grosvenor Square; the gardens and buildings are so beautiful, and Jonnie likes to see all the horses and carriages; they're far grander than anything we see in Devon."

"Very well, but you cannot go alone; you must be accompanied. I can spare Lena for the afternoon so she can be your chaperone. London is an amazing city, but it can be a dangerous place full of pickpockets and thieves, even though this is one of the most respectable areas. Now, have you had enough to eat?"

"Oh, yes, thank you; we'll see you later."

Lena was delighted to take a walk that afternoon and avoid more cleaning. They had walked about a mile when they noticed a man coming toward them, a wide grin on his face. Glancing at the maid, Millie noticed Lena blushing and guessed this must be her young man.

"Lena, would you like a few minutes to chat with your friend?"

"Oh, ma'am, that is so kind of you. Yes, I would appreciate that, thank you."

"Very well, we'll stroll around the corner to the next road to give you a little privacy, and you can catch us up."

Sir Clive could not believe his luck when he saw Millicent and Jonathan alone on a quiet road, as for days, he had been racking his brains about how he could abduct them. He was en route to a friend who lived close to the Chichester house, and he had asked if he could stay for a few days, thinking that if he were in the vicinity, he would have a better chance of seeing them. He was amazed to see the youngsters out and about, unchaperoned, for he had expected to have to kidnap a maid as well.

Millie and Jonathan had only walked a couple of hundred yards when, to their surprise, a grand carriage stopped beside them. A distinguished gentleman alighted from the vehicle and, smiling broadly, asked if they could help him.

"I'm sorry to bother you, my dears, but do you live in this area?"

"No, we don't live here, sir, but we are staying in the neighbourhood for a while; how can we help you?"

"I'm trying to locate the house of Sir Percy Chichester; he's a friend of my sister, and as I was going to be in this area, she asked me to drop off a parcel for him. Stupidly, I've left his address behind and can't quite remember it."

"Oh, yes, sir, we can help you then, for that's where we're staying."

"What a marvellous coincidence; what is the exact address?"

The girl looked blank. "Oh dear, I don't know, though I can direct you there, or my maid will know. She's just around the corner chatting with her friend."

"Is this your little brother? I wonder if you're ready to head back to the house, only I see the young man is quite taken with the horses, and maybe I could offer you both a lift back? He could ride with the driver on the dickey seat if he wished."

"Ooh, yes, Millie, I'd like to do that; I've had enough walking anyway."

"Thank you, sir. That is kind of you, but my maid will wonder where we are."

"No problem, we can collect her on the way."

"Very well; it's not far from the house. Mr Percy's not at home, but I can take the parcel inside if you like."

"Splendid; now, young man, you climb up beside the driver, and you, my dear, allow me to help you into the carriage."

Millie climbed into the luxurious carriage whilst the gentleman gave his driver instructions. He then joined her and entertained her with interesting chit-chat. Jonnie, loving his lofty position on the dickey seat beside the driver, was delighted when the man allowed him to hold the reins.

It was not until several minutes later that Millie suddenly realised they had not seen Lena. The carriage appeared to be travelling in the wrong direction and passing scenery she was unfamiliar with.

"Oh, dear, sir, we must stop, for your driver has taken a wrong turn somewhere along the way; we should have seen my maid by now, but I don't recognise this road at all."

"Never mind, my dear; I have somewhere much more interesting to take you; indeed, it could change your life forever."

Mrs Miggs was taking her customary afternoon stroll around the square when the carriage drove past her. She was amazed to see young Jonathan, with a broad smile, holding the horses' reins. She shouted and waved, but to no avail, and the carriage sped by, taking her two charges with it.

CHAPTER 30

HARTFORD

Sabina and Liza had been busy all morning preparing the vegetables to accompany a large leg of lamb for their Sunday roast. The garden outside the Lodge House was Sabina's pride and joy, and now, in early July, she was delighted to pick her own peas, dig new potatoes and carrots, and gather fresh mint. She paused from chopping the fragrant mint leaves with a sharp knife and inhaled deeply.

"Ah, I love the smell of fresh mint, and lamb just isn't the same without it. It's a pity the runner beans aren't ready, but that will be a pleasure for another day."

"Yes, I'm looking forward to my dinner. New potatoes and garden peas go so nicely with lamb. Now, have I scrubbed enough potatoes? How many of us are there today?"

"Um, let's see; well, you, me, and Arthur, of course, then there's Betsey and Ned, Theresa and Louis, Willie, Edward, Mary, Stephen and Helen. I think that's twelve of us, and we'll mash up some dinner for Katel; she's beginning to like her food. Could you do another half a dozen potatoes, Liza? We've got plenty, and if there's some left, we can fry them up tomorrow. I'm glad Willie, Edward, and Mary could all get the day off today; it's not often that we all get together, and it will take my mind off Danny. I do hope he's all right."

"I'm sure he is; you know Annie and Robert will take care of him, and he's got Jonathan to play with when he gets out of the hospital. It's not like he hasn't been to London before or had an operation; he knows what to expect. At least this should be the last one, and it's incredible what the doctors have done for him. When Annie first brought that poor little mite into the house, I never expected him to live."

"No, neither did I; it was so difficult to feed him. I wonder if his mother regrets giving him up; it must be hard for her knowing he lives down the road."

"It serves her right. What kind of mother gives up her child because he's deformed? Especially as she had enough money to give him the best care possible."

"I've been wondering if I should tell him that he's Robert's brother and his parents are Lord and Lady Fellwood. Do you think I should?"

"I can't see it would do any good. Robert will ensure he never wants for anything, and it would only upset the child. I'd let sleeping dogs lie, but if you decide to tell him, I'd ask Robert and Annie what they think first."

"Yes, I will, though; like you, I think, in this case, ignorance is bliss."

Willie and Edward were the first to arrive and were hugged tightly by Sabina and Liza. Stephen, now eight, was delighted to see his brothers and, taking Edward by the arm, led him outside to show him his baby rabbit. Helen, a pretty little girl of six, tagged along behind, and together, they took turns cuddling their new pet.

"Are you going to church this morning, Willie?"

"No, not today, Mum; I've been a lot lately, so I thought I'd spend the morning with all of you. Is Mary coming?"

"You have been to church a lot recently, Willie, though I'm not sure religion has had much to do with it; I suspect your improved attendance has more to do with a certain young lady. And yes, Mary should be here any time now."

Willie blushed. "I've grown fond of Millie, and I wish she were here today, but I'm glad Robert and Annie are helping to clear her name about the theft of that brooch; she's been so worried. If they can resolve that matter and find her granny, then I think she'll be willing to settle here."

"Yes, let's hope they have good news when they get back from London. Ah, here's Mary, now, and Betsey and Ned, too."

Sabina opened the back door and welcomed them all in, giving her daughter, Mary, a tight hug.

"Hello, Betsey, hello, Ned, how are you both?"

"Fine, thank you, Sabina, and thank you for inviting us to dinner; it's so quiet in the cottage without Millie and Jonnie. It was quite a change for us when we left The Red Lion after so many years of being busy with everything, but having the two youngsters staying with us helped a lot. Now that they've gone to London, we miss them, even though they only came into our lives recently. I hope they get everything sorted out; I'm anxious to find out what's happened to my half-sister, Emily."

"Yes, fingers crossed, Robert will solve the mystery of her whereabouts, and we can welcome her into the family soon. If anyone can sort it all out, he will; I've every confidence in him. Now, why don't you relax in the sitting room while Liza and I finish seeing to the dinner?"

"Is everyone here now?"

"No, there's just Louis and Theresa to come, and hopefully, they won't be too long. Liza thinks of Louis as her long-lost son since he turned up here, and he's such a caring young man; I believe Theresa's quite taken with him. They said they wouldn't be here until one o'clock because Louis has to work at the inn this morning, and Theresa's helping Mary Ann because she has her hands full with the little ones and nursing George. Unfortunately, he's got another abscess where that rat bit him months ago; his arm's never healed properly for some reason, and he's back in bed with a fever."

Theresa and Louis arrived just in time for lunch, and a couple of hours later, the family was enjoying a chat and relaxing with a nice hot cup of tea. Katel had smacked her lips at the mashed-up roast dinner and now, with a full belly, was taking a nap in her cot.

"How are you enjoying living in Fred's cottage, Ned? Has anyone attended to the garden lately?"

"No, sadly not, Arthur. It grieves me to see it so neglected, but I can't do it any more with this weak heart of mine. Millie and Betsey have kept the flower bed free of weeds, but no vegetables have been planted, and it's such a waste of ground. Fred intended to do it, but he's been so busy settling in at The Red Lion and getting the barges up and running that he hasn't had the time. Llewie's been doing a lot of the routine carpentry work, and Fred's employed another worker now, so he's getting on top of things. Maybe next year, he'll have time to plant the ground, but, of course, by that time, it will be overgrown."

"That's a pity, Ned; would you like me to dig it over?"

"That's kind of you, Arthur, but do you have the time? The nursery and the garden here must keep you busy."

"Yes, it does, but Sabina does most of the gardening here, and I'm only allowed to interfere occasionally. Mind you, I'm not complaining because she certainly has green fingers, but yes, I can spare a little time to tidy up your garden, Ned. I'll come along tomorrow and have a look. I'm thinking about what we could plant now in July."

Ned scratched his head. "A few peas should crop by the fall, and radish, lettuce, and beetroot should still grow."

"Yes, that's what I was thinking, and I have some spare cauliflower, cabbage, and sprout plants that are ready to transplant, so they'll keep you going through the winter."

"Marvellous; thank you. There's plenty of ground, so that will leave enough room for some broad beans to be planted in November and a few onions in March."

"Have you thought of a name for the cottage yet, Betsey? It's never had a name, and we've all been calling it Fred's cottage, but it's yours now. I know you named your old home Bluebell Cottage, so you should name this one, too."

"Funnily enough, we were only talking about that last night. We were sitting in the back garden watching the sunset, and it was so beautiful that we decided to call our new home Sunset Cottage. I'll ask Fred to make us a wooden sign when he has the time."

"That's perfect, and yes, I know there's a stunning view out the back. What about Bluebell Cottage? Is anyone living there yet?"

"Yes, a family from South Molton moved in a couple of months ago. It's only a short let because they're renovating an old cottage that was left to them. The place is nearly falling down, so they have a lot of work to do, but they were pleased to find somewhere. Unless we find some reliable tenants, we'll only let it out for a maximum of six months at a time. The last family that rented it was there for years, and they left it in such a mess that we want to keep a better eye on it. The rent money's handy, though, now we're retired."

"Gran, when that family moves out, Louis and I might be interested in renting the cottage; could we do that?"

"Yes, of course, my dear, but I think you'd need to be married first, or you would set tongues wagging."

"Louis has asked me to marry him, Gran, and I've said yes, but he hasn't asked Dad for my hand yet. We've been waiting for him to feel better, and I'm not sure he'll approve because Louis is quite a bit older than me."

"I think you might be surprised, my love; since we nearly lost you a while ago, your dad's changed, and for the better. I think you should ask him; I'm pretty sure he'll only want you to be happy, and he will be if you're living in the village. No parent likes their child to move away; we missed our William terribly when he sailed to China, the naughty boy."

"Thank you, Gran; is that all right with you, too, Grandad? I think Dad will be more agreeable if we have somewhere to live."

"Yes, I'd love you two to rent Bluebell Cottage, and if you have any trouble with George, we'll put in a word for you, Louis. I think you make the perfect couple. Congratulations."

"Oh, thank you." Theresa took Louis' hand. "Do you want to ask Dad when you walk me home this evening?"

"Yes, I will; we'll know where we stand then, and if he approves, maybe we could be married by the time Betsey and Ned are seeking new tenants for Bluebell Cottage. It would be handy to live there; it's next door to the inn where I work and not far from your dad's shop, where you work. Can you tell me how much the rent will be, please, Ned?"

"Oh, let Betsey and I have a chat about that, Louis. As we know you'll be reliable tenants and are related to us, rest assured we'll make sure you can afford it. You can tell George you have somewhere to live."

Theresa threw her arms around Ned and kissed his cheek. "Thank you, Grandad."

Theresa and Louis were the first to leave the family gathering, as Louis was keen to put the question to George, and he had to work the evening shift at The Red Lion. At the cottage, they found a rather harassed Mary Ann, trying to cope with the three children and nurse George. She was on her own as Cissie, their servant, was also in bed with a nasty cold, and Harriet had gone to stay at a friend's house for a couple of days.

"Hello, Mary Ann, is everything all right? You seem a bit flustered."

"Oh, I'm glad to see you, Theresa. Yes, I'm all right, but I need to bathe the children, and I haven't given George,

Cissie, and Mickey their tea yet. Could you give me a hand, please?"

"Yes, of course; what do you want me to do?

"We had a tender piece of pork for dinner, so if you could cut some sandwiches with what's left over for Cissie and Mickey, that would help. Take Cissie's tea to her because she's in bed; she didn't want to go, but she looked so ill I insisted. Mickey's outside chopping firewood so he can have it when he comes in. I don't think your dad will want anything; he feels too poorly. Perhaps take him a cup of tea."

"What about you, Mary Ann? Shall I cut sandwiches for you and the children?"

"Yes, please; did you have a nice time at Sabina's?"

"We did, thank you; Willie, Edward, and Mary were there too, and Granny and Grandad. We have some news: Mary Ann, Louis has asked me to marry him, and Grandad has said we can rent Bluebell Cottage. Louis needs to ask Dad's permission, but do you think we should wait until he's better?"

"I think he'd be pleased to hear that, Theresa, so Louis should ask him. He's not been himself for a while, so some good news might cheer him up."

Rather nervously, Louis carried a cup of tea upstairs, knocked on the bedroom door and entered the room.

"Hello, George. I'm sure you weren't expecting to see me, but here's a cup of tea for you. How are you?"

"Aw, not too good, as you can see, Louis. The wound on my arm is painful, and I'm so shaky on my legs that I've had no choice but to take to my bed. My head swims as soon as I try to get up. I'm fed up with it all, but it's no use complaining. Now, I think I can guess why you're here to see me."

Despite feeling so ill, George smiled weakly, and, thus encouraged, Louis got straight to the point.

"Aye, and I'm sure you're right in your thinking, sir. I've been courting Theresa for some time now, and as you've guessed, I'm here to ask you for her hand in marriage. I promise you that I love her with all my heart and will take care of her. I have a reliable job with Fred and Charlotte at the inn, so I can provide for her. I've already spoken to Ned, and he's agreed that we can rent Bluebell Cottage when the current tenants leave."

"You certainly have everything organised, Louis; I must confess you're a little older than I'd like, but then again, with age comes maturity, and I know you're a trustworthy man who will care for my daughter. After all the worry last year when she was abducted, it would be a relief for me to know she was in a loving and stable marriage, so yes, Louis, you have my blessing. Go ahead and propose to my daughter and marry her as soon as you like."

Louis was taken aback at how well the conversation had gone and, grinning broadly, shook his future father-in-law's hand. "Oh, thank you so much, sir; I'm so pleased, and I hope you feel much better soon."

Louis descended the stairs and entered the kitchen, where Mary Ann was drying Etheline after her bath and Theresa was sitting with Nellie and Sophie and giving them their tea. The two women looked up at him expectantly, and his broad smile answered their question.

"Oh, did Dad say yes?"

Louis nodded happily. "Yes, he was pleased for us; I'm so surprised."

Theresa hugged Louis and kissed him before rushing past him and running up the stairs. In the bedroom, she sat on the bed and hugged her father.

"Oh, thank you so much, Dad; I thought you'd say Louis is too old for me, but I love him, and he's the right man for me."

"Yes, I think he'll look after you, my dear, and that's the main thing. Could you ask Mary Ann to bring me some more of that potion she gives me for my headaches, please?

My head's throbbing, and you can take that tea away; I can't face it."

"Oh, dear, I'm sorry, Dad; Mary Ann's feeding the baby, but I'll fetch it for you; we must get you better to walk me down the aisle."

CHAPTER 31

After an enjoyable day with their family at the Lodge House, Betsey and Ned walked the short distance to their cottage and once more sat in the garden to enjoy the sunset. So far, the month of July had been glorious, and they were enjoying their retirement.

"I wonder how Louis will get on with George; do you think he'll give his permission for him to marry Theresa?"

"I hope so, and I think he will; he'll be a fool if he refuses, for Louis is a hard worker, and it's easy to see he thinks the world of Theresa. Now, would you like some ale while we're sitting here, or perhaps some hot chocolate?"

"I think I'll have some hot chocolate, please; I had ale at Sabina's, and too much doesn't agree with me these days. I certainly can't drink like I used to."

"No, but that may not be a bad thing, Ned."

They enjoyed the view for a little longer and then, as dusk fell, decided to have an early night, for their day had tired them out. However, a few minutes shy of midnight, their slumber was interrupted by someone knocking loudly on their door.

"Oh, what now! I don't know what the time is, but it's still dark." Betsey gathered a shawl around her shoulders and carefully felt her way down the stairs. "All right, all right, I'm coming."

Opening the front door, she was surprised to see Theresa standing there.

"Oh, Gran, I'm so sorry to disturb you, but Mary Ann thinks you should come. Dad's so ill, she's sent Mickey to fetch Doctor Luckett, but she thought you might have a remedy that might help."

"Oh, my goodness, I was going to come and see him in the morning. You get back home, my love, and tell Mary Ann I'll be there in a few minutes. I'll get dressed."

Betsey hurried back up the stairs, where Ned demanded to know what was happening.

"It was Theresa. She came to fetch me because George has taken a turn for the worse. Mary Ann's sent for the doctor, but she wants to know if any of my potions might help."

"Oh, poor lad, I saw his arm was festering again when I saw him the other day. Hang on a minute, and I'll come with you."

"No, you stay in bed and get some rest. You've had a busy day already, and I don't want you overdoing things. I've enough to worry about with George ill, I don't want you to join him. I'll see what's what, and if I need you, I'll come and get you, all right?"

"Aye, if you say so, love, but fetch me if it's serious, won't you?"

"Yes, I will, I promise, but hopefully, it's just a fever."

Betsey kissed her husband and pulled the covers over him before hurrying down the stairs and walking to the village shop where George and Mary Ann lived. Theresa saw her coming and opened the door before she could knock.

"Hello, Gran, can you go on up? Mary Ann wants me to wait here to let Doctor Luckett in."

Betsey hurried up the stairs as fast as she could and entered George's bedroom. Mary Ann was sitting on a chair beside him, holding his hand.

"Oh, Betsey, I don't know what's wrong with him, but he's desperately ill. Is there anything you can do?"

Betsey approached the bed, a grim expression on her old face as she looked at her eldest son with deep concern. George was breathing rapidly and seemed short of breath. Although his eyes were open, they were unfocused, and he showed no recognition of his mother. Betsey took his other hand and leaned over him.

"Hello, George; what's all this about then? It's Mum; I've come to see if I can make you feel better. Can you talk to me, George?"

The ailing man gave no response and shivered, though when Betsey felt his brow, it was hot to the touch.

"How long has he been like this, Mary Ann?"

"Only a few hours. He had a chat with Louis earlier and gave him permission to marry Theresa, and then, when Louis had gone, he asked for one of your mixtures to calm his headache. I brought that to him, and he went to sleep. Theresa kept an eye on him for me while I fed the little ones and got them to bed, and then I came to sit with him, but he hasn't been properly awake since. He's barely eaten or drunk anything for days, and I don't think he's even passed water today. He's been too weak to get out of bed, so I've been bringing him a bottle to use."

"Help me to lift his nightshirt and have a look at him."

Together, the two women removed the covers and pulled up George's nightshirt. Both were horrified to see small, reddish-purple spots across his chest and over most of his body.

"Oh, Betsey, what is it? Is it the measles? That rash wasn't there this morning when I washed him."

"I'm not sure, but it's not the measles. I think it's blood poisoning; the doctor will know more. Let me see his rat-bite wound."

They lowered the man's nightshirt and pulled the covers over him, for his body felt cold. Mary Ann gently removed the bandage around his arm, exposing the wound that had caused so much trouble. Betsey gasped at the sight of the large abscess, which was oozing pus.

"I don't think there's much doubt that this is the source of all the trouble. We'll wait for the doctor, but if he agrees, I'll mix up a lotion to bathe it, though I gave you some last week. Have you been using it?"

"Yes, twice a day, like you said, but it hasn't made much difference. Oh, listen, I think that's the doctor now."

Within a few seconds, the doctor entered the room and went straight to his patient.

"How long has George been like this?"

"Only a few hours, doctor, though, of course, he's had the wound for months; the blasted thing refuses to heal."

The doctor looked into George's eyes, took his pulse, and lifted his shirt, just as Betsey and Mary Ann had done. He drew a sharp breath at the sight of the ugly rash.

"It's blood poisoning, isn't it, doctor?"

"Yes, Betsey, I'm afraid this rash, or purpura, is indicative of blood poisoning, or septicaemia, as we doctors call it; George is seriously ill."

"Is there anything you can do for him?"

"Not much, unfortunately. I'll bleed him, and we can bathe and dress his wound and keep him warm, but that's about it. I fear you must prepare yourselves for the worst."

"Oh no! Betsey, what about your potions; is there nothing you can give him?"

"If only I could, Mary Ann, but I've given him everything I could think of over the last few months, and none of it has encouraged that rat bite to heal. It's continued to fester, and now there's an abscess; I think all we can do is pray. My faith does not equal that of George, but I know it's what he would want us to do. I must fetch Ned, for I promised him I would if I was worried about George, and I couldn't be more worried."

Betsey, Ned, Mary Ann, and the doctor sat with the ailing man all night long, but sadly, neither the doctor bleeding his patient nor Betsey bathing his wound made any difference, and by dawn, Mary Ann was a widow. Betsey and Ned could scarcely believe that they had outlived and must bury a third son.

"Oh, Ned, not another of our children! Why doesn't God see fit to take one of us instead; we've lived our lives. Why must He take another of our sons? He must surely want to punish us, for losing a child is worse than dying."

Ned had no answers but held his wife close as she sobbed, and unashamedly, he, too, had tears running down his wrinkled cheeks.

When folk visited the village shop the next day and found it closed, they were curious about what was wrong and shocked when they heard the sad news. George Carter had not always been a popular man, for although strictly religious, he showed little sympathy for those worse off than himself. Many remembered his lack of compassion for his sister-in-law, Sabina, when her first husband, Tom, died of consumption, and she and her family faced moving to the workhouse. However, since marrying Mary Ann, and particularly since his eldest daughter, Theresa, had been abducted, he had, no doubt, mellowed and changed for the better, and so most folk spoke kindly of him, if only out of respect for his parents.

Betsey and Ned were resting quietly in their cottage the next morning when their son, Fred, arrived from The Red Lion. He hugged them both and insisted on making tea with lots of sugar for them.

"I'm told it helps with the shock, so drink it up. I only saw George yesterday morning, and he wasn't well, but I never expected this."

"None of us did, lad. Do you know if anyone has been to Barnstaple to tell Francis?"

"Yes, I've sent Louis. Theresa and Harriet offered to ride there, but they weren't in any fit state to do so, and anyway, Mary Ann needed them here. Oh, here's Eveline."

He opened the door and let his sister in, and Eveline hugged her mother and then her father.

"I'm so sorry to hear about George; you don't deserve to lose another son after Tom and William. Life's so cruel. I didn't realise George was so ill."

"No, nor me. His condition worsened so quickly that it took us all by surprise. Louis spoke to him at tea time yesterday, and he gave his blessing for him to marry Theresa. According to Mary Ann, he was pleased about it, too. We all knew he wasn't in the best of health, but he deteriorated within hours. Poor man; he's suffered these last few months, and now Mary Ann's widowed and left with three little daughters to raise. At least she's got Theresa and Harriet to help her and run the shop."

Having reassured themselves that their parents were all right, Fred and Eveline left them and visited Mary Ann to offer their condolences and find out how they could best help.

CHAPTER 32

LONDON

Having left Danny at the hospital to await the operation on his foot, Robert summoned a carriage to take Annie and himself to the Highgate Cemetery. They alighted from the carriage, and Annie was delighted to see a flower stall not far from the entrance to the cemetery.

"Oh, look, Robert, that's handy. I can buy some flowers to put on Uncle William's grave."

A stunning array of flowers was displayed on the strategically placed stall, and after some deliberation, Annie chose a large bunch of red roses. She sniffed them.

"Hmm, they don't smell as nice as the roses in our gardens, but they are beautiful. I hope there's a pot we can put them in."

Having visited the grave before, they went straight to it, and to Annie's relief, they found a metal pot containing some artificial flowers. They were bedraggled and faded, so she replaced them with her bunch of fresh blooms.

"Your Mum put them there when Percy brought her here the last time Danny came to London. She thought they would last better than real flowers."

"Yes, I suppose they will; I'll take them to that water butt and wash them off. I saw a few spare pots there, too, so I could put them back on the grave."

Leaving Annie to attend to the flowers and have a few moments alone at her uncle's graveside, Robert wandered off and admired some of the more ornate gravestones. A few were elaborate with stone angels, doves, and other grand statuary, whilst many looked long-forgotten and covered in sinuous ivy that threatened to obscure them completely. He enjoyed the peaceful silence away from the busy city, thinking it was not a bad place to be laid to rest and returned to find his wife kneeling before the grave.

"The flowers are pretty; are you pleased with them?"

"Yes, and the immortelles have spruced up nicely, too; at least people can see someone cares about this grave. Poor Uncle William; it's such a shame he died so young. Granny and Grandad will be pleased I tended his grave again. I know they would like to visit, but they're never likely to come to London at their age."

"No, but at least you can tell them all about it. Are you ready to go yet? I can take another walk if you want a bit more time."

"No, that's all right. I'm ready, but where are we going now?"

"When I brought your mother to London, I took her to the Rosherville Gardens at Gravesend, and we enjoyed our day there. It's a fantastic place, and I think you'd love it. Would you like to go there?"

"Oh, yes, let's do that; Mum told me about it. She was so impressed with the flowers and statues. How do we get there?"

"We'll take a carriage to the Thames and then travel on a paddle steamer to Rosherville Pier. I don't expect you've ever been on a paddle steamer, have you?"

"No, and yes, let's do that."

Within the hour, they were boarding a paddle steamer, and Annie thoroughly enjoyed the boat trip, for she had never been on such a large vessel. As the boat meandered along the river, the man pointed out places of interest and, before long, announced their arrival at Rosherville Pier.

They followed the crowd from the boat, and Robert led the way around the gardens, where Annie was in awe of the beds of magnificent flowers and shrubs. Having explored the zoo, they sat outside a tea room and enjoyed some lunch whilst listening to the music from a brass band.

"Oh, Robert, this is such a magical place; I can see why Mum loved it. She adores her garden, and she found so much inspiration here. I've never seen so many flowers and in so many colours."

"When I brought your Mum, she was pregnant with Katel and didn't fancy walking around the maze. How about you? Shall we see if we can find our way to the middle and back again?"

"Oh, yes, that would be fun. I hope we don't get too lost."

The maze was cleverly planted with thick beech hedges, just too high to see over, and they giggled together like children as, time after time, they found themselves in a familiar place with no clue of the right way to go. After an hour, they finally reached the middle and triumphantly climbed to the top of a wooden platform, enjoying the view over the gardens.

"My goodness, that took a while. I'm hot now." Annie sank onto one of the wooden benches.

"Yes, the sun is scorching today. All we have to do now is find our way out."

Annie groaned. "We'd better get started then if we're to be home in time for our evening meal with Percy. I hope Millie and Jonnie have had a good day, too."

It was after five o'clock by the time Robert and Annie arrived back at Grosvenor Square, and they were greeted in the hallway by an overwrought cook.

"Oh, I'm so glad you're back, sir; I've been beside myself with worry."

"Why, whatever's wrong, Mrs Miggs? Are Millie and Jonnie all right?"

"That's just it, sir; I don't know! They spent the morning in the garden and then came in for some lunch, and after that, they went for a walk around the square. I insisted they were accompanied, and Lena, one of our kitchen maids, went with them. They met Lena's young man along the way, and Millie offered to let them chat for a few minutes. She and Jonnie strolled onto the next road to allow the couple some privacy, but Lena never saw them again, and she is distraught, and they still haven't returned."

"Oh, dear, is Percy here?"

"No, sir, but he should be back from his business meeting any time now, I should think. The thing is, sir, I went for a stroll around the square myself this afternoon, and I swear I saw young Master Jonnie sitting beside the driver on the dickey seat of a smart carriage. He looked like he was having the time of his life, and the driver was letting him hold the reins."

"Did you recognise the carriage or the horses?"

"No, sir, but it must have been owned by someone rich, for it was a grand vehicle."

"Are you sure you've never seen it before? Could it have been a friend of Percy's, perhaps?"

"No, I don't think so, and I suppose I could have been mistaken, but I don't think so."

"What about Millie? Did you see her inside the carriage?"

"No, I didn't get a chance to see inside. I was so shocked to see Jonnie sitting with the driver, and the carriage was going at quite a pace."

Whilst they were considering this surprising news, Percy arrived and, seeing their worried faces, enquired what was wrong. Robert explained their concerns about Millie and Jonathan and asked Mrs Miggs to describe the carriage and horses, but Percy did not think it was anyone he knew. When the doorbell rang, Mrs Miggs left the group to answer the door and returned holding a telegram that she had handed to Robert.

"It's for you, sir."

Robert swiftly opened the message and exclaimed in surprise.

"Why, it's from the solicitors, Parkham, Glover, and Brown, asking us to visit their offices with Millie and Jonnie as soon as possible. How strange. We only saw them a day or two ago; I wonder what they want?"

"Perhaps they have news of Emily."

"Oh, yes, that must be it. We'll visit them tomorrow and find out, but where can those two youngsters have got to? I wouldn't have thought they'd get into a carriage with strangers."

Percy, Robert, and Annie questioned Lena, who was in tears and feared for her job. However, as she could shed no light on the youngster's whereabouts, they decided to report the matter to the police. They set off in Percy's carriage for the nearest police station, where they reported the disappearance of the two youngsters. The constable they saw did his best to reassure them, saying the youngsters were probably off on an adventure and would turn up in their own time. For less important people, he would probably have done little more, but he could see the two gentlemen were wealthy and influential, so he took down all the details and promised to send out a search party. However, Percy felt less than confident that the young man was treating the matter with the seriousness it deserved.

"I'm a friend of Mr Symes, the Police Commissioner. Is he around at the moment?"

"Yes, sir, he's in his office, but I'm not sure he'll be able to see you."

"Then I suggest you find out and tell him it is of the utmost importance."

"Yes, sir, of course."

As the man scurried off, now realising that this gentleman was not to be fobbed off, Percy drew Robert and Annie to one side.

"I suggest you two start searching the streets in my carriage, and I'll stay here and make sure a thorough police search is underway as soon as possible. I'll make my own way back to the house and see you there later."

Robert and Annie scoured the surrounding streets for hours but found no trace of Millie and Jonathan or anyone who could remember seeing them. At last, when darkness had fallen and they were exhausted, they were forced to abandon their search until the next day. They found Percy had returned to the house minutes before them, and although he assured them the police were searching for Millie and Jonathan, so far, there was no news.

Annie was awake at sunrise, having barely slept a wink. She rose and went downstairs, finding Percy asleep on a sofa in the spacious hallway. He stirred as she tried to creep past him, but he mumbled sleepily.

"Have Millie and Jonnie come home yet?"

"No, not that I know of. Have you slept there all night, Percy?"

"Er, yes, I stayed up late in case they came to the front door, but I must have fallen asleep."

"Oh, you didn't have to do that; I would have sat up."

"No, I couldn't let you do that, Annie; I feel terrible that they've gone missing from my home. Mrs Miggs offered to sit up, but I sent her to bed, for I knew she was tired. Oh, dear, where can they be? Is Robert awake?"

"Yes, he's getting dressed. We want to go to the police station as soon as possible to find out if they have any news, but I don't suppose it will be open until nine o'clock, and then we need to visit the solicitors to find out why they want to see us."

Annie, Robert, and Percy breakfasted together, though none had much appetite. They agreed Percy would return to the police station for news, and Annie and Robert would visit the solicitors' office.

"You should be able to flag down a carriage easily enough in the street outside. I suggest we meet back here for lunch at one o'clock to catch up on each other's news. Are you able to visit Danny today?"

"No, not for a couple more days. The doctors like him to have complete rest after his operations, and Danny knows we can't visit for a while. Doctor Turner would have informed us if there were any problems, though, so no news is good news. Thank you for helping us, Percy; we'll see you later."

Having flagged down a carriage, Annie and Robert were soon at the solicitors and were kept waiting only a matter of minutes before being shown into the same office as before, where Mr Glover and Mr Brown were waiting for them.

"Good morning, Lord Fellwood, and you, ma'am, thank you for coming to see us so promptly," Mr Glover leant over and kissed Annie's hand, "and the two youngsters? Millicent and Jonathan, did they accompany you?"

"No, sir, I'm afraid not. We left them at our friend's house yesterday, and they went out for a walk in the afternoon and didn't return; we're so worried."

"Oh, my goodness. Where can they be? Do they know anyone else in the city?"

"No, and even more worrying is that the cook is almost sure she saw Jonnie riding on the dickey seat of a fashionable carriage. We can't imagine how that could be."

"Hmm, that is strange, and I wonder if my news will have any bearing on the matter. Please be seated, and I'll explain why we asked you to visit with Millicent and Jonathan." When Annie and Robert were comfortably seated, the solicitor continued to speak. "We were amazed at the timing of the two visits, but not long after you left our office the other day, Lady Lilliana Grantley arrived and quite likely saw you leave. She came, as requested, for the reading of the will. As you know, the will was sealed, and the instructions were that it should only be read in the presence of Lady Lilliana and Emily and Rosemary Gibbs. However, as we knew Rosemary had passed away, and we had been unable to trace Emily, we decided it was best to proceed."

The solicitor glanced at the young couple before him and smiled. "I'm afraid the reading of the will was a huge shock for Lady Lilliana, for though she felt it would merely be a formality, it turned out to be a different matter entirely. Sir Edgar confessed to being a bigamist as he was already married to Rosemary Gibbs before his marriage to Lady Lilliana."

"What? No, surely not!"

"Oh, yes, I'm afraid it's true. Sir Edgar enclosed his certificate of marriage to Rosemary and the birth certificates of Millicent and Jonathan."

"Goodness, me; she must have been furious."

"She certainly was, and I'm afraid worse news was to come. Although Sir Edgar left Lady Lilliana a great deal of money, his townhouse, and a letter apologising for his behaviour and begging her forgiveness, the bulk of his estate and Grantley House will pass to his heir, Jonathan Gibbs. In fact, the boy is named after Sir Edgar's father, and it's clear Sir Edgar always intended that he should be recognised as his son. The one stipulation in the will is that the boy must reside at Grantley House to inherit. His daughter, Miss Millicent, has also been left a considerable lump sum of money, an annual income from the estate, and a spacious cottage. Also, of course, the sapphire brooch, which we have here for her to collect. There are also bequests for Sir Edgar's wife, Rosemary, and his mother-in-law, Emily, which I'm not at liberty to share with you."

"Can Lady Lilliana contest the will?"

"Not that we can see. Sir Edgar was of sound mind and admitted to being a bigamist, so in the eyes of the law, Lady Lilliana was never his wife. The will is witnessed and correctly drawn up, and we can find no grounds to contest it, though the lady will, no doubt, seek a second opinion."

"When we came in and explained Millie and Jonnie are missing, you seemed to think your news might have some bearing on their disappearance; what did you mean?"

"I'm only guessing, but given that Lady Lilliana must have seen you leave my office the other day and the fact that your cook saw the boy sitting beside the driver of a grand carriage, it's not a great leap of the imagination to wonder if they have been abducted to prevent them from inheriting."

"Oh, good Lord! Yes, I'll bet you're right. We must call on Lady Lilliana without delay."

CHAPTER 33

Jonnie was having the time of his life riding beside the driver in the dickey seat. From his vantage point, he could see all that was going on around him and was completely unaware that the carriage was travelling away from Percy's house. The driver was an affable middle-aged man with a large family, and he enjoyed the boy's company. He wished he could allow his own young son to join him on such a journey.

Inside the carriage, Millie was becoming agitated. The convivial Sir Clive Robinson, who had charmed her with his impeccable manners and winning smile, had vanished, only to be replaced by a sullen man who scowled at her every time she tried to persuade him to turn the carriage around and take them back to Grosvenor Square.

"Sir, I implore you to return to Grosvenor Square immediately. Where are you taking us? I don't even know you."

"Look, I can't take you back, and all will be explained later. As long as you behave yourself, you have nothing to fear, so stop all the questions and be quiet."

Millie sat in stony silence, staring out of the window and wondering if she could find her way back to Percy's house should they manage to escape when the carriage finally stopped. However, she soon realised it was impossible, for after half an hour of travelling through one busy street after another, the girl had no idea where she was. Still, she considered her options. If they could escape from the man, she would summon a carriage like she had seen Robert do and instruct the driver to take them to Grosvenor Square. Of course, she had no money to pay for the journey, but the driver wouldn't know that until they arrived at their destination, and she was sure that Robert or Percy, or even Mrs Miggs, would gladly pay the fare.

Eventually, the carriage stopped, and Sir Clive helped Millie down the steps. However, he kept a firm grip on her arm, and she knew escape was futile. She couldn't kick him in the shins and run as she wanted to, for she couldn't leave her little brother behind. She looked around and realised they had come to a busy dockland. There were large warehouses full of merchandise, and many ships moored along the quayside where gangs of men were carrying goods onto the ships or unloading them. The driver had stopped the carriage alongside a particularly large vessel called The Ocean Queen, and he descended from his seat, lifted Jonnie down, and looked expectantly at his master.

"Right, Johnson, keep a firm grip on the boy and come with me."

The driver looked uncomfortable as Millie pleaded with him. "Sir, I beg you, do not help this man. He's abducting us against our will; please, let us go."

Sir Clive gave her a shake. "Enough! I told you to be quiet. Your fate depends on me now, and if you give me any trouble, I'll instruct my crew to throw you overboard when the ship sails."

The driver looked shocked. "Sir Clive, I'm not sure I want any part of this. Surely, we should let the young lady and the boy go?"

"Johnson, you forget who pays your wages. You'll do as you're told or be out of a job and that miserable family of yours without a roof over their heads. Do I make myself clear? This is none of your business, so just do what you're told."

The man looked pained as he mouthed an apology to Millie, for much as he would have liked to help, with a large family to support and another child on the way, he couldn't risk losing his home and livelihood. Pulling the two youngsters along, the men led them up the gangplank and onto the ship. Sir Clive bade one of the sailors fetch the captain immediately, and within a few minutes, a middle-aged man with a beard and bushy eyebrows appeared.

"Sir Clive, I wasn't expecting to see you today. Is everything all right?"

"Yes, Jim, but there's a little job I need you to do for me. Can you lock these two away somewhere while I explain?"

The captain looked surprised but nodded and called to a sailor to take Millie and Jonnie away. He then invited his employer to join him for a tot of rum in his cabin. Sir Clive dismissed his driver and told him to wait with the carriage. Mr Johnson looked apologetically at the children but turned obediently on his heel and descended the gangplank.

In his cabin, Captain Lethaby poured his visitor a generous tot of rum and then, one for himself. The two men sat facing each other in the small room.

"What time do you sail tomorrow?"

"High tide will be about seven o'clock in the evening. Why do you ask?"

"This is a delicate matter, Jim, but I know I can rely on your discretion. There's no point in beating about the bush; these two youngsters are causing a great deal of trouble to a friend of mine, and they need to vanish. I want you to take them to Australia with you; that should be far enough away to prevent them ever coming back."

The captain looked uncomfortable and said nothing for a moment or two. "And when I get to Australia, what do I do with them? Do they have folk to go to?"

"No, they don't. I'll leave that to you, and I don't want to know the details. I've nothing against the pair, but their presence is unwanted, so do with them as you see fit. Sell them as servants if you wish; it will probably make you a few bob, which can be your reward."

"Oh, I don't know, sir; I'm a law-abiding man, and I could hang for less. What about their folk; won't they be missed?"

"No, they're orphans, so no one will be looking for them. You'd be doing them a favour, taking them to the new world. There's nothing for them here in London, and two children on their own like that would likely be captured and put to work in a brothel in no time. Either that, or they'd starve to death. You have nothing to worry about, and I'll even throw in twenty guineas for your trouble; how does that sound?"

"'Tis kind of you, sir, but I'm not sure. I was always brought up honest, and I don't want to start committing crimes now."

Sir Clive suddenly scowled. "Look, you talk as if you have a choice, man. Let me put it a different way: if you don't help me with this, you can pack your bags and leave right now, and I'll find another captain who will do my bidding. You can find your own way back to that pretty little wife you have in Australia, too; how many children have you given her now?"

Captain Lethaby's shoulders slumped, for he knew he was beaten. "Very well, but I'm not happy about it. Why did you want to know when we sail?"

"You don't have to like it; just do as you're told. The reason I asked when you sail is that although the children have no parents, the police are searching for them, and I would prefer them not to be found. Could you sail on the tide tonight?"

"No, we're far from ready. There's no way we can get all the provisions we need for such a long journey organised in time to sail tonight, and the cargo's not yet fully loaded.

We'll be flat out to be ready for the tide tomorrow night as it is."

"So be it then. Now, here's your twenty guineas, do with the children as you see fit. Like I say, I've nothing against them personally, so I'd prefer you to treat them well, but keep them in line and tell them if they misbehave, you'll throw them overboard! That should ensure they give you no trouble."

Sir Clive left the captain brooding over his predicament. A father himself, he was most unhappy with the situation but knew he had no choice but to comply. He decided to visit the children and ensure they were all right. He discovered they had been imprisoned in a small cabin on the lowest deck. One of the least popular cabins in the centre of the ship, it was normally only purchased by the poorest of passengers, for it had no porthole and was extremely cramped. This one happened to be empty only because the intended passenger had died. He found that the sailor who had imprisoned Millie and Jonnie had left them with a lantern, for which he was glad. He opened the door and was greeted by two anxious pairs of eyes.

"Now, it's all right; I'm sure you're both frightened, but I'll see to it that no harm comes to you. I'm the captain of the ship, and once we're out at sea, I'll let you up on deck, and you can enjoy the voyage."

"But, sir, we don't want to go on a voyage, and I must insist you let us go immediately. The gentleman who handed us over to you abducted us and brought us here against our will. Please, take us to the nearest police station, or let us go, and we'll find our own way."

"I'm sorry, my dear, but I have no choice. You see, I have a wife and family back in Australia, and if I don't agree to take you with me on this voyage, then I'll lose my job and have no way of getting back to them."

"Australia!"

"Yes, that's where the ship will sail tomorrow evening; it's a grand country, and I'm sure you'll like living there."

Millie looked at the man in horror.

CHAPTER 34

HARTFORD

Wanting to spare his parents and sister-in-law further anguish, Fred took it upon himself to make the arrangements for his brother George's funeral. He visited the Reverend Rees to arrange a date for the service and offered to hold the wake at The Red Lion Inn, which met with approval from Betsey, Ned, and Mary Ann. Having been George's childhood home and still owned by the family, the inn was the obvious venue. He discussed the wake with his wife, Charlotte.

"I'm not going to charge Mary Ann anything for the food, though I think we'll need a lot of it, for I suspect the funeral will be well attended. George wasn't popular with everyone, but he was well thought of by the congregations of both the chapel and the church and his fellow committee members of the Overseers of the Poor. I want to give him a decent send-off; is that all right with you?"

Charlotte put her arms around her husband's neck and kissed him fondly. "Yes, of course, it is. Don't worry; I'll make sure there's plenty of food. As we know, there's nothing like a funeral with a wake and a generous spread of food to attract more mourners. It's probably a bit sceptical of me to say that, but it's true nonetheless. Still, there's no way I'd let Betsey and Ned down. I'm so sorry for them to have lost yet another son, and we must make the day as easy for them as possible. Do you have a coffin that will fit George?"

"I do, but it's a run-of-the-mill, cheap, pine one, and it's not good enough for my brother. No, I shall make him a solid oak coffin with shiny brass handles; it's the last thing I can do for him, and it will be my best work."

"Do you have the time? What about the barges and your other carpentry work? I know you said you were rushed off your feet the other day."

"I am, but the rest will have to wait; this is more important. I'm going to see Mary Ann this afternoon to check that she agrees with my suggestions, and then I must get on with it, for the funeral is next week."

A knock on the back door halted their conversation, and Charlotte answered to find her sister-in-law, Sabina, outside.

"Come in, Sabina; you don't need to knock; you're family."

"Thanks, Charlotte; I hope I haven't called at an inconvenient time?"

"No, of course not. We were discussing George's funeral; will you be going?"

"That's why I'm here. 'Tis no secret that George and I didn't get on, though we tolerated each other better in recent years, and I've been wondering if I should attend the funeral or not. I should go because he was Tom's brother, but I don't want to be a hypocrite. I've just called on Betsey and Ned to see what they thought."

"And what did they say?"

"They understand my feelings and are happy for me to go or not, whichever suits me, so I made a suggestion, which they both approved of. As all the family will be attending the funeral, and you're having the wake here, I wondered if it would be more helpful if I looked after Doris and Nicholas for the day to leave you free to deal with everything. I've already told Eveline and Charlie that I'll have Martha, and Joseph, Matthew, and Amelia can come to the Lodge House after school, so Rosella and Eddie could come as well; two more won't make any difference."

"Are you sure, Sabina? 'Tis kind of you, but that's an awful lot of children to mind."

"Oh, you know me, Fred, children are no trouble to me, and most of them are big enough not to need much supervision. It's summer, so the bigger ones can play in the garden, and I've plenty of toys to keep the babies amused. Liza will help me."

"If you're sure, that would be helpful; thank you."

"Good, that's settled then; bring them around as early as you like. I'm always up with the lark these light mornings. What about coffin bearers? Have you got enough?"

"Yes, I think so. There'll be me and Llewellyn; he's only a teenager but nearly as tall as me. George's son, Francis; Eveline's husband, Charlie; Theresa's young man, Louis; and Mary Ann's brother, Cecil. That's the six."

"That's good. I was worried you might want our Willie to be a bearer, but he hasn't forgotten what George was like when Tom died, and I don't think he'd do it. As it is, he needn't even go to the funeral. Arthur will be there to represent our family, so that makes it respectable, and I wouldn't want to upset Mary Ann or the children."

Fred worked hard for the next few days to finish the coffin for his brother. He allowed his son, Llewellyn, to help him, for they seldom had an order for an oak coffin, as most were made of less expensive pine or poplar. Llewellyn had been apprenticed to Fred for a couple of years, and his father was impressed with his skills.

Finally, the day of the funeral arrived, and it was warm and sunny. Charlotte took Doris and Nicholas to Sabina at the Lodge House at eight o'clock in the morning, for they had a lot of baking yet to do.

"This is so kind of you, Sabina, and I appreciate it. We're busy all the time now, what with the stagecoaches, and the visitors using the barges, and the funeral is on top of all that. I mustn't grumble, though; it's better to be busy than to have no customers."

"It's no trouble at all, Charlotte, and after school, the children can all play together."

"Well, thank you, anyway. Now, where shall I put Nicholas? He fell asleep on the way here."

"I'll wheel his pram into the sitting room until he wakes up; it'll be quieter for him in there. Now, you get back and help Sarah, and don't worry about the children; take as long as you like."

The funeral was to be held at eleven o'clock, and at ten o'clock, Eveline, Charlie, and Alfred Chugg arrived at the Lodge House with Martha. By this time, Nicholas was awake and sitting on the floor, playing with Doris, and Martha made a beeline for the toys.

"Would you like a cup of tea before you go, Eveline? You have plenty of time, and Liza has made some fresh cakes."

"Thank you, Sabina, but no, I want to see Mum and Dad before the funeral, and I thought we'd walk to the church with them. It's such a difficult day for them to be burying yet another son. Alfred wants to pay his respects too, for he was at school with Betsey and Ned and has known them all his life."

"Yes, of course; I'll see you later."

As Fred had predicted, the village church was packed, with some mourners having to listen to the service through the open door. With Betsey and Ned having long been the owners of The Red Lion Inn, George, the owner of the village shop, and Fred, the carpenter, there were few folk who didn't know and respect the Carter family. Following the service and burial, the congregation made its way the short distance to the inn, where trestle tables had been set up in Betsey's Kitchen and outside in the garden, where it was already crowded with holidaymakers using the canal boats.

Fred and Charlotte had been busy all morning making sure everything was ready, but then relied on the additional staff they had taken on to leave them free to spend time with their family. Betsey was distraught and leaned heavily on Ned's arm, tears running down her face.

By mid-afternoon, most of the mourners had departed, leaving only family members, and Francis closed the doors of Betsey's Kitchen and asked all present to be seated.

"Mary Ann and I discussed this a few days ago, and we thought now was the best time to read Dad's will while everyone is present. Mr Watson, Dad's solicitor from Barnstaple, attended the funeral and has stayed on to deal with the formalities. So, Mr Watson, I'll hand the proceedings over to you if I may."

"Thank you, Francis. First, may I offer my condolences to all of you present, particularly you, Mary Ann, Francis, Theresa, and Harriet; 'tis so sad to have lost George, for he was not an old man by any means. Betsey and Ned, and your family too; please accept my sympathies, though I know there is little I can say to ease your pain. That said, I will tell you all of George's last wishes, and I must say he was an organised man who left his affairs in good order.

"George has left the Hartford shop and his house to his wife, Mary Ann, with the proviso that his daughters, Theresa and Harriet, be allowed to live and work there until they marry or choose to leave. The shop in Barnstaple he has left to you, Francis. He has left money to several family members, and I'll deal with this by giving you each a letter written by George himself. Once these bequests are dealt with, the remainder of his money is left to his wife, Mary Ann. So, I think that is all straightforward, but are there any questions?"

As his comments were met with silence, the solicitor reached for a bundle of letters and handed one each to George's wife and children, then Betsey and Ned, Eveline and Charlie, and Fred and Charlotte. He looked around the room.

"Is Sabina Webber not here?"

"Er, no, sir, she volunteered to look after the children today to allow all of us to attend the funeral without them. Her husband, Arthur, was here earlier, but he's left now. Why, is there a letter for her?"

"Yes, still, not to worry, I'll drop it into the Lodge House on my way home. Now, unless anyone has any questions, I'll be on my way and bid you all a good day."

Leaving the inn, Mr Watson rode the short distance to the Lodge House and knocked on the door. He was amazed at the number of children, some playing happily in the garden, others in the parlour, and some seated around the kitchen table drawing pictures.

"My goodness, Mrs Webber, you have your hands full today. I have a letter for you from Mr George Carter." He handed her a brown envelope.

"For me?"

"Yes, ma'am. Mr Carter wrote a letter to all his nearest and dearest to advise them of his wishes."

"Oh, I am surprised, for I was certainly never one of his nearest or dearest, but please take a seat."

"Thank you, ma'am. Would you like me to read the letter to you?"

Sabina knew the man meant no offence. "No, it's all right, Mr Watson, I can read."

She tore the letter open and was amazed at its contents. The high and mighty George Carter begged her forgiveness for treating her and her family so shabbily when his brother, Tom, died of consumption. Furthermore, he left her the princely sum of ten guineas and his best wishes for the future.

CHAPTER 35

On a scorching hot day in early August, Marrok, Willie, and a few other workers were stripped to the waist as they harvested the ripened corn with razor-sharp scythes. With the sun glistening on their sweaty bodies, the men worked contentedly alongside each other whilst singing the ancient song, *One Man Went to Mow*, and timing the sweep of their blades to the rhythm of the music. Edward had wanted to join them, but not yet fully grown, he was not strong enough to wield a scythe for long, and Willie insisted he help Sam with the other jobs in the farmyard.

Jinnie and Eliza had been helping Florrie in the kitchen all morning. They had taken to the old woman, who enjoyed teaching them to cook, knit, and sew. Their presence, along with that of their little brothers, Martin and Paul, had given the housekeeper a new lease of life and allowed her to employ her motherly instincts in a way that had never been possible before.

"There now, I think it's time we packed some food for the men. The sun is so hot today that they'll need a drink. Jinnie, you slice the bread now that it's cooled and wrap it in a clean cloth with some chunks of cheese. Then slice the fruit cake and take that, too. Eliza, fetch two flagons of cider from the pantry, please, and Martin, you go into the yard and ask Sam to get the donkey and cart ready for Edward to take the men their lunch. Would you all like to go and see how they're getting on?"

"Yes, please, Florrie; can we join them for lunch in the cornfield?"

"Yes, if you like; put your sunhats on, though. I don't want you getting sunstroke and being sick everywhere. And if Willie has his shirt off, tell him I said he must put it back on. Having red hair, he should know by now that he can't stay in the sun for too long, or he'll be sunburnt, but he always forgets. Ah, here's Sam and Edward, now."

"Are you coming, Grandad and Florrie?"

Florrie answered. "No, I'm not; there won't be enough room on the cart for all of us, and anyway, it's too hot for me today. What about you, Sam? You might be able to squeeze onto the cart if you want to go."

"No, it's too hot for me, too, Florrie; I'll stay here with you."

"Very wise, Sam. Now, enjoy yourselves and pick me a bunch of wildflowers, please; there should be plenty in the hedgerows. Don't walk into the corn, though, or you'll flatten it and have Marrok after you for making it difficult to cut. Here you are; you can each carry a basket and bring it back when the men have finished eating. Sam, I suggest we have a cup of tea and put our feet up for an hour."

Edward hoisted the food baskets and the cider flagons onto the small cart, and the four children clambered aboard. Neddy, the old donkey, was partially sighted, but he was sure-footed, and when Edward flicked the reins, he trotted off happily enough along the familiar track. They didn't take long to travel across three fields and reach the cornfield. The men had cut around a quarter of the corn, and the remainder gleamed golden yellow and was full of wildflowers. With barely a cloud in the azure blue sky, the scarlet poppies, blue cornflowers, and pink scabious were in full bloom, and it was an amazing sight.

"Oh, look, Eliza, isn't it pretty? I can see why Florrie wanted a bunch of flowers."

The men were delighted to see their lunch arrive and, having finished the row they were cutting, laid down their scythes and walked to the side of the field where Edward had left the donkey and cart under the shady branches of a sycamore tree.

"Phew, it's so hot today. Are you going to stay and eat with us?"

"Yes, Dad; Florrie said we could, and she wants us to pick her a bunch of flowers. We'll do that later, or they'll wilt in this heat. Oh, and Willie, Florrie says to remind you to put your shirt back on."

"Good old Florrie, she does fuss; she's right, though. I want to leave it off, but I know I'll burn; it's all right for you lot who are dark-skinned. What have we got to eat today, then?"

"There's some fresh, crusty bread that Jinnie and I made this morning, lots of cheese and a jar of pickled onions. Then there's a big fruit cake that Florrie made, too. She's cut it into slices already. There are two flagons of cider and some water, too; Florrie knew you'd be thirsty."

"She's not wrong there." Marrok took a large swig of the cider and then passed the flagon to Willie. He squinted up at the sun. "Did you happen to see the time before you left the farmhouse?"

"Yes, it was a quarter to twelve. Florrie said it was a bit early for your dinner, but she thought you'd be ready for it, and she said to remind you that Aunty Margery is coming this afternoon."

"Yes, that's right. I can spend another hour or so out here, and then I'll have to go in and get ready. I hope we can get at least half of this field cut today and finish it tomorrow. I reckon the weather will stay fine for the rest of the week and give the straw time to dry out. It shouldn't take long in this heat."

Following their lunch, the children strolled around the field's perimeter, and the two girls collected bunches of poppies, cornflowers and yellow corn marigolds for Florrie.

They surrounded their posies with long green ferns and held them at arm's length to admire them. Suddenly, Martin cried out.

"Oh, look, the scythe has killed a bird; what a shame."

The children gathered around the bird and were joined by Edward, who was distraught. Gently, he checked that the injured bird was dead, and as he moved it, they saw that beneath it was a nest full of tiny chicks.

"Oh no, look, it has babies. What sort of bird is it?"

"I don't know; what shall we do? The babies might die now that their nest is destroyed and their mother is dead."

Edward, who was deaf and unable to speak, had quickly set off back to the cart, and he returned minutes later carrying one of the baskets that had held the food. Lining the bottom with corn stalks, he gently scooped up the chicks and put them into the basket. He then picked up the dead bird, laid it gently in the hedgerow, and covered its body with branches before returning to the cart with the basketful of cheeping baby birds.

"Dad, Dad, we've found some baby birds and their mother was killed with the scythe. Edward has rescued them. Do you know what birds they are?"

Marrok peered into the basket and looked at the brown and yellow speckled chicks. "Hmm, baby partridges, I think. They nest on the ground. What was the mother like?"

"It was grey with an orangy-brown head and not quite as big as a chicken."

"Oh, yes, it was a partridge then, but not the mother; that was the cock bird. I don't know what Edward thinks he'll do with them; it's almost certain they'll die. Mind you, they'll die anyway if we leave them here now that their nest is exposed. The rats or the foxes will have them in no time, even if the mother bird does come back. We'll let him take them home because he'll only get upset if we make him leave them. Tell Florrie I'll be along shortly to meet Aunty Margery."

The children rode back on the cart with Edward, and having found a wooden crate in the barn, he lined it with soft hay and gently put the chicks inside. Florrie groaned when he carried the crate into the kitchen and put it near the Bodley stove.

"Oh no, what have you rescued now, Edward?" Florrie was used to Edward and the seemingly endless menagerie of creatures that he was forever bringing into her kitchen.

"Dad says they're baby partridges, Florrie, and he says they'll probably die, but he's happy to let Edward try to save them."

The housekeeper sighed. "Very well, then. If anyone can save them, he will. Are these flowers for me? Thank you. Now, I'd like you all to wash your hands and face and be ready to greet Lady Margery. Jinnie and Eliza, please put on a clean pinafore and find some clean shirts for the boys; we must have you all looking your best."

Sam grinned. "You needn't go to any trouble, Florrie. Although she's a lady, Margery is easy-going."

"Nevertheless, there are standards to maintain, Sam, and if you don't mind me saying, it wouldn't do any harm for you to change your shirt."

By the time Lady Margery's carriage arrived, the Fellwood family had smartened up, and Florrie had given the kitchen a last-minute clean. This time, Margery had brought Peter Webber with her, and following the introductions, Marrok led them all into the sitting room where they could relax in comfort whilst Florrie made a pot of tea using the late Mrs Houle's best china tea set that so seldom saw the light of day.

"How are you getting on, Marrok? Are the repairs to the house finished yet?"

"No, not quite, but I'll show you around later when we've had tea. The roof's finished, and most of the bedrooms have been decorated, though we need to buy some new furniture when we can get around to it. Dad reckons it would be best to ask Fred Carter to make some for us when he has the time. Still, there's no rush. Dad and I have mended a lot of the fences and gates on the farm, and I've gradually been buying new stock, but I reckon it will be a year or two until I have everything as I want it."

"Did you hear that George Carter passed away, Sam?"

"Yes, I did because he was Willie and Edward's uncle. Marrok told Willie they could both take the day off to attend the funeral, but Willie didn't want to. I think George was quite uncaring when their father, Tom, died, and Willie hasn't forgotten. I certainly wasn't a fan either, for he was always unpleasant to me, though probably with cause, seeing as I was a tramp and a nuisance back then. Sad for a man to die so young, though; rat bite, wasn't it?"

"Yes, apparently so, though it was months ago, he was bitten, but the wound became infected, and he died of blood poisoning, or so I hear."

Peter joined the conversation. "We called at the Lodge House on the way here today to see my son, Arthur, and he was telling me that George left a letter to Sabina apologising for his meanness when his brother, Tom, died. He left her ten guineas, too."

"He had a guilty conscience then, didn't he? Still, at least he tried to make amends, I suppose. We must tell Willie when he comes in from the fields; I don't think he's heard that."

"What will happen to the shops and his house?"

"Arthur said that his wife, Mary Ann, will continue living in the house, and Theresa and Harriet will run the shop in Hartford. George left the Barnstaple shop to his son, Francis, which is only right. I've heard that only hours before he passed away, he gave his blessing for Theresa to marry Louis Blaquiere, you know, the chap who was washed up on the beach and now works at the inn. He's quite a bit older than Theresa, but she could do a lot worse. Of course, I expect they'll have to wait a while now before they can wed, what with George dying. A wedding would hardly be appropriate while the family is in mourning."

"How are Victoria and the children? Have they moved from Hartford Manor yet?"

"Yes, a few weeks ago. I've visited their new home in Lynton once, and Victoria has settled in well, and no wonder for it's such an idyllic spot. She has her mother-in-law staying with her at the moment whilst she decides whether she wants to move to Devon and into the cottage, which is situated on the grounds. Charles and Eleanor miss Victoria and the children, but at least they're much nearer than if they were in London."

"Has anyone heard from Robert and Annie? I take it they're still in London with Danny?"

"Yes, they are. Eleanor received a letter from Robert saying they had arrived safely, but they always planned to stay a month to give Danny's foot time to heal, and of course, this time, they have Millie and Jonathan with them. I believe they want to clear Millie's name over the theft of a brooch. I hope they get it all sorted out and find their granny, Emily. She's Betsey's half-sister, too, of course, and it would be beneficial for Betsey to meet her and take her mind off losing George a little."

"It's strange where the old woman can be, isn't it? I heard that Robert and Annie discovered she had left the workhouse, and that being so, you'd think she would have arrived in Hartford by now if she intended to follow her grandchildren there."

"Yes, it's worrying; I fear the poor lady might have perished on the journey, for she was unwell, and the weather was harsh. The trouble is, no one knows where to look for her now. Even if she has passed away, it would be best to know, and then Millie and Jonathan could move on with their lives. Fortunately, they now have a roof over their heads with Betsey and Ned. Anyway, do you like living here at Sugworthy Farm, Sam? We miss you, don't we, Peter?"

"Yes, I love living here, thank you, though I miss you, too. I used to enjoy a brandy with you of an evening, Peter, when we would put the world to rights. And our little excursions in your carriage, Margery; I miss them too."

"There's no reason we can't have a day out together again soon. I've been thinking I'd like to visit Clovelly; I haven't been there for years. Have you ever been there, Sam?"

"No, I can't say I have, but yes, I'd enjoy that. I've heard it's a pretty village."

"Yes, it is, but incredibly steep, and they use donkeys to carry goods and people up and down the main street to the harbour. The incline is too much for a carriage or a horse and cart and certainly too much for me these days. Shall we go one day next week, perhaps Friday? We can collect you on the way."

"Thank you, yes. I'll look forward to it. How are Christopher, Clarice, and the new baby?"

"Yes, all well, thanks, Sam. Peter Junior is a couple of months old now and smiling at everyone. He's a contented little chap, and I spend a lot of time talking to him. I've just had an idea. When we've visited Clovelly, why don't you come back to Primrose Cottage for a few days? Christopher and Clarice would be pleased to see you, and I'd enjoy your company again."

"Thank you, Peter; yes, I'd like that. Now, would you like to inspect the house and garden to see what Marrok and I have been up to? We've been busy; I think you'll be impressed."

CHAPTER 36

LONDON

Robert and Annie left the solicitors' office, barely believing what they had been told and realising they must waste no time locating Millie and Jonathan.

"That's a turn-up for the books, isn't it? I bet Lady Lilliana was furious when she found out she was not legally married, and who can blame her? It just shows we aren't the only couple to fall in love with someone from a different class, are we? But how scandalous of Sir Edgar to commit bigamy."

"It doesn't sound as if he had much choice, though I suppose he could have maintained Rosemary as his mistress."

"Yes, but then his children would have been illegitimate and unable to inherit Grantley House and all the rest of it. It's hard on Lady Lilliana. I don't like the woman, but she has had a rough deal."

"It's a pity the solicitor wouldn't tell us where she lives."

"I don't think he could, legally. After all, everything he deals with has to be confidential. No matter, let's get back to Grosvenor Square as quickly as we can because Percy might know where Edgar's townhouse is situated. There's not much he doesn't know about the well-to-do in London, and even if he doesn't know, I'm sure he'll be able to find out because he knows a lot of influential people. If all else fails, I'll send a telegram to Roger Everson because I suspect he'll know the address, but that will take longer, and I think we need to find those youngsters as quickly as possible."

"Oh, Robert, you don't think they'll be harmed, do you?"

"Hopefully not, but I think the solicitor is right, and Lady Lilliana has something to do with their disappearance, and she certainly won't want them found."

Having hailed a carriage, they returned to Percy's house and were delighted to find him at home. He listened with interest to their tale and was as surprised as they had been to hear that Sir Edgar was a bigamist. Percy assured them that he knew where Sir Edgar's house was situated and had been there for many social occasions in the past.

"I'll come with you to visit Lady Lilliana. We are acquainted, and I suspect she's more likely to receive me than you, though whether she'll tell us anything useful is another matter. However, it's the only lead we have, so we must try, though I think it will need to be handled extremely delicately."

An hour or so later, Percy, Robert, and Annie alighted from their carriage, and whilst they were waiting to be admitted by the butler, they noticed a smart carriage leave the grounds of the grand townhouse. Percy gazed after the carriage thoughtfully, trying to recall where he had seen it before. However, before he could share his thoughts with his companions, they were welcomed inside and shown into a lavishly decorated drawing room whilst a maid went to enquire whether her mistress would receive them.

Lady Lilliana was dismayed to hear she had visitors, particularly considering who they were, and, at first, told her maid to say she was indisposed. However, she thought better of it, knowing it would look suspicious, and decided to appear as helpful as possible. She swept down the grand staircase and into the drawing room.

"Sir Percy, how kind of you to call. How are you?"

"I'm well, thank you, my dear. I was in the neighbourhood and felt I must call to express my condolences on your loss. I know it's been a while since you lost your dear husband, and I understand you've been ill yourself. I trust you are now fully recovered?"

"Thank you. Yes, it's several months now since we lost poor Edgar, and I am much better, thank you, though I was laid low for some considerable time. But please, won't you introduce me to your friends? I don't think we're acquainted."

"Yes, of course. This is Lord and Lady Fellwood. Lord Fellwood is a cousin on my mother's side of the family, though as they normally reside in North Devon, we do not see as much of each other as we would like."

Lady Lilliana invited her guests to be seated and rang the bell for some refreshments. After a little small talk, Percy enquired, as delicately as he could, whether she had ever met any members of the Gibbs family, whom he understood were the tenants of a tied cottage on the Grantley estate in Brampford Speke.

The lady was taken aback at his sudden and rather blunt question and floundered a little. However, she soon recovered her decorum and, with a smile, confirmed she was aware of the family.

"What a strange question, Percy; why do you ask? Do you know the family?"

"Only recently, my dear, but it has come to light that they're distantly related to Lady Fellwood."

"I see, how intriguing. How exactly are you connected, if I may ask?" Lilliana looked enquiringly at Annie.

Annie took up the story and explained how Millie and Jonathan Gibbs had arrived in Hartford seeking their long-lost relatives in the hope they would give them a home.

"You see, many years ago, my great-grandfather, Adam Lovering, abandoned his family in Hartford when my granny was a little girl. He left the village after his wife died and was never seen again. He moved to Exeter, remarried, and had another daughter called Emily. Emily Gibbs is the grandmother of Millicent and Jonathan, and so Emily is a half-sister to my grandmother, Betsey Carter."

"My goodness, how complicated, and how interesting, but I'm not sure how this concerns me?"

"Well, you see, following Sir Edgar's death, Emily Gibbs was evicted from her tied cottage. Her daughter, Rosemary, had died of typhoid, and Emily, too, was seriously ill."

"Oh dear, I'm so sorry to hear that. It sounds as if my estate manager was a little overzealous. I confess I gave instructions for some of the tied cottages to be repossessed as their inhabitants no longer worked on the estate, but I certainly never meant for anyone to be evicted until they had found somewhere else to live. My husband was so soft-hearted that he never managed the estate efficiently, but I will speak to my manager about his harsh actions when I return to Brampford Speke. However, I'm pleased to hear the youngsters arrived safely in North Devon. Where are they now? Are they reunited with their grandmother?"

"No, sadly not. No one knows the whereabouts of Emily Gibbs, but Millie and Jonathan travelled to London with us recently to deposit a brooch with Sir Edgar's solicitors. As you must be aware, they had been accused of stealing the brooch, though we understand Sir Edgar gave it to Rosemary Gibbs before she died."

"Yes, I must confess, I know of the brooch. It belonged to my mother-in-law and was left to me, but unfortunately, following Edgar's death, it disappeared, and my maid was convinced she saw the young Gibbs girl leaving with it in her hand. However, I'm delighted to hear it has been returned and her name cleared. Hopefully, that's the end of the matter."

"No, not quite; you see, Millie and Jonathan went for a walk around Grosvenor Square yesterday afternoon and never returned. Our cook was almost sure she saw Jonathan sitting beside the driver of a smart carriage, and we're at a loss to explain this. As the children know no other people in London, we wondered if you might have arranged for them to be collected to visit you here?"

"Oh, I see. No, I'm afraid I can't help you. I've never met the children, but I hope you find them."

"Yes, we are concerned. You see, Sir Edgar's solicitor has asked to see them urgently. Do you know why that might be?"

"No, I'm afraid not, but as I say, Edgar was always soft-hearted. Maybe he left them a trinket or two if they were acquainted with him. I do hope you find them safe and sound. Now, may I offer any of you another piece of cake? I recommend the fruit loaf; it's a speciality with my cook."

After a little more pleasant conversation, Percy, Robert, and Annie left Lady Lilliana and resumed their places in their carriage.

"That wasn't much help, was it? I thought you were far too nice to her, Percy; we all know she's behind this. I wanted to pin her to the ground and beat the truth out of her!"

Percy laughed. "Yes, I rather thought you did, Annie, and I confess I was concerned you might do just that, but I'm so glad you didn't; it wouldn't have helped and would only have alerted her to the fact that we know more than I let on. Anyway, we have another lead to follow now."

Annie and Robert looked at him in puzzlement. "We do?"

"We do. I recognised the carriage that was leaving as we arrived and have been racking my brains about where I've seen it before, and now I've remembered. It belongs to Sir Clive Robinson, an extremely rich businessman. I also recall hearing Lady Lilliana's name linked to his romantically in the past. The lady has had quite a string of lovers over the years, which is perhaps more understandable now we know how her husband treated her."

"Do you know where he lives? We must go there straight away."

"I do, Robert, but I doubt we'd find Millie and Jonnie there. I think it's unlikely he'd hide them in his own house, and I have another theory. Sir Clive owns a fleet of magnificent ships that sail far and wide, even as far as the Americas and Australia. Where better to dispose of two unwanted children than to send them on a one-way voyage to the other side of the world?"

CHAPTER 37

Millie and Jonnie had spent a restless night, for it was stuffy in the tiny cabin where they were imprisoned. When they awoke, they didn't know whether it was night or day, for their only light was from the lantern they had kept lit. It had been hours since the captain had visited them, and Millie began to wonder if they had been forgotten. The ship did not appear to be moving, though they could hear distant clanging noises from time to time. They were hungry and thirsty, and Millie took off one of her boots and began banging on the door. It took some time to attract attention, and the girl had almost given up when she heard a key in the lock.

"All right, all right! Enough of the noise!" A swarthy, middle-aged man opened the door and scowled at them. "As if I haven't enough to do without babysitting the pair of you. Now pack it in."

The man was carrying some bread, cheese, and two tankards of ale, which he set down on the small table.

"Can you tell us what time it is, mister?"

"Aye, it's dawn, and I have a lot to do before we sail, so if you know what's good for you, you'll eat your breakfast and keep quiet. Why the captain saw fit to pick me to look after you, I'll never know. I can't abide children, not even my own, so you'd better not give me any trouble."

"I know how you can make a lot of money, mister. If you let us go, we have a rich friend who'll pay you handsomely. How about it? Can you smuggle us off the ship? I'll see you're rewarded."

The man laughed, revealing a few blackened teeth.

"Nice try, my dear, but I can't help you. I daren't get on the wrong side of Sir Clive. He owns this ship, and though he never gets his own hands dirty, he'd make sure I'd not live to enjoy the money, even if your friend did pay up. No, I'm happy with my lot, and I have a loving wife waiting for me in Australia, so thank you, but no, I can't help you. No one on this ship will go against Sir Clive, not even the captain, and I know he doesn't want to take you with us. You might as well accept that you're going to the new world. It's all right there, though it's far too hot for me. Eat your breakfast, and I'll be back in a few hours with some dinner for you; don't worry, I won't forget you, and the lantern should last until then."

The man left, locking the door behind him, and the youngsters thirstily drank some of the ale before nibbling at the hard cheese and stale bread.

"Oh, Millie, what are we going to do? I don't want to go to Australia, do you?"

"No, I don't, and I don't know what we can do, but I'm sure Robert and Percy will be looking for us."

"Yes, but how will they know where to look?"

"Did you notice Mrs Miggs when we were in the carriage? I'm sure I saw her walking along the road not long after Sir Clive tricked us into his carriage. I tried to attract her attention, but Sir Clive stopped me. She might have noticed you sitting beside the driver. Did she wave to you?"

"I didn't even see her; the driver was kind, and he let me hold the reins."

"Never mind, eat your breakfast; we'll just have to hope they find us before the ship sails."

Having left Lady Lilliana's house, Annie, Robert, and Percy discussed their next move.

"I think we should go straight to the docks, find Sir Percy's ships, and search whichever one is next to sail, for no doubt that's where he'll have taken Millie and Jonnie."

"Yes, probably, but Annie, that's much easier said than done. There are several docks in London, and we don't know which one Sir Clive's ships sail from, and the crew would hardly welcome us aboard. No, I think we'll have to return to my friend Mr Symes, the Police Commissioner and ask for his help. His officers are already searching for Millie and Jonathan, though they don't know where to look. What do you think, Robert?"

"I agree, Percy, and we'll come with you this time."

The carriage took them to the police station, where Percy again insisted on seeing the Commissioner. This time, the officer on the desk remembered Percy and the reprimand he had received earlier for not taking the matter seriously. In no time, they were being shown into Mr Syme's office. Percy introduced Robert and Annie and explained their theory about where the children might be.

"That sounds plausible, and yes, I agree it would be worth checking Sir Clive's ships. I believe most large ships bound for Australia sail from the East India or West India Docks. Both are situated in the Poplar area in the eastern part of the city, though they're not adjacent to each other. It's a few miles from here, so we'd better get moving. I suggest you return home to await news, and I'll gather as many men as possible to initiate a search."

Annie opened her mouth to protest, and despite the seriousness of the situation, Robert grinned as he accurately read her thoughts.

"With all due respect, sir, I think you need as many men for the search as possible, and I'm sure I speak for Percy, too, when I say we would prefer to accompany you. Annie, I think you should return to Grosvenor Square, though; things might get rough."

Annie was indignant. "Please let me come, Robert. I promise I'll keep out of any trouble, but if we find Millie and Jonnie, I want to be there to comfort them; they must be so frightened." She raised her eyes pleadingly to her husband.

"Very well, but you must wait on the quayside or in the carriage. Do you promise me?"

Annie nodded reluctantly, for she would have liked nothing better than to storm on board the ships with the men and demand the youngsters' return.

Without further ado, Mr Symes sent his officers to other police stations to organise a search party, and within the hour, they were travelling to the city's east end. Robert, Annie, and Percy followed the police in their carriage and became frustrated because the streets were busy, hindering their progress. It was late afternoon when they arrived at the East India Docks.

Mr Symes went to the shipping office and demanded to see whoever was in charge. Given his position, he was afforded prompt service, and the manager told him that only one of Sir Clive's ships was currently docked there. It had recently arrived from America and would not sail for another two weeks.

Having decided they could safely delay searching that ship until another day, the group headed towards the West India Docks, some five miles away. Again, the roads were busy with carriages and carts, and it was after six o'clock that they approached the second shipping office, where, again, the manager was willing to help.

"Yes, sir, many of Sir Clive Robinson's ships use this dock; he's one of our best customers. I'm pretty sure he has three ships here, and I think one is due to sail within the hour. Please excuse me whilst I check." The man rifled through some paperwork on his desk. "Yes, here we are. *The Ocean Queen* will sail on the tide at a quarter past seven."

"Where is the ship headed?"

"Australia; many of Sir Clive's fleet sail there."

"That ship cannot be allowed to sail; we have reason to believe two youngsters who have been abducted are on board and being held against their will."

"I don't know about that. Sir Clive is a rich and influential merchant, and he'll not be best pleased if his ship misses the tide; it would mean delaying the voyage by at least a day."

"You misunderstand me, sir. I'm the Commissioner of the Metropolitan Police, and I'm not asking you; I'm telling you that the ship cannot sail. Or at least, it cannot sail until it has been searched. Now, please, lead me and my officers to the ship in question."

Somewhat disgruntled and realising he would not be going home for his tea any time soon, the manager led the way along the busy quayside. It was a chaotic scene with cargo being loaded and unloaded from the many large ships. Crowds of people milled around, barrels were rolled along, and sacks of grain were winched aboard the ships as they took on enough supplies to last for their journey. Eventually, the manager stopped beside a vessel where the gangplank was about to be hoisted, and the sailors on deck could be seen fitting iron bars into the capstan, ready to begin the gruelling job of hoisting the heavy anchor. The manager waved his arms and shouted to the men who were about to winch the gangplank aboard the ship.

"Stop. Stop what you're doing. I am impounding this ship."

The sailors looked startled and, glancing at each other, debated whether to obey. However, Percy, Robert, and several policemen took command of the situation by jumping onto the fast-vanishing gangplank and forcing them to abandon their actions. Once the walkway was secured to the ground, Mr Symes mounted it and instructed one of the sailors to take him to the captain. Leaving most of his search party on deck to ensure no further preparations were made to sail, Mr Symes, followed by Percy, Robert, and Annie, trailed after the man along narrow passageways. Annie was keeping unusually quiet as Robert seemed to have forgotten her presence, and she didn't want to be sent back to the carriage.

Captain Lethaby was in his cabin preparing to go up on deck and supervise his ship leaving the dock, and he was most surprised to see three gentlemen and a lady at his door.

"I'm sorry to disturb you, captain, but this policeman says he has impounded our ship, and we cannot sail; he insists on talking to you."

Captain Lethaby had little doubt about why the law had come to his door, but, fearing for his livelihood, knew he must attempt to bluff his way out of the situation.

"This is rather unexpected, sir; how can I help you? We must sail shortly, or we'll miss the tide."

"I'm Mr Symes, the Commissioner of the Metropolitan Police, sir, and this is Sir Percy Chichester and Lord and Lady Fellwood. I'm investigating a serious crime, and one with which I suspect you might be able to assist us. Am I right in thinking Sir Clive Robinson owns this ship?"

"Yes, sir, that is correct."

"And when was the last time you saw Sir Clive?"

"Er, I'm not sure, sir; why do you ask?"

"I'm not going to beat about the bush, sir. To save time, I'll tell you what I suspect. I think Sir Clive visited this ship within the last twenty-four hours and probably had a young woman and a boy with him. They are close relatives of the folk I have with me. Now, I put it to you that he ordered you to imprison them on this ship and sail with them to Australia." The captain paled but said nothing. "You should know that I have twenty policemen waiting on the deck as we speak, and they will turn over every inch of this ship until I am satisfied the two youngsters are not on board. It may be that you had no choice but to obey your employer, and I will take that into consideration if you cooperate. If not, and the people we seek are found on your ship, then I doubt you'll ever see the outside of a jail cell again."

The captain rapidly considered his options, but knew there was little doubt that a thorough search would reveal the whereabouts of the two detainees, and he grimaced.

"You are correct in what you say, sir. Sir Clive visited this ship yesterday afternoon, accompanied by a young woman and a boy, and insisted I hold them captive and take them to Australia with me. You are also right that I had no choice, although I can assure you I protested strongly. I have a wife and family in Australia, and without this job, I would have no way of returning to them. Sir Clive made it clear that unless I complied with his wishes, I would be sacked, and he'd make sure no other ship would ever employ me, and I couldn't take the risk."

"Thank you for your honesty, sir. Now, where are they? They had better not have been harmed."

"No, I assure you, they have been well treated and are confined in a cabin on the lower deck. I even visited them myself and promised to let them up on deck once we had left the English Channel. I was also going to find them a suitable position in Australia; I am not a bad man."

"Can you take us to them, please?"

"Yes, of course, follow me."

The captain led the way along further passageways, down steep stairs and finally to the cabin where Millie and Jonathan were imprisoned. He unlocked the door, and two frightened faces peered out, their expressions changing to relief as they recognised Annie, Robert, and Percy. Annie pushed her way forward and rushed into the cabin, hugging both youngsters at once.

"Oh, thank goodness you're safe; have you been harmed?"

"No, but I'm so glad to see you. They were going to take us to Australia. A man called Sir Clive Robinson brought us here, but I don't know why."

"Ah, well, a lot has happened while you've been missing, but all of that can wait until later. Let's get you out of this awful cabin and into the fresh air."

CHAPTER 38

Mrs Miggs was overjoyed to see Millie and Jonathan and confirmed she had seen the boy riding beside the driver on Sir Clive's carriage.

"I couldn't believe my eyes, and I waved and tried to attract your attention, Jonnie, but you were concentrating on holding the reins. What a terrible man to abduct you both like that, and thank goodness you didn't get taken to Australia; I've heard tales of the terrible life folk endure there. Now, you must be hungry. Give me a few minutes, and I'll rustle up some supper for you."

The cook rushed off to do what she did best and returned in no time with cold chicken, game pie, a large chunk of cheese, a large jar of pickles, and crusty bread and butter.

"Now, I'll leave you all in peace, but ring the bell if you need anything else."

When Mrs Miggs had left, Millie asked why Sir Clive, a man they had never seen before, had taken them prisoner. Robert and Annie glanced at each other, wondering whether the youngsters should get a sound night's sleep and recover from their ordeal before they told them their news.

"You must be so tired, my dears. Maybe it would be better to get some rest, and we'll tell you all that's been happening tomorrow."

"No, please tell us now, Robert, or we'll only lie awake all night wondering what you have to tell us. Is it bad news? Have you found Gran? Is she dead?"

"Oh, no, nothing like that, Millie. No, it's wonderful news, though I suspect it might keep you awake all night, anyway. Not long after the two of you went missing, I received a telegram from Sir Edgar's solicitors asking us to visit their office again with you and Jonnie as soon as possible. After we had reported to the police that you had been abducted, Annie and I went to see Mr Glover again and explained you were missing, and he told us a strange story.

"Lady Lilliana had recently attended the solicitor's office for the reading of her late husband's will. Given that your mother had passed away and your granny was missing, they decided there was no point in delaying the proceedings any longer. The will was correctly written and witnessed and was accompanied by a letter from Sir Edgar. In the letter, he explained that he had married your mother before he married Lady Lilliana and was a bigamist."

"Sorry, but what's a bigamist?"

"That's all right; let me explain. It's a person who gets married for a second time while their first wife or husband is still alive and they have not divorced. It's against the law and is a punishable offence."

"So, Sir Edgar was married to Mum first?"

"Yes, and that means his marriage to Lady Lilliana was a sham and not legal."

"Why would he do that? And why did Mum never tell us?"

"I'm sure there was nothing Sir Edgar would have liked better than to recognise your mother as his wife and live with her at Grantley House. However, if he had, he would not have inherited the house and estate from his father, nor the family title. He was an only child and didn't want to see his inheritance seized by the crown. His marriage to Lady

Lilliana had been arranged many years earlier, and he had to go along with his parents' wishes."

"Oh, how awful for Lady Lilliana; no wonder she hates us."

"Yes, the poor lady was completely unaware that Sir Edgar was already married to your mother and that he was a bigamist. She hated your mother because she thought she was his mistress, but this is far worse, and there's more. With the will and the letter, Sir Edgar enclosed his marriage certificate to your mother and your birth certificates; you are his legitimate children."

"So, what does that mean, and what's it got to do with Sir Clive Robinson? I still don't understand."

"It means that Jonathan will become Sir Jonathan Grantley and Grantley House, and the estate now belongs to him. Your father has not forgotten you, either, Millie; he's left you a large cottage on the estate, a considerable lump sum and an annual allowance. He was determined to recognise you as his children, though he could not do so when he was alive. You are both incredibly wealthy. He may have left money to your mother, Rosemary, and your granny, Emily, too, but we don't know about that yet."

Millie and Jonnie looked at Robert with shocked expressions, and it was the girl who found her voice first.

"I can't believe it. Why did he never tell us? He visited every week and never said a word."

"He couldn't risk any of this getting out, or Lady Lilliana would certainly have ensured he was jailed. She was wronged by Sir Edgar through no fault of her own, and perhaps understandably, she's a bitter woman. Also, if the truth had come out when his parents were alive, they may have disinherited their son and bequeathed the house and estate to someone else. Sir Edgar left a letter to Lilliana begging her forgiveness, but I suspect that will be a long time coming."

"So, how does Sir Clive fit into all this?"

"Sir Clive has been Lady Lilliana's lover for many years. He's an extremely wealthy shipping magnate with ships that travel all over the world. After we left the solicitors' office, we called on Lady Lilliana to see if she could shed any light on your whereabouts, and Percy went with us. As we arrived, a grand carriage was leaving, and luckily, Percy remembered it belonged to Sir Clive and that it matched the description Mrs Miggs had given us of the carriage she saw Jonnie riding on. We put two and two together and went to the police. Percy is a friend of the Police Commissioner, and he quickly got a search underway. We suspected Lady Lilliana would like both of you to disappear because then the courts might find in her favour, considering how shabbily she'd been treated, and may have allowed her to inherit Grantley House and everything else."

"So, what will happen now?"

"The police have gone to arrest Sir Clive Robinson, and he may face some years in jail. However, being so rich and probably with friends in high places, I wouldn't be surprised if he gets away with it. Lady Lilliana will also be implicated, but again, given her high standing in society, the courts may be lenient, given Sir Edgar's terrible treatment of her. Sir Edgar has left her their London townhouse and a considerable sum of money so she will not suffer financially."

"What about me and Jonnie? We have no idea how to run an estate like Grantley Manor. We just want to find our gran, return to Hartford, and live with Aunty Betsey and Uncle Ned. I miss Willie, too." Millie blushed. "We've become fond of each other."

Annie sent a warning glance to her husband, not wanting him to tell the youngsters they would need to reside in Grantley House to inherit. She felt they'd had enough to cope with for one day. Robert picked up on her thoughts and smiled reassuringly at Millie.

"Don't worry about any of that now. I think you and Jonnie need to take it easy and spend some time here with

Mrs Miggs for the next couple of days. Maybe stay in the garden rather than wander around the streets, though you should be safe enough now. Tomorrow we'll make an appointment to take you both to the solicitors' office again, and you can hear the latest news from them. I'm sure, given your inheritance, they will be even keener to discover your granny's whereabouts."

Annie rose to her feet. "Now, I think it's high time you two were in bed. I doubt you got much sleep last night in that horrible poky cabin, worrying about being taken to a strange country. You can rest easy tonight. You're safe, and we'll get all of this sorted out over the next few days. Come on, I'll come and tuck you in."

CHAPTER 39

The next morning was chilly, and despite it still being August, Annie was sure she could feel an autumnal nip in the air. She dressed quickly and pulled a warm shawl around her shoulders. Leaving Robert to enjoy a little longer in bed, the young woman tiptoed along the landing to the rooms of Millie and Jonathan and found them both still fast asleep. She descended the grand staircase, but rather than go to the formal dining room, she went to the kitchen, where she found Mrs Miggs making bread.

"Good morning, my dear. How can I help you? Are you ready for your breakfast?"

"No, it's all right, thank you, Mrs Miggs; I'll have my breakfast with Robert and Percy later, but can I sit with you and have a cup of tea?"

"Yes, of course; I'd like that. If you give me a minute to clean this dough off my hands, I'll make you a brew in no time."

"No, that's all right; you finish what you're doing. I'm quite capable of making a cup of tea. Would you like one?"

"That is kind of you, but a lady like you shouldn't be making tea. The two maids are lighting the fires in the drawing room and the dining room, for I feel it's a different air this morning and quite chilly, and I thought a fire wouldn't go amiss. When they return, we'll get on with cooking breakfast."

"I was a kitchen maid before I married Robert, Mrs Miggs, so I have no problem making tea."

"Were you, my dear? I must say you've learned well; I would never have known you were not born a lady, though you're so much more friendly than most ladies, I should perhaps have guessed. Tell me, do you have a family of your own?"

"Yes, I have a little girl called Selina, who is five, from my first marriage. Sadly, my husband, Harry, died in a terrible fire. A few years later, I married Robert, and we have twin boys, David and Thomas, who are just a year old. Robert and I had known each other for years and had been fond of each other for a long time, but we never thought we'd be able to marry, being from such different walks of life. However, fate smiled on us, and we're happy."

"My goodness, you must miss your children. Was your mother, Sabina, unable to come with Danny this time? I liked her when she came last time."

"Yes, I do miss the children terribly, and between you and me, I can't wait to go home. Mum remarried a while ago and has a baby girl called Katel. She's only a few months old and not yet weaned, and it would have been a long way to travel with a child of that age. I didn't like leaving my children, but I have a nursemaid whom the children adore, and I know Mum and my granny will visit them regularly."

"Yes, I remember your mother was carrying a child when she was here for Danny's last operation; I'm glad all went well. She was telling me she had lost a couple of children to diphtheria, and that's hard for any mother to bear. I'm glad she's found happiness again after losing her husband and then her children. Please give her my best wishes when you return to Hartford."

"I will, and hopefully, we should be on our way back to Devon soon. We'll visit Danny today and have our fingers crossed that we might bring him home. He's been so brave, and what the doctors have done is amazing. He was terribly deformed when he was born, and he's so lucky to have had the opportunity to get his mouth and his feet improved. He's a different child since his surgery, and this should be the last operation. Do you have any children, Mrs Miggs?"

"Yes, I have a son and a daughter, and they live nearby, so I see them regularly. Before I lost my husband, Les, he looked after the horses and drove the carriage for Mr Percy and his father before him. My daughter has asked me to live with her many a time, but I like it here and I enjoy caring for Mr Percy; he's almost like a son to me."

"I know he'd be sorry if you left. I've always thought it's such a pity he's never married; he loves children and would make such a good father. Perhaps when he comes to Devon, I might engineer a little matchmaking. Thank you for the tea and the chat; I've enjoyed talking to you, Mrs Miggs, but I think I hear the men in the dining room, so I'll join them for breakfast, and then we can get off to the hospital."

"Yes, of course, my dear."

As Mrs Miggs watched Annie leave the room, she realised young Lady Fellwood did not fully understand why Percy was unmarried and likely to remain so, but knew it was not her place to enlighten her.

Leaving Millie and Jonnie in the care of the elderly cook, Annie and Robert, accompanied by Percy, headed towards the hospital in his carriage. The driver stopped outside the hospital gates, and Annie and Robert alighted, leaving Percy to continue on his way. He planned to visit his friend, Mr Symes, the Police Commissioner, to hear the latest gossip about the arrest of Sir Clive and Lady Lilliana. Percy was worried that money might talk and that Sir Clive would try to wriggle his way out of the situation. However, Percy was also wealthy and determined that the gentleman would pay for his actions.

Geoffrey Turner and his colleague, Michael Brown, did not keep the Fellwoods waiting long, and the doctors shook the hands of their visitors.

"How lovely to see you again, Doctor Brown; we're so grateful to you for operating on Danny's other foot. Has the operation been successful?"

The skilled orthopaedic surgeon smiled reassuringly at the anxious couple. "Yes, indeed. This operation was much simpler than the one on Danny's other foot, and I'm confident it will be a complete success. I'm hoping he'll walk with only the slightest of limps, if at all, though, of course, we won't know for certain until the plaster comes off in a few weeks. Will you be staying in London or returning to Devon?"

"If Danny can travel, we'd prefer to head back to Devon. We have three young children, and my wife is missing them. She only came instead of Danny's mother, Sabina Webber, as she has recently given birth to a little girl, who is not yet weaned. I, too, have various business matters that demand my attention."

"I see. Are you travelling home by carriage? Danny will need to keep his leg raised if at all possible."

"We came to London on the train as it's so much quicker than by road, but thankfully, our host, Percy Chichester, kindly offered us his carriage to travel back to Devon. We planned this before we came to London. Percy fancies a trip on the train, and so he's going to visit us in a week or two for a holiday and will use his carriage to return to London afterwards."

"Then, yes, that will be fine. Now, shall we visit the patient? He's longing to see you, though, as usual, he has not complained at all and has been stoic throughout the whole procedure. He's a brave and determined young man."

Danny spotted Annie as soon as she entered the room. With a wide grin, he rose, picked up his crutches, and hobbled over to her.

"Oh, Annie, I'm so pleased to see you, and you, too, Robert."

With tears in her eyes, Annie hugged her little brother. "How are you, Danny? Does your foot hurt?"

"A bit, but not as bad as last time. This operation has been the least painful, and Doctor Brown says it should be my last. I hope I can run fast when it's healed. Can I come back to Percy's house with you today?"

Annie and Robert looked at the two doctors enquiringly, thinking they should have asked about this before meeting with Danny, for they did not want him to be disappointed.

"Yes, Danny, you may return to Grosvenor Square today, for we know you will receive the best care. It's been a pleasure to see you again, and I can't wait to see how fast you can run when your foot has mended. You must give it time, though, and not rush matters. Do you promise me you'll do that? It's important."

"Yes, I promise. Will you take the plaster off again like you did last time?"

"Yes, I will. I shall return to my home in Cullompton in a few weeks, and I'll visit you in Hartford to remove the plaster. In the meantime, you must rest as much as possible to give the bones time to knit back together." He turned his attention to Robert and Annie. "Do you have time to come for an evening meal with Clara and me before you leave the city? Clara is making one of her rare visits to the capital, and I was under strict instructions not to let you leave London until I persuaded you to come."

"Oh, yes, I'd love to see Clara again; can we do that, Robert?"

"Yes, of course; thank you so much, Geoffrey."

"Good, and please extend the invitation to Percy, too. How about you, Michael? Would you and your wife like to join us, maybe tomorrow night?"

"Yes, thank you, I'd like that, and I'm sure Esme would too."

"Good, that's settled then. Shall we say seven o'clock?"

CHAPTER 40

Danny was delighted to be back at Percy's home in Grosvenor Square and received a warm welcome from Millie, Jonnie, and Mrs Miggs. Robert carried him upstairs to his bedroom, where Annie insisted he must rest his foot. However, although Percy was not home when they arrived, he had left a parcel for Danny, who opened it with great excitement. Inside, he found a box with a picture on the front, and when he shook it, something inside rattled.

"Oh, what is it?"

"I think it's some sort of puzzle."

Robert was able to shed some light on the mystery. "It's a jigsaw, Danny. I used to have a few when I was a boy. Inside, you'll find lots of wooden pieces, and you have to fit them together to make a picture like the one on the front of the box. How clever of Percy. He knew you'd have to rest your foot, but you could sit at the table and make your puzzle at the same time. Millie and Jonnie can help you."

"Ooh, yes, can we do it now, Annie?"

"Yes, of course. Now, Robert and I would like to do some shopping; will you three be all right here with Mrs Miggs for the rest of the day?"

"Yes, we'll be fine. Are you going to buy something nice?"

Yes, Millie, I want to buy a new dress to wear tomorrow evening as Robert, Percy, and I have been invited to dinner with Doctor Turner and his wife. I also want to buy a few gifts to take home to Hartford. I haven't had much chance yet, what with everything else that's been happening. Millie and Jonnie, you can tell Danny what an exciting time you've had."

Jonnie brightened. "Oh yes, Danny, we have such a story to tell you. Me and Millie were kidnapped, and we were held prisoner in a tiny cabin on a huge ship, but then Robert and Percy fetched the police, and we were rescued. We're rich now, too. I'll buy you another jigsaw when I get some money."

Leaving Jonnie enjoying himself, telling Danny all about their adventure, Robert and Annie left the house and took a carriage to Oxford Street.

"Are you sure you don't mind taking me shopping, Robert? I know it's something you're not keen on."

"No, I don't mind. You never ask for much, and I like to treat you. We'll go to one of the classy shops and find a stunning dress for you to wear tomorrow night. I know; I'll take you to Liberty's and let them find you a complete outfit."

"Won't that be terribly expensive?"

"Yes, it will, but I'm in a good mood, and I like to treat you. When we've finished shopping, would you mind if we went to Sotheby's with the Spanish pieces of eight Fred asked me to get valued? I've been meaning to do it ever since we arrived in London, but there's been so much else going on."

"Yes, of course, I'd forgotten all about them."

A few hours later, Annie and Robert returned to Percy's house. They were exhausted from their shopping trip, but Annie was in high spirits, having purchased a stylish bustle dress. It was a deep emerald green, a colour she knew enhanced her coppery red hair and green eyes; it reminded her of a dress she had worn to a staff Christmas party when she was a maid at Hartford Manor. That dress had once belonged to Robert's sister, Victoria, and Annie had turned many heads that night, much to the housekeeper, Miss Wetherby's annoyance. Robert had also insisted on purchasing some new underwear and petticoats, gloves, stockings and shoes for Annie, and the ladies at Liberty's, the stylish outfitters, had thoroughly enjoyed assisting Annie in her purchases.

They spent far longer in the boutique than expected, but made time to visit many other shops where Annie bought presents for their children, her siblings, and Sabina, Arthur, and Liza. She still found it hard to believe she could spend so much money after being only a step away from the workhouse a few years earlier. At Sotheby's, they were told that the expert numismatist was unavailable that day, and Robert agreed to return later in the week. They arrived home to find that Percy had just arrived, and they asked him what he had learned from Mr Symes.

"I'm glad I went to see him, for Sir Clive also has friends in high places, one of them being a Chief Inspector in the Metropolitan Police, and that particular gentleman was willing to consider the whole matter a simple misunderstanding and take no further action. However, when I explained the full story to Gordon Symes, he lost no time in having Sir Clive arrested, and I'm pleased to tell you that he's behind bars as we speak and will stand trial for kidnapping. I'm not sure how he will explain this situation to his wife or his father-in-law, but I'd dearly like to be a fly on the wall! The case against Lilliana is weaker, for it will be difficult to prove she knew what Sir Clive had arranged, but she has been held for questioning.

"Captain Lethaby is cooperating with the police and has told them Sir Clive forced him to take the children aboard by threatening him that he would lose his job and be unable to return to his family in Australia if he refused. Sir Clive also told him that if Millie and Jonathan gave him any trouble, no one would miss them should they fall overboard!"

"Oh no, how terrible. They could have been murdered!"

"Yes, and I'm sure it would have suited Lady Lilliana perfectly if they were no longer in the picture. Anyway, I have assured Captain Lethaby that I know a few wealthy ship owners and, should he lose his job, I will ensure he finds another. I think he might choose to leave the employ of Sir Clive anyway, for he does not like the man and with reason.

"Now, I hope this is all right with you, but I've said you'll take Millie and Jonathan to Marlborough Street Police Station tomorrow so they can answer some questions; will that be convenient?"

"Yes, that's not a problem because we're taking them to the solicitor's office so they can hear about their inheritance. Danny can stay here with Mrs Miggs and rest for the day."

"I have nothing on tomorrow, apart from our meal with the Turners in the evening, so I can spend some time with Danny. As you know, we enjoy each other's company."

Early the following day, Robert and Annie borrowed Percy's carriage to travel to the police station with Millie and Jonathan. They were interviewed individually and questioned about how Sir Clive had tricked them into his carriage and then taken them to the ship where they were imprisoned. They confirmed they had not been harmed and that the captain had treated them kindly. After their interviews, Robert asked if the youngsters would need to be present at the trial. However, knowing the family was soon to be returning to Devon, the Police Commissioner felt that their statements and the testimony of Captain Lethaby would be sufficient.

Pleased that the matter had been dealt with, their carriage next took them to the solicitors' office, where they once more met with Mr Glover and Mr Brown. The receptionist showed them in, and the two learned gentlemen rose to their feet to welcome them.

"Come in, come in; we're so pleased to see you're safe and sound after your terrible ordeal. It is quite the talk of the town. Please, be seated, and we can explain a few matters to you, but first, may I offer you some refreshments?"

"Thank you. A drink would be most welcome."

When tea, lemonade, and cakes had been provided, Mr Brown pushed his spectacles up his rather bony nose and put his two hands together as if he were about to pray.

"Now, Millicent and Jonathan, I have some excellent news to share with you, though I'm sure Lord and Lady Fellwood have told you a few details. It turns out that Sir Edgar Grantley married your mother, Rosemary Gibbs, before his bigamous marriage to Lady Lilliana. This means you are his legitimate children, and he has recognised you as such in his will. He also left an inheritance to his wife, Rosemary, and her mother, Emily Gibbs. Sadly, the former has passed away, and, at present, the latter is missing, but we'll come to that.

"Jonathan, you will inherit Sir Edgar's title, which means you will be known as Sir Jonathan Grantley. You also own Grantley House and the surrounding estate, which is extensive. However, there is one condition to this inheritance, and that is that you must reside in Grantley House."

Millie and Jonnie glanced at each other and then at the solicitor, concern written all over their faces. Millie found her voice first.

"Oh, but sir, we like living with our Aunty Betsey and Uncle Ned in Hartford. We wouldn't know what to do in Grantley House; is there any way around this?"

"Not for Jonathan, no; I'm afraid he has to live most of the time on the estate to inherit. However, although you, too, have an inheritance, Millicent, you do not have to live there. Your father has left you a substantial lump sum and an annual allowance from the estate, plus a desirable cottage on the grounds. When you return to Devon, I suggest that you both visit Grantley House and see what a wonderful place it would be to live. Perhaps your aunt and uncle would like to live there with you?"

"I don't think Aunty Betsey and Uncle Ned would ever leave Hartford. They've lived there all their lives, and all their family are there. What do you think, Annie?"

"No, I'm sure Gran and Grandad won't leave Hartford, but don't worry, Robert and I will help you with everything. This is an amazing opportunity for you both, and at least you know the village of Brampford Speke and have friends there."

"That's true, Annie, but you see, Willie and I have feelings for each other, and he's asked me to marry him, though we were waiting for the right time to tell people."

Annie was about to say that at sixteen, Millie was far too young to consider marriage, but then she glanced at her husband and remembered that she had only been that age when she first wanted to marry Robert.

"Millie, I don't want to live in Grantley House on my own. You will come with me, won't you?"

The solicitor took control of the situation. "Now, Jonathan, don't worry about this. These details can be sorted out in good time, and there's no rush to do anything. I suggest you visit Grantley House and inspect the estate to see what you think of it. Maybe you'll find a satisfactory way of complying with the terms of the will. In the meantime, we must find your granny, Emily Gibbs, for she, too, is a beneficiary of the will. We have placed advertisements in several newspapers throughout Devon, for that is where she's most likely to be, and we've offered a reward for information as to her whereabouts; hopefully, someone will come forward. However, in the meantime, I would like to congratulate you on your inheritance, and Millicent, I have something here for you."

The solicitor reached into his drawer and withdrew something wrapped in soft tissue paper.

"This is the brooch that Sir Edgar left to your mother, and now it is yours, as he wished. You may now wear it with pride, for it is an exquisite piece."

Slowly, Millie unwrapped the sparkling sapphire and diamond brooch and her eyes misted with tears, as Annie gently pinned it to her lapel.

CHAPTER 41

NEWTON ST CYRES

A few days later, Robert and Annie, accompanied by Millie and Jonnie, said their goodbyes to Mrs Miggs and Percy and set off in the carriage on the long journey back to North Devon. They would be travelling for several days, as they wanted to make sure Danny got plenty of rest. Although he would sit with his foot raised in the carriage, the roads were in poor condition, and the constant jolting was tiring.

After a few days, they arrived in Newton St Cyres, and Millie nudged Jonnie as she recognised some of the scenery.

"Look, Jonnie, this is where we stayed at Hilldale Farm with the March family; I wonder if they're all right and if Mrs March had a boy or a girl. I think her baby was due in June."

"Do you know the way to the farm where you stayed?"

"Yes, it's down the next lane on the left."

"Would you like to visit your friends? I'd like to thank them for taking you in."

"Oh, yes, I'd love to see them all again. We got on so well with Gertie, Rosie, Albert, and Walter, didn't we, Jonnie?"

"Yes, and perhaps we can see the calf we helped deliver. You know, I called her Holly because it was Christmas time."

"We'll do that, then. We're staying at the Fox and Hounds Inn in Eggesford tonight, and that's not far from here, so we can easily call in and see the March family, as long as they don't mind us turning up unexpectedly."

"No, I don't think they'll mind; I think they'd like to know we're all right and that we found our relatives."

Robert called to the driver and gave him directions, and in no time, the carriage entered the farmyard.

Hubert March was feeding the pigs, and as he stood up and eased his back, he squinted in surprise at the grand carriage that had come to a halt before him. He removed his cap and scratched his bald head before climbing over the pigsty wall and approaching the vehicle. His puzzled expression became one of joy as he caught sight of Millie and Jonnie through the window. The two youngsters leapt out of the carriage and hugged the old man.

"Oh, Mr March, I'm so pleased to see you again."

"And I, you, Millie, but what a grand carriage you're riding in. Won't you introduce me to your friends?"

"Yes, of course. This is Lord and Lady Fellwood, and this is Danny Carter, who has recently had an operation on his foot in London. We have such a lot to tell you, Mr March."

Hubert held out his hand to Robert and Annie and smiled at Danny. "I'm pleased to meet you, sir, and you, ma'am. I take it you must be related to Millie and Jonnie?"

"Hello, Mr March. Yes, my wife is their cousin, and I'm pleased to meet you, too. We were passing in the carriage on our way back to Hartford and decided to call in and thank you and your wife for taking care of Millie and Jonnie when they were in such desperate need. We're so grateful to you."

"We found our relatives in Hartford, Mr March, but we're so worried about Gran. We thought she would be in the Exeter workhouse, but she left there and never arrived in Hartford, so we don't know where else to look for her."

"Oh, I'm sorry to hear that, my dear, but maybe she'll turn up safe and sound yet. It was a pleasure to offer you a roof over your heads, but now, you must come in and see Angela and the children, and another guest we have staying at the moment." With an amused expression, Hubert led his visitors through the back door and into the kitchen.

It was a cosy scene. Angela had just fed her new baby and gently laid the sleeping child in its crib. Albert and Walter were playing with some toys on the floor, and they cried out excitedly when they spotted Millie and Jonnie.

"Millie and Jonnie, you've come back."

Hubert introduced everyone, and Angela, too, seemed amused about something.

"Where are Gertie and Rosie? And how is your new baby? Did you have a boy or a girl, Mrs March?"

"Gertie and Rosie are in the parlour doing some sewing with a friend we have staying, and yes, Jessica is a few weeks old now and doing well. I'll take you to see the girls and introduce you to my friend."

Angela led the way into the parlour, and she and her husband enjoyed seeing Millie and Jonnie's shocked expressions as the old lady in the rocking chair suddenly smiled broadly and struggled to her feet.

"Oh, Millie and Jonnie! I can't believe my eyes! Thank goodness you're both all right. I've been so worried about you. How did you know I was here? Come here, both of you." Emily put her arms around both grandchildren and held them tightly, tears running down her wrinkled old cheeks.

"Gran! Oh, Gran, we thought we'd lost you! We didn't know you were here. This is Annie and Robert Fellwood, and Annie is my cousin. It's a long story, but we're on our way home from London, and we called in to say hello to the March family, for they were so kind to Jonnie and me. But how did you get here? And why didn't you come to Hartford?"

"I think you all have a lot of catching up to do, by the sound of it. I'll make us a pot of tea, and you can relax and sort things out. Gertie and Rosie, come and give me a hand, please. Now, Danny and Jonnie, would you like to play with Albert and Walter in the kitchen, or do you want to sit in the parlour?"

Danny quickly elected to play with the other boys, but Jonnie wanted to stay near his granny and happily crept onto her knee to enjoy a cuddle.

"How about your husband, Mrs March; is he well?"

"Yes, Vivian's fine, thank you, but he's outside working in the fields as usual. He'll be in for his tea a bit later, and you're all welcome to stay and eat with us if you like?"

"That's kind of you, Mrs March, but no, we'll eat at the Fox and Hounds Inn later. There are rather a lot of us, and we don't want to put you to too much trouble."

It's no trouble, though it won't be anything fancy. I have plenty of potatoes, bacon and eggs, but it's up to you. I just thought you had a lot of catching up to do."

"That's true if you're sure. It's generous of you, thank you."

"That's settled, then, and it won't take you long to get to the Fox and Hounds, for it's only a short distance down the road. I'm afraid I don't have enough beds to offer you all to stay."

Once they were settled with a cup of tea and a piece of fruit cake, Millie urged Emily to tell her story.

"Well, after you left me that night in Brampford Speke, I was so worried about you, and I wondered if I'd done the right thing by sending you off on such a journey in the middle of winter. I felt so ill, though, and I honestly thought my time was up. I didn't want you to find me dead in my bed like you did your poor mother. I spent a restless night, and early the next morning, I was awoken by someone hammering on the door. I couldn't think who it was because Ollie and Agnes from next door always let themselves in.

Anyway, I tried to get out of bed, but I was too weak, and then, to my amazement, Lady Lilliana Grantley burst into my room and demanded to know where you both were."

"What did you say?"

"I told her your mother had died and that I expected to join her soon, and I said I'd sent you to relatives in Somerset."

"That was clever, Gran, sending her the wrong way."

"She didn't believe me. She stormed off and searched the entire house, and then she had her men search all the other houses nearby, but of course, they found nothing. She was so angry and insisted you had stolen her brooch and said she would send the police after you. I demanded she leave my house, but that infuriated her even more, and she reminded me it wasn't my house but her house and that I must leave immediately. I begged for some time to gain a little more strength, but she was having none of it and instructed her groom to carry me downstairs and put me outside on the ground."

"That's terrible. You were so ill, and it was bitterly cold."

"Aye, but she didn't care. She let my neighbours gather a few of my bits and pieces and then locked the door and went off with the key. She wouldn't even let the neighbours or the vicar take me in. She threatened them with eviction, too, if they did."

"What a horrible woman."

"Yes, but after all, she knew my Rosemary had been her husband's lover for many years. I can understand why she was bitter; I think I would have been in the same circumstances."

Millie, Robert, and Annie grinned to themselves but said nothing, leaving their news until Emily had finished telling her story.

"So what happened next? Is that when the vicar took you to the workhouse?"

"Yes, he was so disgusted with Lady Lilliana's lack of compassion that he insisted on taking me to the Exeter workhouse on his cart. A few kind neighbours gave me a pillow and some blankets, but it was so cold that I wondered if I would make it there alive. Anyway, I did, and the vicar took me to their infirmary, for he knew I would be better looked after there. Once they knew I had typhoid, they didn't want me mixing with the other inmates anyway."

"Robert and Annie took me to the workhouse searching for you, Gran, but the lady said you'd discharged yourself and didn't know where you'd gone. How did you get from Exeter to here? Did you walk? I'm surprised you were strong enough."

"No, my dear, I didn't walk. I was rescued by a kind and loyal friend. After you left here, Hubert kept worrying about me and hated to think of me sick and all alone in my cottage. When the weather improved, he decided to go to Brampford Speke to see if I was all right, and Ollie and Agnes told him I'd been taken to the workhouse. He was sorry to hear that because we were raised there together as children and were always close friends. He didn't like to think of me back there on my own. I'd been there for two or three weeks when I was told I had a visitor. I thought it must be you two, but then Hubert walked in, wearing a huge grin. It was such a wonderful surprise."

"Oh, Mr March, thank you so much for rescuing Gran. I expect we have you to thank that she's still alive. But Gran, why didn't you come to Hartford and find us when you were better? We've been so worried."

"I wanted to do that, but I had to regain my strength first. Then, just when I thought I was fit enough to travel, I fell and broke my ankle. It was so stupid. It was the first time I'd been outside since I got here, and I slipped on the cobbles. Hubert took me to the hospital, and they put a plaster on, and I've been laid up ever since. The plaster came off last week, and I'm beginning to hobble around. Hubert was going to come to Hartford with me on the train in a week or two to try to find you. I would have written if I'd known where you were. But now you must tell me how you got on. Did you find my father's family? And Millie, I can't believe you're wearing that pretty brooch so blatantly on your collar when I told you to keep it hidden. You'll end up in jail if Lady Lilliana sees it."

"Ah, well, we have a lot to tell you, too, Gran. Our journey to Hartford took us some weeks, and we had quite a few problems. Most folk were kind to us, but not all, and I'll tell you more about that another time. When we finally got to Hartford, we didn't know how to find our relatives. We asked at an inn called The Three Pigeons, and the landlord said he had lived there a long time, but he knew of no one in the village by the name of Lovering. Then we asked the vicar, and he said the same. We were desperate that night, for we didn't know what to do, and it was cold and raining hard. We had nowhere to sleep, but then I remembered what you'd said, and we sheltered in the church. In the morning, the vicar found us and offered to take us to the workhouse, but I said we wanted to search for our relatives a bit longer. He was kind and took us to the vicarage, where his cook gave us a big bowl of porridge, and we were so glad of it. She didn't know anyone called Lovering, but suggested we look at the gravestones in the churchyard in case they had died.

"It was a good idea because eventually, we found the grave of Ellen Lovering, who died in 1821. Her son, Norman, who also died in 1821, was only three, and he was buried with her. The grave was well tended, and there was a bunch of snowdrops on it, so we could see someone was looking after it. We decided to ask at the village shop if they knew who the grave belonged to."

"And were the people at the shop able to help?"

"Yes, two sisters worked there, Harriet and Theresa Carter, and Theresa knew the grave and said it was her granny, Betsey, who cared for the grave. She wasn't sure, but she thought Ellen was Betsey's mother, and Norman was her brother."

Angela had been busy cooking the tea and half listening to the story unfold, but she now appeared in the doorway.

"I'm sorry to interrupt, but Vivian has come in from work, and the tea is ready. Would you all like to come and eat and then continue with your tale afterwards?"

The guests thanked Angela and, not wanting to appear rude, went to eat, though they were all desperate to hear the rest of the story.

CHAPTER 42

Having enjoyed a hastily put-together tea of bacon, sausages, eggs and fried potato, Emily was keen to hear the rest of their story.

"So, did you find Betsey? And was she called Lovering?"

"Yes, Gran, we did, and she was. She was attending a funeral that afternoon, and when Theresa accompanied us back to the churchyard, Betsey was actually standing by the Lovering grave with two men. It was raining, and it wasn't until it stopped and she removed her shawl from her head that we could see her properly, and we had such a shock."

"Why? Is there something wrong with her?"

"No, not at all, but she's the spitting image of you, Gran. I couldn't believe the likeness, but I knew then that you must be related."

"Do you know how?"

"Yes, her mother was called Ellen, and she was the first wife of your father, Adam Lovering. They had ten children together, but most died as infants. The only two living now are Barney and Betsey; you have a half-brother and half-sister, Gran."

"Do I? That's amazing. Since my mother died when I was little, I've always thought I was completely alone in the world with no kin. I'm so pleased, and I can't wait to meet them."

"Yes, and they want to meet you, too. Betsey is married to Ned Carter, and they have a large family. Until recently, they were the innkeepers of The Red Lion in Hartford. They've retired to a little cottage now, and when they realised we were related, they offered us a home. They've been so kind to us. Uncle Barney lives in Wales, and he's married with a family, too."

"So why did my father leave Ellen, Barney, and Betsey?"

"He wasn't a good man, Gran, but I think you already know that. He was having an affair with another woman in the village, and he was also an alcoholic. When he was drunk, he used to beat Ellen, and on the last occasion he did so, she went into labour prematurely, and she and the baby boy she was carrying died."

"Oh, what a hateful man. How sad. Was that the little boy in the grave with her? Norman, I think you said his name was?"

"No, the premature baby is in the grave with her, but he was unnamed. No, the little boy called Norman was three when he died. I'm afraid Adam Lovering ran away with his lover and left Betsey and Norman to fend for themselves. It was Christmas, and he told them he had to go away for a few days and to stay in the cottage and not answer the door. They soon ran out of food and wood for the fire, but were afraid to seek help and upset their father. By the time they were found, they were both seriously ill from the lack of food and being so cold. Fortunately, Betsey, who was six, survived, but poor little Norman died."

"That's terrible. What an awful thing to do. What happened to Betsey?"

"She was taken in by Mal and Kezia Carter, who owned The Red Lion Inn next door. They were Betsey's husband, Ned's parents. She was raised with him and his brother, Silas, and eventually she married Ned."

"Goodness, what a tale. You couldn't make it up. And how do you fit into this family, Annie?"

"Betsey and Ned are my grandparents. My dad, Tom Carter, was their son, but sadly, he died of consumption several years ago. There are a lot of us in the Carter family, Aunty Emily; you certainly have a lot of kin now."

"It's lovely to hear you call me Aunty Emily, and I'm sorry to hear about your dad. This is all such a shock, but I'm delighted that some good has come out of bad. If I hadn't been so worried about Lady Lilliana throwing us out of our cottage and making trouble for you, Millie, I would never have sent you on such a dangerous journey, and we would never have known all this. I must insist you take that brooch off, though, my dear. It's not safe to flaunt it; Lady Lilliana will not give up, and she could yet have you sent to jail or hanged."

"There's still a lot you don't know, Gran, and this is even more unbelievable; I'm glad you're sitting down. It turns out that Sir Edgar married Mum before he married Lady Lilliana; he was a bigamist, and he left a letter with his will confessing his sins. He was never legally married to Lady Lilliana."

"What! No, I don't believe it. Rosemary would have told me."

"She couldn't. They kept it a secret between themselves so that Sir Edgar could inherit Grantley House and the estate, but he was never a true husband to Lady Lilliana, and it's no wonder she's bitter. There's more to come, too, Gran. Jonnie, come here, a minute."

Jonnie tore himself away from playing with his friends. "What do you want, Millie?"

"Gran, I want to introduce you to Sir Jonathan Grantley!"

Emily's face was a picture as she gaped open-mouthed at her grandson. "What do you mean?"

"As Mum was married to Sir Edgar, Jonnie and I are not bastards; we're his rightful heirs and Jonathan will take his title. We're rich, Gran, and the brooch is mine."

By the time the rest of the story had been told, it was late evening, and Robert said they must drive to The Fox and Hounds Inn before it was too dark to see the way and the doors might be locked. He promised they would return in the morning to discuss the next steps.

The following day, Robert, Annie, and the three youngsters returned to Hilldale Farm, where Emily confessed she had spent a restless night.

"There's so much to think about; my mind was in a whirl last night, and there's something Hubert and I want to tell you all. We haven't said anything about this until now, not even to Angela and Vivian, but now that I'm better, we're planning to get married. We've known each other all our lives and have always had feelings for each other, though we both ended up marrying someone else. We want to be together now, even though we haven't decided where we'll live yet."

"Oh, my goodness! Congratulations; I'm so pleased for you both." Vivian shook his father's hand and kissed Emily's cheek. "Dad, it's years since you lost Mum, and you deserve some happiness."

Angela joined in. "That's great news, Dad, and needless to say, Hilldale Farm will always be your home, and we'd be happy for you and Emily to continue living here."

"Thanks, Angela; I thought you'd say that, and we'll see, but I think we might try to get a little place of our own. I want to take it easy in my last few years and enjoy Emily's company."

"I couldn't sleep last night, either, Gran, because there's something else I haven't told you yet. I've fallen in love with Annie's brother, Willie, and before I left for London, he proposed to me. I said yes, but with so much else going on, we haven't told many people."

"Oh, my goodness, but you're only sixteen, Millie. Are you sure about this?"

"Yes, definitely, Gran. Willie's a farm manager living in a tied cottage. He has a reliable job and can provide for me, and we love each other. I know he's the man for me."

"Well, I suppose I was only a teenager when I married Lenny, so I can't say too much. Congratulations, my dear. I'm not sure my heart will take many more shocks after the last day or two. Hubert and I were talking last night, and now that my ankle has mended, I want to travel to Hartford to meet Betsey and Ned."

"Annie and I were discussing that last night, too, Emily, and if you like, we thought we could hire another carriage for you to travel to Hartford with us. It would be much more comfortable for you than the train, and you're welcome to stay at Hartford Manor with us. Annie can't wait to introduce you to Betsey."

"Thank you, Robert, but I'm not sure we can afford to hire a carriage. We can catch the next stagecoach that calls into Newton St Cyres, though that would have to be tomorrow now."

"No, I'm willing to pay, and I'd like us all to travel together. Millie and Jonnie can ride with you; they've been so worried about you and need to spend some time with you. It will give Danny more space to stretch out his leg, too. Our journey has been a little cramped, to say the least."

"That would be wonderful if you're sure. Thank you so much."

CHAPTER 43

HARTFORD

There was great excitement when the two carriages pulled into Hartford Manor's driveway. It was late in the afternoon, and Naomi, the children's nursemaid, was taking the twins, Thomas and David, for a walk in their pram whilst Selina walked beside them. Selina came bounding over to the carriage and climbed onto the step before Annie had time to alight.

"Mummy, Mummy, you're home! Hello Papa and Danny, is your foot mended?"

Annie took the little girl into her arms and hugged her tightly. "Oh, Selina, I've missed you so much; are you all right?"

"Yes, I'm fine, thank you, Mummy. I've been to Granny Sabina's and Granny Betsey's houses a lot. Can you walk, Danny?"

Robert lifted the little boy from the carriage and handed him his crutches.

"Yes, of course, I can walk, and soon I'll be able to run faster than you."

"Huh, I don't think so, but you can try."

Robert also hugged Selina whilst Annie went to the pram to see her two babies. "Is everything all right, Naomi?"

"Yes, ma'am."

The two little boys, who were now fifteen months old, were a little shy of their parents at first, but when Robert and Annie held out their arms to them and picked them up, they soon snuggled in and were chuckling away.

"Oh, it's so nice to be home. I wonder where Mum and Liza are? It's not like the Lodge House to be empty, though I know the children are at school."

"Oh, ma'am, I happen to know that they're with your grandparents, Betsey and Ned, today. I took the twins to see Sabina yesterday, and she mentioned that she and Liza were going to take baby Katel and spend the day with them. They've both been a bit under the weather for the last week or two since losing George."

"What do you mean, Naomi? Since losing George? Do you mean my Uncle George?"

"Oh, yes, ma'am; I'm sorry if you didn't know, but George Carter passed away quite suddenly a few weeks ago. It's been a difficult time for his family."

"Oh, my goodness. I knew he'd not been himself for a while, but I didn't think it was anything serious. What did he die of?"

"The word is that a rat bite he'd had for some time had never healed properly and became infected. He died of blood poisoning."

"Oh, poor Gran and Grandad, how awful to lose another son. Poor George, too, of course. Robert, I must go and see them all later and take Danny home."

"Yes, of course, but let's get our visitors settled in first."

Emily, Hubert, Millie, and Jonathan had been patiently waiting while Annie and Robert were reunited with their children, and now Annie turned to them.

"I'm so sorry; how rude of me to leave you standing there. Please come inside, and we'll get you settled in. Millie and Jonnie, we'll take you to your Aunty Betsey and Uncle Ned's a little later."

Leaving Emily and Hubert to rest after the long journey, Annie and Robert, accompanied by Danny, their three children, and Millie and Jonnie, walked to the Lodge House. Robert pushed Danny in a wheelchair as it was too far for him to walk on his crutches. Thankfully, Sabina, Liza, and the children were now home, and Sabina hugged Danny and then Annie.

"Oh, my dears, how wonderful to see you both. Danny, how's your foot? Does it hurt?"

"Not much, Mum. Doctor Brown says I won't need any more operations, and he thinks that when the plaster is taken off, I'll soon be able to run as fast as everyone else."

"I hope so, Danny, you deserve to. You've been so brave. You, Selina, and Jonnie can play with Helen and Stephen if you like. They're in the sitting room." Turning to Millie, she asked, "And how about you, my dear? Did you return the brooch and clear your name? And how about your granny; is there any news?"

Annie grinned. "You'd better put the kettle on, Mum. Millie has a long story to tell you, and then we must call on Granny and Grandad, for we have good news for them, and it sounds like they need some. I was shocked to hear about Uncle George. I never liked him much, but he was not an old man and had improved in recent years."

"Yes, I'm afraid it's hit Betsey and Ned hard. George is the third son they've lost, and that's difficult for any parents to take. His death happened so suddenly, though he'd been unwell for a while. Louis Blaquiere had only visited him hours before he died to ask for Theresa's hand in marriage, and to everyone's surprise, George gave his blessing. Now, of course, they'll have to wait at least a few months before a wedding would be acceptable."

An hour later, having divulged all of their news and leaving Selina and the twins to play with the other children, Annie and Robert accompanied Millie and Jonathan to Sunset

Cottage. It was a warm evening, and they found Betsey and Ned sitting in their favourite spot in the back garden.

"Hello, Granny and Grandad; it's lovely to see you both." Annie hugged the elderly couple. "We've brought Millie and Jonnie back to you, safe and sound, and I'm so sorry to hear about Uncle George; it was such a shock."

"Aye, for us, too, poor man. Although he'd not been in the best of health, none of us saw that coming, not even Doctor Luckett, and he usually knows his stuff. Anyway, it's no use dwelling on it; how did you get on in London? Is Danny all right? Have you cleared your name about the brooch? And is there any sign of your granny? I can tell you someone who'll be glad to see you back, Millie, and that's Willie. He's been like a lost sheep these last few weeks. He's called every few days to see if we know when you'd be coming home. Got it bad he has, poor lad; I only hope you feel the same, or his heart will be broken."

"Goodness, Gran; one question at a time. Danny's operation was a success, and yes, we have cleared Millie's name of theft, though that's a long story, but perhaps best of all, we've found Emily. We have found your half-sister, Gran, and she and Hubert, her husband-to-be, are resting at Hartford Manor as we speak. We'll bring them to see you tomorrow." She grinned. "Millie, I'll leave you to tell Gran about Willie."

"Oh, that's wonderful news, isn't it, Ned? We can't wait to meet Emily. We'll have to write to Barney and tell him he has a new half-sister. I wonder if he'll come and visit. Now, what about Willie? Have you missed him, Millie?"

"Yes, Aunty Betsey, I've missed Willie a lot because before I went to London, he asked me to marry him, and I said yes."

"Oh, my dear. I'm so pleased. Congratulations!"

Betsey and Ned were astounded to hear the story of the bigamous Sir Edgar and delighted that Millie and Jonnie would now be recognised as his children.

"My goodness, today is full of surprises. It sounds as if we'll need to call you, sir, from now on, Jonnie. I hope you won't become too high and mighty to live in our little cottage."

Millie frowned. "That's the one problem with all of this, Uncle Ned. One of the conditions of the will is that to inherit, Jonnie has to live in Grantley House. Sir Edgar left me a cottage on the grounds, too, but Willie and I planned to live in a tied cottage at Sugworthy Farm after we were married so that he could continue working for Marrok Fellwood. Willie has worked there for years and loves the place. I don't want to move to Brampford Speke without him, even if it is to a lovely cottage. We wondered if you and Aunty Betsey would like to live in Grantley House with Jonnie."

Ned looked at the girl in surprise. "Oh, my dear, that's a generous offer, thank you, but no, I don't even need to discuss it with Betsey to know that neither of us would ever want to leave Hartford. No, we've lived here all our lives and will die here, surrounded by our family. I'm sorry, but I'm afraid you'll have to find another solution to that difficult problem."

"Before we go, Ned, I have good news for you and Betsey." Robert smiled at the elderly couple. "I think this will come as quite a surprise, but do you remember that old trunk that your father found in the attic when you and your brother, Silas, were boys?"

"Aye, of course; we were so excited. Dad was desperately hard up at the time, and we hoped it contained treasure, but no such luck. There was an old map showing tunnels in the village that Raymond Chugg found useful for his smuggling. What makes you mention that? It was so many years ago."

"Well, when you and Betsey left the inn, Fred and George brought the trunk down again as you suggested, and they asked me if I would take the foreign coins to London and get them valued. There was a bundle of old papers too, all tied up with ribbon, and they were written in faded Latin that I struggled to read, although I learned the language at school."

"That was a good idea to take them to an expert; what did he say? Are they worth anything? I've always been curious, but at the time, we were worried that if we let people know about the coins, we might be accused of stealing them, for we didn't know where they came from."

"I had to leave the coins and the bundle of papers with two experts in Sotheby's to be examined. That's an auction house in London. Just before I left London, I received a letter from them, and I haven't even told Annie this yet because I wanted to surprise you all together. The numismatist, or coin expert, says the coins are Spanish pieces of eight, and they are made of solid silver. As you know, the coins were large and called pieces of eight because they were worth eight reales. Silver is a soft metal, and the coins could be split into eight bits, which people used as smaller denominations."

"Ah, Raymond Chugg thought they were pieces of eight, but they had stopped being legal tender by the time we found them. It was interesting to see them; I remember they all had Spanish heads of royalty on one side, and on the other, some had the Pillars of Hercules, and others had the Catholic Church orb with a cross. Worthless, then, are they?"

"No, far from it. Quite apart from the value of the considerable amount of silver in each coin, they are of historical value, and coin collectors will be interested in buying them because, as you say, they were last minted in 1825, and the coins we found were much older than that. The expert at Sotheby's asked in his letter if we would like him to auction the coins at their next sale, and he thinks they will make a lot of money."

"No! Really? Well, when I think about how Mum and Dad struggled to meet the repayments on their loan for a new roof, and all the time, the means to pay for it were sitting just beneath it. I wish I could tell them. I wonder where the coins came from in the first place; perhaps my ancestor, Jago Carter, was a pirate after all!" Ned grinned at Betsey. What do you think, love? Should the coins be sold?"

"Aye, I think so. It's what Uncle Mal and Auntie Kezzie would want, especially if it can benefit the whole family."

"When George and Fred gave me the coins, they insisted that if they were worth anything, then the money should come to you, Ned, and your brother, Silas, and I think that's right, don't you?"

"Aye, it would be grand to help Silas out; he's never had much, and plenty of people in our family would benefit from a nice inheritance. What do you say, Betsey?"

"Yes, I think we should share it fifty-fifty with Silas, and then we can do what we like with our half. I always felt sorry for Silas because, as the eldest son, you inherited The Red Lion Inn, Ned, and he didn't get anything. This legacy will make up for it."

"Ah, now that brings me on to my other news. The document expert at Sotheby's managed to read the Latin on those old papers, and they are the deeds to The Red Lion Inn. They date from around 1450 and make interesting reading. One of my ancestors, Lord John Fellwood, gifted the land and the inn to one Jeremiah Carter in return for saving the life of his son when he was set upon by robbers. It seems our families have been looking out for each other for a very long time!"

The following day, Annie, Emily, and Hubert travelled to Sunset Cottage in a small pony and trap to meet Betsey and Ned, as it was too far for Emily to walk on her newly mended ankle. It was an emotional time as the two half-sisters looked at one another in disbelief.

"Oh, my dear, I'm so pleased to finally meet you. I can hardly believe I have a little sister after all these years!"

"Me, too, Betsey. I'm so pleased to find I have living relatives when all my life I thought I had no one. Mind you, no one can doubt we're related, can they? It's almost like looking in the mirror."

"It is. I never thought about Dad going on to marry someone else, but then, there was no reason why he shouldn't after Mum died."

"I was so sorry to hear about your little brother, Norman, Betsey; what a terrible thing to leave you both like that. I don't know how Adam Lovering slept at night. Your son, too. I'm so sorry you've lost another child, for we always think of them as children, don't we, no matter how old they are? I understand how you feel because I lost my only daughter, Rosemary, to typhoid just before Christmas. I wish it had been me instead of her, but of course, we don't get to choose. Only God can do that, but it's not right for parents to bury their children; 'tis the wrong order of things."

"I'm sorry to hear about Rosemary, Emily. Do you remember your father? What happened to Adam?"

"No, I don't remember him at all. I believe I was only about one when he died, and Mum had to move into the workhouse with me. Then she died when I was still a toddler, though I do vaguely remember her. A woman at the workhouse once told me that my father drank himself to death, but I don't know if that's true."

"I expect it is. Dad always drank like a fish and never gave my mother enough money to feed us. I think he had his own problems, but don't we all? Still, at least we've found each other now and have a large family to comfort us in our old age. It will be a pleasure to get to know you and Hubert better."

CHAPTER 44

HARTFORD

It had been over a month since Annie, Robert, and their companions had returned to Hartford Manor, and during that time, a lot had happened. Emily and Hubert had taken Annie and Robert up on their offer to stay in Hartford Manor for as long as they liked, giving Betsey and Emily a chance to get to know each other. It had been a welcome distraction for both women, grieving as they were for their lost children.

Robert's cousin, Percy, had arrived on the train as planned and stayed for a couple of weeks before returning to London in his carriage. He brought news that Sir Clive's trial had not yet taken place, but that his friend, the Police Commissioner, was convinced the wealthy aristocrat would go to jail for some time. It was felt that the evidence against Lady Lilliana was not strong enough to charge her with abduction or kidnap, and she had been released with a caution. However, she had packed up her belongings and left Brampford Speke, and now resided in the London townhouse left to her by Sir Edgar.

Millie and Willie Carter were inseparable and longed to get married. Millie told him about hers and Jonnie's inheritance, and he was amazed she should still want to marry him.

"But Millie, think about it; you're a rich lady now, and I'm a poor farm manager. I can't buy you the expensive clothes and jewellery that you deserve. No, I release you from our betrothal, and you must look for a better man."

"I could never find a better man, Willie Carter, and it's you I love, so I don't want to hear another word about it. I wondered, though, could you bear to leave Sugworthy Farm and move to the cottage I've been left on the Grantley Estate? I'm sure you could work there, or maybe I'd have enough money that you wouldn't need to. Marrok Fellwood is the tenant at Sugworthy now, and he knows what he's doing. He could easily find another farm manager or probably do the job himself; it wouldn't be like you were leaving poor old Tommy Houle in the lurch."

"It's a thought, I suppose, if you're sure. What about Jonnie, though? It still doesn't solve the problem of him living in Grantley House. He can't live there alone, and we can't live in two places."

"No, though I might have a solution to that problem. I won't say any more now as there's someone else I need to talk to first."

"That's rather mysterious, but if I say I'll move to your cottage, does that mean we could get married as soon as possible?"

"I don't see why not."

Willie pulled her to him and kissed her passionately. "In that case, I'll give my notice to Marrok tomorrow, and we can get married as soon as the banns are called. "I can't wait to marry you, Millie; I love you so much. I promise I'll be a faithful husband and always care for you."

"I know you will, and I feel the same way. Let me see if I can sort out the other problem with Jonnie having to live in Grantley House, and then we can set a date for our wedding."

Later that day, Emily went to visit Betsey in the afternoon, and, as had become their custom over the last few weeks, they were soon enjoying a cup of tea in the kitchen of Sunset Cottage. Millie had been waiting for her gran to arrive, and when the two women were settled, she asked if she could join them.

"Yes, of course, my dear; there's nothing we'd like better."

"Good, because I want to talk to you about something."

"Go on then, you have our attention."

"I've asked Willie if he'll come to live in Brampford Speke in the cottage my father left me after we're married. He says he will and would like to work on the Grantley estate if possible. I might have enough money that he doesn't need to work, but he'd rather have something to do, and he doesn't want to be dependent on me."

"Quite right, too; no self-respecting man should live off his wife's money. Seeing as the estate belongs to Jonnie now, I'm sure if Willie wants to work there, then it won't be a problem. Marrok and Sam Fellwood will miss him, but no doubt they'll soon find a new manager. They've had a few months to find their feet at Sugworthy Farm, and that sounds like a fantastic opportunity for you both."

"Yes, it will be, but it doesn't solve the problem of Jonnie having to live at Grantley House, and I think I may have a solution. Gran, you and Hubert want to get married, don't you?"

"Yes, as soon as we get back to Hilldale Farm, we intend to get the banns called. Hubert has left it to me to decide when to return, and I've enjoyed spending time with Betsey and Ned and getting to know all the family, but I think we should go back soon. Why, what has it to do with us?"

"Well, Gran, you've lived in Brampford Speke for years, and Hilldale Farm isn't far away, and I know you haven't decided yet where to live. What about if, after you're married, you moved into Grantley House with Jonnie?

Willie and I would be living in my cottage, and we'd all be close to one another."

The two elderly women looked at Millie thoughtfully, and Emily found her voice first.

"Do you know, Millie, I think you might have something there. Hubert would be close to his family, and Jonnie and I would be near you. It's not that far from Hartford either, and I understand Jonnie will also inherit a grand carriage and horses, so we could visit whenever we liked. You clever girl. I think that could be the answer to meet the regulations in the will."

Millie beamed at her grandmother. "In that case, Gran, I have another suggestion. Why don't we get the banns called and have a double wedding here in Hartford? Most of our relations are here, and it's not far for Vivian, Angela, and the children to travel."

Millie's plan met with approval from all concerned, and so, in late October, on a warm sunny morning, Hartford Church was packed, with many villagers standing outside hoping to catch a glimpse of the two blushing brides. It had nearly become a triple wedding, for Millie had kindly offered for Theresa and Louis to join them. However, out of respect for her father, George, and stepmother, Mary Ann, Theresa had declined, saying they would wait until the spring. Fortunately, the tenants of Bluebell Cottage had asked to stay for another six months, and then, Betsey and Ned had promised the cottage to the young couple.

The joint wedding was a grand affair, with the reception held at Hartford Manor and attended by people from all walks of life. Sam, who had been a tramp for most of his life; his son, Marrok, who had spent some lonely weeks in the workhouse with his family; and Sabina and Liza, who a few years ago had nearly starved to death, all rubbed shoulders with members of the rich Fellwood family, and everyone got along fine.

Emily was delighted to finally meet her half-brother, Barney, who had travelled from Wales with his wife, Bronwen. He had been as amazed to hear the story of Adam Lovering's second family as the rest of them.

Ned, too, was thrilled that his brother, Silas, and his wife, Josie, travelled from the Somerset border to see everyone, and he and Betsey had thoroughly enjoyed themselves telling the couple about the Spanish pieces of eight and the deeds to the inn. The auction to sell the coins would be held in the next few days, but a reserve had been put on the many individual lots, and whatever happened, the Carter family would become wealthy in its own right. For now, the coins had been kept a secret from their families, but Ned and Silas were delighted to know they could help out so many of their descendants and make their lives more comfortable. It was a far cry from their childhood when every penny mattered.

The only people not at the celebration were Robert's parents, Charles and Eleanor, who steadfastly refused to accept their son's connection to the Carter family.

Robert's aunt, Lady Margery, had a quiet word with him.

"Did you invite your parents, Robert?"

"Yes, of course, I did, but I knew they wouldn't come. I'm glad we've swapped accommodation with them now, for there's far more space here in the main part of Hartford Manor than in the West Wing, and it's been a wonderful day."

"Yes, it has, and it's their loss. Are they comfortable in the west wing?"

"Yes, I think so, and I hope to get everything up and running to offer the fishing and shooting parties from next Easter."

"I wish you every success, my boy, and if I can do anything to help, you only have to ask."

"Thank you, Aunty Margery; I've always been able to depend on you. Look at Danny, running around outside with the other children; you'd never know now that he was so deformed."

"No, it's a small miracle."

A miracle that was not lost on his birth mother, Eleanor Fellwood, who watched wistfully from an upstairs window.

Betsey and Ned, Silas and Josie, and Barney and Bronwen were the first to leave the celebrations, for Ned tired easily these days. Robert had insisted on sending them home to Sunset Cottage in the carriage, and they enjoyed a quiet mug of cocoa together, speculating on their good fortune and wondering what their families would spend their surprise inheritance on. Eventually, they hugged each other goodnight and went upstairs to bed.

Betsey and Ned snuggled down under the covers, and Ned put his arm around his wife.

"Well, Betsey, what a lovely day we've had."

"Yes, it was grand to have all our family around us. Well, most of them, anyway. We'll always miss our Tom, George, and William, and it's the one thing in my life that I wish I could change, but we have a lot to be thankful for."

"Yes, we do, and as long as I have you, that's all I need. I love you so much, Betsey Carter."

"I love you too, Ned."

AUTHOR'S NOTE

I hope you enjoyed reading this book as much as I enjoyed writing it. If so, I would really appreciate it if you could leave a short review on Amazon or Goodreads.

An honest review is the highest compliment you can pay to any author, and it would mean so much to me.

If you would like to find out more about me and my books, and keep up to date with new releases, please visit https://marciaclayton.co.uk/ and join my mailing list.

Thank you.

Marcia

ABOUT THE AUTHOR

Marcia Clayton writes historical fiction with a sprinkling of romance and mystery in a heart-warming family saga that stretches from the Regency period through to Victorian times.

A farmer's daughter, Marcia, was born in North Devon, a rural and picturesque area in the far South West of England. When she left school at sixteen, Marcia worked in a bank for several years until she married her husband, Bryan, and then stayed at home for a few years to care for her three sons, Stuart, Paul and David.

Now a grandmother, Marcia enjoys spending time with her family and friends. She's a keen researcher of family history, and this hobby inspired some of the characters in her books. A keen gardener, Marcia grows many of her own vegetables. She is also an avid reader and enjoys historical fiction, romance, and crime books.

Marcia has written seven books in the historical family saga, "The Hartford Manor Series". You can read her free short story, "Amelia", a spin-off tale from the first book, "The Mazzard Tree". Amelia, a little orphan girl of 4, is abandoned in Victorian London with her brothers, Joseph and Matthew. To find out what happens to her, download the story here: https://marciaclayton.co.uk/amelia-free-download/ In addition to writing books, Marcia produces blogs to share with her readers in a monthly newsletter. If you would like to join Marcia's mailing list, you can subscribe here: https://marciaclayton.co.uk/

If you enjoyed reading *A Woman Scorned,* you might enjoy the other books in the series:

Betsey

The Prequel to the Hartford Manor Series

1820 North Devon, England

Betsey, a sadly neglected child, is shouldering responsibilities far beyond her years. As she does her best to care for her little brother, Norman, she is befriended by Gypsy Freda, an old woman whose family is camped nearby. Freda's granddaughter, Jane, is also fond of the little girl and is concerned about her.

Thomas, the second son of Lord Fellwood, happens across the gypsy camp and becomes besotted with Jane. However, Jasper Morris, the local miller, also has designs on the young gypsy, and inevitably, the two men do not see eye to eye.

Betsey is drawn into their rivalry for the attention of the beautiful young woman, and she finds herself promising to keep a dangerous secret for many years to come.

The Mazzard Tree

Book One in The Hartford Manor Series

1880 North Devon, England

Annie Carter is a farm labourer's daughter, and life is a continual struggle for survival. When her father dies of consumption, her mother, Sabina, is left with seven hungry mouths to feed and another child on the way. To save them from the workhouse or starvation, Annie steals vegetables from the Manor House garden, risking jail or transportation. Unknown to her, she is watched by Robert, the wealthy heir to the Hartford Estate, but far from turning her in, he befriends her.

Despite their different social backgrounds, Annie and Robert develop feelings they know can have no future. Harry Rudd, the village blacksmith, has long admired Annie, and when he proposes, her mother urges her to accept. She reminds Annie that as a kitchen maid, she will never be allowed to marry Robert. Harry is a good man, and Annie is fond of him. Her head knows what she should do, but will her heart listen?

Set against the harsh background of the rough, class-divided society of Victorian England, this heart-warming and captivating novel portrays a young woman who uses her determination and willpower to defy the circumstances of her birth in her search for happiness.

The Angel Maker

Book Two in The Hartford Manor Series

1884 North Devon, England

When carpenter Fred Carter finds a young woman in dire straits by the roadside, he takes her to the local inn, where she gives birth to a daughter. Charlotte Mackie is an unmarried mother and has run away from home, where she would have no sympathy from her strict parents. A few days later, Fred takes Charlotte to her aunt's house and does not expect to see her again.

When their paths unexpectedly cross, Fred finds Charlotte is distraught as her aunt has arranged an adoption behind her back. Charlotte is desperate to find her baby, and Fred promises to help.

However, they are unprepared for the sinister discoveries that lie before them. Set alongside the absorbing detail of country life and budding village romances, dark forces are at work which ultimately test the bravery and resourcefulness of the whole community.

The Angel Maker is the sequel to The Mazzard Tree, and the second novel in a compelling series which follows the lives and loves of the villagers of Hartford. A rare treat for lovers of historical fiction.

The Rabbit's Foot

Book Three in The Hartford Manor Series

1885 North Devon, England

Mr Edward Snell was more than a little curious when Robert Fellwood, the heir to Hartford Manor, and Lady Margery, his elderly aunt, begged an audience on a Saturday morning. However, being such valued clients, the solicitor was happy to oblige. As his clerk showed the visitors in, he was intrigued to see them followed by an older man who, though respectably dressed, had something of a vagrant about him. The crisp suit in which he was attired could not disguise his weather-beaten face or his missing teeth.

Robert introduced his Uncle Sam and explained he had come to claim his inheritance. The solicitor was old enough to remember the extensive search for Thomas Fellwood when his father, Ephraim, died in 1840. However, that was some forty-five years ago, and the young man had never been found. Yet, here was Sam, who claimed to be Thomas

Fellwood's son, and even more surprising was the fact that the Fellwood family appeared to have accepted him as such.

The Rabbit's Foot tells the tale of how an old man who has spent his life with barely a penny to his name suddenly finds himself rich beyond his wildest dreams. However, there is only one thing that Sam Fellwood truly wants, and that is to be reunited with his son, Marrok, whom he abandoned at the age of five.

Millie's Escape

Book Four in The Hartford Manor Series

1885 North Devon, England

It is winter in the small Devon village of Brampford Speke, and a typhoid epidemic has claimed many victims. Millie, aged fifteen, is doing her best to nurse her mother and grandmother as well as look after Jonathan, her five-year-old brother. One morning, Millie is horrified to find that her mother, Rosemary, has passed away during the night and is terrified the same fate may befall her granny, Emily.

When Emily's neighbours inform her that Sir Edgar Grantley has also perished from the deadly disease, the old woman is distraught, for the kindly gentleman has been their benefactor for many years, much to the disgust of his wife, Lilliana. Emily is well aware that Sir Edgar's generosity has long been a bone of contention between him and his spouse, and she is certain Lady Grantley will evict them from their cottage at the first opportunity.

As she racks her brain for a solution, Emily remembers her father came from Hartford, a seaside village in North Devon and had relatives there. Desperate and too weak to travel, she insists Millie and Jonathan leave home and make their way to Hartford before the embittered woman can cause trouble for them. There, she tells them, they must throw themselves on the mercy of their family and hope they will offer them a home.

With Emily promising to follow them as soon as possible, the two youngsters reluctantly set off on their fifty-mile journey on foot and in the harshest weather conditions. Emily warns them to be cautious, for she suspects Lady Grantley may well pursue them to seek her revenge.

Annie's Secret

Book Six in The Hartford Manor Series

North Devon, England, 1887

When Lady Eleanor Fellwood gave birth to a badly deformed baby, she insisted that the child be adopted as far away as possible. However, that proved difficult to accomplish, and so, in return for payment, Sabina Carter, an impoverished widow living locally, agreed to raise the little boy as a foundling. The child's father, Lord Charles Fellwood of Hartford Manor, warned Sabina that the matter must be treated in the strictest confidence or her family would be evicted from their home. As far as Lady Eleanor was concerned, the child was being cared for miles away.

All was well for several years until fate took a hand and, against his parents' wishes, Robert Fellwood, the heir to the Hartford Estate, married Sabina's daughter, Annie. Robert arranged for his mother-in-law, Sabina, and her family to reside in the Lodge House, situated at the end of the Manor House driveway. A house that Lady Eleanor passed regularly, and it was not long before she spotted Danny's dark curls among the Carter redheads. As she looked into the child's eyes and noted his disabilities, she recognised her son.

Now, at seven years old, Danny has had numerous operations to correct his disabilities and is a happy, healthy child. However, his presence is a source of constant anguish for his birth mother as, day after day, she watches him play in the garden. Her husband, Charles, and son, Robert, are aghast when she announces that she wants him back! An impossible situation for all concerned, and a rift develops between Robert and Annie as he struggles to find a solution to suit everyone.

Over the years, Lady Eleanor has steadfastly refused to acknowledge her daughter-in-law, for she disapproves of Annie's lower-class origins. When a freak accident forces the two women to spend time together, they inevitably find themselves drawn into conversation. Before long, the years of pent-up resentment and family secrets surface as home truths are aired.

Will the two women be rescued from their precarious situation unscathed? And, if so, will the family survive the scandal that is about to be unleashed?